THE BIG BOOK

SELECTED AND EDITED BY FLORENCE PETERSON

ILLUSTRATED BY HAMILTON GREENE

FOREWORD BY FARLEY MOWAT

OF FAVORITE
Dog Stories

PLATT & MUNK, *Publishers* / NEW YORK

Acknowledgments

ADAMS COUNTY NATIONAL BANK, Gettysburg, Penna. "A Pair of Lovers" by Elsie Singmaster; © Elsie Singmaster Lewars; by permission of the Elsie Singmaster Lewars Estate. APPLETON-CENTURY-CROFTS, INC. "Gulliver the Great" from *Gulliver the Great and Other Dog Stories,* by Walter A. Dyer; copyright 1916 by The Century Company. MRS. GEORGE BAMBRIDGE and THE MACMILLAN COMPANY OF CANADA, LTD. for the Canadian rights on "Garm—A Hostage" from *Actions and Reactions,* by Rudyard Kipling. LURTON BLASSINGAME. "Pat'tidge Dog" by Jim Kjelgaard; reprinted as it first appeared in *Boy's Life,* March, 1944; copyright 1944 by The Boy Scouts of America. CALLING ALL GIRLS. "Marty and the Monster," by Vela DePeugh; first appeared in *Calling All Girls* magazine, November, 1960; copyright 1960 by the Better Reading Foundation, Inc. COWARD-MCCANN, INC. "Buried Treasure" from *Clarence Turns Sea Dog,* by Patricia Lauber; copyright © 1959 by Coward-McCann, Inc. "The Story of Verdun Belle," from *Two Gentlemen and a Lady* by Alexander Woollcott, copyright 1928 by Coward-McCann, Inc. CURTIS BROWN, LTD. "Lassie Come Home," by Eric Knight; reprinted by permission of the author's estate; copyright 1938 by the Curtis Publishing Company; an expanded and novel length form of the story is published by the John C. Winston Company. DOUBLEDAY & COMPANY, INC. *"Blood Will Tell,"* by Don Marquis, copyright 1915 by The Crowell Publishing Company, from *The Revolt of the Oyster* by Don Marquis. "Dog for Defense," selection from *Valiant Comrades,* by Ruth Adams Knight; copyright 1943 by Ruth Adams Knight. "One Minute Longer," from *The Heart of the Dog;* copyright 1924, George H. Doran Company. "Trail of Danger," from *Luck of the Trail,* by Esther Birdsall Darling; copyright 1933 by Esther Birdsall Darling. HARCOURT, BRACE & WORLD, INC. "A Dog of Pompeii" from *The Donkey of God,* by Louis Untermeyer; copyright 1932 by Harcourt, Brace & World, Inc.; renewed 1960 by Louis Untermeyer. HOLIDAY HOUSE. "Turtle Hound" from *Bristle Face,* by Zachary Ball; copyright © 1962 by Kelly R. Masters. HOLT, RINEHART AND WINSTON, INC. "The Truest of the Breed" from *Valiant, Dog of the Timberline,* by Jack O'Brien; copyright 1935 by Holt, Rinehart and Winston, Inc.; copyright renewed © 1963 by Wallace Wyatt. MRS. RUTH HULL. "Justice in the Painted Hills," by Alexander Hull; first appeared in *The American Magazine,* July, 1923; copyright 1923 by Alexander Hull. ALFRED A. KNOPF, INC. "Crisis in the Storm," from *Pat: The Story of a Seeing Eye Dog,* by Col. S. P. Meek; copyright 1947 by S. P. Meek. LITTLE, BROWN AND COMPANY—The Atlantic Monthly Press. "Battle Tactics" from *The Dog Who Wouldn't Be,* by Farley Mowat; copyright © 1957 by the Curtis Publishing Company; © 1957 by Farley Mowat; also Little, Brown & Company (Canada) Limited for the Canadian rights. "Dog of Good Omen," selection from *The Incredible Journey,* by Sheila Burnford; copyright © 1960, 1961 by Sheila Burnford. MCGRAW-HILL BOOK COMPANY, INC.—Whittlesey House. "Reddy As Always," from *Always Reddy,* by Marguerite Henry and Wesley Dennis; copyright © 1947 by the McGraw-Hill Book Company, Inc. THE NEW YORKER. "Snapshot of a Dog," by James Thurber, copyright © 1935, 1963 by The New Yorker Magazine, Inc. G. P. PUTNAM'S SONS. "A Hunter's Horn," from *The Trail of the Hunter's Horn,* by Billy C. Clark; © 1957 by Billy C. Clark. MISS RUTH ELIZABETH TANNER. "A Wild Dog," by Ruth Elizabeth Tanner; copyright by Ruth Elizabeth Tanner. THE VIKING PRESS, INC. "Dog Story" from *Small Beer* in *The World of Bemelmans,* by Ludwig Bemelmans; copyright 1939 by Ludwig Bemelmans; first appeared in *The New Yorker.* "Mind-Reading Dog," selection from *Travels With Charley in Search of America* by John Steinbeck; copyright © 1961, 1962 by The Curtis Publishing Co., Inc., copyright © 1962 by John Steinbeck.

Library of Congress Catalog Card No. 64-14546

ISBN number: 0-8228-2640-2

Contents

Foreword

by FARLEY MOWAT

ONE OF these gadget-ridden days it is probably inevitable that someone will invent an electronic machine which will enable us to communicate directly with dogs. This may well turn out to be a mistake, since I am not at all sure that the human ego can stand up to the shock of knowing what dogs really think about us and of us. Nevertheless it will probably come to pass, and then some astute publisher will score a coup by printing the first book *written* by a dog. It will no doubt be a best seller, but it will also, no doubt, put a period to any further dog stories written by mere men and women.

But in the meantime, until the machine becomes operative, we shall continue to depend for our understanding of dogs on what human beings have said and written about them. Humanity has said a good deal on the subject. Probably no other animal has been the subject of so many books, articles, short stories and poems. There is hardly a writer of any stature in all human history who has been able to refrain from the temptation to immortalize a dog or two, or several hundreds in some extreme cases. A few blacklegs, like Henry James, have preferred to write about cats; but such rare malcontents have thereby forfeited their chance at achieving a lasting immortality.

The first authentic writings to be concerned with dogs go right back to the earliest period of written history and consist of some fragments of baked mud from Babylon, whereon a scribe has listed the hunting qualities of a species of hound belonging to one of the Babylonian kings. From this rather slow start dogs burgeoned into literature on all sides and through all the subsequent ages. Thus when the editor of this present book took on the task of surveying the whole canine field with a view to assembling the best dog anthology yet produced, she took on a truly gargantuan task. Close associates of hers have informed me that toward the final phases of her work she would growl at strangers, chase cats casually encountered on the street, and that she betrayed a marked penchant for raw hamburger for breakfast.

There can be no doubt but that she threw herself into the task body and soul, and such was her diligence and her dedication that she has compiled one of the finest collections of stories about dogs which has ever been brought between covers. Nor do I come to this conclusion *solely* because she has had the wisdom and acumen to include a story written by me. There are any number of other good stories in this book as well.

A quick glance at the list of authors involved will demonstrate the truth of my contention. Here you will find such diverse bedfellows as John Steinbeck and Sheila Burnford; such unusual collaborators as Rudyard Kipling and James Thurber; and even such confirmed antagonists as Alexander Woollcott and Don Marquis. Yet all are brought together and united by their common infatuation with the dog. The variety of these selections is endless, ranging from the purely romantic to the purely zany; name it, and if it is canine, you will probably find it in these pages.

The fact of the matter is that although I never buy books, I am personally so impressed by the present volume that I have ordered a copy. It is not intended for myself. It is intended as a gift for a rather decrepit gentleman named Rover P. Mackenzie who lives in a small cabin on the banks of the Barachoix River in Newfoundland.

Rover shares the cabin with another elderly gentleman called Uncle Peter Barfitt and although both are rather shaggy fellows and unkempt to a degree, Uncle Peter gets about on two legs while Rover uses four. This is one of the few real distinctions between them. In fact Uncle Peter (who sleeps in the upper of the two bunk berths built into the wall) is convinced that Rover (who sleeps in the lower berth) is not only his intellectual equal but even, in some respects, Peter's superior.

As proof of this Peter points out that while he himself "had no larnin' " and never learned to read, Rover is a pretty able hand with the printed word. Peter subscribes to a weekly newspaper called the *Northern Star* and each week when the current issue arrives he carefully unfolds it and spreads it out on the rough floor of the shack. Rover sits sedately by until the preparations are completed whereupon he moves stiffly from in front of the pot-bellied stove and lowers his hindquarters into a comfortable position before beginning to scan the printed columns. When you watch him you observe, with a prickling of your back hair, that his nose is going from left to right, and from top to bottom of each page. Once in a while he raises his head—perhaps to rest his aging eyes—but on catching the enthusiastic and ardent glance of old Peter bent proudly upon him he lowers his gaze resolutely to the page once more.

I don't know what Peter gets out of it—for if I were to tell you that Rover gives him a resumé of the news after he finishes reading it, you would—with reason—call me a liar. Perhaps Peter's reward lies in his transparent pride in Rover's accomplishment.

I am not even prepared to state with absolute certainty whether or not Rover really *can* read at all. I have heard it said by certain skeptics that all he does is look at the photographs and the advertisements. Nevertheless I intend to take a chance and I am going to send him a copy of *The Big Book of Favorite Dog Stories,* for if any dog can enjoy it as it ought to be enjoyed, then Rover P. MacKenzie is that dog.

And gentle readers, I hope that you will enjoy it just as much.

Burgeo, Newfoundland
January, 1964

Editor's Preface

"LOVE ME, love my dog" is true not only for dog owners. Millions who have never owned a pet nonetheless feel a fierce, partisan passion for favorite dogs that have in some way captured their hearts—by a look of understanding, a noble act, a comic performance, or even a wag of the tail. Dogs, we know, can win over the most timid child or the toughest hunter.

It is not surprising, then, that as Farley Mowat indicates in his foreword, many important authors have been moved to write stories about dogs. Some, like Kipling and Terhune, have written numerous dog stories; others, only one or two. This collection is made up of thirty favorite stories by as many different authors. Each story recreates a very special dog whose qualities called forth the finest art of storytelling. Yet all the stories are different —even when the subject is the same. Compare, for instance, what Terhune says about a dog of Pompeii in "One Minute Longer" with Louis Untermeyer's story, "The Dog of Pompeii."

Whichever your favorite dog may be, you will thrill as well to the heroism and loyalty of all these real and fictional dogs, or laugh at their hilarious exploits, or perhaps weep at others.

It has been a joyous task for me to assemble from hundreds of books and short stories the most outstanding, interesting and exciting dog stories ever written. Each of them stands alone, although a few stories, taken from the heart of full length novels, are the clearer for brief opening explanatory notes which set the background. And to tell you something about the authors of these stories a biographical section has been included in the back of the book.

I cannot conclude without expressing my deepest appreciation to Phyllis Braun, editor, and to David B. Dreiman, publisher, for their unfailing help, understanding and enthusiasm in this project.

FLORENCE PETERSON
New York, N. Y.

A separation that couldn't last

Lassie Come Home

BY ERIC KNIGHT

*T*HE DOG had met the boy by the school gate
for five years. Now she couldn't understand that times were
changed and she wasn't supposed to be there any more. But the
boy knew.

So when he opened the door of the cottage, he spoke before
he entered.

"Mother," he said, "Lassie's come home again."

He waited a moment, as if in hope of something. But the
man and woman inside the cottage did not speak.

"Come in, Lassie," the boy said.

He held open the door, and the tricolor collie walked in
obediently. Going head down, as a collie does when it knows

13

something is wrong, it went to the rug and lay down before the hearth, a black-white-and-gold aristocrat. The man, sitting on a low stool by the fireside, kept his eyes turned away. The woman went to the sink and busied herself there.

"She were waiting at school for me, just like always," the boy went on. He spoke fast, as if racing against time. "She must ha' got away again. I thought, happen this time, we might just—"

"No!" the woman exploded.

The boy's carelessness dropped. His voice rose in pleading.

"But this time, mother! Just this time. We could hide her. They wouldn't ever know."

"Dogs, dogs, dogs!" the woman cried. The words poured from her as if the boy's pleading had been a signal gun for her own anger.

"I'm sick o' hearing about tykes around this house. Well, she's sold and gone and done with, so the quicker she's taken back the better. Now get her back quick, or first thing ye know we'll have Hynes round here again. Mr. Hynes!"

Her voice sharpened in imitation of the Cockney accent of the south. "Hi know you Yorkshiremen and yer come-'ome dogs. Training yer dogs to come 'ome so's yer can sell 'em hover and hover again.

"Well, she's sold, so ye can take her out o' my house and home to them as bought her!"

The boy's bottom lip crept out stubbornly, and there was silence in the cottage. Then the dog lifted its head and nudged the man's hand, as a dog will when asking for patting. But the man drew away and stared, silently, into the fire.

The boy tried again, with the ceaseless guile of a child, his voice coaxing.

"Look, feyther, she wants thee to bid her welcome. Aye, she's that glad to be home. Happen they don't tak' good care on her up there? Look, her coat's a bit poorly, don't ye think? A bit o' linseed strained through her drinking water—that's what I'd gi' her."

Still looking in the fire, the man nodded. But the woman, as if perceiving the boy's new attack, sniffed.

14

"Aye, tha wouldn't be a Carraclough if tha didn't know more about tykes nor breaking eggs we' a stick. Nor a Yorkshireman. My goodness, it seems to me sometimes that chaps in this village thinks more on their tykes nor they do o' their own flesh and blood. They'll sit by their firesides and let their own bairns starve so long as t' dog gets fed."

The man stirred, suddenly, but the boy cut in quickly.

"But she does look thin. Look, truly—they're not feeding her right. Just look!"

"Aye," the woman chattered. "I wouldn't put it past Hynes to steal t' best part o' t' dog meat for himself. And Lassie always was a strong eater."

"She's fair thin now," the boy said.

Almost unwillingly the man and woman looked at the dog for the first time.

"My gum, she is off a bit," the woman said. Then she caught herself. "Ma goodness, I suppose I'll have to fix her a bit o' summat. She can do wi' it. But soon as she's fed, back she goes. And never another dog I'll have in my house. Never another. Cooking and nursing for 'em, and as much trouble to bring up as a bairn!"

So, grumbling and chatting as a village woman will, she moved about, warming a pan of food for the dog. The man and boy watched the collie eat. When it was done, the boy took from the mantelpiece a folded cloth and a brush, and began prettying the collie's coat. The man watched for several minutes, and then could stand it no longer.

"Here," he said.

He took the cloth and brush from the boy and began working expertly on the dog, rubbing the rich, deep coat, then brushing the snowy whiteness of the full ruff and the apron, bringing out the heavy leggings on the forelegs. He lost himself in his work, and the boy sat on the rug, watching contentedly. The woman stood it as long as she could.

"Now will ye please tak' that tyke out o' here?"

The man flared in anger.

"Well, ye wouldn't have me tak' her back looking like a mucky Monday wash, wouldta?"

15

He bent again, and began fluffing out the collie's petticoats.

"Joe!" the woman pleaded. "Will ye tak' her out o' here? Hynes'll be nosing round afore ye know it. And I won't have that man in my house. Wearing his hat inside, and going on like he's the duke himself—him and his leggings!"

"All right, lass."

"And this time, Joe, tak' young Joe wi' ye."

"What for?"

"Well, let's get the business done and over with. It's him that Lassie runs away for. She comes for young Joe. So if he went wi' thee, and told her to stay, happen she'd be content and not run away no more, and then we'd have a little peace and quiet in the home—though heaven knows there's not much hope o' that these days, things being like they are." The woman's voice trailed away, as if she would soon cry in weariness.

The man rose. "Come, Joe," he said. "Get thy cap."

The Duke of Rudling walked along the gravel paths of his place with his granddaughter, Philippa. Philippa was a bright and knowing young woman, allegedly the only member of the duke's family he could address in unspotted language. For it was also alleged that the duke was the most irascible, vile-tempered old man in the three Ridings of Yorkshire.

"Country going to pot!" the duke roared, stabbing at the walk with his great blackthorn stick. "When I was a young man! Hah! Women today not as pretty. Horses today not as fast. As for dogs—ye don't see dogs today like—"

Just then the duke and Philippa came round a clump of rhododendrons and saw a man, a boy and a dog.

"Ah," said the duke, in admiration. Then his brow knotted. "Damme, Carraclough! What're ye doing with my dog?"

He shouted it quite as if the others were in the next county, for it was also the opinion of the Duke of Rudling that people were not nearly so keen of hearing as they used to be when he was a young man.

16

"It's Lassie," Carraclough said. "She runned away again and I brought her back."

Carraclough lifted his cap, and poked the boy to do the same, not in any servile gesture, but to show that they were as well brought up as the rest.

"Damme, ran away again!" the duke roared. "And I told that utter nincompoop Hynes to—where is he? Hynes! Hynes! Damme, Hynes, what're ye hiding for?"

"Coming, your lordship!" sounded a voice, far away behind the shrubberies. Soon Hynes appeared, a sharp-faced man in check coat, riding breeches, and the cloth leggings that grooms wear.

"Take this dog," roared the duke, "and pen her up! And damme, if she breaks out again, I'll—I'll—"

The duke waved his great stick threateningly, and then, without so much as a thank you or kiss the back of my hand to Joe Carraclough, he went stamping and muttering away.

"I'll pen her up," Hynes muttered, when the duke was gone. "And if she ever gets awye agyne, I'll—"

He made as if to grab the dog, but Joe Carraclough's hobnailed boot trod heavily on Hynes' foot.

"I brough my lad we' me to bid her stay, so we'll pen her up this time. Eigh—sorry! I didn't see I were on thy foot. Come, Joe, lad."

They walked down the crunching gravel path, along by the neat kennel buildings. When Lassie was behind the closed door, she raced into the high wire run where she could see them as they went. She pressed close against the wire, waiting.

The boy stood close, too, his fingers through the meshes touching the dog's nose.

"Go on, lad," his father ordered. "Bid her stay!"

The boy looked around, as if for help that he did not find. He swallowed, and then spoke, low and quickly.

"Stay here, Lassie, and don't come home no more," he said. "And don't come to school for me no more. Because I don't want to see ye no more. 'Cause tha's a bad dog, and we don't love thee no more, and we don't want thee. So stay there forever and leave us be, and don't never come home no more."

17

Then he turned, and because it was hard to see the path plainly, he stumbled. But his father, who was holding his head very high as they walked away from Hynes, shook him savagely, and snapped roughly: "Look where tha's going!"

Then the boy trotted beside his father. He was thinking that he'd never be able to understand why grownups sometimes were so bad-tempered with you, just when you needed them most.

After that, there were days and days that passed, and the dog did not come to the school gate any more. So then it was not like old times. There were so many things that were not like old times.

The boy was thinking that as he came wearily up the path and opened the cottage door and heard his father's voice, tense with anger: ". . . walk my feet off. If tha thinks I like—"

Then they heard his opening of the door and the voice stopped and the cottage was silent.

That's how it was now, the boy thought. They stopped talking in front of you. And this, somehow, was too much for him to bear.

He closed the door, ran out into the night, and onto the moor, that great flat expanse of land where all the people of that village walked in lonesomeness when life and its troubles seemed past bearing.

A long while later, his father's voice cut through the darkness.

"What's tha doing out here, Joe lad?"

"Walking."

"Aye."

They went on together, aimlessly, each following his own thoughts. And they both thought about the dog that had been sold.

"Tha maun't think we're hard on thee, Joe," the man said at last. "It's just that a chap's got to be honest. There's that to it. Sometimes, when a chap doesn't have much, he clings right hard to what he's got. And honest is honest, and there's no two ways about it.

"Why, look, Joe. Seventeen year I worked in that Clarabelle

18

Pit till she shut down, and a good collier too. Seventeen year! And butties I've had by the dozen, and never a man of 'em can ever say that Joe Carraclough kept what wasn't his, nor spoke what wasn't true. Not a man in his Riding can ever call a Carraclough mishonest.

"And when ye've sold a man summat, and ye've taken his brass, and ye've spent it—well, then done's done. That's all. And ye've got to stand by that."

"But Lassie was—"

"Now, Joe! Ye can't alter it, ever. It's done—and happen it's for t' best. No two ways, Joe, she were getting hard to feed. Why, ye wouldn't want Lassie to be going around getting peaked and pined, like some chaps round here keep their tykes. And if ye're fond of her, then just think on it that now she's got lots to eat, and a private kennel, and a good run to herself, and living like a varritable princess, she is. Ain't that best for her?"

"We wouldn't pine her. We've always got lots to eat."

The man blew out his breath, angrily. "Eigh, Joe, nowt pleases thee. Well then, tha might as well have it. Tha'll never see Lassie no more. She run home once too often, so the duke's taken her wi' him up to his place in Scotland, and there she'll stay. So it's good-by and good luck to her, and she'll never come home no more, she won't. Now, I weren't off to tell thee, but there it is, so put it in thy pipe and smoke it, and let's never say a word about it no more—especially in front of thy mother."

The boy stumbled on in the darkness. Then the man halted.

"We ought to be getting back, lad. We left thy mother alone."

He turned the boy about, and then went on, but as if he were talking to himself.

"Tha sees, Joe, women's not like men. They have to stay home and manage best they can, and just spend the time in wishing. And when things don't go right, well, they have to take it out in talk and give a man hell. But it don't mean nowt, really, so tha shouldn't mind when thy mother talks hard.

"Ye just got to learn to be patient and let 'em talk, and just let it go up t' chimney wi' th' smoke."

Then they were quiet, until, over the rise, they saw the

lights of the village. Then the boy spoke: "How far away is Scotland, feyther?"

"Nay, lad, it's a long, long road."

"But how far, feyther?"

"I don't know—but it's a longer road than thee or me'll ever walk. Now, lad. Don't fret no more, and try to be a man— and don't plague thy mother no more, wilta?"

Joe Carraclough was right. It is a long road, as they say in the North, from Yorkshire to Scotland. Much too far for a man to walk—or a boy. And though the boy often thought of it, he remembered his father's words on the moor, and he put the thought behind him.

But there is another way of looking at it; and that's the distance from Scotland to Yorkshire. And that is just as far as from Yorkshire to Scotland. A matter of about four hundred miles, it would be, from the Duke of Rudling's place far up in the Highlands, to the village of Holdersby. That would be for a man, who could go fairly straight.

To an animal, how much farther would it be? For a dog can study no maps, read no signposts, ask no directions. It could only go blindly, by instinct, knowing that it must keep on to the south, to the south. It would wander and err, quest and quarter, run into firths and lochs that would send it sidetracking and backtracking before it could go again on its way—south.

A thousand miles, it would be, going that way—a thousand miles over strange terrain.

There would be moors to cross, and burns to swim. And then those great, long lochs that stretch almost from one side of that dour land to another would bar the way and send a dog questing a hundred miles before it could find a crossing that would allow it to go south.

And, too, there would be rivers to cross, wide rivers like the Forth and the Clyde, the Tweed and the Tyne, where one must go miles to find bridges. And the bridges would be in towns. And in the towns there would be officials—like the one in Lanarkshire. In all his life he had never let a captured dog get away

—except one. That one was a gaunt, snarling collie that whirled on him right in the pound itself, and fought and twisted loose to race away down the city street—going south.

But there are also kind people, too; ones knowing and understanding in the ways of dogs. There was an old couple in Durham who found a dog lying exhausted in a ditch one night—lying there with its head to the south. They took that dog into their cottage and warmed it and fed it and nursed it. And because it seemed an understanding, wise dog, they kept it in their home, hoping it would learn to be content. But, as it grew stronger, every afternoon toward four o'clock it would go to the door and whine, and then begin pacing back and forth between the door and the window, back and forth as the animals do in their cages at the zoo.

They tried every wile and every kindness to make it bide with them, but finally, when the dog began to refuse food, the old people knew what they must do. Because they understood dogs, they opened the door one afternoon and they watched a collie go, not down the road to the right, or to the left, but straight across a field toward the south; going steadily at a trot, as if it knew it still had a long, long road to travel.

Ah, a thousand miles of tor and brae, of shire and moor, of path and road and plowland, of river and stream and burn and brook and beck, of snow and rain and fog and sun, is a long way, even for a human being. But it would seem too far—much, much too far—for any dog to travel blindly and win through.

And yet—and yet—who shall say why, when so many weeks had passed that hope against hope was dying, a boy coming out of school, out of the cloakroom that always smelled of damp wool drying, across the concrete play yard with the black, waxed slides, should turn his eyes to a spot by the school gate from force of five years of habit, and see there a dog?

Not a dog, this one, that lifted glad ears above a proud, slim head with its black-and-gold mask; but a dog that lay weakly, trying to lift a head that would no longer lift, trying to wag a tail that was torn and blotched and matted with dirt and burs, and managing to do nothing much except to whine in a weak, happy, crying way as a boy on his knees threw arms about

21

it, and hands touched it that had not touched it for many a day.

Then who shall picture the urgency of a boy, running, awkwardly, with a great dog in his arms, running through the village, past the empty mill, past the Labor Exchange, where the men looked up from their deep ponderings on life and the dole? Or who shall describe the high tones of a voice—a boy's voice, calling as he runs up a path: "Mother! Oh, mother! Lassie's come home! Lassie's come home!"

Nor does anyone who ever owned a dog need to be told the sound a man makes as he bends over a dog that has been his for many years; nor how a woman moves quickly, preparing food—which might be the family's condensed milk stirred into warm water; nor how the jowl of a dog is lifted so that raw egg and brandy, bought with precious pence, should be spooned in; nor how bleeding pads are bandaged, tenderly.

That was one day. There was another day when the woman in the cottage sighed with pleasure, for a dog lifted itself to its feet for the first time to stand over a bowl of oatmeal, putting its head down and lapping again and again while its pinched flanks quivered.

And there was another day when the boy realized that, even now, the dog was not to be his again. So the cottage rang again with protests and cries, and a woman shrilling: "Is there never to be no more peace in my house and home?" Long after he was in bed that night the boy heard the rise and fall of the woman's voice, and the steady, reiterative tone of the man's. It went on long after he was asleep.

In the morning the man spoke, not looking at the boy, saying the words as if he had long rehearsed them.

"Thy mother and me have decided upon it that Lassie shall stay here till she's better. Anyhow, nobody could nurse her better than us. But the day that t' duke comes back, then back she goes, too. For she belongs to him, and that's honest, too. Now tha has her for a while, so be content."

In childhood, "for a while" is such a great stretch of days when seen from one end. It is a terribly short time when seen from the other.

22

The boy knew how short it was that morning as he went to school and saw a motorcar driven by a young woman. And in the car was a gray-thatched, terrible old man, who waved a cane and shouted: "Hi! Hi, there! Damme, lad! You there! Hi!"

Then it was no use running, for the car could go faster than you, and soon it was beside you and the man was saying: "Damme, Philippa, will you make this smelling thing stand still a moment? Hi, lad!"

"Yes, sir."

"You're What's-'is-Name's lad, aren't you?"

"Ma feyther's Joe Carraclough."

"I know. I know. Is he home now?"

"No, sir. He's away to Allerby. A mate spoke for him at the pit and he's gone to see if there's a chance."

"When'll he be back?"

"I don't know. I think about tea."

"Eh, yes. Well, yes. I'll drop round about fivish to see that father of yours. Something important."

It was hard to pretend to listen to lessons. There was only waiting for noon. Then the boy ran home.

"Mother! T'duke is back and he's coming to take Lassie away."

"Eigh, drat my buttons. Never no peace in this house. Is tha sure?"

"Aye. He stopped me. He said tell feyther he'll be round at five. Can't we hide her? Oh, mother."

"Nay, thy feyther—"

"Won't you beg him? Please, please. Beg feyther to—"

"Young Joe, now it's no use. So stop thy teasing! Thy feyther'll not lie. That much I'll give him. Come good, come bad, he'll not lie."

"But just this once, mother. Please beg him, just this once. Just one lie wouldn't hurt him. I'll make it up to him. I will. When I'm growed up, I'll get a job. I'll make money. I'll buy him things—and you, too. I'll buy you both anything you want if you'll only—"

For the first time in his trouble the boy became a child,

23

and the mother, looking over, saw the tears that ran openly down his contorted face. She turned her face to the fire, and there was a pause. Then she spoke.

"Joe, tha mustn't," she said softly. "Tha must learn never to want nothing in life like that. It don't do, lad. Tha mustn't want things bad, like tha wants Lassie."

The boy shook his clenched fists in impatience.

"It ain't that, mother. Ye don't understand. Don't ye see— it ain't me that wants her. It's her that wants us! Tha's wha made her come all them miles. It's her that wants us, so terrible bad!"

The woman turned and stared. It was as if, in that moment, she were seeing this child, this boy, this son of her own, for the first time in many years. She turned her head down toward the table. It was surrender.

"Come and eat, then," she said. "I'll talk to him. I will that, all right. I feel sure he won't lie. But I'll talk to him, all right. I'll talk to Mr. Joe Carraclough. I will indeed."

At five that afternoon, the Duke of Rudling, fuming and muttering got out of a car at a cottage gate to find a boy barring his way. This was a boy who stood, stubbornly, saying fiercely: "Away we' thee! Thy tyke's net here!"

"Damme, Philippa, th' lad's touched," the duke said. "He is. He's touched."

Scowling and thumping his stick, the old duke advanced until the boy gave way, backing down the path out of reach of the waving blackthorn stick.

"Thy tyke's net here," the boy protested.

"What's he saying?" the girl asked.

"Says my dog isn't here. Damme, you going deaf? I'm supposed to be deaf, and I hear him plainly enough. Now, ma lad, what tyke o' mine's net here?"

As he turned to the boy, the duke spoke in broadest Yorkshire, as he did always to the people of the cottages—a habit which the Duchess of Rudling, and many more members of the duke's family, deplored.

"Coom, coom, ma lad. Whet tyke's net here?"

"No tyke o' thine. Us hasn't got it." The words began running faster and faster as the boy backed away from the fearful
old man who advanced. "No tyke could have done it. No tyke
can come all them miles. It isn't Lassie. It's another one that
looks like her. It isn't Lassie!"

"Why, bless ma heart and sowl," the duke puffed. "Where's
thy father, ma lad?"

The door behind the boy opened; a woman's voice spoke.

"If it's Joe Carraclough ye want, he's out in the shed—and
been there shut up half the afternoon."

"What's this lad talking about—a dog of mine being here?"

"Nay," the woman snapped quickly. "He didn't say a tyke
o' thine was here. He said it wasn't here."

"Well, what dog o' mine isn't here, then?"

The woman swallowed, and looked about as if for help.
The duke stood, peering from under his jutting eyebrows. Her
answer, truth or lie, was never spoken, for then they heard the
rattle of a door opening, and a man making a pursing sound
with his lips, as he will when he wants a dog to follow, and then
Joe Carraclough's voice said, "This is t' only tyke us has here.
Does it look like any dog that belongs to thee?"

With his mouth opening to cry one last protest, the boy
turned. And his mouth stayed open. For there he saw his father,
Joe Carraclough, the collie fancier, standing with a dog at his
heels—a dog that sat at his left heel patiently, as any well-
trained dog should do—as Lassie used to do. But this dog was
not Lassie. In fact, it was ridiculous to think of it at the same
moment as you thought of Lassie.

For where Lassie's skull was aristocratic and slim, this dog's
head was clumsy and rough. Where Lassie's ears stood in twin-
lapped symmetry, this dog had one ear draggling and the other
standing up Alsatian fashion in a way to give any collie breeder
the cold shivers. Where Lassie's coat was rich tawny gold, this
dog's coat had ugly patches of black; and where Lassie's apron
was a billowing stretch of snow-white, this dog had puddles of
off-color blue-merle mixture. Besides, Lassie had four white
paws, and this one had one paw white, two dirty-brown, and one
almost black.

That is the dog they all looked at as Joe Carraclough stood there, having told no lie, having only asked a question. They all stood, waiting the duke's verdict.

But the duke said nothing. He only walked forward, slowly, as if he were seeing a dream. He bent beside the collie, looking with eyes that were as knowing about dogs as any Yorkshireman alive. And those eyes did not waste themselves upon twisted ears, or blotched marking, or rough head. Instead they were looking at a paw that the duke lifted, looking at the underside of the paw, staring intently at five black pads, crossed and recrossed with the scars where thorns had lacerated, and stones had torn.

For a long time the duke stared, and when he got up he did not speak in Yorkshire accents any more. He spoke as a gentleman should, and he said: "Joe Carraclough, I never owned this dog. 'Pon my soul, she's never belonged to me. Never!"

Then he turned and went stumping down the path, thumping his cane and saying: "Bless my soul. Four hundred miles! Damme, wouldn't ha' believed it. Damme—five hundred miles!"

He was at the gate when his granddaughter whispered to him fiercely.

"Of course," he cried. "Mind your own business. Exactly what I came for. Talking about dogs made me forget. Carraclough! Carraclough! What're ye hiding for?"

"I'm still here, sir."

"Ah, there you are. You working?"

"Eigh, now. Working," Joe said. That's the best he could manage.

"Yes, working, working!" The duke fumed.

"Well, now—" Joe began.

Then Mrs. Carraclough came to his rescue, as a good housewife in Yorkshire will.

"Why, Joe's got three or four things that he's been considering," she said, with proper display of pride. "But he hasn't quite said yes or no to any of them yet."

"Then say no, quick," the old man puffed. "Had to sack Hynes. Didn't know a dog from a drunken filly. Should ha'

26

known all along no Londoner could handle dogs fit for Yorkshire taste. How much, Carraclough?"

"Well, now," Joe began.

"Seven pounds a week, and worth every penny," Mrs. Carraclough chipped in.

"Five," roared the duke—who, after all, was a Yorkshireman, and couldn't help being a bit sharp about things that pertained to money.

"Six," said Mrs. Carraclough.

"Five pound ten," bargained the duke, cannily.

"Done," said Mrs. Carraclough, who would have been willing to settle for three pounds in the first place.

"But, o' course, us gets the cottage too."

"All right," puffed the duke. "Five pounds ten and the cottage. Begin Monday. But—on one condition. Carraclough, you can live on my land, but I won't have that thick-skulled, screw-lugged, gay-tailed eyesore of a misshapen mongrel on my property. Now never let me see her again. You'll get rid of her?"

He waited, and Joe fumbled for words. But it was the boy who answered, happily, gaily: "Oh, no, sir. She'll be waiting at school for me most o' the time. And, anyway, in a day or so we'll have her fixed up and coped up so's ye'd never, never recognize her."

"I don't doubt that," puffed the duke, as he went to the car. "I don't doubt ye could do just exactly that."

It was a long time afterward, in the car, that the girl said: "Don't sit there like a lion on the Nelson column. And I thought you were supposed to be a hard man."

"Fiddlesticks, m'dear. I'm a ruthless realist. For five years I've sworn I'd have that dog by hook or crook, and now, egad, at last I've got her."

"Pooh! You had to buy the man before you could get his dog."

"Well, perhaps that's not the worst part of the bargain."

Blood Will Tell

BY DON MARQUIS

I A M a middle-sized dog, with spots on me here and there, and several different colors of hair mixed in even where there aren't any spots, and my ears are frazzled a little on the ends where they have been chewed in fights.

At first glance you might not pick me for an aristocrat. But I am one. I was considerably surprised when I discovered it, as nothing in my inmost feelings up to that time, nor in the treatment which I had received from dogs, humans or boys, had led me to suspect it.

28

I can well remember the afternoon on which the discovery was made. A lot of us dogs were lying in the grass, up by the swimming hole, just laying around, and the boys were doing the same. All the boys were naked and comfortable, and no humans were about, the only thing near being a cow or two and some horses, and although large they are scarcely more human than boys. Everybody had got tired of swimming, and it was too hot to drown out gophers or fight bumblebees, and the boys were smoking grapevine cigarettes and talking.

Us dogs was listening to the boys talk. A Stray Boy, by which I mean one not claimed or looked out for or owned by any dog, says to Freckles Watson, who is my boy, "What breed would you call that dog of yours, Freck?"

I pricked up my ears at that. I cannot say that I had ever set great store by breeds up to the time that I found out I was an aristocrat myself, believing as Bill Patterson, a human and the town drunkard used to say when intoxicated, that often an honest heart beats beneath the outcast's ragged coat.

"Spot ain't any *one* particular breed," says Freckles. "He's considerably mixed."

"He's a mongrel," says Squint Thompson, who is Jack Thompson's boy.

"He ain't," says Freckles, so huffy that I saw a mongrel must be some sort of a disgrace. "You're a link, link liar, and so's your Aunt Mariar," says Freckles.

I thought there might be a fight then, but it was too hot for any enjoyment in a fight, I guess, for Squint let it pass, only saying, "I ain't got any Aunt Mariar, and you're another."

"A dog," chips in the Stray Boy, "has either got to be a thoroughbred or a mongrel. He's either an aristocrat or else he's a common dog."

"Spot ain't any common dog," says Freckles, sticking up for me. "He can lick any dog in town within five pounds of his weight."

"He's got some spaniel in him," says the Stray Boy.

"His nose is pointed like a hound's nose," says Squint Thompson.

29

"Well," says Freckles, "neither one of them kind of dogs is a common dog."

"Spot has got some bulldog blood in him too," says Tom Mulligan, an Irish boy owned by a dog by the name of Mutt Mulligan. "Did you ever notice how Spot will hang on so you can't pry him loose when he gets into a fight?"

"That proves he is an aristocratic kind of dog," says Freckles.

"There's some bird dog blood in Spot," says the Stray Boy, sizing me up careful.

"He's got some collie in him too," says Squint Thompson. "His voice sounds just like a collie's when he barks."

"But his tail is more like a coach dog's tail," says Tom Mulligan.

"His hair ain't, though," says the Stray Boy. "Some of his hair is like a setter's."

"His teeth are like a mastiff's," says Mutt Mulligan's boy Tom. And they went on like that; I never knew before there were so many different kinds of thoroughbred dog.

Finally Freckles says, "Yes, he's got all them different kinds of thoroughbred blood in him, and he's got other kinds you ain't mentioned and that you ain't slick enough to see. You may think you're running him down, but what you say just *proves* he ain't a common dog."

I was glad to hear that. It was beginning to look to me that they had a pretty good case for me being a mongrel.

"How does it prove it?" asked the Stray Boy.

"Well," says Freckles, "you know who the King of Germany is, don't you?"

They said they'd heard of him from time to time.

"Well," says Freckles, "if you were a relation of the King of Germany you'd be a member of the German royal family. You fellows may not know that, but you would. You'd be a swell, a regular high-mucky-muck."

They said they guessed they would.

"Now, then," says Freckles, "if you were a relation to the

King of Switzerland, too, you'd be just *twice* as swell, wouldn't you, as if you were only related to one royal family? Plenty of people are related to just *one* royal family."

Tom Mulligan butts in and says that way back, in the early days, his folks was the Kings of Ireland; but no one pays any attention.

"Suppose, then, you're a cousin of the Queen of England into the bargain and your granddad was King of Scotland, and the Prince of Wales and the Emperor of France and the Sultan of Russia and the rest of those royalties were relations of yours, wouldn't all that royal blood make you *twenty times* as much of a high-mucky-muck as if you had just *one* measly little old king for a relation?"

The boys had to admit that it would.

"You wouldn't call a fellow with all that royal blood in him a *mongrel,* would you?" says Freckles. "You bet your sweet life you wouldn't! A fellow like that is darned near on the level with a congressman or a vice-president. Whenever he travels around in the old country they turn out the brass band; and the firemen and the Knights of Pythias and the Modern Woodmen parade, and the mayor makes a speech, and there's a picnic and fire-crackers, and he gets blamed near anything he wants. People kowtow to him, just like they do to a swell left-handed pitcher or a champion prizefighter. If you went over to the old country and called a fellow like that a mongrel, and it got out on you, you would be sent to jail for it."

Tom Mulligan says yes, that is so; his granddad came to this country through getting into some kind of trouble about the King of England, and the King of England ain't anywhere near as swell as the fellow Freckles described, nor near so royal, neither.

"Well, then," says Freckles, "it's the same way with my dog, Spot, here. *Any* dog can be full of just *one* kind of thoroughbred blood. That's nothing! But Spot here has got more different kinds of thoroughbred blood in him than any dog you ever saw. By your own say-so he has. He's got *all* kinds of thoroughbred blood in him. If there's any kind he ain't got, you just name it."

"He ain't got any Great Dane in him," yells the Stray Boy, hating to knuckle under.

"You're a liar, he has too," says Freckles.

The Stray Boy backed it, and there was a fight. All us dogs and boys gathered around in a ring to watch it, and I was more anxious than anybody else. For the way that fight went, it was easy to see, would decide what I was.

Well, Freckles licked that Stray Boy and rubbed his nose in the mud, and that's how I come to be an aristocrat.

Being an aristocrat may sound easy. And it may look easy to outsiders. And it may really be easy for them that are used to it. But it wasn't easy for *me*. It came on me suddenly, the knowledge that I was one, and without warning. I didn't have any time to practice up being one. One minute I wasn't one, and the next minute I was; and while, of course, I felt important over it, there were spells when I would get kind of discouraged, too, and wish I could go back to being a common dog again. I kept expecting my taste and habits to change. I watched and waited for them to. But they didn't. No change at all set in on me. But I had to pretend I was changed. Then I would get tired of pretending, and be downhearted about the whole thing, and say to myself, "There has been a mistake. I am *not* an aristocrat after all."

I might have gone along like that for a long time, partly in joy over my noble birth, and partly in doubt, without ever being certain, if it had not been for a happening which showed, as Freckles said, that blood will tell.

It happened the day Wilson's World's Greatest One Ring Circus and Menagerie came to our town. Freckles and me, and all the other dogs and boys, and a good many humans, too, followed the street parade around through town and back to the circus lot. Many went in, and the ones that didn't have any money hung around outside a while and explained to each other they were going at night, because a circus is more fun at night anyhow. Freckles didn't have any money, but his dad was going to take him that night, so when the parade was over him and me went back to his dad's drugstore on Main Street, and I crawled under the soda water counter to take a nap.

Freckles's dad, that everyone calls Doc Watson, is a pretty good fellow for a human, and he doesn't mind you hanging around the store if you don't drag bones in or scratch too many fleas off. So I'm there considerable in right hot weather. Under the soda water counter is the coolest place for a dog in the whole town. There's a zinc tub under there always full of water, where Doc washes the soda water glasses, and there's always considerable water slopped onto the floor. It's damp and dark there always. Outdoors it may be so hot in the sun that your tongue hangs out of you so far you tangle your feet in it, but in under there you can lie comfortable and snooze, and when you wake up and want a drink there's the tub with the glasses in it. And flies don't bother you because they stay on top of the counter where soda water has been spilled.

Circus day was a hot one, and I must have drowsed off pretty quick after lying down. I don't know how long I slept, but when I waked up it was with a start, for something important was going on outside in Main Street. I could hear people screaming and swearing and running along the wooden sidewalk, and horses whinnying, and dogs barking, and old Tom Cramp, the city marshal, was yelling out that he was an officer of the law, and the steam whistle on the flour mill was blowing. And it all seemed to be right in front of our store. I was thinking I'd better go out and see about it, when the screen doors crashed like a runaway horse had come through them, and the next minute a big yellow dog was back of the counter, trying to scrouch down and scrooge under it like he was scared and was hiding. He backed me into the corner without seeing me or knowing I was there, and like to have squashed me.

No dog—and it never struck me that maybe this wasn't a dog—no dog can just calmly sit down on me like that when I'm waking up from a nap, and get away with it, no matter *how* big

33

he is, and in spite of the darkness under there I could see and feel that this was the biggest dog in the world. I had been dreaming I was in a fight, anyhow, when he crowded in there with his hindquarters on top of me, and I bit him on the hind leg.

When I bit him he let out a noise like a thrashing machine starting up. It wasn't a bark. Nothing but the end of the world coming could bark like that. It was a noise more like I heard one time when the boys dared Freckles to lie down between the cattle guards on the railroad track and let a train run over him about a foot above his head, and I laid down there with him and it nearly deafened both of us. When he let out that noise I says to myself, "Great guns! What kind of a dog have I bit?"

And as he made that noise he jumped, and over went the counter, marble top and all, with a smash, and jam into the show window he went, with his tail swinging, and me right after him, practically on top of him. It wasn't that I exactly intended to chase him, you understand, but I was rattled on account of that awful noise he had let out, and I wanted to get away from there, and I went the same way he did. So when he bulged through the window glass onto the street I bulged right after him, and as he hit the sidewalk I bit him again. The first time I bit him because I was sore, but the second time I bit him because I was so nervous I didn't know what I was doing, hardly. And at the second bite, without even looking behind him, he jumped clean over the hitch rack and a team of horses in front of the store and landed right in the middle of the road with his tail between his legs.

And then I realized for the first time he wasn't a dog at all. He was the circus lion.

Mind you, I'm not saying that I would have bit him at all if I'd a-known at the start he was a lion.

And I ain't saying I *wouldn't* 'a' bit him, either.

But actions speak louder than words, and records are records, and you can't go back on them, and the fact is I *did* bite him. I bit him twice.

And that second bite, when we came bulging through the window together, the whole town saw. It was getting up telephone poles, and looking out of second-story windows, and crawling under sidewalks and into cellars, and trying to hide behind the town pump; but no matter where it was trying to get to, it had one eye on that lion, and it saw me chasing him out of that store. I don't say I would have chased him if he hadn't been just ahead of me, anyhow, and I don't say I wouldn't have chased him, but the facts are I *did* chase him.

The lion was just as scared as the town—and the town was so scared it didn't know the lion was scared at all—and when his trainer got hold of him in the road he was tickled to death to be led back to his cage, and he lay down in the far corner of it, away from the people, and trembled till he shook the wagon it was on.

But if there was any further doubts in any quarter about me being an aristocrat, the way I bit and chased that lion settled 'em forever. That night Freckles and Doc went to the circus, and I marched in along with them. And every kid in town, as they saw Freckles and me marching in, says, "There goes the dog that licked the lion!"

And Freckles, every time anyone congratulated him on being the boy that belonged to that kind of a dog, would say, "Blood will tell! Spot's an aristocrat, he is."

And him and me and Doc Watson, his dad, stopped in front of the lion's cage that night and took a good look at him. He was a kind of an old moth-eaten lion, but he was a lion all right, and he looked mighty big in there. He looked so big that all my doubts come back on me, and I says to myself, "Honest, now, if I'd *a-known* he was a lion and that *big* a lion when I bit him, *would* I have bit him or would I not?"

But just then Freckles reached down and patted me on the head and said, "You wasn't afraid of him, was you, old Spot! Yes, sir, blood will tell!"

One Minute Longer

BY ALBERT PAYSON TERHUNE

WOLF was a collie, red-gold and white of coat, with a shape more like his long-ago wolf ancestors' than like a domesticated dog's. It was from this ancestral throwback that he was named Wolf.

He looked not at all like his great sire, Sunnybank Lad, not like his dainty thoroughbred mother, Lady. Nor was he like them in any other way, except that he inherited old Lad's stanchly gallant spirit and loyalty, and uncanny brain. No, in traits as well as in looks he was more wolf than dog. He almost never barked, his snarl supplying all vocal needs.

36

The Mistress, or the Master, or the Boy—any of these three could romp with him, roll him over, tickle him or subject him to all sorts of playful indignities, and Wolf entered gleefully into the fun of the romp. But let any human besides these three lay a hand on his slender body and a snarling plunge for the offender's throat was Wolf's invariable reply to the caress.

It had been so since his puppyhood. He did not fly at accredited guests, nor indeed pay any heed to their presence as long as they kept their hands off him. But to all of them the Boy was forced to say at the very outset of the visit:

"Pat Lad and Bruce all you want to, but please leave Wolf alone. He doesn't care for people. We've taught him to stand for a pat on the head from guests—but don't touch his body."

Then to prove his own immunity, the Boy would proceed to tumble Wolf about to the delight of them both.

In romping with humans whom they love most dogs will bite, more or less gently—or pretend to bite—as a part of the game. Wolf never did this. In his wildest and roughest romps with the Boy or with the Boy's parents, Wolf did not so much as open his mighty jaws. Perhaps he dared not trust himself to bite gently or perhaps he realized that a bite is not a joke but an effort to kill.

There had been only one exception to Wolf's hatred for mauling at strangers' hands. A man came to The Place on a business call, bringing along a chubby two-year-old daughter. The Master warned the baby that she must not go near Wolf, although she might pet any of the other collies. Then he became so much interested in the business talk that he and his guest forgot all about the child.

Ten minutes later the Master chanced to shift his gaze to the far end of the room. And he broke off with a gasp in the very middle of a sentence.

The baby was seated astride Wolf's back, her tiny heels digging into the dog's sensitive ribs, and each of her chubby fists gripping one of his ears. Wolf was lying there with an idiotically happy grin on his face and wagging his tail in ecstasy.

No one knew why he had submitted to the baby's tugging

hands, except because she *was* a baby, and the gallant heart of the dog had gone out to her helplessness.

Wolf was the official watchdog of The Place; and his name carried dread to the loafers and tramps of the region. Also, he was the Boy's own special dog. He had been born on the Boy's tenth birthday, five years before this story of ours begins, and ever since then the two had been inseparable chums.

One sloppy afternoon in late winter Wolf and the Boy were sprawled side by side on the fur rug in front of the library fire. The Mistress and the Master had gone to town for the day. The house was lonely, and the two chums were left to entertain each other.

The Boy was reading a magazine. The dog beside him was blinking in drowsy comfort at the fire. Presently, finishing the story he had been reading, the Boy looked across at the sleepy dog.

Wolf," he said, "here's a story about a dog. I think he must have been something like you. Maybe he was your great-great-great-great-grandfather. He lived an awfully long time ago—in Pompeii. Ever hear of Pompeii?"

Now, the Boy was fifteen years old, and he had too much sense to imagine that Wolf could possible understand the story he was about to tell him. But long since, he had fallen into a way of talking to his dog sometimes, as if to another human. It was fun for him to note the almost pathetic eagerness wherewith Wolf listened and tried to grasp the meaning of what he was saying. Again and again, at sound of some familiar word or voice inflection, the collie would prick up his ears or wag his tail, as if in joyous hope that he had at last found a clue to his owner's meaning.

"You see," went on the Boy, "this dog lived in Pompeii, as I told you. You've never been there, Wolf."

Wolf was looking up at the Boy in wistful excitement, seeking vainly to guess what was expected of him.

"And," continued the Boy, "the kid who owned him seems to have had a regular knack for getting into trouble all the time. And his dog was always on hand to get him out of it. It's a true story, the magazine says. The kid's father was so grateful to the dog that he bought him a solid silver collar. Solid silver! Get that, Wolfie?"

Wolf did not "get it." But he wagged his tail hopefully, his eyes alight with bewildered interest.

"And," said the Boy, "what do you suppose was engraved on the collar? Well, I'll tell you: *This dog has thrice saved his little master from death. Once by fire, once by flood, and once at the hands of robbers!'* How's that for a record, Wolf? For *one* dog, too!"

At the words "Wolf" and "dog" the collie's tail smote the floor in glad comprehension. Then he edged closer to the Boy as the narrator's voice presently took on a sadder note.

"But at last," resumed the Boy, "there came a time when the dog couldn't save the kid. Mount Vesuvius erupted. All the sky was pitch dark, as black as midnight, and Pompeii was buried under lava and ashes. The dog could easily have got away by himself—dogs can see in the dark, can't they, Wolf?—but he couldn't get the kid away. And he wouldn't go without him. You wouldn't have gone without me, either, would you, Wolf? Pretty nearly two thousand years later, some people dug through the lava that covered Pompeii. What do you suppose they found? Of course they found a whole lot of things. One of them was that dog—silver collar and inscription and all. He was lying at the feet of a child. The child he couldn't save. He was one grand dog— hey, Wolf?"

The continued strain of trying to understand began to get on the collie's high-strung nerves. He rose to his feet, quivering, and sought to lick the Boy's face, thrusting one upraised white forepaw at him in appeal for a handshake. The Boy slammed shut the magazine.

"It's slow in the house, here, with nothing to do," he said to his chum. "I'm going up the lake with my gun to see if any wild ducks have landed in the marshes yet. It's almost time for them. Want to come along?"

The last sentence Wolf understood perfectly. On the instant he was dancing with excitement at the prospect of a walk. Being a collie, he was of no earthly help in a hunting trip; but, on such tramps, as everywhere else, he was the Boy's inseparable companion.

Out over the slushy snow the two started, the Boy with his light single-barreled shotgun slung over one shoulder, the dog trotting close at his heels. The March thaw was changing to a sharp freeze. The deep and soggy snow was crusted over, just thick enough to make walking a genuine difficulty for both dog and Boy.

The Place was a promontory that ran out into the lake, on the opposite bank from the mile-distant village. Behind, across the highroad, lay the winter-choked forest. At the lake's northerly end, two miles beyond The Place, were the reedy marshes where, a month hence, wild ducks would congregate. Thither, with Wolf, the Boy plowed his way through the biting cold.

The going was heavy and heavier. A quarter mile below the marshes, the Boy struck out across the upper corner of the lake. Here the ice was rotten at the top where the thaw had nibbled at it, but beneath it was still a full eight inches thick, easily strong enough to bear the Boy's weight.

Along the gray ice field the two plodded. The skim of water, which the thaw had spread an inch thick over the ice, had frozen in the day's cold spell. It crackled like broken glass as the chums walked over it. The Boy had on big hunting boots. So, apart from the extra effort, the glasslike ice did not bother him. To Wolf it gave acute pain. The sharp particles were forever getting between the callous black pads of his feet, pricking and cutting him acutely.

Little smears of blood began to mark the dog's course, but it never occurred to Wolf to turn back or to betray by any sign that he was suffering. It was all a part of the day's work—a cheap price to pay for the joy of tramping with his adored young master.

Then, forty yards or so on the hither side of the marshes, Wolf beheld a right amazing phenomenon. The Boy had been walking directly in front of him, gun over shoulder. With no warning at all the youthful hunter fell, feet foremost, out of sight through the ice.

The light shell of new-frozen water that covered the lake's thicker ice also masked an air hole nearly three feet wide. Into this, as he strode carelessly along, the Boy had stepped. Straight down he had gone, with all the force of his hundred-and-twenty pounds and with all the impetus of his forward stride.

Instinctively he threw out his hands to restore his balance. The only effect of this was to send the gun flying ten feet away.

Down went the Boy through less than three feet of water (for the bottom of the lake at this point had started to slope upward toward the marshes) and through nearly two feet more of sticky marsh mud that underlay the lake bed.

His outflung hands struck against the ice on the edges of the air hole and clung there.

Sputtering and gurgling, the Boy brought his head above the surface and tried to raise himself by his hands, high enough to wriggle out upon the surface of the ice. Ordinarily this would have been simple enough for so strong a lad. But the gluelike mud had imprisoned his feet and the lower part of his legs and held them powerless.

Try as he would, the Boy could not wrench himself free of the slough. The water, as he stood upright, was on a level with his mouth. The air hole was too wide for him, at such a depth, to get a good purchase on its edges and lift himself bodily to safety.

Gaining such fingerhold as he could, he heaved with all his might, throwing every muscle of his body into the struggle. One leg was pulled almost free of the mud, but the other was driven deeper into it. And, as the Boy's fingers slipped from the smoothly wet ice edge, the attempt to restore his balance drove the free leg back, knee-deep into the mire.

Ten minutes of this hopeless fighting left the Boy panting and tired out. The icy water was numbing his nerves and chilling his blood into torpidity. His hands were without sense of feeling as far up as the wrists, Now, even if he could have shaken free his legs from the mud he hadn't the strength to crawl out of the hole.

He ceased his uselessly frantic battle and stood dazed. Then he came sharply to himself. For as he stood, the water crept upward from his lips to his nostrils. He knew why the water seemed to be rising. It was not rising. It was he who was sinking.

As soon as he stopped moving the mud began very slowly, but very steadily, to suck him downward.

This was not a quicksand, but it was a deep mud bed. And only by constant motion could he avoid sinking farther and farther down into it. He had less than two inches to spare at best before the water should fill his nostrils, less than two inches of life, even if he could keep the water down to the level of his lips.

There was a moment of utter panic. Then the Boy's brain cleared. His only hope was to keep on fighting—to rest when he must for a moment or so, and then to renew his numbed grip on the ice edge and try to pull his feet a few inches higher out of the mud. He must do this as long as his chilled body could be scourged into obeying his will.

He struggled again, but with virtually no result in raising himself. A second struggle, however, brought him chin-high above the water. He remembered confusedly that some of these earlier struggles had scarce budged him, while others had gained him two or three inches. Vaguely, he wondered why. Then turning his head, he realized.

Wolf, as he turned, was just loosing his hold on the wide collar of the Boy's mackinaw. His cut forepaws were still braced against a flaw of ragged ice on the air hole's edge, and all his tawny body was tense.

His body was dripping wet, too. The Boy noted that; and he realized that the repeated effort to draw his master to safety must have resulted, at least once, in pulling the dog down into the water with the floundering Boy.

"Once more, Wolfie! *Once more!*" chattered the Boy through teeth that clicked together like castanets.

The dog darted forward, caught his grip afresh on the edge of the Boy's collar, and tugged with all his fierce strength, growling and whining ferociously the while.

The Boy seconded the collie's tuggings by a supreme struggle that lifted him higher than before. He was able to get one arm and shoulder clear. His numb fingers closed about an upthrust tree limb which had been washed downstream in the autumn freshets and had been frozen into the lake ice.

With this new purchase, and aided by the dog, the boy

tried to drag himself out of the hole. But the chill of the water had done its work. He had not the strength to move farther. The mud still sucked at his calves and ankles. The big hunting boots were full of water that seemed to weigh a ton.

He lay there, gasping and chattering. Then, through the gathering twilight his eyes fell on the gun lying ten feet away.

"Wolf!" he ordered, nodding toward the weapon. "Get it! *Get* it!"

Not in vain had the boy talked to Wolf for years as if the dog were human. At the words and the nod the collie trotted over to the gun, lifted it by the stock, and hauled it awkwardly along over the bumpy ice to his master, where he laid it down at the edge of the air hole.

The dog's eyes were cloudy with trouble, and he shivered and whined as with ague. The water on his thick coat was freezing to a mass of ice. But it was from anxiety that he shivered, and not from cold.

Still keeping his numb grasp on the tree branch, the boy balanced himself as best he could, and thrust two fingers of his free hand into his mouth to warm them into sensation again.

When this was done, he reached out to where the gun lay and pulled its trigger. The shot boomed deafeningly through the twilight winter silences. The recoil sent the weapon sliding sharply back along the ice, spraining the boy's trigger finger and cutting it to the bone.

"That's all I can do," said the Boy to himself. "If anyone hears it, well and good. I can't get at another cartridge. I couldn't put it into the breech if I had it. My hands are too numb."

For several minutes he clung there, listening. But this was a desolate part of the lake, far from any road; and the season was too early for other hunters to be abroad. The bitter cold, in any case, tended to make sane folk hug the fireside rather than to venture so far into the open. Nor was the single report of a gun uncommon enough to call for investigation in such weather.

All this the Boy told himself as the minutes dragged by. Then he looked again at Wolf. The dog, head on one side, still stood protectingly above him. The dog was cold and in pain. But being only a dog it did not occur to him to trot off home to the comfort of the library fire and leave his master to fend for himself.

Presently, with a little sigh, Wolf lay down on the ice, his nose across the Boy's arm. Even if he lacked strength to save his beloved master, he could stay and share the Boy's sufferings.

But the Boy himself thought otherwise. He was not at all minded to freeze to death, nor was he willing to let Wolf imitate the dog of Pompeii by dying helplessly at his master's side. Controlling for an instant the chattering of his teeth, he called:

"Wolf!"

The dog was on his feet again at the word, alert, eager.

"Wolf!" repeated the boy. *"Go! Hear me? Go!"*

He pointed homeward.

Wolf stared at him, hesitant. Again the boy called in vehement command, *"Go!"*

The collie lifted his head to the twilight sky with a wolf howl hideous in its grief and appeal—a howl as wild and discordant as that of any of his savage ancestors. Then, stooping first to lick the numb hand that clung to the branch, Wolf turned and fled.

Across the sharp rim of ice he tore at top speed, head down, whirling through the deeping dusk like a flash of tawny light.

Wolf understood what was wanted of him. Wolf always understood. The pain in his feet was nothing. The stiffness of his numbed body was forgotten in the urgency for speed.

The Boy looked drearily after the swift-vanishing figure which the dusk was swallowing. He knew the dog would try to bring help, as has many another and lesser dog in times of need. Whether or not that help could arrive in time, or at all, was a point on which the Boy would not let himself dwell. Into his benumbed brain crept the memory of an old Norse proverb he had read in school:

"Heroism consists in hanging on one minute longer."

Unconsciously he tightened his feeble hold on the tree branch and braced himself.

From the marshes to The Place was a full two miles. Despite the deep and sticky snow, Wolf covered the distance in less than nine minutes. He paused in front of the gate lodge, at the highway entrance to the drive. But the superintendent and his wife had gone to Paterson, shopping, that afternoon.

Down the drive to the house he dashed. The maids had taken advantage of their employers' day in New York to walk across the lake to the village, to a motion picture show.

Wise men claim that dogs have not the power to think or to reason things out in a logical way. So perhaps it was mere chance that next sent Wolf's flying feet across the lake to the village. Perhaps it was chance, and not the knowledge that where there is a village there are people.

Again and again, in the car, he had sat upon the front seat alongside the Mistress when she drove to the station to meet guests. There were always people at the station. And to the station Wolf now raced.

The usual group of platform idlers had been dispersed by the cold. A solitary baggageman was hauling a trunk and some boxes out of the express coop on to the platform to be put aboard the five o'clock train from New York.

As the baggageman passed under the clump of station lights, he came to a sudden halt. For out of the darkness dashed a dog. Full tilt, the animal rushed up to him and seized him by the skirt of the overcoat.

The man cried out in scared surprise. He dropped the box he was carrying and struck at the dog, to ward off the seemingly murderous attack. He recognized Wolf and he knew the collie's repute.

But Wolf was not attacking. Holding tight to the coat skirt he backed away, trying to draw the man with him, and all the while whimpering aloud like a nervous puppy.

A kick from the heavy-shod boot broke the dog's hold on the coat skirt, even as a second yell from the man brought four or five other people running out from the station waiting room.

One of these, the telegraph operator, took in the scene at a single glance. With great presence of mind he bawled loudly: "MAD DOG!"

This, as Wolf, reeling from the kick, sought to gain another grip on the coat skirt. A second kick sent him reeling over and over on the tracks, while other voices took up the panic cry of "Mad dog!"

Now, a mad dog is supposed to be a dog afflicted by rabies. Once in ten thousand times, at the very most, a mad-dog hue and cry is justified. Certainly not oftener. A harmless and friendly dog loses his master on the street. He runs about, confused and frightened, looking for the owner he has lost. A boy throws a stone at him. Other boys chase him. His tongue hangs out and his eyes glaze with terror. Then some fool bellows: "Mad dog!"

And the cruel chase is on—a chase that ends in the pitiful victim's death. Yes, in every crowd there is a voice ready to raise that asinine and murderously cruel shout.

So it was with the men who witnessed Wolf's frenzied effort to take aid to the imperiled Boy.

Voice after voice repeated the cry. Men groped along the platform edge for stones to throw. The village policeman ran puffingly upon the scene, drawing his revolver.

Finding it useless to make a further attempt to drag the baggageman to the rescue, Wolf leaped back, facing the ever larger group. Back went his head again in that hideous wolf howl. Then he galloped away a few yards, trotted back, howled once more, and again galloped lakeward.

All of which only confirmed the panicky crowd in the belief that they were threatened by a mad dog. A shower of stones hurled about Wolf as he came back a third time to lure these dull humans into following him.

One pointed rock smote the collie's shoulder, glancingly, cutting it to the bone. A shot from the policeman's revolver fanned the fur of his ruff as it whizzed past.

Knowing that he faced death, he nevertheless stood his ground, not troubling to dodge the fusillade of stones, but continuing to run lakeward and then trot back, whining with excitement.

A second pistol shot flew wide. A third grazed the dog's hip. From all directions people were running toward the station. A

man darted into a house next door and emerged carrying a shot‑
gun. This he steadied on the veranda rail, not forty feet away
from the leaping dog, and made ready to fire.

It was then the train from New York came in. And momen‑
tarily the sport of "mad-dog" killing was abandoned, while the
crowd scattered to each side of the track.

From a front car of the train the Mistress and the Master
emerged into a bedlam of noise and confusion.

"Best hide in the station, ma'am!" shouted the telegraph
operater, at sight of the Mistress. "There's a mad dog loose
out here! He's chasing folks around, and—"

"Mad dog!" repeated the Mistress in high contempt, "If
you knew anything about dogs, you'd know mad ones never
'chase folks around,' any more than diptheria patients do.
Then—"

A flash of tawny light beneath the station lamp, a scurrying
of frightened idlers, a final wasted shot from the policeman's
pistol—as Wolf dived headlong through the frightened crowd
toward the voice he heard and recognized.

Up to the Mistress and Master galloped Wolf. He was
bleeding, his eyes were bloodshot, his fur was rumpled. He
seized the astounded Master's gloved hand lightly between his
teeth and sought to pull him across the tracks and toward the
lake.

The Master knew dogs. Especially he knew Wolf. And with‑
out a word he suffered himself to be led. The Mistress and one or
two inquisitive men followed.

Presently, Wolf loosened his hold on the Master's hand
and ran on ahead, darting back every few moments to make
certain he was followed.

"*Heroism—consists—in—hanging—on—one—minute—
longer,*" the Boy was whispering deliriously to himself for the
hundredth time, as Wolf pattered up to him in triumph across
the ice with the human rescuers a scant ten yards behind.

Mind-Reading Dog

BY JOHN STEINBECK

The author and his poodle, Charley, share here some of the experiences they found together when they set out in a truck named Rocinante to discover America.

C*HARLEY* is a mind-reading dog. There have been many trips in his lifetime, and often he has to be left at home. He knows we are going long before the suitcases come out, and he paces and worries and whines and goes into a state of mild hysteria, old as he is. During the weeks of preparation he was underfoot the whole time and made a nuisance of himself.

He took to hiding in the truck, creeping in and trying to make himself look small. . . .

Charley is a tall dog. As he sat in the seat besides me, his head was almost as high as mine. He put his nose close to my ear and said, "Ftt." He is the only dog I ever knew who could pronounce the consonant *F*. This is because his front teeth are crooked, a tragedy which keeps him out of dog shows; because his upper front teeth slightly engage his lower lip Charley can pronounce *F*. The word "Ftt" usually means he would like to salute a bush or a tree. I opened the cab door and let him out, and he went about his ceremony. He doesn't have to think about it to do it well. It is my experience that in some areas Charley is more intelligent than I am, but in others he is abysmally ignorant. He can't read, can't drive a car, and has no grasp of mathematics. But in his own field of endeavor, which he was now practicing, the slow, imperial smelling over and anointing of an area, he has no peer. Of course his horizons are limited, but how wide are mine? . . .

Charley likes to get up early, and he likes me to get up early too. And why shouldn't he? Right after his breakfast he goes back to sleep. Over the years he has developed a number of innocent-appearing ways to get me up. He can shake himself and his collar loud enough to wake the dead. If that doesn't work he gets a sneezing fit. But perhaps his most irritating method is to sit quietly beside the bed and stare into my face with a sweet and forgiving look on his face; I come out of deep sleep with the feeling of being looked at. But I have learned to keep my eyes tight shut. If I even blink he sneezes and stretches, and that night's sleep is over for me. Often the war of wills goes on for quite a time, I squinching my eyes shut and he forgiving me, but he nearly always wins. He liked traveling so much he wanted to get started early, and early for Charley is the first tempering of darkness with the dawn. . . .

49

Upon arrival in Chicago, John Steinbeck leaves Charley in a kennel to be stored, bathed and Hollanderized. Upon picking him up. . . .

Charley was torn three ways—with anger at me for leaving him, with gladness at the sight of Rocinante, and with pure pride in his appearance. For when Charley is groomed and clipped and washed he is as pleased with himself as is a man with a good tailor or a woman newly patinaed by a beauty parlor, all of whom can believe they are like that clear through. Charley's combed columns of legs were noble things, his cap of silver blue fur was rakish, and he carried the pompon of his tail like the baton of a bandmaster. A wealth of combed and clipped mustache gave him the appearance and attitude of a French rake of the nineteenth century, and incidentally concealed his crooked front teeth. I happen to know what he looks like without the tailoring. One summer when his fur grew matted and mildewed I clipped him to the skin. Under those sturdy towers of legs are spindly shanks, thin and not too straight; with his chest ruff removed one can see the sagging stomach of the middle-aged. But if Charley was aware of his deep-down inadequacy, he gave no sign. If manners maketh man, then manner and grooming maketh poodle. He sat straight and nobly in the seat of Rocinante and he gave me to understand that while foregiveness was not impossible, I would have to work for it.

He is a fraud and I know it. Once when our boys were little and in summer camp we paid them the deadly parents' visit. When we were about to depart, a lady parent told us she had to leave quickly to keep her child from going into hysterics. And with brave but trembling lips she fled blindly, masking her feeling to save her child. The boy watched her go and then with infinite relief went back to his gang and his business, knowing that he too had played the game. And I know for a fact that five minutes after I had left Charley he had found new friends and had made his arrangements for his comfort. But one thing Charley did not fake. He was delighted to be traveling again, and for a few days he was an ornament to the trip. . . .

Charley has always associated with the learned, the gentle, the literate, and the reasonable both in France and in America. And Charley is no more like a dog dog than he is like a cat. His perceptions are sharp and delicate and he is a mind reader. I don't know that he can read the thoughts of other dogs, but he can read mine. Before a plan is half formed in my mind, Charley knows about it, and he also knows whether he is to be included in it. There's no question about this. I know too well his look of despair and disapproval when I have just thought that he must be left at home. . . .

Mr. Steinbeck and Charley arrive at Yellowstone National Park . . .

A pleasant-looking National Park man checked me in and then he said, "How about that dog? They aren't permitted in except on leash."

"Why?" I asked.

"Because of the bears."

"Sir," I said, "this is an unique dog. He does not live by tooth or fang. He respects the right of cats to be cats although he doesn't admire them. He turns his steps rather than disturb an earnest caterpillar. His greatest fear is that someone will point out a rabbit and suggest that he chase it. This is a dog of peace and tranquility. I suggest that the greatest danger to your bears will be pique at being ignored by Charley."

The young man laughed. "I wasn't so much worried about the bears," he said. "But our bears have developed an intolerance for dogs. One of them might demonstrate his prejudice with a clip on the chin, and then—no dog."

"I'll lock him in the back, sir. I promise you Charley will cause no ripple in the bear world, and as an old bear-looker, neither will I."

"I just have to warn you," he said. "I have no doubt your dog has the best of intentions. On the other hand, our bears

51

have the worst. Don't leave food about. Not only do they steal but they are critical of anyone who tries to reform them. In a word, don't believe their sweet faces or you might get clobbered. And don't let the dog wander. Bears don't argue."

We went on our way into the wonderland of nature gone nuts, and you will have to believe what happened. The only way I can prove it would be to get a bear.

Less than a mile from the entrance I saw a bear beside the road, and it ambled out as though to flag me down. Instantly a change came over Charley. He shrieked with rage. His lips flared, showing wicked teeth that have some trouble with a dog biscuit. He screeched insults at the bear, which hearing, the bear reared up and seemed to me to overtop Rocinante. Frantically I rolled the windows shut and, swinging quickly to the left, grazed the animal, then scuttled on while Charley raved and ranted beside me, describing in detail what he would do to that bear if he could get at him. I was never so astonished in my life. To the best of my knowledge Charley had never seen a bear, and in his whole history had showed great tolerance for every living thing. Besides all this, Charley is a coward, so deep-seated a coward that he has developed a technique for concealing it. And yet he showed every evidence of wanting to get out and murder a bear that outweighed him a thousand to one. I don't understand it.

A little farther along two bears showed up, and the effect was doubled. Charley became a maniac. He leaped all over me, he cursed and growled, snarled and screamed. I didn't know he had the ability to snarl. Where did he learn it? Bears were in good supply, and the road became a nightmare. For the first time in his life Charley resisted reason, even resisted a cuff on the ear. He became a primitive killer lusting for the blood of his enemy, and up to this moment he had had no enemies. In a bearless stretch, I opened the cab, took Charley by the collar, and locked him in the house. But that did no good. When we passed other bears he leaped on the table and scratched at the windows trying to get out at them. I could hear canned goods crashing as he struggled in his mania. Bears simply brought out

52

the Hyde in my Jekyll-headed dog. What could have caused it? Was it a pre-breed memory of a time when the wolf was in him? I know him well. Once in a while he tries a bluff, but it is a palpable lie. I swear that this was no lie. I am certain that if he were released he would have charged every bear we passed and found victory or death.

It was too nerve-racking, a shocking spectacle, like seeing an old, calm friend go insane. No amount of natural wonders, of rigid cliffs and belching waters, of smoking springs could even engage my attention while that pandemonium went on. After about the fifth encounter I gave up, turned Rocinante about, and retraced my way. If I had stopped the night and bears had gathered to my cooking, I dare not think what would have happened.

At the gate the park guard checked me out. "You didn't stay long. Where's the dog?"

"Locked up back there. And I owe you an apology. That dog has the heart and soul of a bear killer and I didn't know it. Heretofore he has been a little tenderhearted toward an under-done steak."

"Yeah!" he said. "That happens sometimes. That's why I warned you. A bear dog would know his chances, but I've seen a Pomeranian go up like a puff of smoke. You know, a well-favored bear can bat a dog like a tennis ball."

I moved fast, back the way I had come, and I was reluctant to camp for fear there might be some unofficial non-government bears about. That night I spent in a pretty auto court near Livingston. I had my dinner in a restaurant, and when I had settled in a comfortable chair, I inspected Charley. He was dazed. His eyes held a faraway look and he was totally ex-hausted, emotionally no doubt. He couldn't eat his dinner, he refused the evening walk, and once we were in he collapsed on the floor and went to sleep. In the night I heard him whining and yapping, and when I turned on the light his feet were making running gestures and his body jerked and his eyes were wide open, but it was only a night bear. I awakened him and gave him some water. This time he went to sleep and didn't stir

53

all night. In the morning he was still tired. I wonder why we think the thoughts and emotions of animals are simple.

In New Mexico, after days of driving, the author feels he is no longer "seeing and hearing," every hill looks alike. To add to his mood, the cabin is cold and cluttered.

Charley had not returned. I opened the door and whistled him and got no response. I grabbed my searchlight and turned its spearing beam up the canyon. The light flashed on two eyes about fifty yards away. I ran up the trail and found him standing staring into space.

"What's the matter, Charley, aren't you well?"

His tail slowly waved his replies. "Oh yes, Quite well, I guess."

"Why didn't you come when I whistled?"

"I didn't hear you whistle."

"What are you staring at?"

"I don't know. Nothing I guess."

"Well, don't you want your dinner?"

"I'm really not hungry. But I'll go through the motions."

Back in the cabin he flopped down on the floor and put his chin down on his paws.

"Come on up on the bed, Charley. Let's be miserable together." He complied but without enthusiasm and I riffled my fingers in his topknot and behind his ears the way he likes it. "How's that?"

He shifted his head. "A little more to the left. There. That's the place."

"We'd be lousy explorers. A few days out and we get the mullygrubs. The first white man through here—I think he was named Narváez and I'm under the impression his little jaunt took six years. Move over. I'll look it up. Nope, it was eight years—1528 to 1536. And Narváez himself didn't make it this far. Four of his men did, though. I wonder if they ever got the mullygrubs. We're soft, Charley. Maybe it's time for a little gallantry. When's your birthday?"

54

"I don't know. Maybe it's like horses, the first of January."

"Think it might be today?"

"Who knows?"

"I could make you a cake. Have to be hotcake mix because that's what I have. Plenty of syrup and a candle on top."

Charley watched the operation with some interest. His silly tail made delicate conversation. "Anybody saw you make a birthday cake for a dog that he don't even know when's his birthday would think you were nuts."

"If you can't manage any better grammar than that with your tail, maybe it's a good thing you can't talk."

It turned out pretty well—four layers of hotcakes with maple syrup between and a stub of a miner's candle on top. . . .

Charley licked the syrup from his whiskers. "What makes you so moony?"

"It's because I've stopped seeing. When that happens you think you'll never see again."

He stood up and stretched himself, first fore and then aft. "Let's take a stroll up the hill," he suggested. "Maybe you've started again." . . .

The dry, frozen air came out of us in plumes of steam. Some fairly large animal went leaping up the broken stone hill, or maybe a small animal and a big little avalanche.

"What does your nose say that was?"

"Nothing I recognize. Kind of a musky smell. Nothing I'm going to chase, either."

So dark was the night that it was prickled with fiery dots. My light brought an answering flash up the steep rocky bank. I climbed up, slipping and floundering, lost the echoed light and found it again, a good little new-split stone with a piece of mica in it—not a fortune but a good thing to have. I put it in my pocket and we went to bed.

Two orphans make a team

The Dog of Pompeii

BY LOUIS UNTERMEYER

TITO and his dog Bimbo lived (if you could call it living) under the wall where it joined the inner gate. They really didn't live there; they just slept there. They lived anywhere. Pompeii was one of the gayest of the old Latin towns, but although Tito was never an unhappy boy, he was not exactly a merry one. The streets were always lively with shining chariots and bright red trappings; the open-air theatres rocked with laughing crowds; sham battles and athletic sports were free for the asking in the great stadium. Once a year the Caesar visited the pleasure city and the fireworks lasted for days; the sacrifices in the Forum were better than a show. But Tito saw none of these things. He was blind—had been blind from birth. He was known to everyone in the poorer quarters. But no one could say how old he was, no one remembered his parents, no one could tell where he came from. Bimbo was another mystery. As long as people could remember seeing Tito—about twelve or thirteen years—they had seen Bimbo. Bimbo had never left his side. He was not only dog, but nurse, pillow, playmate, mother and father to Tito.

Did I say Bimbo never left his master? (Perhaps I had better say comrade, for if anyone was the master, it was Bimbo.) I was wrong. Bimbo did trust Tito alone exactly three times a day. It was a fixed routine, a custom understood between boy and dog since the beginning of their friendship, and the way it worked was this.

Early in the morning, shortly after dawn while Tito was still dreaming, Bimbo would disappear. When Tito awoke, Bimbo would be sitting quietly at his side, his ears cocked, his stump of a tail tapping the ground, and a fresh-baked bread—more like a large round roll—at his feet. Tito would stretch himself; Bimbo would yawn; then they would breakfast. At noon, no matter where they happened to be, Bimbo would put his paw on Tito's knee and the two of them would return to the inner gate. Tito would curl up in the corner (almost like a dog) and go to sleep, while Bimbo, looking quite important (almost like a boy) would disappear again. In half an hour he'd be back with their lunch. Sometimes it would be a piece of fruit or a scrap of meat; often it was nothing but a dry crust. But sometimes there would be one of those flat rich cakes, sprinkled with raisins and sugar, that Tito liked so much. At suppertime the same thing happened, although there was a little less of everything, for things were hard to snatch in the evening with the streets full of people. Besides, Bimbo didn't approve of too much food before going to sleep. A heavy supper made boys too restless and dogs too stodgy—and it was the business of a dog to sleep lightly with one ear open and muscles ready for action.

But, whether there was much or little, hot or cold, fresh

57

or dry, food was always there. Tito never asked where it came from and Bimbo never told him. There was plenty of rainwater in the hollows of soft stones; the old egg-woman at the corner sometimes gave him a cupful of strong goat's milk; in the grape season the fat winemaker let him have drippings of the mild juice. So there was no danger of going hungry or thirsty. There was plenty of everything in Pompeii—if you knew where to find it—and if you had a dog like Bimbo.

As I said before, Tito was not the merriest boy in Pompeii. He could not romp with the other youngsters and play hare-and-hounds and I-spy and follow-your-master and ball-against-the-building and jackstones and kings-and-robbers with them. But that did not make him sorry for himself. If he could not see the sights that delighted the lads of Pompeii he could hear and smell things they never noticed. He could really see more with his ears and nose than they could with their eyes. When he and Bimbo went out walking he knew just where they were going and exactly what was happening.

"Ah," he'd sniff and say, as they passed a handsome villa, "Glaucus Pansa is giving a grand dinner tonight. They're going to have three kinds of bread, and roast pigling, and stuffed goose, and a great stew—I think bear stew—and a fig pie." And Bimbo would note that this would be a good place to visit tomorrow.

Or, "H'm," Tito would murmur, half through his lips, half through his nostrils. "The wife of Marcus Lucretius is expecting her mother. She's shaking out every piece of goods in the house; she's going to use the best clothes—the ones she's been keeping in pine needles and camphor—and there's an extra girl in the kitchen. Come, Bimbo, let's get out of the dust!"

Or, as they passed a small but elegant dwelling opposite the public baths, "Too bad! The tragic poet is ill again. It must be a bad fever this time, for they're trying smoke fumes instead of medicine. Whew! I'm glad I'm not a tragic poet!"

Or, as they neared the Forum, "Mm-m! What good things they have in the Macellum today!" (It really was a sort of butcher-grocer-market-place, but Tito didn't know any better. He called it the Macellum.) "Dates from Africa, and salt oysters from sea caves, and cuttlefish, and new honey, and sweet onions, and—ugh!—water-buffalo steaks. Come, let's see what's what in the Forum." And Bimbo, just as curious as his comrade, hurried on. Being a dog, he trusted his ears and nose (like Tito) more than his eyes. And so the two of them entered the center of Pompeii.

The Forum was the part of the town to which everybody came at least once during each day. It was the central square and everything happened here. There were no private houses; all was public—the chief temples, the gold and red bazaars, the silk shops, the town hall, the booths belonging to the weavers and jewel merchants, the wealthy woolen market, the shrine of the household gods. Everything glittered here. The buildings looked as if they were new—which, in a sense, they were. The earthquake of twelve years ago had brought down all the old structures and, since the citizens of Pompeii were ambitious to rival Naples and even Rome, they had seized the opportunity to rebuild the whole town. And they had done it all within a dozen years. There was scarcely a building that was older than Tito.

Tito had heard a great deal about the earthquake though, being about a year old at the time, he could scarcely remember it. This particular quake had been a light one—as earthquakes go. The weaker houses had been shaken down, parts of the outworn wall had been wrecked; but there was little loss of life, and the brilliant new Pompeii had taken the place of the old. No one knew what caused these earthquakes. Records showed they had happened in the neighborhood since the beginning of time. Sailors said that it was to teach the lazy city folk a lesson and make them appreciate those who risked the dangers of the sea to bring them luxuries and protect their town from invaders. The priests said that the gods took this way of showing their anger to those who refused to worship properly and who failed to bring enough sacrifices to the altars and (though they didn't say it in so many words) presents to the priests. The tradesmen said that the foreign merchants had corrupted the ground and it was no longer safe to traffic in imported goods that came from strange places and carried a curse with them. Everyone had a different explanation—and everyone's explanation was louder and sillier than his neighbor's.

They were talking about it this afternoon as Tito and Bimbo came out of the side street into the public square. The Forum was the favorite promenade for rich and poor. What with the priests arguing with the politicians, servants doing the day's shopping, tradesmen crying their wares, women displaying the latest fashions from Greece and Egypt, children playing hide-and-seek among the marble columns, knots of soldiers, sailors, peasants from the provinces—to say nothing of those who merely came to lounge and look on—the square was crowded to its last inch. His ears even more than his nose guided Tito to the place where the talk was loudest. It was in front of the Shrine of the Household Gods that, naturally enough, the householders were arguing.

"I tell you," rumbled a voice which Tito recognized as bath-master Rufus', "there won't be another earthquake in my lifetime or yours. There may be a tremble or two, but earthquakes, like lightnings, never strike twice in the same place."

"Do they not?" asked a thin voice Tito had never heard. It had a high, sharp ring to it and Tito knew it as the accent of a stranger. "How about the two towns of Sicily that have been ruined three times within fifteen years by the eruptions of Mount Etna? And were they not warned? And does that column of smoke above Vesuvius mean nothing?"

"That?" Tito could hear the grunt with which one question answered another. "That's always there. We use it for our weather guide. When the smoke stands up straight we know we'll have fair weather; when it flattens out it's sure to be foggy; when it drifts to the east—"

"Yes, yes," cut in the edged voice. "I've heard about your mountain barometer. But the column of smoke seems hundreds of feet higher than usual and it's thickening and spreading like a shadowy tree. They say in Naples—"

"Oh, Naples!" Tito knew this voice by the little squeak that went with it. It was Attilio, the cameo cutter. *"They* talk while we suffer. Little help we got from them last time. Naples commits the crimes and Pompeii pays the price. It's become a proverb with us. Let them mind their own business."

"Yes," grumbled Rufus, "and others, too."

"Very well, my confident friends," responded the thin voice which now sounded curiously flat. "We also have a proverb—and it is this: Those who will not listen to men must be taught by the gods. I say no more. But I leave a last warning. Remember the holy ones. Look to your temples. And when the smoke tree above Vesuvius grows to the shape of an umbrella pine, look to your lives."

Tito could hear the air whistle as the speaker drew his toga about him and the quick shuffle of feet told him the stranger had gone.

"Now what," said the cameo cutter, "did he mean by that?"

"I wonder," grunted Rufus, "I wonder."

Tito wondered, too. And Bimbo, his head at a thoughtful angle, looked as if he had been doing a heavy piece of pondering. By nightfall the argument had been forgotten. If the smoke had increased no one saw it in the dark. Besides, it was Caesar's birthday and the town was in holiday mood. Tito and Bimbo were among the merrymakers, dodging the charioteers who shouted at them. A dozen times they almost upset baskets of sweets and jars of Vesuvian wine, said to be as fiery as the streams inside the volcano, and a dozen times they were cursed and cuffed. But Tito never missed his footing. He was thankful for his keen ears and quick instinct—most thankful of all for Bimbo.

They visited the uncovered theatre and, though Tito could not see the faces of the actors, he could follow the play better than most of the audience, for their attention wandered—they were distracted by the scenery, the costumes, the by-play, even by themselves—while Tito's whole attention was centered in what he heard. Then to the city walls, where the people of Pompeii watched a mock naval battle in which the city was attacked by the sea and saved after thousands of flaming arrows had been exchanged and countless colored torches had been

61

burned. Though the thrill of flaring ships and lighted skies was lost to Tito, the shouts and cheers excited him as much as any and he cried out with the loudest of them.

The next morning there were *two* of the beloved raisin and sugar cakes for his breakfast. Bimbo was unusually active and thumped his bit of a tail until Tito was afraid he would wear it out. The boy could not imagine whether Bimbo was urging him to some sort of game or was trying to tell something. After a while, he ceased to notice Bimbo. He felt drowsy. Last night's late hours had tired him. Besides, there was a heavy mist in the air—no, a thick fog rather than a mist—a fog that got into his throat and scraped it and made him cough. He walked as far as the marine gate to get a breath of the sea. But the blanket of haze had spread all over the bay and even the salt air seemed smoky.

He went to bed before dusk and slept. But he did not sleep well. He had too many dreams—dreams of ships lurching in the Forum, of losing his way in a screaming crowd, of armies marching across his chest, of being pulled over every rough pavement of Pompeii.

He woke early. Or, rather, he was pulled awake. Bimbo was doing the pulling. The dog had dragged Tito to his feet and was urging the boy along. Somewhere. Where, Tito did not know. His feet stumbled uncertainly; he was still half asleep. For a while he noticed nothing except the fact that it was hard to breathe. The air was hot. And heavy. So heavy that he could taste it. The air, it seemed, had turned to powder, a warm powder that stung his nostrils and burned his sightless eyes.

Then he began to hear sounds. Peculiar sounds. Like animals under the earth. Hissings and groanings and muffled cries that a dying creature might make dislodging the stones of his underground cave. There was no doubt of it now. The noises came from underneath. He not only heard them—he could feel them. The earth twitched; the twitching changed to an uneven shrugging of the soil. Then, as Bimbo half-pulled, half-coaxed him across, the ground jerked away from his feet and he was thrown against a stone fountain.

The water—hot water—splashing in his face revived him. He got to his feet, Bimbo steadying him, helping him on again. The noises grew louder; they came closer. The cries were even more animal-like than before, but now they came from human throats. A few people, quicker of foot and more hurried by fear, began to rush by. A family of two—then a section—then, it seemed, an army broken out of bounds. Tito, bewildered though he was, could recognize Rufus as he bellowed past him, like a water buffalo gone mad. Time was lost in a nightmare.

It was then the crashing began. First a sharp crackling, like a monstrous snapping of twigs; then a roar like the fall of a whole forest of trees; then an explosion that tore earth and sky. The heavens, though Tito could not see them, were shot through with continual flickerings of fire. Lightnings above were answered by thunders beneath. A house fell. Then another. By a miracle the two companions had escaped the dangerous side streets and were in a more open space. It was the Forum. They rested here a while—how long he did not know.

Tito had no idea of the time of day. He could *feel* it was black—an unnatural blackness. Something inside—perhaps the lack of breakfast and lunch—told him it was past noon. But it didn't matter. Nothing seemed to matter. He was getting drowsy, too drowsy to walk. But walk he must. He knew it. And Bimbo knew it; the sharp tugs told him so. Nor was it a moment too soon. The sacred ground of the Forum was safe no longer. It was beginning to rock, then to pitch, then to split. As they stumbled out of the square, the earth wriggled like a caught snake and all the columns of the temple of Jupiter came down. It was the end of the world—or so it seemed. To walk was not enough now. They must run. Tito was too frightened to know what to do or where to go. He had lost all sense of direction. He started to go back to the inner gate; but Bimbo, straining his back to the last inch, almost pulled his clothes from him. What did the creature want? Had the dog gone mad?

Then, suddenly, he understood. Bimbo was telling him the way out—urging him there. The sea gate of course. The sea gate —and then the sea. Far from falling buildings, heaving ground.

63

He turned, Bimbo guiding him across open pits and dangerous pools of bubbling mud, away from buildings that had caught fire and were dropping their burning beams. Tito could no longer tell whether the noises were made by the shrieking sky or the agonized people. He and Bimbo ran on—the only silent beings in a howling world.

New dangers threatened. All Pompeii seemed to be thronging toward the marine gate and, squeezing among the crowds, there was the chance of being trampled to death. But the chance had to be taken. It was growing harder and harder to breathe. What air there was choked him. It was all dust now—dust and pebbles, pebbles as large as beans. They fell on his head, his hands—pumice stones from the black heart of Vesuvius. The mountain was turning itself inside out. Tito remembered a phrase that the stranger had said in the Forum two days ago: "Those who will not listen to men must be taught by the gods." The people of Pompeii had refused to heed the warnings; they were being taught now—if it was not too late.

Suddenly it seemed too late for Tito. The red hot ashes blistered his skin, the stinging vapors tore his throat. He could not go on. He staggered toward a small tree at the side of the road and fell. In a moment Bimbo was beside him. He coaxed. But there was no answer. He licked Tito's hands, his feet, his face. The boy did not stir. Then Bimbo did the last thing he could—the last thing he wanted to do. He bit his comrade, bit him deep in the arm. With a cry of pain, Tito jumped to his feet, Bimbo after him. Tito was in despair, but Bimbo was determined. He drove the boy on, snapping at his heels, worrying his way through the crowd; barking, baring his teeth, heedless of kicks or falling stones. Sick with hunger, half-dead with fear and sulphur fumes, Tito pounded on, pursued by Bimbo. How long he never knew. At last he staggered through the marine gate and felt soft sand under him. Then Tito fainted. . . .

Some one was dashing sea water over him. Some one was carrying him toward a boat.

"Bimbo," he called. And then louder, "Bimbo!" But Bimbo had disappeared.

Voices jarred against each other. "Hurry—hurry!" "To the boats!" "Can't you see the child's frightened and starving!" "He keeps calling for someone!" "Poor boy, he's out of his mind." "Here, child—take this!"

They tucked him in among them. The oarlocks creaked; the oars splashed; the boat rode over toppling waves. Tito was safe. But he wept continually.

"Bimbo!" he wailed. "Bimbo! Bimbo!"

He could not be comforted.

Eighteen hundred years passed. Scientists were restoring the ancient city; excavators were working their way through the stones and trash that had buried the entire town. Much had already been brought to light—statues, bronze instruments, bright mosaics, household articles; even delicate paintings had been preserved by the fall of ashes that had taken over two thousand lives. Columns were dug up and the Forum was beginning to emerge.

It was at a place where the ruins lay deepest that the Director paused.

"Come here," he called to his assistant. "I think we've discovered the remains of a building in good shape. Here are four huge millstones that were most likely turned by slaves or mules —and here is a whole wall standing with shelves inside it. Why! It must have been a bakery. And here's a curious thing. What do you think I found under this heap where the ashes were thickest? The skeleton of a dog!"

"Amazing!" gasped his assistant. "You'd think a dog would have had sense enough to run away at the time. And what is that flat thing he's holding between his teeth? It can't be a stone."

"No. It must have come from this bakery. You know it looks to me like some sort of cake hardened with the years. And, bless me, if those little black pebbles aren't raisins. A raisin cake almost two thousand years old! I wonder what made him want it at such a moment?"

"I wonder," murmured the assistant.

Was Red too special?

Pat'tidge Dog

BY JIM KJELGAARD

*A*S SOON as the train lurched to a stop at
the little wayside station, Danny Pickett jumped from the express
car. He turned to help Red, but almost before he had turned
around the big Irish setter had leaped to the cinders beside him.
Danny started at once for the beechwoods that began almost
where the railroad property ended. The fuss and glamor of the
dog show were behind them. Mr. Haggin had the blue ribbon
and silver cup that Red had won. But Danny had the dog. And
now they were home, here in the Wintapi.

Red paced sedately beside the boy. Nominally the property
of Mr. Haggin, a millionaire sportsman who had built an estate

in the wild Wintapi, the red dog had attached himself to Danny, son of a hillbilly trapper and farmer. Together, they had trailed and killed an outlaw bear that no hounds had dared follow. Mr. Haggin, an understanding man, had figured out for himself exactly what had happened on that bear hunt, had known that both Danny and the dog had played fair throughout. He had hired Danny to take care of Red, his first duty being to handle him at the New York show. But now that responsibility was ended and Red was Danny's, to do with as he saw fit.

Once in the woods, screened by trees from prying eyes that might see and comment on any letdown in dignity, the boy broke into a wild run. It seemed an eternity since he had seen the rough shanty where he and his father lived, smelled the good scent of streams, forests and mountains, or had any part at all in the only life he had ever loved. With the dog racing beside him Danny ran over the jutting nose of a mountain, trotted up a long valley, climbed the ridge at its head and descended the other side. He ran in almost a perfectly straight line through the beechwoods to his father's home. Ross Pickett would naturally be out scouting around the ridges on a fine day like this.

But his father's four hounds strained at the ends of their chains and bayed a vociferous welcome. Danny grinned at them and watched Red go up to sniff noses with Old Mike, leader of the hound pack. The three younger dogs sat on their haunches and awaited quizzically their boss's reaction to this dazzling, red-coated invader of their home. But the setter did not falter and Mike knew too much about other animals not to know when one was his superior. The two dogs wagged stiff tails, and Mike sat down to blink indifferently at Danny. Red was accepted.

Danny chuckled and tickled the old hound's tattered ears while the three pups begged for attention. Red sat back with his head cocked to one side and watched jealously. The boy stooped and unsnapped the chains. Wild to be free after a long day's confinement, the four hounds went in a mad race across the field. They came tearing back and were away again. Red raced with them, but wheeled and came back when Danny whistled. The boy tickled his silken ears.

67

"Leave 'em go," he said. "Leave 'em go, Red. They'll find an' tree somethin' an' Pappy'll get it when he comes in. But you got mo' impawtant work to do, Red. Youah a pat'tidge dog."

The setter walked beside him when Danny went into the house. Outside, everything had been warm sunshine. But inside, where only glancing sunbeams strayed through the single-paned windows that Ross Pickett had set in the walls of his shanty, a definite chill prevailed. Danny stuffed tinder into the stove, lighted it and added wood when it was blazing. He pulled aside the burlap curtain that hung over the cupboard and took out a pot and skillet. Red trotted beside him when he went out to the springhouse for a piece of pork that Ross had left there to cool and returned to the house to lie in the center of the floor while Danny cooked the meat.

A little before sundown the setter got up and went to sit before the door. Three minutes later there was a heavy tread on the porch and Ross Pickett came in.

"Danny!" he exclaimed. "I knowed you was home on account I heer'd the haouns a 'bayin'. I whistled 'em in an' they come back wi' me. They had a little coon up, an' coons ain't prime yet."

"Hello, Pappy! It shuah is good to be home. You been scoutin' out a trap line?"

"Yup. Stoney Lonesome Ridge fo' foxes. Ought to be a nice take of pelts this yeah; they's lots of rabbits fo' pelt animals to eat off."

But the shine in Ross's eyes belied the workaday talk, and the warm glow inside Danny was far too intense ever to be put into words. He and his father had been so close for so long that they felt and acted and almost thought alike. Each was lost without the other, and now that they were together once more, they could be happy again.

Danny said with affected carelessness that could not hide the enormous pride he felt, "I fetched the Red dog home. Theah he is."

"Well, so you did!" Ross whirled about as though he had just noticed the magnificent setter. "That is a dog, Danny! I reckon you'n him must of cut some swath in Noo Yawk, huh?"

"Red did in the dog ring. He got some prizes fo' Mistah Haggin."

"How'd you like Noo Yawk, Danny?"

"Gosh, I dunno. It's nice but it's awful big. It's a right smart place for them that likes it, but I'd ruther abide in the Wintapi."

Ross Pickett was on the floor beside Red. His expert hands strayed over the dog's back, his legs, his withers, his chest. Danny waited breathlessly until his father finally rose.

"Danny," he said profoundly, "if that Red dog's got a nose, he's got evah'thin' any six dogs should have."

Danny's heart leaped. "He smelt you when you was still three minutes away."

"I should of knowed it," Ross breathed. "He run that big killah heah right into the groun'. Danny, that dog is goin' to be the best vahmint killah we evah had."

Danny turned away. All the joy of homecoming was suddenly gone, and a smothering hand came to still his singing heart. He should have known what his father would say. But until now it had never occurred to him that hunting to Ross meant hunting bears, wildcats, foxes and raccoons. Every other kind of hunting was only to get meat. Danny gulped. Maybe he could explain but he felt before he started that his father wouldn't understand.

"I—I guess Red ain't goin' be no vahmint dog."

"Huh! What use would you put such a dog to?"

"Well, he could hunt pat'tidges." Danny continued desperately, "Look, they's some things a man can do an' some he cain't. Makin' Red hunt vahmints would be like makin' one of Mistah Haggin's blooded hosses do a mule's work. It's right in Red's blood to be a pat'tidge dog."

"Oh! Maybe Mistah Haggin tol' you to make him hunt pat'tidges?"

"Mistah Haggin didn' say nothin'," Danny answered miserably. "I jus' know Red's a pat'tidge dog."

"How do you know it?"

Danny tried and failed to put into words some of the things he had learned on his brief visit to New York and in his association with Mr. Haggin. Always before he had accepted his father's notion that a dog was a dog, something to be bent to the will of its master. But that wasn't so. For thousands of years there had been special dogs for special functions—dachshunds for entering badger holes and subduing their occupants, greyhounds for coursing swift game, malemutes for sledge work, and only when you knew something of their blood lines could you really appreciate the fascinating story of dogdom. It was in Red's blood to hunt birds, and partridges were the only game birds in the Wintapi. Making him hunt anything else would verge on the criminal. But how to explain all this to his father?

"I jus' know it," Danny said miserably. "Red on'y hunted the beah on account he thought it was goin' to hurt me."

"Well—if that's the way you feel—" Ross's voice trailed off. He sat down stiffly and ate his supper. After eating, he helped wash the dishes and took his accustomed chair beside the stove. He ignored Red when the big setter tried to thrust his nose into his cupped hand and sensing the rebuff, Red went back to Danny. The boy sat moodily alone. Ross was deeply hurt. He wouldn't have been had his son been able to furnish a good reason why Red should be a partridge dog. But Danny himself knew of no reason save that the setter had been born to hunt partridges. And that sounded silly.

They went silently to bed.

The next morning when Danny got up Ross had already gone. He had taken one of the hounds with him.

But he hadn't asked Danny to go along.

Partridge season was not open yet, but it was legal to have dogs afield for training. Danny's heart was heavy within him while he ate a lonely breakfast. After eating he opened the door and a flood of the sparkling October sunshine came spilling in. Red rushed outside and went over to sniff noses with Mike. He came galloping back to Danny and reared to put both front paws on the boy's chest. Danny pulled his silky ears and stroked his smooth muzzle. If only his father were there to see Red as he saw him! Then the autumn and the sunshine worked their magic.

It was enough to be afield with Red. Pappy would understand in time.

Crisp frost-curled leaves crackled underfoot when the pair entered the beechwoods. Red went racing among the trees as a gray squirrel stopped his busy digging for nuts and leaped to a tree trunk. But when Danny whistled he stopped, turned around and came trotting back. For a space he walked beside the boy. Then he leaped a few feet ahead and stopped in his tracks.

He stood with his body rigid and his tail stiff behind him. With a quick little rush he went a dozen feet and stopped again. Then, in a slow, steady stalk, he advanced a hundred feet and stopped on a knoll. He raised one forefoot, stiffened his body and tail.

Danny murmured very softly, "Easy. Easy theah, Red."

The dog trembled, but held his point. Danny leaned over and, as quietly as possible, brushed the leaves from a half-buried limb. He hurled it into the brush at which the setter was pointing and a lone partridge thundered up. The dog took three nervous steps forward, but halted at Danny's, "Back heah, Red."

Danny's knees were suddenly weak and he sat down. Red came over with wagging tail and grinning tongue, and the boy passed both arms about his neck. Starry-eyed he sat still, in his mind living and reliving the scene he had just witnessed. It was a thrill to hear hounds strike a trail, to listen to them baying their quarry and their final frenzy when they cornered it. But this! The hounds were good workmen, but the setter was an artist. And not even Ross had suspected how keen his nose really was.

The early autumn twilight was just dimming out the day when the pair arrived home. A light in the window told that Ross was there before them. Danny opened the door and Red slid unobtrusively in to lie on the floor. Ross, who was standing over the stove, turned and spoke briefly.

"Hi-ya."

"Hi-ya," Danny replied and busied himself setting the table. From time to time he stole a furtive glance at Red, and once looked with mute appeal at his father's back. But his eyes

71

squinted slightly and the same stubborn mouth that was his father's tightened in grim lines. Once more he looked at Ross's back—and found the determination not to speak until his father did melting away. He tried to make his voice casual.

"Wheah'd you go today, Pappy?"

"Out."

Danny flushed, and his face set in lines ten times more stubborn. Maybe his father thought he couldn't make a pat'tidge dog out of Red. He'd show him! He'd prove such a dog was much more valuable than a hound, and that setters were as practical as hounds. Danny hesitated. Proving to Ross that a partridge dog was worth the food he ate wasn't going to be any harder job than moving Staver Plateau with a tin shovel!

After supper Danny sat by Red for a while, stroking his ears and tickling his chin. But Ross ignored the dog completely. As though he understood, the setter had nothing to do with him.

Partridge season and the first snow came together. Ross as usual was up long before daylight and away on his trap line. When Danny went out with his shotgun and Red he looked longingly at the tracks in the snow. Always before he and his father had gone trapping together. Resolutely he shouldered his gun and walked in an opposite direction, toward the pine and hemlock thickets where the partridges would certainly be seeking a refuge from the storm.

They approached a thick growth of hemlock and Red ranged ahead. He came to a stiff point, and Danny edged up.

A partridge burst out of the hemlocks, showing itself for a split second between the branches, and Danny shot. A ruffled heap of brown feathers, the bird came down in the snow. Red hesitated, turned around to look at Danny as though asking for instructions.

The boy waved a hand forward. "Go on," he said. "Get him."

Red padded forward and stood uncertainly over the fallen partridge. He looked up, then back at the bird.

"Give it to me," Danny said gently.

The setter lowered his head to sniff the partridge and grasped it gently in his mouth. The boy took it in his hand. He threw it down in the snow and Red picked it up again.

They went on, and the setter pointed three more grouse. The last one Danny shot the dog picked up and brought back, though he went about it in an awkward fashion. His tail wagged furiously and his eyes glistened at the lavish praise that the feat called forth from his master. But four birds were the limit.

Danny arrived home first that night, and had supper ready when his father came in. Ross had no furs, as he had set his traps only that day, but he opened his hunting jacket and took out four partridges. He laid them on the table and turned silently away to remove his coat and wash his hands.

Danny's cheeks burned. His father had had no dog. And every one of the partridges had been shot through the head with the little .22 pistol he carried on his trap line.

By the last day of the season Danny knew that his hunch had been the correct one. Red was not only a partridge dog, but he was a great partridge dog, one in a million. He found the birds and pointed them so carefully that only the wildest ones flushed before the gunner could get in his shot. It had taken him only nine trips afield to learn perfectly the art of retrieving, regardless of how thick the brush or brambles in which the bird fell might be. Red paid no attention to the rabbits that scooted before him or the chattering squirrels that frisked through the trees. And when he hunted, no scent save that of partridges drew the slightest interest. Now, on this last day of the season he and Danny were going out for one last hunt.

Ross as usual had already gone, and a few flakes of snow hovered in the air. Little wind stirred and the naked trees were silent. But the blue-black horizon and the clouded sky foretold a heavier storm to come. Danny went back into the shanty and buttoned a woolen jacket over the wool hunting shirt he already wore. He dropped half a dozen twelve-gauge shells into his pocket.

"Goin' be weathah shuah 'nough," he murmured. "Wintah's nigh heah, Red."

The hard little snowflakes rustled against the frozen leaves,

73

and it seemed to Danny that they were falling faster even before he came to the edge of his father's field. But he forgot them then because Red came to a point. Steady as a rock, he stopped just a little way within the woods. Danny flushed the bird. It soared up and out, dodging behind tree trunks and twisting about. But for one split second it showed through the crotch of a big beech and Danny shot. The bird dropped to the ground and Red brought it in.

They went on deeper into the beechwoods where they had found so many partridges before. But Red worked for an hour before he pointed another, and that one flushed so wild that Danny had no shot at it. It was noon before he killed a second bird—and at the same time he awoke to the necessity of getting back to the cabin before he had trouble finding it. The snow was falling so fast now that the trees were only wavering shadows. And there was a rising wind, which meant that the heavy snow would be accompanied by a gale. Danny snapped his fingers.

"Heah, Red."

It was nearly dusk when they reached the cabin. Danny opened the door, stamped the snow from his feet and sank into a chair. Red crouched full length on the floor, looking at the boy from the corners of his eyes.

Danny cut thick slices from a ham and peeled a great potful of potatoes. His father would be hungry after bucking the storm, would want good things to eat and plenty of them. But the boy worked with deliberate slowness, trying in the accustomed routine of household chores to still the small worried voice that was rising in him. Pappy should have been home before this.

He went to a window and peered into the inky blackness outside. He fought back a rising panic; this was no time for a man to lose his head. He waited another ten minutes.

Then he made up a pack, a thermos of hot coffee, enough food for three days, a knife and ax, plenty of matches and two woolen blankets. He put on his warmest coat, pulled a felt hat down over his eyes and took his snowshoes from their peg on the wall.

With a happy little whine and a furiously wagging tail, Red

74

sprang up to join him. Danny looked at the setter. The dog could not be of any use. He would hunt only partridges, would pay no attention to Pappy's scent, even though they passed within ten feet of him. Danny shook his head.

"Reckon not, Red. This heah's one hunt I got to run alone. Not even the other dogs are trained for this."

Red flattened his ears and begged mutely. Danny looked away, and back again. The setter wouldn't help any, but he would be company and certainly he could do no harm.

"Aw ri'. Come on."

Red waited impatiently in the snow while Danny took a toboggan from its elevated platform, and when he started off on his snowshoes through the night the dog ran a little ahead. Danny watched him work carefully toward a briar patch and grinned wryly. The setter was still ashamed of his inability to locate more than two partridges, and he was trying to make up for it.

The snow was drifting down in great feathery flakes that dropped softly to earth. The wind had abated and it was not as cold as it had been. But if Pappy were helpless he could freeze. Danny put the thought from his mind and plodded grimly on. Lately he had scarcely spoken to his father, but he still knew where to look for him. Last night Ross had brought in two muskrats and a mink, pelts that could be trapped only along waterways. Therefore he must have run the traps in Brant Marsh and along Elk River. Today he would cover his fox line on Stoney Lonesome Ridge.

But even though he would search until he found his father Danny was aware of the near hopelessness of his mission. If Pappy were lying unconscious after having been caught in a slide or struck down by a falling limb, the snow would cover him and he might not be found until it melted. Danny admitted this. Nobody was too good at anything to guard against unforeseen accidents, not even a skilled woodsman like his father. It was just as well to face possibilities as to close his eyes to them. He must be ready for any emergency.

Red came trotting happily back and was away again. As

Danny dragged the toboggan up the long steep trail his father took to Stoney Lonesome, he looked down at his feet. They seemed barely to move. Yet he saw by a dead stub of a tree that stood beside the trail and served as a landmark when they were away from it, that in an hour he had come almost four miles. That was fast travel in deep snow when a man had to drag a toboggan.

It was too fast. A quarter of a mile farther on Danny stopped to rest. He panted heavily, and perspiration streamed down his face and back. He took the felt hat off and opened his jacket. Red returned to stand anxiously beside him.

"If only I'd taught you to hunt men 'stead of pat'tidge," Danny half sobbed. "If only I had!"

He turned to go on. Pappy had to be somewhere, and he was as likely to be near the trail as anywhere else. But if he wasn't, his son would go to all the traps, and from them he would branch out to scour every inch of Stoney Lonesome. Pappy just couldn't die! Why there would be hardly anything worthwhile if it weren't for his father. That foolish quarrel over Red. Danny should have let him hunt varmints or anything else Pappy wanted. If only he could talk to his father once more and tell him how sorry he was!

Danny stumbled and sprawled in the snow. He rose, annoyed and grumbling. He had fallen over Red, who had come to a point in the trail, headed off to the side.

"Go on!" Danny snapped.

Red took three uncertain steps forward beside the trail, then he stopped again. Danny rushed toward him, angry at the dog for the first time. He reached down to grasp his collar, but the toes of his snowshoes crossed and he stumbled sideways. His bare hands plunged deeply into the drifted snow. And they found something soft and yielding, something that gave before them. It was a man's trousered leg. Danny dug frantically and lifted Ross Pickett from his snowy bed. His hand went under his father's shirt.

His body was warm and his heart still beat.

76

Two days later, back at the cabin, Danny served his father two roasted partridges and a great heap of mashed potatoes. He propped him up on pillows and grinned when his patient began to wolf the food.

"Fo' a man as should of been daid, you shuah hungry," he observed. "How come you can eat so much?"

Ross grinned back. "Cain't kill an old he-bear like me." He tore off a great strip of breast meat and held it up in his fingers, saying, "Come heah an' have some vittles."

Red padded daintily across the floor, and his wagging tail thanked Ross for the offering. Danny's eyes shone, because the two things that he loved best now loved each other.

" 'Twas a mighty lot of foolishment to fight over the dog, wan't it? But even if I hadn't got ovah my mad an' like the mule-haid I am wan't waitin' fo' you to say somethin', I shuah would know what a pointin' dog is now. When the side of that ol' trail give way beneath me, I thought I was a cooked goose fo' certain. How come the dog foun' me, Son?"

Danny answered soberly. "Red foun' you on account he's got a better nose as any houn' dog."

It was the first time he had ever deceived his father—but it was more evasion than lie. Red was a partridge dog through and through. And when he had pointed there in the snow, he had pointed, not Ross, but the two partridges the trapper had shot and put in his pocket.

A shipwreck and two castaways

Gulliver the Great

BY WALTER A. DYER

*I*T WAS a mild evening in early spring, and the
magnolias were in bloom. We motored around the park, turned
up a side street, and finally came to a throbbing standstill before the Churchwarden Club.

There was nothing about its exterior to indicate that it was
a clubhouse at all, but within there was an indefinable atmosphere of early Victorian comfort. There was something about it
that suggested Mr. Pickwick. Old prints of horses and ships and
battles hung upon the walls, and the oak was dark and old.
There seemed to be no decorative scheme or keynote, and yet
the atmosphere was utterly distinctive. It was my first visit to the
Churchwarden Club, of which my quaint, old-fashioned Uncle
Ford had long been a member, and I was charmed.

78

We dined in the rathskeller, the walls of which were completely covered with long churchwarden pipes, arranged in the most intricate and marvelous patterns; and after our mutton chop and ale and plum pudding, we filled with the choicest of tobaccos the pipes which the old major-domo brought us.

Then came Jacob R. Enderby to smoke with us.

Tall and spare he was, with long, straight black hair, large aquiline nose, and piercing eyes. I disgraced myself by staring at him. I didn't know such a man existed in New York, and yet I couldn't decide whether his habitat should be Arizona or Cape Cod.

Enderby and Uncle Ford were deep in a discussion of the statesmanship of James G. Blaine when a waiter summoned my uncle to the telephone.

I neglected to state that my uncle in his prosaic hours is a physician, and this was a call. I knew it the moment I saw the waiter approaching. I was disappointed and disgusted.

Uncle Ford saw this and laughed.

"Cheer up!" said he. "You needn't come with me to visit the sick. I'll be back in an hour, and meanwhile Mr. Enderby will take care of you; won't you, Jake?"

For answer Enderby arose, and refilling his pipe took me by the arm, while my uncle got into his overcoat. As he passed us on the way out he whispered in my ear:

"Talk about dogs."

I heard and nodded.

Enderby led me to the lounge or loafing-room, an oak-paneled apartment in the rear of the floor above, with huge leather chairs and a seat in the bay window. Save for a gray-haired old chap dozing over a copy of *Simplicissimus*, the room was deserted.

But no sooner had Enderby seated himself on the window seat than there was a rush and a commotion, and a short, glad bark, and Nubbins, the steward's bull terrier, bounded in and landed at Enderby's side with canine expressions of great joy.

I reached forward to pat him, but he paid absolutely no attention to me.

79

At last his wrigglings subsided, and he settled down with his head on Enderby's knee, the picture of content. Then I recalled my uncle's parting injunction.

"Friend of yours?" I suggested.

Enderby smiled. "Yes," he said, "we're friends, I guess. And the funny part of it is that he doesn't pay any attention to anyone else except his master. They all act that way with me, dogs do." And he pulled Nubbins' stubby ears.

"Natural attraction, I suppose," said I.

"Yes, it is," he answered, with the modest frankness of a big man. "It's a thing hard to explain, though there's a sort of reason for it in my case."

I pushed toward him a little tobacco-laden teakwood stand hopefully. He refilled and lighted.

"It's an extraordinary thing, even so," he said, puffing. "Every dog nowadays seems to look upon me as his long-lost master, but it wasn't always so. I hated dogs and they hated me."

Not wishing to say "Really" or "Indeed" to this big, outdoor man, I simply grunted my surprise.

"Yes, we were born enemies. More than that, I was afraid of dogs. A little fuzzy toy dog, ambling up to me in a room full of company with his tail wagging, gave me the shudders. I couldn't touch the beast. And as for big dogs outdoors, I feared them like the plague. I would go blocks out of my way to avoid one.

"I don't remember being particularly cowardly about other things, but I just couldn't help this. It was in my blood, for some reason or other. It was the bane of my existence. I couldn't see what the brutes were put in the world for, or how anyone could have anything to do with them.

"All the dogs reciprocated. They disliked and distrusted me. The most docile old Brunos would growl and show their teeth when I came near."

"Did the change come suddenly?" I asked.

"Quite. It was in 1901. I accepted a commission from an importing and trading company to go to the Philippines to do a little quiet exploring, and spent four months in the sickly place.

80

Then I got the fever, and when I recovered I couldn't get out of there too soon.

"I reached Manila just in time to see the mail steamer disappearing around the point, and I was mad. There would be another in six days, but I couldn't wait. I was just crazy to get back home.

"I made inquiries and learned of an old tramp steamer, named the *Old Squaw,* making ready to leave for Honolulu on the following day with a cargo of hemp and stuff, and a bunch of Moros for some show in the States, and I booked passage on that.

"She was the worst old tub you ever saw. I didn't learn much about her, but I verily believe her to have been a condemned excursion boat. She wouldn't have been allowed to run to Coney Island.

"She was battered and unpainted, and she wallowed horribly. I don't believe she could have reached Honolulu much before the regular boat, but I couldn't wait, and I took her.

"I made myself as comfortable as possible, bribed the cook to insure myself against starvation, and swung a hammock on the forward deck as far as possible from the worst of the vile smells.

"But we hadn't lost sight of Manila Bay when I discovered that there was a dog aboard—and such a dog! I had never seen one that sent me into such a panic as this one, and he had free range of the ship. A Great Dane he was, named Gulliver, and he was the pride of the captain's rum-soaked heart.

"With all my fear, I realized he was a magnificent animal, but I looked on him as a gigantic devil. Without exception, he was the biggest dog I ever saw, and as muscular as a lion. He lacked some points that show judges set store by, but he had the size and the build.

"I had seen Vohl's Vulcan and the Württemberg breed, but they were fox terriers compared with Gulliver. His tail was as big around as my arm, and the cook lived in terror of his getting into the galley and wagging it; and he had a mouth that looked to me like the crater of Mauna Loa, and a voice that shook the planking when he spoke.

81

"I first caught sight of him appearing from behind a huge coil of cordage in the stern. He stretched and yawned, and I nearly died of fright.

"I caught up a belaying pin, though little good that would have done me. I think he saw me do it, and doubtless he set me down for an enemy then and there.

"We were well out of the harbor, and there was no turning back, but I would have given my right hand to be off that boat. I fully expected him to eat me up, and I slept with that belaying pin sticking into my ribs in the hammock, and with my revolver loaded and handy.

"Fortunately, Gulliver's dislike for me took the form of sublime contempt. He knew I was afraid of him, and he despised me for it. He was a great pet with the captain and crew, and even the Moros treated him with admiring respect when they were allowed on deck. I couldn't understand it. I would as soon have made a pet of a hungry boa constrictor.

"On the third day out the poor old boiler burst and the *Old Squaw* caught fire. She was dry and rotten inside and she burned like tinder. No attempt was made to extinguish the flames, which got into the hemp in the hold in short order.

"The smoke was stifling, and in a jiffy all hands were struggling with the boats. The Moros came tumbling up from below and added to the confusion with their terrified yells.

"The davits were old and rusty, and the men were soon fighting among themselves. One boat dropped stern foremost, filled, and sank immediately, and the *Old Squaw* herself was visibly settling.

"I saw there was no chance of getting away in the boats, and I recalled a life raft on the deck forward near my hammock. It was a sort of catamaran—a double platform on a pair of hollow, watertight, cylindrical buoys. It wasn't twenty feet long and about half as broad, but it would have to do. I fancy it was a forgotten relic of the old excursion-boat days.

"There was no time to lose, for the *Old Squaw* was bound to sink presently. Besides, I was aft with the rest, and the flames were licking up deck and running gear in the waist of the boat.

"The galley, which was amidships near the engine room, had received the full force of the explosion, and the cook lay moaning in the lee scuppers with a small water cask thumping against his chest. I couldn't stop to help the man, but I did kick the cask away.

"It seemed to be nearly full, and it occurred to me that I should need it. I glanced quickly around, and luckily found a tin of biscuits that had also been blown out of the galley. I picked this up, and rolling the cask of water ahead of me as rapidly as I could, I made my way through the hot stifling smoke to the bow of the boat.

"I kicked at the life raft; it seemed to be sound, and I lashed the biscuits and water to it. I also threw on a coil of rope and a piece of sailcloth. I saw nothing else about that could possibly be of any value to me. I abandoned my trunk for fear it would only prove troublesome.

"Then I hacked the raft loose with my knife and shoved it over the bulwark. Apparently no one had seen me, for there was no one else forward of the sheet of flame that now cut the boat in two.

"The raft was a mighty heavy affair, but I managed to raise one end to the rail. I don't believe I would ever have been able to heave it over under any circumstances, but I didn't have to.

"I felt a great upheaval, and the prow of the *Old Squaw* went up into the air. I grabbed the ropes that I had lashed the food on with and clung to the raft. The deck became almost perpendicular, and it was a miracle that the raft didn't slide down with me into the flames. Somehow it stuck where it was.

"Then the boat sank with a great roar, and for about a thousand years, it seemed to me, I was under water. I didn't do anything, I couldn't think.

"I was only conscious of a tremendous weight of water and a feeling that I would burst open. Instinct alone made me cling to the raft.

"When it finally brought me to the surface I was as nearly dead as I care to be. I lay there on the thing in a half-conscious

83

condition for an endless time. If my life had depended on my doing something, I would have been lost.

"Then gradually I came to, and began to spit out salt water and gasp for breath. I gathered my wits together and sat up. My hands were absolutely numb, and I had to loosen the grip of my fingers with the help of my toes. Odd sensation.

"Then I looked about me. My biscuits and water and rope were safe, but the sailcloth had vanished. I remember that this annoyed me hugely at the time, though I don't know what earthly good it would have been.

"The sea was fairly calm, and I could see all about. Not a human being was visible, only a few floating bits of wreckage. Every man on board must have gone down with the ship and drowned, except myself.

"Then I caught sight of something that made my heart stand still. The huge head of Gulliver was coming rapidly toward me through the water!

"The dog was swimming strongly, and must have leaped from the *Old Squaw* before she sank. My raft was the only thing afloat large enough to hold him, and he knew it.

"I drew my revolver, but it was soaking wet and useless. Then I sat down on the cracker tin and gritted my teeth and waited. I had been alarmed, I must admit, when the boiler blew up and the panic began, but that was nothing to my terror now.

"Here I was all alone on the top of the Pacific Ocean with a horrible demon making for me as fast as he could swim. My mind was benumbed, and I could think of nothing to do. I trembled and my teeth rattled. I prayed for a shark, but no shark came.

"Soon Gulliver reached the raft and placed one of his forepaws on it and then the other. The top of it stood six or eight inches above the water, and it took a great effort for the dog to raise himself. I wanted to kick him back, but I didn't dare to move.

"Gulliver struggled mightily. Again and again he reared his great shoulders above the sea, only to be cast back, scratching and kicking, at a lurch of the raft.

"Finally a wave favored him, and he caught the edge

of the under platform with one of his hind feet. With a stupendous effort he heaved his huge bulk over the edge and lay sprawling at my feet, panting and trembling."

Enderby paused and gazed out of the window with a big sigh, as though the recital of his story had brought back some of the horror of his remarkable experience.

Nubbins looked up inquiringly, and then snuggled closer to his friend, while Enderby smoothed the white head.

"Well," he continued, "there we were. You can't possibly imagine how I felt unless you, too, have been afflicted with dog-fear. It was awful. And I hated the brute so. I could have torn him limb from limb if I had had the strength. But he was vastly more powerful than I. I could only fear him.

"By and by he got up and shook himself. I cowered on my cracker tin, but he only looked at me contemptuously, went to the other end of the raft, and lay down to wait patiently for deliverance.

"We remained this way until nightfall. The sea was comparatively calm, and we seemed to be drifting but slowly. We were in the path of ships likely to be passing one way or the other, and I would have been hopeful of the outcome if it had not been for my feared and hated companion.

"I began to feel faint, and opened the cracker tin. The biscuits were wet with salt water, but I ate a couple, and left the tin open to dry them. Gulliver looked around, and I shut the tin hastily. But the dog never moved. He was not disposed to ask any favors. By kicking the sides of the cask and prying with my knife, I managed to get the bung out and took a drink. Then I settled myself on the raft with my back against the cask, and longed for a smoke.

"The gentle motion of the raft produced a lulling effect on my exhausted nerves, and I began to nod, only to awake with a start, with fear gripping at my heart. I dared not sleep. I don't know what I thought Gulliver would do to me, for I did not understand dogs, but I felt that I must watch him constantly. In the starlight I could see that his eyes were open. Gulliver was watchful too.

"All night long I kept up a running fight with drowsiness,

I dozed at intervals, but never for long at a time. It was a horrible night, and I cannot tell you how I longed for day and welcomed it when it came.

"I must have slept toward dawn, for I suddenly became conscious of broad daylight. I roused myself, stood up, and swung my arms and legs to stir up circulation, for the night had been chilly. Gulliver arose, too, and stood silently watching me until I ceased for fear. When he had settled down again I got my breakfast out of the cracker tin. Gulliver was restless, and was evidently interested.

"He must be hungry, I thought, and then a new fear caught me. I had only to wait until he became very hungry and then he would surely attack me. I concluded that it would be wiser to feed him, and I tossed him a biscuit.

"I expected to see him grab it ravenously, and wondered as soon as I had thrown it if the taste of food would only serve to make him more ferocious. But at first he would not touch it. He only lay there with his great head on his paws and glowered at me. Distrust was plainly visible in his face. I had never realized before that a dog's face could express the subtler emotions.

"His gaze fascinated me, and I could not take my eyes from his. The bulk of him was tremendous as he lay there, and I noticed the big, swelling muscles of his jaw. At last he arose, sniffed suspiciously at the biscuit, and looked up at me again.

" 'It's all right; eat it!' I cried.

"The sound of my own voice frightened me. I had not intended to speak to him. But in spite of my strained tone he seemed somewhat reassured.

"He took a little nibble, and then swallowed the biscuit after one or two crunches, and looked up expectantly. I threw him another and he ate that.

" 'That's all,' said I. 'We must be sparing of them.'

"I was amazed to discover how perfectly he understood. He lay down again and licked his chops.

"Late in the afternoon I saw a line of smoke on the horizon, and soon a steamer hove into view. I stood up and waved my coat frantically, but to no purpose. Gulliver stood up and looked from me to the steamer, apparently much interested.

" 'Too far off,' I said to Gulliver. 'I hope the next one will come nearer.'

"At midday I dined, and fed Gulliver. This time he took the two biscuits quite without reserve and whacked his great tail against the raft. It seemed to me that his attitude was less hostile, and I wondered at it.

"When I took my drink from the cask, Gulliver showed signs of interest.

" 'I suppose dogs get thirsty, too,' I said aloud.

"Gulliver rapped with his tail. I looked about for some sort of receptacle, and finally pulled off my shoe, filled it with water, and shoved it toward him with my foot. He drank gratefully.

"During the afternoon I sighted another ship, but it was too distant to notice me. However, the sea remained calm and I did not despair.

"After we had had supper, I settled back against my cask, resolved to keep awake, for still I did not trust Gulliver. The sun set suddenly and the stars came out, and I found myself strangely lonesome. It seemed as though I had been alone out there on the Pacific for weeks. The miles and miles of heaving waters, almost on a level with my eye, were beginning to get on my nerves. I longed for someone to talk to, and wished I had dragged the half-breed cook along with me for company. I sighed loudly, and Gulliver raised his head.

" 'Lonesome out here, isn't it?' I said, simply to hear the sound of my own voice.

"Then for the first time Gulliver spoke. He made a deep sound in his throat, but it wasn't a growl, and with all my ignorance of dog language I knew it.

"Then I began to talk. I talked about everything—the people back home and all that—and Gulliver listened. I know more about dogs now, and I know that the best way to make friends with a dog is to talk to him. He can't talk back, but he can understand a heap more than you think he can.

"Finally Gulliver, who had kept his distance all this time, arose and came toward me. My words died in my throat. What was he going to do? To my immense relief he did nothing but sink down at my feet with a grunt and curl his huge body into

87

a semicircle. He had dignity, Gulliver had. He wanted to be friendly, but he would not presume. However, I had lost interest in conversation, and sat watching him and wondering.

"In spite of my firm resolution, I fell asleep at length from sheer exhaustion, and never woke until daybreak. The sky was clouded and our raft was pitching. Gulliver was standing in the middle of the raft, looking at me in evident alarm. I glanced over my shoulder, and the blackness of the horizon told me that a storm was coming, and coming soon.

"I made fast our slender provender, tied the end of a line about my own waist for safety, and waited.

"In a short time the storm struck us in all its tropical fury. The raft pitched and tossed, now high up at one end, and now at the other, and sometimes almost engulfed in the waves.

"Gulliver was having a desperate time to keep aboard. His blunt claws slipped on the wet deck of the raft, and he fell and slid about dangerously. The thought flashed across my mind that the storm might prove to be a blessing in disguise, and that I might soon be rid of the brute.

"As I clung there to the lashings, I saw him slip down to the further end of the raft, his hind quarters actually over the edge. A wave swept over him, but still he clung, panting madly. Then the raft righted itself for a moment, and as he hung there he gave me a look I shall never forget—a look of fear, of pleading, of reproach, and yet of silent courage. And with all my stupidity I read that look. Somehow it told me that I was the master, after all, and he the dog. I could not resist it. Cautiously I raised myself and loosened the spare rope I had saved. As the raft tipped the other way Gulliver regained his footing and came sliding toward me.

"Quickly I passed the rope around his body, and as the raft dived again I hung on to the rope with one hand, retaining my own hold with the other. Gulliver's great weight nearly pulled my arm from its socket, but he helped mightily, and during the next moment of equilibrium I took another turn about his body and made the end of the rope fast.

"The storm passed as swiftly as it had come, and though it

left us drenched and exhausted, we were both safe on the raft.

"That evening Gulliver crept close to me as I talked, and I let him. Loneliness will make a man do strange things.

"On the fifth day, when our provisions were nearly gone, and I had begun to feel the sinking dullness of despair, I sighted a steamer apparently coming directly toward us. Instantly I felt new life in my limbs and around my heart, and while the boat was yet miles away I began to shout and to wave my coat.

" 'I believe she's coming, old man!' I cried to Gulliver. 'I believe she's coming!'

"I soon wearied of this foolishness and sat down to wait. Gulliver came close and sat beside me, and for the first time I put my hand on him. He looked up at me and rapped furiously with his tail. I patted his head—a little gingerly, I must confess.

"It was a big, smooth head, and it felt solid and strong. I passed my hand down his neck, his back, his flanks. He seemed to quiver with joy. He leaned his huge body against me. Then he bowed his head and licked my shoe.

"A feeling of intense shame and unworthiness came over me, with the realization of how completely I had misunderstood him. Why should this great, powerful creature lick my shoe? It was incredible.

"Then, somehow, everything changed. Fear and distrust left me, and a feeling of comradeship and understanding took their place. We two had been through so much together. A dog was no longer a frightful beast to me; he was a dog! I cannot think of a nobler word. And Gulliver had licked my shoe! Doubtless it was only the fineness of his perception that had prevented him from licking my hand. I might have resented that. I put my arms suddenly around Gulliver's neck and hugged him. I loved that dog!

"Slowly, slowly, the steamer crawled along, but still kept to her course. When she was about a mile away, however, I saw that she would not pass as close to us as I had hoped; so I began once more my waving and yelling. She came nearer, nearer, but still showed no sign of observing us.

"She was abreast of us, and passing. I was in a frenzy!

"She was so near that I could make out the figure of the captain on the bridge, and other figures on the deck below. It seemed as though they must see us, though I realized how low in the water we stood, and how pitifully weak and hoarse my voice was. I had been a fool to waste it. Then an idea struck me.

" 'Speak!' I cried to Gulliver, who stood watching beside me. 'Speak, old man!'

"Gulliver needed no second bidding. A roar like that of all the bulls of Bashan rolled out over the blue Pacific. Again and again Gulliver gave voice, deep, full, powerful. His great side heaved with the mighty effort, his red, cavernous mouth open, and his head raised high.

" 'Good, old man!' I cried. 'Good!' And again that magnificent voice boomed forth.

"Then something happened on board the steamer. The figures came to the side. I waved my coat and danced. Then they saw us.

"I was pretty well done up when they took us aboard, and I slept for twenty-four hours straight. When I awoke there sat Gulliver by my bunk, and when I turned to look at him he lifted a great paw and put it on my arm."

Enderby ceased, and there was silence in the room save for the light snoring of Nubbins.

"You took him home with you, I suppose?" I asked.

Enderby nodded.

"And you have him still?" I certainly wanted to have a look at that dog.

But he did not answer. I saw an expression of great sadness come into his eyes as he gazed out of the window, and I knew that Jacob Enderby had finished his story.

A fiery temper and a kindred spirit

Red Wull

BY ALFRED OLLIVANT

T H E winter came and went; the lambing season
was over, and spring already shyly kissing the land. With the
back of the year's work broken and her master well started on
a fresh season, M'Adam's old collie, Cuttie Sark, lay down one
evening and passed quietly away.

The little black-and-tan lady, Parson Leggy used to say,
had been the only thing on earth M'Adam cared for. Certainly
the two had been wondrously devoted; and for many a market
day the Dalesmen missed the shrill chuckling cry which heralded
the pair's approach: "Weel done, Cuttie Sark!"

The little man felt his loss acutely and, according to his wont, vented his ill-feeling on David and the Dalesmen. In return Tammas, whose forte lay in invective and alliteration, called him behind his back, "A wenomous one!" and "A wiralent wiper!" to the applause of tinkling pewters.

A shepherd without his dog is like a ship without a rudder, and M'Adam felt his loss *practically* as well. Especially did he experience this on a day when he had to take a batch of draft ewes over to Grammoch-town. To help him Jem Burton had lent the services of his herring-gutted, herring-hearted greyhound lurcher, Monkey. But before they had well topped Braithwaite Brow, which leads from the village on to the marches, M'Adam was standing in the track with a rock in his hand, a smile on his face, and the tenderest blandishments in his voice as he coaxed the dog to him. But Master Monkey knew too much for that. However, after gamboling a while longer in the middle of the flock, a boulder, better aimed than its predecessors, smote him on the hinder parts and sent him back to the Sylvester Arms with a sore tail and a subdued heart.

For the rest, M'Adam would never have won over the sheep-infested marches alone with his convoy had it not been for the help of old Saunderson and Shep, who caught him on the way and aided him.

It was in a very wrathful mood that on his way home he turned into the Dalesman's Daughter in Silverdale.

The only occupants of the taproom as he entered were Teddy Bolstock the publican, Jim Mason with the faithful Betsy beneath his chair and the post-bags flung into the corner, and one long-limbed, drover-like man—a stranger.

"And he coom up to Mr. Moore," Teddy was saying, "and says he, 'I'll gie ye twal' pun for yon gray dog o' yourn.' 'Ah,' says Moore, 'yo' may gie me twal' hunner'd and yet you'll not get ma Bob'—eh, Jim?"

"And he did thot," corroborated Jim. " 'Twal' hunner'd,' says he."

"James Moore and his dog agin,' " snapped M'Adam. "There's ithers in the warld for bye them twa."

"Ay, but none like 'em," quoth loyal Jim.

92

"Na, thanks be. Gin there were there'd be no room for Adam M'Adam in this 'melancholy vale.'"

There was silence a moment, and then—

"You're wantin' a tyke, bain't you, Mr. M'Adam?" Jim asked.

The little man hopped round all in a hurry.

"What!" he cried in well-affected eagerness, scanning the yellow mongrel beneath the chair. "Betsy for sale! Guid life! Where's ma checkbook!" Whereat Jim, most easily snubbed of men, collapsed.

M'Adam took off his dripping coat and crossed the room to hang it on a chair back. The stranger drover followed the meager shirt-clad figure with shifty eyes; then he buried his face in his mug.

M'Adam reached out a hand for the chair; and as he did so a bomb in yellow leapt out from beneath it, and growling horribly, attacked his ankles.

"Curse ye!" cried M'Adam, starting back. "Ye devil, let me alone!" Then turning fiercely on the drover, "Yours, mister?" he asked. The man nodded. "Then call him aff, can't ye? D—n ye!" At which Teddy Bolstock withdrew, sniggering, and Jim Mason slung the post-bags on to his shoulder and plunged out into the rain, the faithful Betsy following, disconsolate.

The cause of the squall, having beaten off the attacking force, had withdrawn again beneath its chair. M'Adam stooped down, still cursing, his wet coat on his arm, and beheld a tiny yellow puppy, crouching defiant in the dark and glaring out with fiery light eyes. Seeing itself remarked, it bared its little teeth, raised its little bristles, and growled a hideous menace.

A sense of humor is many a man's salvation, and was M'Adam's one redeeming feature. The laughableness of the thing —this ferocious atomy defying him—struck home to the little man. Delighted at such a display of vice in so tender a plant, he fell to chuckling.

"Ye leetle devil!" he laughed. "He! he! ye leetle devil!" and flipped together finger and thumb in vain endeavor to coax the puppy to him.

But it growled and glared more terribly.

"Stop it, ye little snake, or I'll flatten you!" cried the big drover, and shuffled his feet threateningly. Whereat the puppy, gurgling like hot water in a kettle, made a feint as though to advance and wipe them out, these two bad men.

M'Adam laughed again, and smote his leg.

"Keep a ceevil tongue and yer distance," says he, "or I'll e'en ha' to mak' ye. Though he is but as big as a man's thumb, a dog's a dog for a' that—he! he! the leetle devil." And he fell to flipping finger and thumb afresh.

"Ye're maybe wantin' a dog?" inquired the stranger. "Yer friend said as much."

"Ma friend lied; it's his way," M'Adam replied.

"I'm willin' to part wi' him," the other pursued.

The little man yawned. "Weel, I'll tak' him to oblige ye," he said indifferently.

The drover rose to his feet.

"It's givin' 'im ye, fair givin' 'im ye, mind! But I'll do it!"—he smacked a great fist into a hollow palm. "Ye may have the dog for a pun'—I'll only ask *you* a pun'," and he walked away to the window.

M'Adam drew back, the better to scan his would-be benefactor; his lower jaw dropped, and he eyed the stranger with a drolly sarcastic air.

"A poun', man! A poun'—for yon noble dorg!" he pointed a crooked forefinger at the little creature, whose scowling mask peered from beneath the chair. "Man, I couldna do it. Na, na; ma conscience wadna permit me. 'Twad be fair robbin' ye. Ah, ye Englishmen!" he spoke half to himself, and sadly, as if deploring the unhappy accident of his nationality; "it's yer grand, open-hairted generosity that grips a puir Scotsman by the throat. A poun'! and for yon!" He wagged his head mournfully, cocking it sideways the better to scan his subject.

"Take him or leave him," ordered the drover truculently, still gazing out of the window.

"Wi' yer permission I'll leave him," M'Adam answered meekly.

"I'm short o' the ready," the big man pursued, "or I

wouldna part with him. Could I bide me time there's many'd be glad to give me a tenner for one o' that bree——" he caught himself up hastily—"for a dog sic as that."

"And yet ye offer him me for a poun'! Noble indeed!"

Nevertheless the little man had pricked his ears at the other's slip and quick correction. Again he approached the puppy, dangling his coat before him to protect his ankles; and again that wee wild beast sprang out, seized the coat in its small jaw, and worried it savagely.

M'Adam stooped quickly and picked up his tiny assailant; and the puppy, suspended by its neck, gurgled and slobbered; then wriggling desperately around, made its teeth meet in its adversary's shirt. At which M'Adam shook it gently and laughed. Then he set to examining it.

Apparently some six weeks old, a tawny coat, fiery eyes, a square head with small, cropped ears, and a comparatively immense jaw, the whole giving promise of great strength if little beauty. And this effect was enhanced by the manner of its docking. For the miserable relic of a tail, yet raw, looked little more than a red button adhering to its wearer's stern.

M'Adam's inspection was as minute as it was apparently absorbing; he omitted nothing, from the square muzzle to the lozenge-like scut. And every now and then he threw a quick glance at the man at the window, who was watching the careful scrutiny a thought uneasily.

"Ye've cut him short," he said at length, swinging round on the drover.

"Ay; strengthens their backs," the big man answered with averted gaze.

M'Adam's chin went up in the air; his mouth partly opened and his eyelids partly closed as he eyed his informant.

"Oh, ay," he said.

"Gie him back to me," ordered the drover surlily. He took the puppy and set it on the floor; whereupon it immediately resumed its former fortified position. "Ye're no buyer; I knoo that all along by that face on ye," he said in insulting tones to the little man.

"Ye wad ha' bought him yerself', nae doot?" M'Adam inquired blandly.

"In course, if you says so."

"Or airblins ye bred him?"

" 'Appen I did."

"Ye'll no be from these parts?"

"Will I no?" answered the other.

A smile of genuine pleasure stole over M'Adam's face. He laid his hand on the other's arm.

"Man," he said gently, "ye mind me o' hame." Then almost in the same breath, "Ye said ye found him?"

It was the stranger's turn to laugh.

"Ha! ha! Ye teeckle me, little mon. Found 'im? Nay! I was give 'im by a friend. But there's nowt amiss wi' his breedin', ye may believe me."

The great fellow advanced to the chair under which the puppy lay. It leaped out like a lion and fastened on his huge boot.

"A rare bred un, look 'ee! a rare game un. Ma word, he's a big-hearted un! Look at the back on him; see the jaws to him; mark the pluck of him!" He shook his booted foot fiercely, tossing his leg to and fro like a tree in a wind. But the little creature, now raised ceilingward, now dashed to the ground, held on with incomparable doggedness, till its small jaw was all bloody, and its muzzle wrinkled with the effort.

"Ay, ay, that'll do," M'Adam interposed, irritably.

The drover ceased his efforts.

"Now, I'll mak' ye a last offer." He thrust his head down to a level with the other's, shooting out his neck. "It's throwin' him at ye, mind. 'Tain't buyin' him ye'll be—don't go for to deceive yourself. Ye may have him for fifteen shillin'. Why do I do it, ye ask? Why, 'cos I think ye'll be kind to him," as the puppy retreated to its chair, leaving a spotted track of red along its route.

"Ay, ye wadna be happy gin ye thocht he'd no a comfortable hame, conseederate man?" M'Adam answered, eyeing the dark track on the floor. Then he put on his coat.

"Na, na, he's no for me. Weel, I'll no detain ye. Goodnicht to ye, mister!" and he made for the door.

"A gran' worker he'll be," called the drover after him.

"Ay; muckle wark he'll mak' amang the sheep wi' sic a jaw and sic a temper. Weel, I maun be steppin'. Good-nicht to ye."

"Ye'll niver have sich anither chanst."

"Nor niver wush to. Na, na; he'll never mak' a sheep-dog." And the little man turned up the collar of his coat.

"Will he not?" cried the other scornfully. "There niver yet was one o' that line——" he stopped abruptly.

The little man spun round.

"Iss?" he said, as innocent as any child. "Ye were sayin'?"

The other turned to the window and watched the rain falling monotonously.

"Ye'll be wantin' wet," he said adroitly.

"Ay, we could do wi' a drappin'. And he'll never mak' a sheep dog." He shoved his cap down on his head. "Weel, good-nicht to ye!" and he stepped out into the rain.

It was long after dark when the bargain was finally struck.

Adam M'Adam's Red Wull became that little man's property for the following realizable assets: ninepence in cash—three coppers and a doubtful sixpence, a plug of suspicious tobacco in a well-worn pouch, and an old watch.

"It's clean givin' 'im ye," said the stranger bitterly, at the end of the deal.

"It's mair the charity than aught else mak's me sae leeberal," the other answered gently. "I wad not like to see ye pinched."

"Thank ye kindly," the big man replied with some acerbity, and plunged out into the darkness and rain. Nor was that long-limbed drover-man ever again seen in the countryside. And the puppy's previous history—whether he was honestly come by or no, whether he was indeed of the famous Red McCulloch [1] strain, ever remained a mystery in the Daleland.

[1] You may know a Red McCulloch anywhere by the ring of white upon his tail some two inches from the root.

Dog Story

BY LUDWIG BEMELMANS

F O R   many years our summer vacations were
spent in an old peasant house, and everybody who came to see us
was breathless, partly on account of the beauty of the scenery,
but chiefly because the house stood atop a steep hill, overlooking
a village on the shore of a remote Austrian lake.

The landscape was as simple as bread and water. A ring
of dark, green mountains which anyone could climb reflected
themselves in the silent lake. At one side of this lake, a string
of gay rowboats shifted back and forth in the currents of the
green water. Each boat had the name of a girl painted on its

side, and from the end of the pier to which they were tied I went swimming while Wally, my dachshund (she was so small that I carried her home in my coat pocket whenever we had walked too far), slept in one of the boats, in the shade of the bench that spans the center. Wally disliked both sun and water.

From the pier one walked into the garden of the White Horse tavern, a cool space, filled with yellow tables and chairs, shaded by an arbor of wild grapevines.

Here usually sat a man of good appetite; he was a butcher and Wally's best friend, a plain fat man with a round shaven head, a large mustache, the caricature of a German, and certainly a butcher. He owned the house to the left of ours, on the hill.

After he had finished eating and laid knife and fork aside, he would take a piece of bread, break it into two pieces, call for Wally, and, mopping up the rest of the sauce on his plate, carefully feed it to the dog.

He paid his bill, said good morning, blew his nose into a large blue handkerchief, finished his beer, and took his cane from a hook, put on an alpine hat, and in a wide circle walked around the baroque, salmon-colored church.

Next to the church was a fountain, with a statue of St. Florian, the patron saint of firemen, standing on a tall column above it. As the butcher passed this fountain, the lower half of him was always hidden by the wide basin and only his hat, coat and arms—rowing in the air—seemed to walk up the street. In a while we followed him up the hill.

The sounds of this remote place were as comfortable as its panorama. In the morning twilight, Wally was at the garden gate, barking at the cattle that were driven up to the high meadows. From their necks hung bronze bells, suspended from heavy, quill-embroidered leather straps. The bells clanged away into the distance, and their place was taken by the church bells below calling to early mass at about seven.

The little motor boat that zigzagged back and forth over the lake had another bell, which announced its first departure half an hour later. The bell on the schoolhouse rang at eight.

As the sun rose over the high wall of mountains it changed all the colors in the valley and lit up the underside of the clouds that hung in the thin clear air above. Children sang in the school-house, the birds in the trees, carpets were beaten in gardens, and the cobbler started hammering.

At half-past ten followed the screech of the small wheels of the daily train from Salzburg as it slowed down to negotiate the sharp curve which carried it into the village. At this sound Wally sent up a long, high flutelike cry. She took that up again for another sound that came from the same direction as the train, the tearing howl of the whistle which announced that it was nocn in the sawmill at the far end of the lake.

The worst sound, one that made the little dog's hair stand on end and sent her for protection under a couch, was the music that started at one, Mozart, Bach, Haydn, Schubert, and Bee-thoven. It came from the house on our right. In its living room, little girls, in one-hour shifts, glared at études, cramped their small fingers into claws, and performed awful concertos on two old Bechstein grand pianos.

This went on until four. When the last of the little blond girls had left, Frau Dorothea von Moll, the music teacher, came out of the house, held her temples for a moment, and then walked slowly up and down in her kitchen garden. She wandered between even rows of spinach, kohlrabi, beets, celery, peas and carrots and the large leaves of rhubarb.

She wore a severe black costume, on cold days a mantle trimmed with worn Persian lamb, an old gray bonnet, and a watch on a long thin golden chain. She looked like someone deliberately and carefully made up to play the role of a distin-guished old lady in reduced circumstances.

She went out little; a few gentle, little old ladies formed a group that met in her garden house on Thursdays. She enter-tained them with coffee and gugelhupf, a native cake, and with anecdotes of musicians and the great people she had known when her husband, the famous pianist Arnulf von Moll, was still alive.

As soon as the pianos were stilled, Wally ran down the steep stairs that led to Frau Dorothea's garden as if to thank her because the terrible concert was over. Wally seesawed down the incline—front legs first, back legs after. Then she squeezed through an opening in the fence and attended the Thursday teas, eating cake and drinking milk. On other days she just walked up and down between the rows of vegetables, behind Frau Dorothea.

Wally's initial cost was very small, notwithstanding the fact that her father was the Bavarian champion Hasso von der Eulenburg, and that she personally was entered on her distinguished pedigree as Waltraut von der Eulenburg. However, she became expensive almost immediately.

One Sunday morning she pulled the cloth off the breakfast table and with it every cherished cup and saucer of a Sèvres tea set. The hot water from a falling pot scalded her, and Wally walked about for a week wrapped in bandages. As soon as this was forgotten, she ate a box of matches, and when she had recovered from that experience and come back from the veterinary, she worked a whole night to rip the satin cover off a Biedermeier love seat, took all the horsehair carefully out of it, carrying small tufts of it all over the house, down to Frau Dorothea's, and over to the butcher's garden.

There were many more nice things in this old house of which we were very fond, and it seemed best to send Wally away to be trained. One day a forest ranger, who had trained many dogs, took her away in his knapsack. To this experience I owe the knowledge that dogs can recognize a picture, a fact often disputed.

The forest rangers are government employees; they wear green mountain uniforms and faded felt hats with plumes. Most of them have Santa Claus beards, and usually they smoke long pipes that hang down the middle of the beard and end over heavy silver watch chains that are weighted down with old thalers. They carry knapsacks and over their shoulders hang double-barreled shotguns.

This forester found Wally more stubborn than any dachshund he had ever trained. He was very strict with her, rubbed her nose on the floor whenever she had done indignities to his clean house, gave her a few slaps on the backside, and threw her out into the forest.

Wally came back to us a few weeks later a completely changed dog. A model dog. Soon after her return a new tobacco was put on the market. It was called "Forester's Cut" and was wonderfully and widely advertised. Large posters were pasted up everywhere; on them appeared a package of "Forester's Cut," and the picture of a forester smoking it with delight. He wore the rakish hat with the plume, the grass-green uniform, the white beard, the shotgun, and was just such a one as Wally had been living with.

Wherever Wally saw this picture, she went for it. She strained on her leash, the little hairy chest became a bellows and started to work in and out, the lips were pulled up from over her teeth, and long rolls of thunder came from her throat. She shook with anger and looked like an old woodcut of the devil in a peasant Bible. She did nothing about the picture when it was shown to her in magazines, where it appeared in full colors but was reduced to half a page, nor did she recognize it when she saw a poster that was life-sized but printed in black and white.

At the end of that summer's vacation, we took Wally to America with us. It was not a happy idea and we should have followed the advice of Frau Dorothea, who wanted to keep Wally for us until our return. Wally hated the big liner. She was in a good kennel and had the company of two theatrical black poodles, good-natured animals, used to travel, and able to ride a bicycle and to count up to ten. The food was excellent, the sailor who took care of her a friendly fellow. But Wally remained curled up in a corner of her compartment, an unhappy, defiant coil of dachshund. She looked with mistrust at the ocean, with despair at the masts, the funnels, and the ventilators of the ship. She never played with the other dogs and stopped trembling only when she was wrapped up and resting on my lap in a deck chair.

Wally did not like New York any better than the ship. Her memories were a nightmare of fire-engine sirens, revolving doors, backfiring automobiles, the absence of grass and bushes, the rarity of trees. We decided the next summer to leave her with Frau Dorothea, who took care of our house while we were away.

This also was a sad arrangement. Frau Dorothea wrote that Wally came home only for meals, that she ate little, became thinner and thinner, sat in front of the closed door of our house, and that even her friend the butcher, leaning over the fence from his side of the garden and holding up choice pieces of meat, could not console her. Once she almost bit him when he came up to the house to speak to her.

We asked a dog specialist for advice and he suggested that we send her some piece of personal wearing apparel. A pair of old slippers, an old skiing mitten to which I had lost the mate, and a sweater with a few holes were dispatched with the next mail.

This helped a good deal. We read in happier letters that Wally now had a basket on the porch of our house and busied herself packing and unpacking it. She carried the slippers or the glove proudly through the garden, slept inside, under, and on top of the sweater. She still sat on the porch waiting for us until dark, but she ate now, slept at night in Frau Dorothea's house, and the butcher was allowed to come into the garden, was welcome, with a bone, or even just as he was.

We did not open the house the next summer; it was the year of the Anschluss. From letters we gathered that the village was not noticeably disturbed; a new strategic highway was being built along the lake, new songs were being sung, some people had become very quiet and others too loud, and a few places had been renamed; but to a dog, Hermann Göring Strasse and Adolf Hitler Platz are as good as Heinrich Heine Strasse and Dollfuss Platz.

Early the next year, Frau Dorothea had a visitor at whom Wally barked. He was a portly, serious business man from Salzburg and he offered to buy her house. The man's name was Hermann Brettschneider.

Frau Dorothea said that she loved her home, had no reason

to sell it, and would certainly never sell it at the price he offered her. She told him that our house was for sale. He did not want our house. He left.

A few weeks later he came back again, this time in the parade uniform of a captain of Storm Troopers, the medal of the Order of the Blood, highest Nazi decoration, on his chest. He sat a long while in her garden house and talked, and he left finally, red in the face. Frau Dorothea still did not want to sell.

Soon after he was gone, the piano lessons stopped; the little blond girls were forbidden to come. The old ladies also sent their regrets and stayed away on Thursdays. One night windows were broken, and then the butcher was arrested because he had come out of his garden to beat up a young man in uniform. The young man in uniform had been busy with a pail of red paint and a brush; he had lettered on the wall of Frau Dorothea's house, "Get out of town, Sarah—make haste, go back to Jerusalem."

On the first of the next month the house was newly painted, the windows repaired; the balcony broke out in Nazi bunting, and Herr Hauptmann Brettschneider gave a garden party bright with uniforms.

Frau Dorothea moved out of the village, to a house near the sawmill, and during the daytime she stayed indoors or in her little garden.

Wally, of course, was Aryan. She could run around and she made the long run to our house twice a day. She climbed to the terrace, unpacked the dirty slippers, and carried the skiing glove about. The butcher was in a concentration camp, but the Brettschneider housekeeper gave Wally occasional pieces of ham, ends of sausages, cuts of pork. Storm Troopers keep good kitchens.

When it was time for her to come home, late at night, Frau Dorothea usually walked to meet her in the dark. It was a rather dangerous place to walk. It was a freightyard of a place; its contours were an uncertain smudge, much like a charcoal drawing. There was a lamp about sixty feet from the spot where the railroad tracks crossed the new cement highway. It was here that the wheels of the train screeched at half-past ten in the morning. The highway entered the village in a blind, sudden turn, something the engineers would have liked to avoid, but the alternative would have been to drill a tunnel through two mountains. At the side of the highway, on its outer curve, the ground was soft and the terrain dropped down to the rocky bed of a river, the outflow of the lake. About where the lamp was, the water thundered down over a dam. It was an ideal setting for accidents, this place.

The accident happened on the night of March 7, 1939. A battery of tanks was being rushed to the Eastern Front—Front is the right word, for Germany was in a state of war—and came to the sawmill somewhat ahead of schedule, at the moment that Wally was about to cross the highway.

The beams of the strong headlights, the hellish clatter and tumult of the machinery, and the apparition of terror that a tank is, must have frozen the little dog to the middle of the road.

The driver of tank Number 1 tried to avoid her. He suddenly put on the brakes, that is, he retarded the left tractor belt and advanced the right. Four of the tanks behind him piled into one another, and his had turned too far, left the highway, and rolled over three times as it went down into the river bed.

It went into the shallow water (the sawmill closes the locks at night, to have more water for the turbine the next morning) right side up, and the two men in it, in overalls, loosened their belts and climbed out of the machine. Tanks Numbers 2, 3, 4, and 5 were somewhat damaged.

From the tower of tank Number 6 jumped a baby of a lieutenant with his first mustache. The men had climbed out of the other tanks and stood in a ring about Wally. The lieutenant picked her up, patted her head, spoke soft words to her, and held her to his cheek.

When Frau Dorothea came forward he clicked his heels, saluted, and smiled. "Dear lady, so sorry," he said, and gave the dog to her. While the mechanics set to work repairing the

105

damaged tanks, the young lieutenant lingered a moment or two, asking the dog's name and talking to Frau Dorothea about her. Then he went over to the edge of the highway.

At his direction, pulleys and spades appeared. Chains and cables were carried down the embankment. As two bugs might pull another, a dead one, under a leaf somewhere to eat him, two of the tanks above, without effort or strain, dragged the tank up out of the river bed and set it on the road. The lieutenant waved at Frau Dorothea and Wally as he got into the top of his machine. Tank Number 6 started forward, then the other tanks fell into line, one by one, and the procession continued on its way to the Czechoslovakian frontier.

A new kind of devotion

For the Love of a Man

BY JACK LONDON

Buck, scarcely full grown, had been kidnapped and schooled as a sled dog in the hardships of the far North. When at last John Thornton rescued him, the dog was nearly dead of starvation, beatings and overwork.

WHEN John Thornton froze his feet in the previous December, his partners had made him comfortable and left him to get well, going on, themselves, up the river to get out a raft of sawlogs for Dawson. He was still limping slightly at the time he rescued Buck, but with the continued warm weather even the slight limp left him. And here, lying by the river bank through the long spring days, watching the running water, listening lazily to the songs of birds and the hum of nature, Buck slowly won back his strength.

107

A rest is doubly good after one has traveled three thousand miles, and it must be confessed that Buck waxed lazy as his wounds healed, his muscles swelled out, and the flesh came back to cover his bones. For that matter, they were all loafing—Buck, John Thornton, and Skeet and Nig—waiting for the raft to come that was to carry them down to Dawson. Skeet was a little Irish setter who early made friends with Buck, who, in a dying condition, was unable to resent her first advances. She had the doctor trait which some dogs possess, and as a mother cat washes her kittens, so she washed and cleansed Buck's wounds. Regularly each morning after he had finished his breakfast, she performed her self-appointed task, till he came to look for her ministrations as much as he did for Thornton's. Nig, equally friendly though less demonstrative, was a huge black dog, half bloodhound and half deerhound, with eyes that laughed and a boundless good nature.

To Buck's surprise these dogs manifested no jealousy toward him. They seemed to share the kindliness and largeness of John Thornton. As Buck grew stronger they enticed him into all sorts of ridiculous games, in which Thornton himself could not forbear to join, and in this fashion Buck romped through his convalescence and into a new existence. Love, genuine passionate love, was his for the first time. This he had never experienced at Judge Miller's down in the sun-kissed Santa Clara Valley. With the Judge's sons, hunting and tramping, it had been a working partnership; with the Judge's grandsons, a sort of pompous guardianship; and with the Judge himself, a stately and dignified friendship. But love that was feverish and burning, that was adoration, that was madness, it had taken John Thornton to arouse.

This man had saved his life, which was something; but further, he was the ideal master. Other men saw to the welfare of their dogs from a sense of duty and business expediency; he saw to the welfare of his as if they were his own children, because he could not help it. And he saw further. He never forgot a kindly greeting or a cheering word, and to sit down for a long talk with them ("gas" he called it) was as much his delight as theirs. He had a way of taking Buck's head roughly between his hands, and resting his own head upon Buck's, of shaking him back and forth, the while calling him ill names that to Buck were love names. Buck knew no greater joy than that rough embrace and the sound of murmured oaths, and at each jerk back and forth it seemed that his heart would be shaken out of his body so great was its ecstasy. And when, released, he sprang to his feet, his mouth laughing, his eyes eloquent, his throat vibrant with unuttered sound, and in that fashion remained without movement, John Thornton would reverently exclaim, "God! you can all but speak!"

Buck had a trick of love expression that was akin to hurt. He would often seize Thornton's hand in his mouth and close so fiercely that the flesh bore the impress of his teeth for some time afterward. And as Buck understood the oaths to be love words, so the man understood this feigned bite for a caress.

For the most part, however, Buck's love was expressed in adoration. While he went wild with happiness when Thornton touched him or spoke to him, he did not seek these tokens. Unlike Skeet, who was wont to shove her nose under Thornton's hand and nudge and nudge till petted, or Nig, who would stalk up and rest his great head on Thornton's knee, Buck was content to adore at a distance. He would lie by the hour, eager, alert, at Thornton's feet, looking up into his face, dwelling upon it, studying it, following with keenest interest each fleeting expression, every movement or change of feature. Or, as chance might have it, he would lie farther away, to the side or rear, watching the outlines of the man and the occasional movements of his body. And often, such was the communion in which they lived, the strength of Buck's gaze would draw John Thornton's head around, and he would return the gaze, without speech, his heart shining out of his eyes as Buck's heart shone out.

For a long time after his rescue, Buck did not like Thornton to get out of his sight. From the moment he left the tent to when he entered it again, Buck would follow at his heels. His transient masters since he had come into the Northland had bred in him a fear that no master could be permanent. He was afraid that Thornton would pass out of his life as Perrault and François and the Scotch half-breed had passed out. Even in the night, in his dreams, he was haunted by this fear. At such times he would shake off sleep and creep through the chill to the flap of the tent, where he would stand and listen to the sound of his master's breathing.

But in spite of this great love he bore John Thornton, which seemed to bespeak the soft civilizing influence, the strain of the primitive, which the Northland had aroused in him, remained alive and active. Faithfulness and devotion, things born of fire and roof, were his; yet he retained his wildness and wiliness. He was a thing of the wild, come in from the wild to sit by John Thornton's fire, rather than a dog of the soft Southland stamped with the marks of generations of civilization. Because of his very great love, he could not steal from this man but from any other man, in any other camp, he did not hesitate an instant; while the cunning with which he stole enabled him to escape detection.

His face and body were scored by the teeth of many dogs, and he fought as fiercely as ever and more shrewdly. Skeet and Nig were too good-natured for quarreling—besides, they belonged to John Thornton; but the strange dog, no matter what the breed or valor, swiftly acknowledged Buck's supremacy or found himself struggling for life with a terrible antagonist. And Buck was merciless. He had learned well the law of club and fang, and he never forewent an advantage or drew back from a foe he had started on the way to death. He had lessoned from Spitz, and from the chief fighting dogs of the police and mail, and knew there was no middle course. He must master or be mastered; while to show mercy was a weakness. Mercy did not exist in the primordial life. It was misunderstood for fear, and such misunderstandings made for death. Kill or be killed, eat or be eaten, was the law; and this mandate, down out of the depths of Time, he obeyed.

He was older than the days he had seen and the breaths he had drawn. He linked the past with the present, and the eternity behind him throbbed through him in a mighty rhythm to which he swayed as the tides and seasons swayed. He sat by John Thornton's fire, a broad-breasted dog, white-fanged and long-

110

furred; but behind him were the shades of all manner of dogs, half wolves and wild wolves, urgent and prompting, tasting the savor of the meat he ate, thirsting for the water he drank, scenting the wind with him, listening with him and telling him the sounds made by the wild life in the forest, dictating his moods, directing his actions, lying down to sleep with him when he lay down, and dreaming with him and beyond him and becoming themselves the stuff of his dreams.

So peremptorily did these shades beckon him, that each day mankind and the claims of mankind slipped farther from him. Deep in the forest a call was sounding, and as often as he heard this call, mysteriously thrilling and luring, he felt compelled to turn his back upon the fire and the beaten earth around it, and to plunge into the forest, and on and on, he knew not where or why; nor did he wonder where or why, the call sounding imperiously, deep in the forest. But as often as he gained the soft unbroken earth and the green shade, the love for John Thornton drew him back to the fire again.

Thornton alone held him. The rest of mankind was as nothing. Chance travelers might praise or pet him; but he was cold under it all, and from a too demonstrative man he would get up and walk away. When Thornton's partners, Hans and Pete, arrived on the long-expected raft, Buck refused to notice them till he learned they were close to Thornton; after that he tolerated them in a passive sort of way, accepting favors from them as though he favored them by accepting. They were of the same large type as Thornton, living close to the earth, thinking simply and seeing clearly; and ere they swung the raft into the big eddy by the sawmill at Dawson, they understood Buck and his ways, and did not insist upon an intimacy such as obtained with Skeet and Nig.

For Thornton, however, his love seemed to grow and grow. He alone among men could put a pack upon Buck's back in the summer traveling. Nothing was too great for Buck to do, when Thornton commanded. One day (they had grub-staked themselves from the proceeds of the raft and left Dawson for the headwaters of the Tanana) the men and dogs were sitting on the crest of a cliff which fell away, straight down, to naked bedrock three hundred feet below. John Thornton was sitting near the edge, Buck at his shoulder. A thoughtless whim seized Thornton, and he drew the attention of Hans and Pete to the experiment he had in mind. "Jump, Buck!" he commanded, sweeping his arm out and over the chasm. The next instant he was grappling with Buck on the extreme edge, while Hans and Pete were dragging them back into safety.

"It's uncanny," Pete said, after it was over and they had caught their speech.

Thornton shook his head. "No, it is splendid, and it is terrible, too. Do you know, it sometimes makes me afraid."

"I'm not hankering to be the man that lays hands on you while he's around," Pete announced conclusively, nodding his head toward Buck.

"Py Jingo!" was Hans' contribution. "Not mineself either."

It was at Circle City, ere the year was out, that Pete's apprehensions were realized. "Black" Burton, a man evil-tempered and malicious, had been picking a quarrel with a tenderfoot at the bar, when Thornton stepped good-naturedly between. Buck, as was his custom, was lying in a corner, head on paws, watching his master's every action. Burton struck out, without warning, straight from the shoulder. Thornton was sent spinning, and saved himself from falling only by clutching the rail of the bar.

Those who were looking on heard what was neither bark nor yelp, but a something which is best described as a roar, and they saw Buck's body rise up in the air as he left the floor for Burton's throat. The man saved his life by instinctively throwing out his arm, but was hurled backward to the floor with Buck on top of him. Buck loosed his teeth from the flesh of the arm and drove in again for the throat. This time the man succeeded only in partly blocking, and his throat was torn open. Then the crowd was upon Buck, and he was driven off; but while a surgeon checked the bleeding, he prowled up and down, growling furiously, attempting to rush in, and being forced back by an array of hostile clubs. A "miners' meeting," called on the spot, decided that the dog had sufficient provocation, and Buck was discharged.

But his reputation was made, and from that day his name spread through every camp in Alaska.

Later on, in the fall of the year, he saved John Thornton's life in quite another fashion. The three partners were lining a long and narrow poling boat down a bad stretch of rapids on the Forty-Mile Creek. Hans and Pete moved along the bank, snubbing with a thin Manila rope from tree to tree, while Thornton remained in the boat, helping its descent by means of a pole, and shouting directions to the shore. Buck, on the bank, worried and anxious, kept abreast of the boat, his eyes never off his master.

At a particularly bad spot, where a ledge of barely submerged rocks jutted out into the river, Hans cast off the rope and, while Thornton poled the boat out into the stream, ran down the bank with the end in his hand to snub the boat when it had cleared the ledge. This it did, and was flying downstream in a current as swift as a millrace, when Hans checked it with the rope and checked too suddenly. The boat flirted over and snubbed in to the bank, bottom up, while Thornton, flung sheer out of it, was carried downstream toward the worst part of the rapids, a stretch of wild water in which no swimmer could live.

Buck had sprung in on the instant, and at the end of three hundred yards, amid a mad swirl of water, he overhauled Thornton. When he felt him grasp his tail, Buck headed for the bank, swimming with all his splendid strength. But the progress shoreward was slow; the progress downstream amazingly rapid. From below came the fatal roaring where the wild current went wilder and was rent in shreds and spray by the rocks which thrust through like the teeth of an enormous comb. The suck of the water as it took the beginning of the last steep pitch was frightful, and Thornton knew that the shore was impossible. He scraped furiously over a rock, bruised across a second, and struck a third with crushing force. He clutched its slippery top with both hands, releasing Buck, and above the roar of the churning water shouted: "Go, Buck! Go!"

Buck could not hold his own and swept on downstream, struggling desperately but unable to win back. When he heard Thornton's command repeated, he partly reared out of the water, throwing his head high, as though for a last look, then turned obediently toward the bank. He swam powerfully and was dragged ashore by Pete and Hans at the very point where swimming ceased to be possible and destruction began.

They knew that the time a man could cling to a slippery rock in the face of that driving current was a matter of minutes, and they ran as fast as they could up the bank to a point far above where Thornton was hanging on. They attached the line with which they had been snubbing the boat to Buck's neck and shoulders, being careful that it should neither strangle him nor impede his swimming, and launched him into the stream. He struck out boldly, but not straight enough into the stream. He discovered the mistake too late, when Thornton was abreast of him and a bare half-dozen strokes away while he was being carried helplessly past.

Hans promptly snubbed with the rope, as though Buck were a boat. The rope thus tightening on him in the sweep of the current, he was jerked under the surface, and under the surface he remained till his body struck against the bank and he was hauled out. He was half drowned, and Hans and Pete threw themselves upon him, pounding the breath into him and the water out of him. He staggered to his feet and fell down. The faint sound of Thornton's voice came to them, and though they could not make out the words of it, they knew that he was in his extremity. His master's voice acted on Buck like an electric shock. He sprang to his feet and ran up the bank ahead of the men to the point of his previous departure.

Again the rope was attached and he was launched, and again he struck out, but this time straight into the stream. He had miscalculated once, but he would not be guilty of it a second time. Hans paid out the rope, permitting no slack, while Pete kept it clear of coils. Buck held on till he was on a line straight above Thornton; then he turned, and with the speed of an express train headed down upon him. Thornton saw him coming, and as Buck struck him like a battering ram, with the whole force of the current behind him, he reached up and closed with both arms around the shaggy neck. Hans snubbed the rope around the tree, and Buck and Thornton were jerked under the water.

114

Strangling, suffocating, sometimes one uppermost and sometimes the other, dragging over the jagged bottom, smashing against rocks and snags, they veered in to the bank.

Thornton came to, belly downward and being violently propelled back and forth across a drift log by Hans and Pete. His first glance was for Buck, over whose limp and apparently lifeless body Nig was setting up a howl, while Skeet was licking the wet face and closed eyes. Thornton was himself bruised and battered, and he went carefully over Buck's body, when he had been brought around, finding three broken ribs.

"That settles it," he announced. "We camp right here." And camp they did, till Buck's ribs knitted and he was able to travel.

That winter, at Dawson, Buck performed another exploit, not so heroic, perhaps, but one that put his name many notches higher on the totem pole of Alaskan fame. This exploit was particularly gratifying to the three men for they stood in need of the outfit which it furnished, and were enabled to make a long-desired trip into the virgin East, where miners had not yet appeared. It was brought about by a conversation in the Eldorado Saloon, in which men waxed boastful of their favorite dogs. Buck, because of his record, was the target for these men, and Thornton was driven stoutly to defend him. At the end of half an hour one man stated that his dog could start a sled with five hundred pounds and walk off with it; a second bragged six hundred for his dog, and a third, seven hundred.

"Pooh! pooh!" said John Thornton. "Buck can start a thousand pounds."

"And break it out? and walk off with it for a hundred yards?" demanded Matthewson, a Bonanza King, he of the seven hundred vaunt.

"And break it out, and walk off with it for a hundred yards," John Thornton said coolly.

"Well," Matthewson said, slowly and deliberately, so that all could hear, "I've got a thousand dollars that says he can't. And there it is." So saying, he slammed a sack of gold dust the size of a bologna sausage down on the bar.

Nobody spoke. Thornton's bluff, if bluff it was, had been

called. He could feel a flush of warm blood creeping up his face. His tongue had tricked him. He did not know whether Buck could start a thousand pounds. Half a ton! The enormousness of it appalled him. He had great faith in Buck's strength and had often thought him capable of starting such a load; but never, as now, had he faced the possibility of it, the eyes of a dozen men fixed upon him, silent and waiting. Further, he had no thousand dollars; nor had Hans or Pete.

"I've got a sled standing outside now, with twenty fifty-pound sacks of flour on it," Matthewson went on with brutal directness, "so don't let that hinder you."

Thornton did not reply. He did not know what to say. He glanced from face to face in the absent way of a man who has lost the power of thought and is seeking somewhere to find the thing that will start it going again. The face of Jim O'Brien, a Mastodon King and old-time comrade, caught his eyes. It was as a cue to him, seeming to rouse him to do what he would never have dreamed of doing.

"Can you lend me a thousand?" he asked, almost in a whisper.

"Sure," answered O'Brien, thumping down a plethoric sack by the side of Matthewson's. "Though it's little faith I'm having, John, that the beast can do the trick."

The Eldorado emptied its occupants into the street to see the test. The tables were deserted, and the dealers and gamekeepers came forth to see the outcome of the wager and to lay odds. Several hundred men, furred and mittened, banked around the sled within easy distance. Matthewson's sled, loaded with a thousand pounds of flour, had been standing for a couple of hours, and in the intense cold (it was sixty below zero) the runners had frozen fast to the hard-packed snow. Men offered odds of two to one that Buck could not budge the sled. A quibble arose concerning the phrase "break out." O'Brien contended it was Thornton's privilege to knock the runners loose, leaving Buck to "break it out" from a dead standstill. Matthewson insisted that the phrase included breaking the runners from the frozen grip of the snow. A majority of the men who had

116

witnessed the making of the bet decided in his favor, whereat the odds went up to three to one against Buck.

There were no takers. Not a man believed him capable of the feat. Thornton had been hurried into the wager, heavy with doubt; and now that he looked at the sled itself, the concrete fact, with the regular team of ten dogs curled up in the snow before it, the more impossible the task appeared. Matthewson waxed jubilant.

"Three to one!" he proclaimed. "I'll lay you another thousand at that figure, Thornton. What d'ye say?"

Thornton's doubt was strong in his face but his fighting spirit was aroused—the fighting spirit that soars above odds, fails to recognize the impossible, and is deaf to all save the clamor for battle. He called Hans and Pete to him. Their sacks were slim, and with his own the three partners could rake together only two hundred dollars. In the ebb of their fortunes, this sum was their total capital; yet they laid it unhesitatingly against Matthewson's six hundred.

The team of ten dogs was unhitched, and Buck, with his own harness, was put into the sled. He had caught the contagion of the excitement, and he felt that in some way he must do a great thing for John Thornton. Murmurs of admiration at his splendid appearance went up. He was in perfect condition, without an ounce of superfluous flesh, and the one hundred and fifty pounds that he weighed were so many pounds of grit and virility. His furry coat shone with the sheen of silk. Down the neck and across the shoulders, his mane, in repose as it was, half bristled and seemed to lift with every movement, as though excess of vigor made each particular hair alive and active. The great breast and heavy forelegs were no more than in proportion with the rest of the body, where the muscles showed in tight rolls underneath the skin. Men felt these muscles and proclaimed them hard as iron, and the odds went down to two to one.

"Gad, sir! Gad, sir!" stuttered a member of the latest dynasty, a king of the Skookum Benches. "I offer you eight hundred for him, sir, before the test, sir, eight hundred just as he stands there now."

117

Thornton shook his head and stepped close to Buck's side.

"You must stand off from him," Matthewson protested. "Free play and plenty of room."

The crowd fell silent; only could be heard the voices of the gamblers vainly offering two to one. Everybody acknowledged Buck a magnificent animal, but twenty fifty-pound sacks of flour bulked too large in their eyes for them to loosen their pouch strings.

Thornton knelt down by Buck's side. He took his head in his two hands and rested cheek on cheek. He did not playfully shake him, as was his wont, or murmur soft love curses, but he whispered in his ear. "As you love me, Buck. As you love me," was what he whispered. Buck whined with suppressed eagerness.

The crowd was watching curiously. The affair was growing mysterious. It seemed like a conjuration. As Thornton got to his feet, Buck seized his mittened hand between his jaws, pressing in with his teeth and releasing slowly, half-reluctantly. It was the answer, in terms, not of speech, but of love. Thornton stepped well back.

"Now, Buck," he said.

Buck tightened the traces, then slacked them for a matter of several inches. It was the way he had had learned.

"Gee!" Thornton's voice rang out, sharp in the tense silence.

Buck swung to the right, ending the movement in a plunge that took up the slack and with a sudden jerk arrested his one hundred and fifty pounds. The load quivered, and from under the runners arose a crisp crackling.

"Haw!" Thornton commanded.

Buck duplicated the maneuver, this time to the left. The crackling turned into a snapping, the sled pivoting and the runners slipping and grating several inches to the side. The sled was broken out. Men were holding their breaths, intensely unconscious of the fact.

"Now, MUSH!"

Thornton's command cracked out like a pistol shot. Buck threw himself forward, tightening the traces with a jarring lunge. His whole body was gathered compactly together in the tremendous effort, the muscles writhing and knotting like live things under the silky fur. His great chest was low to the ground, his head forward and down, while his feet were flying like mad, the claws scarring the hard-packed snow in parallel grooves. The sled swayed and trembled, half started forward. One of his feet slipped, and one man groaned aloud. Then the sled lurched ahead in what appeared a rapid succession of jerks, though it never really came to a dead stop again . . . half an inch . . . an inch . . . two inches . . . The jerks perceptibly diminished; as the sled gained momentum, he caught them up, till it was moving steadily along.

Men gasped and began to breathe again, unaware that for a moment they had ceased to breathe. Thornton was running behind, encouraging Buck with short, cheery words. The distance had been measured off, and as he neared the pile of firewood which marked the end of the hundred yards a cheer began to grow and grow, which burst into a roar as he passed the firewood and halted at command. Every man was tearing himself loose, even Matthewson. Hats and mittens were flying in the air. Men were shaking hands, it did not matter with whom, and bubbling over in a general incoherent babel.

But Thornton fell on his knees beside Buck. Head was against head, and he was shaking him back and forth. Those who hurried up heard him cursing Buck, and he cursed him long and fervently, and softly and lovingly.

"Gad, sir! Gad, sir!" spluttered the Skookum Bench king. "I'll give you a thousand for him, sir, a thousand, sir—twelve hundred, sir."

Thornton rose to his feet. His eyes were wet. The tears were streaming frankly down his cheeks. "Sir," he said to the Skookum Bench king, "no, sir. You can go to hell, sir. It's the best I can do for you, sir."

Buck seized Thornton's hand in his teeth. Thornton shook him back and forth. As though animated by a common impulse, the onlookers drew back to a respectful distance; nor were they again indiscreet enough to interrupt.

Perseverance, patience and enterprise

Snapshot of a Dog

BY JAMES THURBER

I RAN across a dim photograph of him the other day. He's been dead twenty-five years. His name was Rex (my two brothers and I named him) and he was a bull terrier. "An American bull terrier," we used to say, proudly; none of your English bulls. He had one brindle eye that sometimes made him look like a clown and sometimes reminded you of a politician with derby hat and cigar. The rest of him was white except for a brindle saddle and a brindle stocking on a hind leg. Nevertheless, there was a nobility about him. He was big and muscular and beautifully made. He never lost his dignity even when trying to

120

accomplish the extravagant tasks my brother and I used to set for him.

One of these was the bringing of a ten-foot wooden rail into the yard through the back gate. We would throw it out into the alley and tell him to get it. Rex was as powerful as a wrestler, and he would catch the rail at the balance, lift it clear of the ground, and trot with great confidence toward the gate. Of course, the gate being only four feet wide, he couldn't bring the rail in broadside. He found that out when he got a few terrific jolts, but he wouldn't give up. He finally figured out how to do it, by dragging the rail, holding onto one end, growling. He got a great, wagging satisfaction out of his work.

He was a tremendous fighter, but he never started fights. He never went for a dog's throat but for one of its ears (that teaches a dog a lesson), and he would get his grip, close his eyes, and hold on. He could hold on for hours. His longest fight lasted from dusk to almost pitch dark, one Sunday. It was fought with a large, snarly nondescript belonging to a large colored man. When Rex finally got his ear grip, the brief whirlwind of snarling turned to screeching. It was frightening to listen to and to watch. The negro boldly picked the dogs up, swung them around his head, and finally let them fly like a hammer in a hammer throw, but although they landed ten feet away, with a great plump, Rex still held on. Working their way to the middle of the car tracks, two or three streetcars were held up by the fight. A motorman tried to pry Rex's jaws open with a switch rod; somebody lighted a stick and held it to Rex's tail but he paid no attention. Rex's joy of battle, when battle was joined, was almost tranquil. He had a kind of pleasant expression during fights, his eyes closed in what would have seemed to be sleep had it not been for the turmoil of the struggle. The fire department finally had to be sent for and a powerful stream of water turned on the dogs for several moments before Rex finally let go.

The story of that Homeric fight got all around town, and some of our relatives considered it a blot on the family name. They insisted that we get rid of Rex, but nobody could have made us give him up. We would have left town with him first. It would have been different, perhaps, if he had ever looked for trouble. But he had a gentle disposition. He never bit a person in the ten strenuous years that he lived, nor ever growled at anyone except prowlers.

Swimming was his favorite recreation. The first time he ever saw a body of water, he trotted nervously along the steep bank for a while, fell to barking wildly, and finally plunged in from a height of eight feet or more. I shall always remember that shining, virgin dive. Then he swam upstream and back just for the pleasure of it, like a man. It was fun to see him battle upstream against a stiff current, growling every foot of the way. He had as much fun in the water as any person I have ever known. You didn't have to throw a stick into the water to get him to go in. Of course, he would bring back a stick if you did throw one in. He would have brought back a piano if you had thrown one in.

That reminds me of the night he went a-roving in the light of the moon and brought back a small chest of drawers he had found somewhere—how far from the house nobody ever knew. There were no drawers in the chest when he got it home, and it wasn't a good one—just an old cheap piece abandoned on a trash heap. Still it was something he wanted, probably because it presented a nice problem in transportation. We first knew about his achievement when, deep in the night, we heard sounds as if two or three people were trying to tear the house down. We came downstairs and turned on the porch light. Rex was on the top step, trying to pull the thing up, but it had caught and he was just holding his own. I suppose he would have held his own until dawn if we hadn't helped him. Next day we carted the chest miles away and threw it out. If we had thrown it out nearby he would have brought it home again, as a small token of his integrity in such matters.

There was in his world no such thing as the impossible. Even death couldn't beat him down. He died, it is true, but only, as one of his admirers said, after "straight-arming the death angel" for more than an hour. Late one afternoon he wandered home, too slowly and uncertainly to be the Rex that had trotted briskly homeward up our avenue for ten years. I think we all knew when he came through the gate that he was dying. He had apparently taken a terrible beating, probably from the owner of some dog he had got into a fight with. His head and body were scarred, and some of the brass studs of his heavy collar were sprung loose. He licked at our hands and, staggering, fell, but got up again. We could see that he was looking for someone. One of his three masters was not home. He did not get home for an hour. During that hour the bull terrier fought against death as he had fought against the cold strong current of the creek. When the person he was waiting for did come through the gate, whistling, ceasing to whistle, Rex walked a few wobbly paces toward him, touched his hand with his muzzle, and fell down again. This time he didn't get up.

Shame warred with love

A Hunter's Horn

BY BILLY C. CLARK

Young mountain-born Jeb wanted to hunt like a man. But he didn't know how to blow the hunter's horn, and his pup, Mooneye, was half blind. Shamed, Jeb refused even to try to hunt and faced the threat of losing his pup. Then Jeb was given a last chance.

*J*E B could tell by the warmness of the wind that it would be a warm and clear night. So clear and warm that Grandma Quildy feared rain. And when Jeb took the hunter's horn and strapped it across his shoulder and picked up the flashlight she cautioned him for the second time.

"Hunt low on the slopes tonight, Jeb," she said. "If it rains you won't have far to get to the cabin. I am afraid of the woods during time of storm. Don't stay out too late. Circle the slopes one time and then come in."

124

Jeb was so anxious to go that he didn't answer Grandma Quildy. He was happy to have a hound like Lucy to hunt with, and on such a clear night there was a good chance he might strike a coon. He did not like to have Grandma Quildy warn him about the woods. He knew the woods well enough to name all of the trees, and almost all the sounds.

But Grandma Quildy knew the woods as well as he and this was why she had told him to hunt the slopes. She knew the danger of the woods during a storm. The tall trees on the ridge would be the first to catch lightning if it were to strike close to the mountain. During a storm there was always a high wind and trees were cracked and thrown across the path. During a storm was the time when the trees shed their dead or weak limbs, and one could hit you without warning.

Jeb walked to the outhouse and got an empty feedsack and tucked it in his belt. Lucy whimpered and sniffed around the yard anxious to get started, and the small pup ran after her trying to play. But Lucy would have no part of the pup. Once in the woods she would hunt the trail, her own trails, and it was up to the pup to keep her pace.

Grandma Quildy stood by the window and Jeb waved at her and started down the path. He followed the creek to where the path turned up the ridge and here he stopped. Lucy went into the beech grove and Jeb waited for her to circle. The pup followed her. Jeb knew that he would wait for Lucy to hunt a section of the ground. If she struck no trails she would come in. This would be a sign to Jeb to move along.

To the left of the path stood a gray rock, and in front of the rock ran a small creek. Under the rock was a good place for coon or possum. If a coon was denned under the rock, Jeb figured he was probably out of his den by now, running the small creek searching for crawdads.[1] The coon would probably work up the creek toward the head of the hollow. On the ridge there was a cornfield—a good place for coon.

While Jeb waited for the dogs to circle he walked over to the rock and flashed his light under it. He could see by her

[1] crawfish

125

prints in the dust that Lucy had been here ahead of him. And beside Lucy's tracks were the tracks of the pup.

There were several holes under the rock and Jeb knew that each hole was a den. He dropped to his knees and reached his hand back in one of the holes. He picked up a handful of dirt and, holding it under the light, let it sift through his hand. Mixed in the dirt were long gray and white hairs. This is the den of a possum, Jeb thought.

The second and third hole belonged to a possum, but the fourth belonged to a skunk. The hair from this hole was black and white and coarser than the possum's.

None of the holes were worn slick, and Jeb figured they were old holes. And he had not really expected to find coon hair here anyway. He knew that a coon took to a tree den more often than a rock den.

The beeches near Jeb were likely to be chosen by a coon. Few beeches grew old and tall without having coon holes in them. And in these holes the coon would stay. Jeb shone his light into the tall beeches. There were several holes.

At some of the beeches Jeb stopped and shone his light on the bark. If a coon climbed the tree often, the bark of the beech would tell on him so. There would be claw marks on the slick, gray bark. Jeb found some marks on the beeches but they were mostly squirrel marks.

Lucy came back down the creek, the pup still with her. She sniffed again at the holes under the rock and started back up the creek. Jeb pulled the rawhide strap of the horn farther up on his shoulder and walked toward the head of the hollow.

Jeb didn't stop until he got to the top of the ridge. There he sat down on a dead log that had fallen across the path on his side of the cornfield, and waited for Lucy and the pup. In a short while Lucy came up the path behind him and he hissed her and the pup into the cornfield. Under the light of the moon he could follow them with his eyes to the edge of the cornfield. Behind Lucy, with his nose to the ground, went the small pup. Lucy stopped, sniffed, and then disappeared.

It seemed to Jeb that he had been sitting on the log a long

126

time. Lucy had stayed out longer than usual. Jeb sat and listened to the wind in the trees. Now and then a bird fluttered from a tree into the darkness and each time Jeb jumped, thinking that Lucy was coming in. But each time when Lucy did not come he knew that the bird had probably been pushed from the limb by another bird and would have to find a new roost.

Jeb listened to the weird sounds of the woods. There was the hoot of an owl from over in the hollow. And from some-where along the creek came the sound of a whippoorwill. Jeb liked to listen to the whippoorwill. Its voice was soft and clear. But not the owl's. Its hoot brought a loneliness to the woods.

A gust of wind swept across the ridge and Jeb listened to the sound in the trees. And then the wind died and the woods were quiet. Almost too quiet, Jeb thought.

Once, he wished that the pup would come in so that he'd have company. Jeb had not thought he would stay out this long. But it would be wrong to call the pup in. And he couldn't call Lucy even if he wanted to. She would only come to the sound of the horn if she were out tracking.

The wind became harder in the trees and still Lucy did not come. Jeb got up to stretch his legs and walked to the edge of the cornfield. The moon was overhead and was so bright that Jeb didn't have to use the flashlight to see the path. Lucy had been gone too long, he thought. He let his hand slide along the smooth horn and he touched the mouthpiece. Then he let his hand fall to his side.

Then, in the stillness of the woods, Jeb heard it. It was Lucy's voice. Loud and clear it sounded through the woods and bounced against the side of the valleys. Jeb jumped with joy and listened. Lucy bawled again and again, each time from a different place. They were short, quick bawls and Jeb knew she was trailing. Whatever she had struck was not far away.

Jeb waited to hear the voice of the pup. But there was only Lucy's voice. The pup is a silent trailer, Jeb thought. And he frowned. Jeb liked to listen to a hound that opened on the trail, first with short, quick barks and then a steady bawl when it had treed the game. To him this was the prettiest of all music. A silent

127

trailer would only bark after it had treed, and some would not bark then.

Jeb listened to Lucy as she trailed the side of the slope and crossed a ridge into another hollow. She came out of the hollow and down a ridge. If she trailed over this ridge, Jeb knew she would be in Hurricane Hollow. Hurricane Hollow was a short hollow. At the head of it stood a large rock cliff. If Lucy could turn the game into this hollow and press it close enough, she could run it into the rock. Here it would have to turn and make its stand. If it was a fighting animal, like a coon, it would make a stand and fight.

Lucy's voice stopped. Then after a short while Jeb heard her open again. She had circled back to the valley. And then her voice sounded farther and farther away until Jeb had to listen close to hear it.

A loud scream came from the far ridge and cold chills swept Jeb's body. He looked into the darkness, toward the far ridge. Then he heard the scream again. At first, Jeb had not been sure. But now he knew the sound. Only once before had he ever heard it. He had been with Jeptha, and Jeptha had told him never to forget it. This was the scream of a wildcat. This was the deadliest of all the game a hound could hunt here in the mountains. It was not often that a hound would stand against one and fight. And most of the hounds that did were either buried or left somewhere on the mountainside, never to be found.

Lucy bawled, and Jeb knew she was following a slow trail. And this was the mark of a good hound. There would be no hurry for Lucy. She would trail slowly, but always moving closer to her game. A fast hound would many times overrun the trail and have to drop back and pick it up again.

The wildcat screamed again and Jeb thought it was egging Lucy on. It was on the far ridge, the ridge that turned into Hurricane Hollow. Jeb thought it would wait until Lucy worked closer and then would turn down the ridge—not into the hollow where it would be trapped. The wildcat must know, Jeb thought, that Lucy was a slow trailer. There was a chance that a fast hound could turn the wildcat into the hollow and force it against the cliff. And against the cliff the wildcat would turn and fight.

Other than its loud scream that seemed to stop all the other sounds of the woods, Jeb was glad it was a wildcat. He loved to hear Lucy bark and he knew on the slow trail she would run all night. That is, if she were not called off. And he couldn't blow the horn.

He was glad in one way he couldn't blow the horn. He could stay on the mountaintop all night and he would be able to tell Grandma Quildy what had happened. Even Grandma Quildy knew that a hunter never left the mountain without his hound.

Jeb found himself a soft place to sit on and started to sit down. Then he jumped to his feet.

Along the far ridge drifted the bawl of another hound. At first Jeb thought it was the voice of Lucy, clear and deep. But the long bawls instead of the short, quick ones told him it wasn't. Other than this, the voice was the same.

Deep and mellow the voice rang through the woods as though it were coming from a hollow log. It was hard to believe that another hound could have a voice so close to Lucy's. And then chills covered his body. He thought of the pup. There was a chance, Jeb knew, that the pup, being young on the trail, had heard the scream of the wildcat and had turned toward it, following sound instead of track.

Jeb caught his breath and listened to the steady bawl. He knew now it was the pup. And he was moving fast along the mountainside. So fast that he was sure to turn the wildcat into Hurricane Hollow. The wildcat screamed again, egging the young pup on, Jeb thought.

Once in the hollow the ground would be cleared by the small creek that came out of it, and the pup would move faster toward the cliff. Once against the cliff, the wildcat would turn. The pup would not have a chance. And yet, the pup had no way of knowing the danger of the wildcat. He was only following the sound.

From two hollows away came the voice of Lucy. For the first time that Jeb could ever remember, Lucy had lost the trail and circled back to pick it up. And into the hollow went the pup.

Jeb thought of the pup pushing the wildcat against the rock cliff, and then being torn to pieces by its sharp teeth and long claws. He thought of the pup sticking his head into the air and bawling to let Jeb know that he was a hound and was pushing his game. And that he had no fear of the wildcat. With the blind eye and stub tail he would face the wildcat, the deadliest of all the game here in the mountains.

Tears came to Jeb's eyes. And he called as loud as he could. "Mooneye!" he yelled. But his voice died in the deep woods.

Jeb called again, and this time he started to run through the trees toward the ridge. His only chance was to try and catch the pup before he reached the cliff. Jeb fell into the thick underbrush and got to his feet. Tree limbs hit him in the face and brought more tears to his eyes. And the horn, swinging back and forth at his side, caught on low bushes and slowed him up. He pulled the horn from his shoulder and held it in his hand, crossing the ridge and into the hollow.

Jeb stopped to catch a short breath and listen. Behind him was the voice of Lucy, working the slow trail. By the time she reaches the cliff, Jeb thought, the pup will be killed.

Again and again the pup bawled, each time nearer the rock. In the hollow Jeb slipped on the slick stems of the wild fern and fell against the side of a large beech. The horn flew from his hand and into the air. Jeb wiped his eyes and found the horn. He yelled again for the pup and headed for the cliff.

Close to the cliff Jeb stopped. Against the rock, its fur bristling, stood the wildcat. In front of the wildcat, his head low, stood the pup. He was not moving in, as Jeb had thought he would, but was baying the wildcat, staying at a safe distance but close enough to press the wildcat against the rock.

Jeb was afraid to call. If the pup knew he was this close, the sound of his voice might encourage it to move in on the wildcat. Jeb stood, tears streaming down his face, the horn hanging limp in his hand. Beneath the moon he could see the stub tail of the pup moving back and forth. His head was turned to one side as if he were favoring the white eye. Then Jeb looked into the red eyes of the wildcat. He could hear the growl and see the sharp, white teeth. Lucy sounded again, closer, but not close enough. She was coming to the ridge, and for the first time Jeb was mad because she followed a slow trail. The wildcat crouched as if it were going to jump.

Jeb felt the horn. There was one way, he thought, to save the pup. He looked at the horn. One long blast and he knew Lucy would move over the ridge, coming to the sound. She was an old hound and had followed many trails. Once Jeb remembered Jeptha's saying that she was the only hound he would pit against a wildcat.

Jeb thought of the many days he had let the horn lie on the mantle while he had gone to the hillside garden. And he remembered why he had left the horn. But now, the white eye or stub tail of the pup no longer mattered. He knew he loved the small pup with all his might. The pup had found his trail and pushed his game like a true hound. It was Jeb who had failed. He knew that he could not blow the horn.

Tears welled in his eyes. Somewhere along the mountain, Jeb thought, Sampson [1] once staggered. Maybe, Jeb thought, it was this same hollow. Sampson had found faith, enough faith to lift a whole mountain. Jeb looked again at the horn. It looked small compared to a mountain. He looked again toward the pup and the wildcat. Then he wiped his eyes and looked toward the moon.

"Lord," he said, "I know that that Book of Yours Grandma Quildy has is lots bigger than a box of doodlebugs. And I was ashamed of the pup You gave me, too. But I'm not ashamed any more. I haven't got the right to be a hunter, being that it takes a hunter to blow a horn. But if You are up there, Lord, like Grandma Quildy says, please let me blow it. I ain't got much time left and I got to call Lucy in."

Jeb raised the horn to his lips and took a deep breath. He blew with all his might. He blew until his face became red. And out of the end of the horn came nothing but wind. Trembling, Jeb pulled the horn from his lips.

"I ain't aiming to try and fool You this time, Lord," he said, and blew again.

The sweet music of the horn drifted through the deep woods

[1] the Biblical hero, Samson

131

and climbed the high ridge. And Jeb heard it echo over in the valley. And then the woods were quiet except for the whimper of the pup that had moved closer and the growl of the wildcat.

Through the brush came Lucy. She stopped in front of Jeb wagging her long tail. Then she sniffed the air and jumped at the whimper of the pup. She turned and leaped onto the back of the wildcat.

Over and over they went, first Lucy on top and then the wildcat. Lucy was grabbing for its throat and the wildcat was trying to reach Lucy's stomach with its powerful claws. The pup jumped upon a ledge of the cliff and stood barking.

Lucy yelped and Jeb saw the red stream of blood come from her shoulder. The wildcat was on top now and Lucy fought to get up. Lucy yelped from the pain of the sharp claws.

The pup bawled into the air and with one long leap landed on the back of the wildcat. The pup rolled over and over on the ground, bouncing off the back of the wildcat. He had knocked the cat loose. The wildcat turned toward the pup. But before it could jump, Lucy had it by the throat. The pup ran around and around the wildcat, barking.

Finally Lucy let go of the wildcat and crawled away. And the wildcat lay still.

Jeb walked over and patted Lucy on the head. Her fur was covered with blood and Jeb wiped it with the sack he had tucked under his belt. Lucy licked his face as he lifted her in his arms and turned down the path that let out of the hollow. In front of him walked the small pup, his head high in the air. He stopped once, looked back at Jeb and Lucy and walked on. Jeb watched the short tail moving back and forth.

The steep walls of the valley were so tall that Jeb could not see the top. The woods were dark with the tall trees of the mountain. Even the small saplings that sprouted in the hollow were taller than Jeb. The horn bounced against his side and he touched it with his hand. Jeb looked again toward the moon and he felt as big as Sampson.

Stickeen

BY JOHN MUIR

*I*N THE summer of 1880 I set out from Fort
Wrangel in a canoe with the Rev. S. H. Young and a crew of
Indians to continue the exploration of the icy region of south-
eastern Alaska. The necessary provisions, blankets, etc., had been
collected and stowed away, and the Indians were in their places
ready to dip their paddles, while a crowd of their friends were
looking down from the wharf to bid them good-by and good luck.
Mr. Young, for whom we were waiting, at length came aboard,
followed by a little black dog that immediately made himself
at home by curling up in a hollow among the baggage. I like

133

dogs, but this one seemed so small, dull and worthless that I objected to his going and asked the missionary why he was taking him.

"Such a helpless wisp of hair will only be in the way," I said. "You had better pass him up to one of the Indian boys on the wharf, to be taken home to play with the children. This trip is not likely to be a good one for toy dogs. He will be rained on and snowed on for weeks, and will require care like a baby."

But the missionary assured me that he would be no trouble at all, that he was a perfect wonder of a dog—could endure cold and hunger like a polar bear, could swim like a seal, and was wondrous wise, etc., making out a list of virtues likely to make him the most interesting of the company.

Nobody could hope to unravel the lines of his ancestry. He was short-legged, bunchy-bodied, and almost featureless—something like a muskrat. Though smooth, his hair was long and silky, so that when the wind was at his back it ruffled, making him look shaggy. At first sight his only noticeable feature was his showy tail, which was about as shady and airy as a squirrel's, and was carried curling forward nearly to his ears. On closer inspection you might see his thin, sensitive ears and his keen dark eyes with cunning tan spots. Mr. Young told me that when the dog was about the size of a woodrat he was presented to his wife by an Irish prospector at Sitka, and that when he arrived at Fort Wrangel he was adopted by the Stickeen Indians as a sort of new good-luck totem, and named "Stickeen" for the tribe, with whom he became a favorite.

On our trip he soon proved himself a queer character—odd, concealed, independent, keeping invincibly quiet, and doing many inexplicable things that piqued my curiosity. Sailing week after week through the long, intricate channels and inlets among the innumerable islands and mountains of the coast, he spent the dull days in sluggish ease, motionless, and apparently as unobserving as a hibernating marmot. But I discovered that somehow he always knew what was going forward. When the Indians were about to shoot at ducks or seals, or when anything interesting was to be seen along the shore, he would rest his chin on the edge of the canoe and calmly look out. When he heard us talking about making a landing, he roused himself to see what sort of place we were coming to, and made ready to jump overboard and swim ashore as soon as the canoe neared the beach. Then, with a vigorous shake to get rid of the brine in his hair, he went into the woods to hunt small game. But though always the first out of the canoe, he was always the last to get into it. When we were ready to start he could never be found, and refused to come to our call. We soon found out, however, that though we could not see him at such times he saw us, and from the cover of the briers and huckleberry bushes in the fringe of the woods was watching the canoe with wary eye. For as soon as we were fairly off he came trotting down the beach, plunged into the surf and swam after us, knowing well that we would cease rowing and take him in. When the contrary little vagabond came alongside, he was lifted by the neck, held at arm's length a moment to drip, and dropped aboard. We tried to cure him of this trick by compelling him to swim farther before stopping for him. But this did no good; the longer the swim, the better he seemed to like it.

Though capable of the most specious idleness, he was always ready for excursions or adventures of any sort. When the Indians went into the woods for a deer, Stickeen was sure to be at their heels, provided I had not yet left camp. For though I never carried a gun, he always followed me, forsaking the hunting Indians and even his master to share my wanderings. The days that were too stormy for sailing I spent in the woods, or on the mountains or glaciers. Wherever I chanced to be Stickeen always insisted on following me, gliding through the dripping huckleberry bushes and prickly *Panax* and *Rubus* tangles like a fox, scarce stirring their close-set branches, wading and wallowing through snow, swimming ice cold streams, jumping logs and rocks and the crusty hummocks and crevasses of glaciers with the patience and endurance of a determined mountaineer, never tiring or gettting discouraged.

Once he followed me over a glacier the surface of which was so rough that it cut his feet until every step was marked with blood; but he trotted on with Indian fortitude until I noticed his pain and taking pity on him, made him a set of moccasins out of a handkerchief. But he never asked for help or made any complaint, as if, like a philosopher, he had learned that without hard work and suffering there could be no pleasure worth having. . . .

We had explored the glaciers of the Sumdum and Tahkoo inlet. Now we sailed through Stephen's Passage into Lynn Canal, and thence through Icy Strait into Cross Sound, looking for unexplored inlets leading toward the ice fountains of the Fairweather Range. . . . At length we discovered the entrance of what is now called Taylor Bay, and about five o'clock reached the head of it, and encamped near the front of a large glacier which extends as an abrupt barrier all the way across from wall to wall of the inlet, a distance of three or four miles.

On first observation the glacier presented some unusual features, and that night I planned a grand excursion for the morrow. I awoke early, called not only by the glacier, but also by a storm. Rain, mixed with trailing films of scud and the ragged, drawn-out nether surfaces of gray clouds, filled the inlet, and was sweeping forward in a thick, passionate, horizontal flood. Everything was streaming with life and motion—woods, rocks, waters, and the sky. The main perennial streams were booming, and hundreds of new ones, born of the rain, were descending in gray and white cascades on each side of the inlet, fairly streaking their rocky slopes, and roaring like the sea.

I had intended making a cup of coffee before starting, but when I heard the storm I made haste to join it; for in storms nature has always something extra fine to show us. . . .

I took my ice ax, buttoned my coat, put a piece of bread in my pocket, and set out.

Mr. Young and the Indians were asleep, and so I hoped, was Stickeen; but I had not gone a dozen rods before he left his warm bed in the tent, and came boring through the blast after me. That a man should welcome storms for their exhilarating music and motion, and go forth to see God making landscapes, is reasonable enough; but what fascination could there be in dismal weather for this poor feeble wisp of a dog, so pathetically small? Anyhow, on he came, breakfastless, through the choking blast. I

136

stopped, turned my back to the wind, and gave him a good, dissuasive talk.

"Now don't," I said, shouting to make myself heard in the storm—"now don't, Stickeen. What has got into your queer noodle now? You must be daft. This wild day has nothing for you. Go back to camp and keep warm. There is no game abroad —nothing but weather. Not a foot or wing is stirring. Wait and get a good breakfast with your master, and be sensible for once. I can't feed you or carry you, and this storm will kill you. . . ."

After ordering him back again and again to ease my conscience, I saw that he was not to be shaken off. . . . The dog just stood there in the wind, drenched and blinking, saying doggedly, "Where thou goest I will go." So I told him to come on, if he must, and gave him a piece of the bread I had put in my pocket for breakfast. Then we pushed on in company, and thus began the most memorable of all my wild days.

The level flood, driving straight in our faces, thrashed and washed us wildly until we got into the shelter of the trees and ice-cliffs on the east side of the glacier, where we rested and listened and looked on in comfort. The exploration of the glacier was my main object. But the wind was too high to allow excursions over its open surface where one might be dangerously shoved while balancing for a jump on the brink of a crevasse. In the meantime the storm was a fine study. Here the end of the glacier, descending over an abrupt swell of resisting rock about five hundred feet high, leans forward and falls in majestic ice cascades. And as the storm came down the glacier from the north, Stickeen and I were beneath the main current of the blast while favorably located to see and hear it. A broad torrent, draining the side of the glacier, now swollen by scores of new streams from the mountains, was rolling boulders along its rocky channel between the glacier and the woods with thudding, bumping, muffled sounds, rushing toward the bay with tremendous energy. . . .

Looking southward from our shelter, we had this great torrent on our left, with mossy woods on the mountain slope above it, the glacier on our right, the wild, cascading portion of it forming a multitude of towers, spires and flat-topped battlements seen through the trees, and smooth gray gloom ahead. . . .

When the wind began to abate I traced the east side of the glacier. All the trees standing on the edge of the woods were barked and bruised, showing high ice mark in a very telling way, while tens of thousands of those that had stood for centuries on the bank of the glacier farther out lay crushed and being crushed. In many places I could see, down fifty feet or so beneath, the margin of the glacier mill, where trunks from one to two feet in diameter were being ground to pulp against outstanding rock-ribs and bosses of the bank. About three miles above the front of the glacier, I climbed to the surface of it by means of ax steps, made easy for Stickeen; and as far as the eye could reach, the level, or nearly level, glacier stretched away indefinitely beneath the gray sky, a seemingly boundless prairie of ice. The rain continued, which I did not mind; but a tendency to fogginess in the drooping clouds made me hesitate about venturing far from land. No trace of the west shore was visible, and in case the misty clouds should settle, or the wind again become violent, I feared getting caught in a tangle of crevasses. Lingering undecided, watching the weather, I sauntered about on the crystal sea. For a mile or two out I found the ice remarkably safe. The marginal crevasses were mostly narrow, while the few wider ones were easily avoided by passing around them, and the clouds began to open here and there. Thus encouraged, I at last pushed out for the other side. . . .

Toward the west side we came to a closely crevassed section, in which we had to make long, narrow tacks and doublings, tracing the edges of tremendous longitudinal crevasses, many of which were from twenty to thirty feet wide, and perhaps a thousand feet deep, beautiful and awful. In working a way through them I was severely cautious, but Stickeen came on as unhesitatingly as the flying clouds. Any crevasse that I could jump he would leap without so much as halting to examine it. . . . He showed neither caution nor curiosity. His courage was so unwavering that it seemed due to dullness of perception, as if he were only blindly bold; and I warned him that he might slip or fall short. His bunchy body seemed all one skipping muscle, and his peg legs appeared to be jointed only at the top.

We gained the west shore in about three hours, the width of the glacier here being about seven miles. Then I pushed northward, in order to see as far back as possible into the fountains of the Fairweather Mountains, in case the clouds should rise. The walking was easy along the margin of the forest, which, of course, like that on the other side, had been invaded and crushed by the swollen glacier. In an hour we rounded a massive headland and came suddenly on another outlet of the glacier, which, in the form of a wild ice-cascade, was pouring over the rim of the main basin toward the ocean with the volume of a thousand Niagaras. . . . It was a dazzling white torrent two miles wide, flowing between high banks black with trees. Tracing its left bank three or four miles, I found that it discharged into a fresh-water lake, filling it with icebergs.

I would gladly have followed the outlet, but the day was waning, and we had to make haste on the return trip to get off the ice before dark. When we were about two miles from the west shore the clouds dropped misty fringes, and snow soon began to fly. Then I began to feel anxiety about finding a way in the storm through the intricate network of crevasses which we had entered. Stickeen showed no fear. He was still the same silent, sufficient, uncomplaining Indian philosopher. When the storm-darkness fell he kept close behind me. The snow warned us to make haste, but at the same time hid our way. . . .

I pushed on as best I could, jumping innumerable crevasses, and for every hundred rods or so of direct advance traveling a mile in doubling up and down in the turmoil of chasms and dislocated masses of ice. . . . Many a mile we thus traveled, mostly up and down, making but little real headway in crossing, most of the time running instead of walking, as the danger of spending the night on the glacier threatened. . . .

At length our way was barred by a very wide and straight crevasse, which I traced rapidly northward a mile or so without finding a crossing or hope of one, then southward down the glacier about as far, to where it united with another crevasse. In all this distance of perhaps two miles there was only one place where I could possibly jump it; but the width of this jump was nearly the utmost I dared attempt, while the danger of slipping on the farther side was so great that I was loath to try it. . . . Because of the dangers already behind me, however, I determined to venture against those that might be ahead, jumped, and landed well. Stickeen followed, making nothing of it.

But within a distance of a few hundred yards we were stopped again by the widest crevasse yet encountered. Of course I made haste to explore it, hoping all might yet be well. About three fourths of a mile up-stream it united with the one we had just crossed, as I feared it would. Then, tracing it down, I found it joined the other great crevasse at the lower end, maintaining a width of forty to fifty feet. We were on an island about two miles long and from one hundred to three hundred yards wide, with two barely possible ways of escape—one by the way we came, the other by an almost inaccessible sliver-bridge that crossed the larger crevasse from near the middle of the island. After tracing the brink, I ran back to the sliver-bridge and cautiously studied it. . . .

This sliver was evidently very old, for it had been wasted until it was the worst bridge I ever saw. The width of the crevasse was here about fifty feet, and the sliver, crossing diagonally, was about seventy feet long, was depressed twenty-five or thirty feet in the middle, and the up-curving ends were attached to the sides eight or ten feet below the surface of the glacier. Getting down the nearly vertical wall to the end of it and up the other side were the main difficulties, and they seemed all but insurmountable.

Of the many perils encountered in my years of wandering in mountain altitudes, none seemed so plain and stern and merciless as this. And it was presented when we were wet to the skin and hungry, the sky was dark with snow, and the night near, and we had to fear the snow in our eyes and the disturbing action of the wind in any movement we might make. But we were forced to face it. It was a tremendous necessity.

Beginning not immediately above the sunken end of the

bridge, but a little to one side, I cut nice hollows on the brink for my knees to rest in; then, leaning over, with my short-handled ax cut a step sixteen or eighteen inches below, which, on account of the sheerness of the wall, was shallow. That step, however, was well made; its floor sloped slightly inward, and formed a good hold for my heels. Then, slipping cautiously upon it, and crouching as low as possible, with my left side twisted toward the wall, I steadied myself with my left hand in a slight notch, while with the right I cut other steps and notches in succession, guarding against glinting of the ax, for life or death was in every stroke, and in the niceness of finish of every foothold. After the end of the bridge was reached, it was a delicate thing to poise on a little platform which I had chipped on its up-curving end, and, bending over the slippery surface, get astride of it.

Crossing was easy, cutting off the sharp edge with careful strokes, and hitching forward a few inches at a time, keeping my balance with my knees pressed against its sides. The tremendous abyss on each side I studiously ignored. The surface of that blue sliver was then all the world. But the most trying part of the adventure was, after working my way across inch by inch, to rise from the safe position astride that slippery strip of ice, and to cut a ladder in the face of the wall—chipping, climbing, holding on with feet and fingers in mere notches. At such times one's whole body is eye, and common skill and fortitude are replaced by power beyond our call or knowledge. Never before had I been so long under deadly strain. How I got up the cliff at the end of the bridge I never could tell. The thing seemed to have been done by somebody else. . . .

But poor Stickeen, the wee, silky, sleekit beastie—think of him! When I had decided to try the bridge, and while I was on my knees cutting away the rounded brow, he came behind me, pushed his head past my shoulder, looked down and across, scanned the sliver and its approaches with his queer eyes, then looked me in the face with a startled air of surprise and concern, and began to mutter and whine, saying as plainly as if speaking with words, "Surely you are not going to try that awful place?" This was the first time I had seen him gaze deliberately into a crevasse or into my face with a speaking look. That he should have recognized and appreciated the danger at the first glance showed wonderful sagacity. Never before had the quick, daring midget seemed to know that ice was slippery, or that there was such a thing as danger anywhere. His looks and the tones of his voice when he began to complain and speak his fears were so human that I unconsciously talked to him as I would to a boy, and in trying to calm his fears perhaps in some measure moderated my own.

"Hush your fears, my boy," I said; "we will get across safe, though it is not going to be easy. No right way is easy in this rough world. We must risk our lives to save them. At the worst we can only slip; and then how grand a grave we shall have! And by and by our nice bones will do good in the terminal moraine."

But my sermon was far from reassuring him; he began to cry, and after taking another piercing look at the tremendous gulf, ran away in desperate excitement, seeking some other crossing. By the time he got back, baffled, of course, I had made a step or two. I dared not look back, but he made himself heard; and when he saw that I was certainly crossing, he cried aloud in despair. The danger was enough to daunt anybody, but it seems wonderful that he should have been able to weigh and appreciate it so justly. No mountaineer could have seen it more quickly or judged it more wisely, discriminating between real and apparent peril.

After I had gained the other side he howled louder than ever, and after running back and forth in vain search for a way of escape, he would return to the brink of the crevasse above the bridge, moaning and groaning as if in the bitterness of death. Could this be the silent, philosophic Stickeen? I shouted encouragement, telling him the bridge was not as bad as it looked, that I had left it flat for his feet, and he could walk it easily. But he was afraid to try it. Strange that so small an animal should be capable of such big, wise fears! I called again and again in a reassuring tone to come on and fear nothing, that he could come if he would only try. Then he would hush for a moment, look again at the bridge, and shout his unshakable conviction that he could never, never come that way, then lie back in despair, as if howling: "Oh-o-o, what a place! No-o-o; I can never go-o-o down there!" His natural composure and courage had vanished utterly in a tumultuous storm of fear. Had the danger been less, his distress would have seemed ridiculous. But in this gulf—a huge, yawning sepulcher big enough to hold everybody in the territory—lay the shadow of death, and his heartrending cries might well have called Heaven to his help. Perhaps they did. So hidden before, he was transparent now, and one could see the workings of his mind like the movements of a clock out of its case. His voice and gestures were perfectly human, and his hopes and fears unmistakable, while he seemed to understand every word of mine. I was troubled at the thought of leaving him. It seemed impossible to get him to venture. To compel him to try by fear of being left, I started off as if leaving him to his fate, and disappeared back of a hummock; but this did no good, for he only lay down and cried. So after hiding a few minutes, I went back to the brink of the crevasse, and in a severe tone of voice shouted across to him that now I must certainly leave him —I could wait no longer; and that if he would not come, all I could promise was that I would return to seek him next day. I warned him that if he went back to the woods the wolves would kill him, and finished by urging him once more by words and gestures to come on. He knew very well what I meant, and at last, with the courage of despair, hushed and breathless, he lay down on the brink in the hollow I had made for my knees, pressed his body against the ice to get the advantage of the friction, gazed into the first step, put his little feet together, and slid them slowly down into it, bunching all four in it, and almost standing on his head. Then, without lifting them, as well as I could see through the snow, he slowly worked them over the edge of the step, and down into the next and the next in succession in the same way, and gained the bridge. Then lifting his feet with the regularity and slowness of the vibrations of a seconds' pendulum, as if counting and measuring one, two, three, holding himself in dainty poise, and giving separate attention to each little step, he gained the foot of the cliff, at the top of which I was kneeling to give him a lift should he get within reach. Here he halted in dead silence, and it was here I feared he might fail, for dogs are poor climbers. I had no cord. If I had had one, I would have dropped a noose over his head and hauled him up. But while I was thinking whether an available cord might be made out of clothing, he was looking keenly into the series of notched steps and finger-holds of the ice-ladder I had made, as if counting them and fixing the position of each one in his mind. Then suddenly up he came, with a nervy, springy rush, hooking his paws into the notches and steps so quickly that I could not see how it was done, and whizzed past my head, safe at last!

And now came a scene! "Well done, well done, little boy! Brave boy!" I cried, trying to catch and caress him, but he would not be caught. Never before or since have I seen anything like so passionate a revulsion from the depths of despair to uncontrollable, exultant, triumphant joy. He flashed and darted hither and thither as if fairly demented, screaming and shouting, swirling round and round in giddy loops and circles like a leaf in a whirlwind, lying down and rolling over and over, sidewise and heels over head, pouring forth a tumultuous flood of hysterical cries and sobs and gasping mutterings. And when I ran up to him to shake him, fearing he might die of joy, he flashed off two or three hundred yards, his feet in a mist of motion; then, turning suddenly, he came back in wild rushes, and launched himself at my face, almost knocking me down, all the time screeching and screaming and shouting as if saying, "Saved! saved! saved!" Then away again, dropping suddenly at times with his feet in the air, trembling, and fairly sobbing. Such passionate emotion was enough to kill him. Moses' stately song of triumph after escaping the Egyptians and the Red Sea was nothing to it. Who could have guessed the capacity of the dull, enduring little fellow for all that most stirs this mortal frame? Nobody could have helped crying with him.

But there is nothing like work for toning down either excessive fear or joy. So I ran ahead, calling him, in as gruff a voice as I could command, to come on and stop his nonsense, for we had far to go, and it would soon be dark. Neither of us feared another trial like this. Heaven would surely count one enough for a lifetime. The ice ahead was gashed by thousands of crevasses, but they were common ones. The joy of deliverance burned in us like fire, and we ran without fatigue, every muscle, with immense rebound, glorying in its strength. Stickeen flew across everything in his way, and not till dark did he settle into his normal foxlike, gliding trot. At last the mountains crowned with spruce came in sight, looming faintly in the gloaming, and we soon felt the solid rock beneath our feet, and were safe. Then came weariness. We stumbled down along the lateral moraine in the dark, over rocks and tree trunks, through the bushes and devil-club thickets and mossy logs and boulders of the woods where we had sheltered ourselves in the morning. Then out on the level mud slope of the terminal moraine. Danger had vanished, and so had our strength. We reached camp about ten o'clock, and found a big fire and a big supper. A party of Hoona Indians had visited Mr. Young, bringing a gift of porpoise-meat and wild strawberries, and hunter Joe had brought in a wild goat. But we lay down, too tired to eat much, and soon fell into a troubled sleep. The man who said, "The harder the toil the sweeter the rest," never was profoundly tired. Stickeen kept springing up and muttering in his sleep, no doubt dreaming that he was still on the brink of the crevasse; and so did I—that night and many others, long afterward, when I was nervous and overtired.

Thereafter Stickeen was a changed dog. During the rest of the trip, instead of holding aloof, he would come to me at night, when all was quiet about the camp fire, and rest his head on my knee, with a look of devotion, as if I were his god. And often, as he caught my eye, he seemed to be trying to say, "Wasn't that an awful time we had together on the glacier?"

Wild Dog

BY RUTH ELIZABETH TANNER

T H E prairie grass was thick and soft beneath Tip's padding feet as he moved through the gathering dusk. Somewhere in the distance a mourning dove raised her voice in a sleepy *coo-coo;* now and then a grasshopper flew blindly up and away; the ceaseless throbbing of locusts filled the air.

A sudden *whirr* rose from a clump of sage as a prairie chicken shot up into the air. She floundered one-sidedly, came down again and, dragging one wing, flopped along on the ground. Tip paused to watch her for a moment, but he did not

146

give chase, for he knew she was trying to lead him away from her nest.

Then he trotted over to the clump of sage and after a little searching found her nest cleverly hidden in the matted grass. Sorely tempted, he sniffed at the eggs. He was very hungry and, though he would never have considered eating an egg in the barn or hen house, these out on the open prairie did not seem quite the same. His hunting instinct told him to take them, they did not belong to his master. But from generations of shepherd and collie forebears he had inherited another instinct. That was to guard faithfully, no matter what the cost.

He licked his lips again, but with a quick shake of his head he turned and marched away without a single backward glance. His better instinct had won.

Two hours later, after dining on a fat prairie dog and a quail, he started for home. When he came to the top of a high hill he sat down, pointed his white nose to the full moon, and sent forth the long mournful howl of a lost or forsaken dog.

Sims, Tip's old master, had sold his ranch in New Mexico and returned to the East. As he could not take a half-grown dog to an apartment in a large city, he gave Tip to a friend in Belmont just before taking the train. But Tip did not understand. He slipped away and traveled the twenty miles back to the only home he had ever known. For a month he had been guarding the empty ranch, waiting for his owner's return.

At first he had gone hungry quite a lot. But the sand hills south of the house were full of cottontails, and the sage-covered prairie was alive with jack rabbits. He soon grew accustomed to finding his own meals. Still, he was lonely, and now he voiced all his uneasiness and his yearning for love and companionship in his mournful appeal to the moon.

To the north on the Flying M Ranch, old Mr. Marvin turned restlessly in his bed. "Bill! Dusty!" he called.

"Yeah," came a sleepy answer.

"Hear that dog? There are too blamed many dogs around here. From now on when you boys see a stray, shoot him. They'll be getting the calves next."

A few evenings later, Tip paused in his wandering to watch a couple of riders coming up the coulee. He was about to make a friendly advance when—*bang!*—a shot rang out, and a bullet flicked sand into his face. *Crack!* A second shot grazed his shoulder like a hot iron.

For a moment he had been confused. Then he came to life, and fled like a tawny streak, dodging behind brush, skimming over the open places. A man on a long-legged black was pounding madly after him. Twice more the rider fired at a flash of yellow and brown, but both bullets went wild.

Finally the pursuer gave up and returned to his companion, a lanky sunburned boy. "He got away! Why didn't you take a hand, Dusty?"

Dusty's gray eyes crinkled as he smiled. "I'm glad you didn't get him. That's a good dog, a collie. He looks like a pup that fellow Sims had."

"Anyway, I nipped him."

"Poor fellow. I'm sorry for that," Dusty said slowly.

"Boss's orders," the cowhand explained.

"The boss can shoot him if he wants to, but I won't," Dusty declared.

Twice more in the next week some of the Flying M men shot at Tip, but after that he saw them first and vanished.

Still they heard him serenading the moon. A dog whose ancestors have for generations lived with men and who has known a loved master cannot so easily break the tie that binds him to mankind. He was very lonely, but as there was no human for him to serve he spent his energy guarding the ranch buildings. Like a wild animal, he had formed the habit of sleeping days and roaming about at night. Perhaps the heat and his avoidance of chance riders started him doing this.

One evening he woke, stretched out, and, yawning like a sleepy child, came out from under the ranch house.

"*Woof!*" he yelped, dodging to one side in surprise. Stretched across the path beside the sagging step was a four-foot rattlesnake! Tip bristled. Ordinarily he would have gladly given the snake the right of way, but this was *his own* yard; he would not stand for the intrusion.

A snarl rose in his throat and like a flash he seized the snake before it could coil. He shook and shook it, then threw it down with all the strength he had. The snake landed with a thump and was coiled like a spring, ready for battle. Tip circled about. The snake was raging with fury. His rattles buzzed. His little eyes glittered with hate. The deadly rattler's head, balanced at least a foot from the ground, swung about, ever facing the dog as Tip minced about the snake.

Finally Tip pretended to step forward, and the rattler struck with every ounce of energy in his powerful coils. His head went fully three feet through the air. His fangs brushed Tip's whiskers as the collie dodged backward. Tip walked away feeling sick. The snake had struck much farther than he had expected him to. Death had missed him only by an inch, but he was not ready to give up.

After a moment he returned to the raging snake. Again he stepped forward, but with more caution this time. As before, the rattler struck, but when he landed on the ground Tip seized him and shook him long and hard. This performance was repeated time after time. The snake was a powerful and experienced fighter, and the battle was long and hard. But finally the snake failed to recoil.

Tip waited and watched him for a moment. Then, shaking his head distastefully, he trotted away toward the creek to wash that hateful taste from his mouth.

The dog gravely herded away stray cattle and horses from the ranch. But he welcomed Mollie and her calf with a friendly, wagging tail, although they wore the Flying M brand now. They had been sold when his old master left, but Tip still felt they belonged here the same as he did.

Autumn came with its yellow-brown grass and its chilly nights. Food was not so plentiful, yet Tip had grown in both size and cunning. He was a beauty. In color and marking, with the white ruff about his throat, he was like a collie. But he resembled his shepherd ancestors in his broad, powerful frame.

One evening as he scouted up wind several miles from his home, his keen nose caught the warm scent of freshly killed meat. Minutes later he found two coyotes feeding on a dead calf.

Bristling with fury, he fell upon the killers and drove them away. Then, after hesitating for a little, he made a good meal of the tempting meat. Nothing would have induced him to kill a calf; all his instincts were against it. But the calf was dead so he ate his fill. Then, circling about the dead animal, leaving plenty of tracks, he went his way.

After that his reputation grew. A wild dog, crafty, powerful, cruel; alone he could kill a two-year-old cow! The boys at the Flying M had strict orders to "get that dog." Of all this Tip was unaware. He went his way as usual, glorying in his strength and in the art of matching his wits, both with the wild things and with men. To him it was a game.

His avoidance of men was even more than a game. He knew of their far-reaching guns and he played safe.

Then winter with its snowy blanket closed down. Dusty was to ride the upper branches of the Little Comanche Creek, keeping watch over the range cattle and sleeping in Sims' old ranch house.

"Don't let that wild dog eat you," one of the men warned him as he was getting ready to leave the main camp.

"Oh, he's no wilder'n I am. I'll have him eating out of my hand by Christmas."

"Two bits says you won't."

"Two bits. It's a bet." Gravely they called a third cowboy to witness the wager.

Tip's home was beneath the kitchen, and at first he resented Dusty's intrusion. He stayed away for two whole days, but the next night he returned. Two saddle horses were munching hay in the barn. He listened for a moment; it was such a friendly sound. Guardedly he approached the house. It seemed as before, but his sharp ears could hear the breathing of a man within. After a long hesitating pause, he crawled under the house and curled up in his own bed.

When Dusty started for the barn the next morning, he stopped short and a slow smile spread over his face. Those fresh tracks in the snow told their story.

"I'll win that two bits yet," he said softly. After that it be-

150

came a game for two. Dusty put out food every day. Tip daintily ate what he chose, though he always left Dusty's biscuits. This amused the cowboy. "If the boys knew this I'd never hear the last of it." Still he knew it was too good to keep. He would tell them sooner or later.

In turn, Tip guarded all of Dusty's things. Each morning found fresh tracks in the snow. But the month passed, and never once had the man seen his newly found friend. Then one day Dusty lost a glove. Next morning it was on the step just outside the door.

Dusty was delighted, so he dropped his old red muffler about a quarter of a mile up the trail where he knew he could find it if Tip didn't. The lost article was on the doorstep the following morning. "Old fellow, I'll bring you a rabbit today to pay for this," he promised, addressing the mouth of Tip's hole.

Staying alone in a cow camp, seeing no one for weeks at a time, is a lonely business at best. Dusty derived a great deal of amusement from Tip's actions. To some people, winning the love of a wild thing is a fascinating pastime. It was even more than that to the big, kindly cowboy. He felt that Tip had not received a square deal.

Tip had grown fond of Dusty, too. He longed to become real friends, to feel the caress of a hand on his head. Yet those burning shots could not be easily forgotten. Thus they lived until the latter part of November, each drawing a great deal of pleasure and satisfaction from his unseen comrade.

Then one cold bitter night Dusty did not come home. As darkness fell Tip grew uneasy. He watched and listened. Dusty had never been so late before. Tip trotted to the top of the nearest hill, then back again. Time dragged, yet no Dusty. The dog grew more and more uneasy.

Some folks declare that dogs cannot reason. Perhaps they cannot, but something had brought an anxious light to Tip's eyes as he trotted restlessly about. Finally, as if he were unable to stand the suspense any longer, he picked up the trail Dusty's horse had left in the snow that morning and followed it at an easy lope. In and out among the rough, choppy hills, re-

151

peatedly doubling back to the creek, he wound. The stinging wind was rising. Sleet beat in his face and clung to his long shaggy coat.

On and on, farther into the flinty badlands he traveled. He was running now, sure that something was wrong. The snow was coming fast, but the trail was still readable. Then suddenly on a steep hillside he came to a big slide in the snow. His keen nose told him the story. The horse had fallen and with his rider had rolled to the bottom. Tip raced on a short distance to the only dark spot in the white expanse.

It was Dusty, stretched out unconscious in the snow. His hat was gone, his face was bared to the driving sleet. Tip whined softly. His fear for the moment was forgotten as he licked the boy's icy face with his red tongue.

Again he whined, but there was no answer. He poked his nose under Dusty's arm and moved it, but the arm was cold and unresponsive. Anxiously he walked about the quiet figure. He noted how one leg was stretched out in a helpless fashion. It had made a furrow in the snow. Dusty was no quitter. Battered and bruised, with a broken leg dragging painfully behind, he had pulled himself fully fifty yards before unconsciousness overcame him.

Tip sat up and howled his longest, most anguished notes. He trotted to the top of the hill and repeated them again and again, returning at intervals to try to arouse the unconscious cowboy. Once Dusty moved a little. A faint moan escaped his lips. Raising his hand, he inadvertently rubbed it against the quivering, eager dog.

In the meantime Dusty's horse, limping badly, with the bridle reins dragging and a stain of blood on the saddle, had returned to the main ranch ten miles away. Six men, grim and steady, started out into the rising storm on what they knew was an almost hopeless hunt. The back trail was dim, and snow was falling fast. Chances were ten to one they would not find Dusty until it was too late. He might be anywhere in an area ten miles one way by six the other. Even if they did find him, after lying out in the bitter cold for hours he—they refused to think of it.

The men spread out in twos after agreeing that three shots fired in rapid succession would mean that Dusty was found.

After what seemed endless hours in the saddle, Mr. Marvin turned to Bob, his companion. "Hear that dog howl! I'd like to shoot him." Then a little later he added, "Funny, him howling on a night like this."

"Say!" Bob brought his horse to an abrupt halt. "Dusty bet me twenty-five cents he could tame that dog. Do you suppose . . ."

"There's a chance," the boss muttered. When hope is nearly dead, men will grasp at straws. Without another word they turned and urged their horses on at a faster pace.

The long eerie howls rose faintly again, but only once more. Then, in spite of straining their ears hopefully, desperately, nothing but the crunching of their horses' feet and the swirling wind could be heard. Still they fought on blindly, refusing to give up that one faint glimmer of hope.

After wailing until his voice was hoarse, Tip gave up calling for help. He tried in vain again to rouse Dusty, then for a few moments he lay down with his warm body close beside the boy.

Presently, as if in answer to some call, he rose and trotted down wind. At the slide he came to Dusty's hat, half buried in a drift. He hesitated a moment, then picking it up he loped away in to the night.

The two men coming to a hill paused uncertainly. "Which way?" called Bob.

The boss drew rein and wiped the snow and frost from his mustache. "Say, what's that?" He pointed.

Dimly through the falling snow they saw a quick-moving shape. It hesitated, then drew near, and laid something on the ground at the feet of Bob's horse. Then it disappeared in a flash.

Bob was on the ground instantly. "Dusty's hat."

They looked anxiously about for the dog, but the gray curtain of the storm had closed. The dog had vanished. "Here, Pup! Come, Shep!" Mr. Marvin called.

From the right-hand trail came a sharp bark. They turned

153

and followed. Bob whistled and Mr. Marvin kept on calling, "Here, Pup. Here, Shep!" Ahead came the sharp, imperative bark.

"And to think I ordered that dog shot," the boss muttered as he urged his weary horse on. "If he takes us to Dusty, I'll . . ." What could a fellow do to square himself with a dog? He couldn't think of any way just then, but he would later.

Thus they went on through the storm. The dog's yelping grew far away on several occasions. Then he would double back with anxious inquiries, to bound ahead again when he was sure they followed.

Suddenly the horses were floundering in the deep snow at the foot of the slide. In a glance the men read the grim story of the fall! Tip raced ahead to Dusty's side to lick his hand and tell him help was coming.

Three shots were fired into the air; the men were off their horses. Shoving aside the drifted snow, they began rubbing Dusty's numb arms and feet. A roll from behind the boss's saddle turned out to be a warm wool blanket and a thermos bottle of steaming coffee. The boss took his sheepskin coat, warm from his own body, and put it on the unconscious cowboy.

Soon two other men arrived. Tip hovered about, watching. At last he saw Dusty open his eyes, choke on the hot coffee, then speak. Tip's work was done. Dusty would be all right now, he was sure, so he turned his steps homeward.

There was a certain pride in his bearing as he went his rounds about the ranch in the days that followed. Again he was gallantly taking care of the place as he waited a loved one's return, and this time he did not wait in vain.

Giving up your best friend

Garm—A Hostage

BY RUDYARD KIPLING

O N E night a very long time ago I drove to an Indian military encampment called Main Mir to see amateur theatricals. At the back of the infantry barracks a soldier, his cap over one eye, rushed in front of the horses and shouted that he was a dangerous highway robber. As a matter of fact he was a friend of mine, so I told him to go home before anyone caught him; but he fell under the pole, and I heard voices of a military guard in search of someone.

The driver and I coaxed him into the carriage, drove home swiftly, undressed him and put him to bed, where he waked next

155

morning with a sore headache, very much ashamed. When his uniform was cleaned and dried, and he had been shaved and washed and made neat, I drove him back to barracks with his arm in a fine white sling, and reported that I had accidentally run over him. I did not tell this story to my friend's sergeant, who was a hostile and unbelieving person, but to his lieutenant, who did not know us quite so well.

Three days later my friend came to call, and at his heels slobbered and fawned one of the finest bull terriers—of the old-fashioned breed, two parts bull and one terrier—that I had ever set eyes on. He was pure white, with a fawn-colored saddle just behind his neck and a fawn diamond at the root of his thin whippy tail. I had admired him distantly for more than a year; Vixen, my own fox terrier, knew him too, but did not approve.

" 'E's for you," said my friend, but he did not look as though he liked parting with him.

"Nonsense! That dog's worth more than most men, Stanley," I said.

" 'E's that and more. 'Tention!"

The dog rose on his hind legs, and stood upright for a full minute.

"Eyes right!"

He sat on his haunches and turned his head sharp to the right. At a sign he rose and barked twice. Then he shook hands with his right paw and bounded lightly to my shoulder. Here he made himself into a necktie, limp and lifeless, hanging down on either side of my neck. I was told to pick him up and throw him in the air. He fell with a howl and held up one leg.

"Part o' the trick," said his owner. "You're going to die now. Dig yourself your little grave an' shut your little eye."

Still limping, the dog hobbled to the garden edge, dug a hole and lay down in it. When told that he was cured he jumped out, wagging his tail and whining for applause. He was put through half a dozen other tricks, such as showing how he would hold a man safe (I was that man, and he sat down before me, his teeth bared, ready to spring), and how he would stop eating at the word of command. I had no more than finished praising him when my friend made a gesture that stopped the dog as though he had been shot, took a piece of blue-ruled canteen paper from his helmet, handed it to me and ran away, while the dog looked after him and howled. I read:

Sir—I give you the dog because of what you got me out of. He is the best I know, for I made him myself, and he is as good as a man. Please do not give him too much to eat, and please do not give him back to me, for I'm not going to take him if you will keep him. So please do not try to give him back any more. I have kept his name back, so you can call him anything and he will answer, but please do not give him back. He can kill a man as easy as anything, but please do not give him too much meat. He knows more than a man.

Vixen sympathetically joined her shrill little yap to the bull terrier's despairing cry, and I was annoyed, for I knew that a man who cares for dogs is one thing, but a man who loves one dog is quite another. Dogs are at best no more than verminous vagrants, self-scratchers, foul feeders, and unclean by the law of Moses and Mohammed; but a dog with whom one lives alone for at least six months in the year, a free thing, tied to you so strictly by love that without you he will not stir or exercise, a patient, temperate, humorous, wise soul who knows your moods before you know them yourself, is not a dog under any ruling.

I had Vixen, who was all my dog to me, and I felt what my friend must have felt, at tearing out his heart in this style and leaving it in my garden.

However, the dog understood clearly enough that I was his master, and did not follow the soldier. As soon as he drew breath I made much of him, and Vixen, yelling with jealousy, flew at him. Had she been of his own sex, he might have cheered himself with a fight, but he only looked worriedly when she nipped his deep iron sides, laid his heavy head on my knee, and howled anew. I meant to dine at the Club that night, but as darkness drew in and the dog snuffed through the empty house like a child trying to recover from a fit of sobbing, I felt that I could not leave him to suffer his first evening alone. So we fed at home,

157

Vixen on one side, and the stranger dog on the other, she watching his every mouthful and saying explicitly what she thought of his table manners, which were much better than hers.

It was Vixen's custom, till the weather grew hot, to sleep in my bed, her head on the pillow like a Christian; and when morning came I would always find that the little thing had braced her feet against the wall and pushed me to the very edge of the cot. This night she hurried to bed purposefully, every hair up, one eye on the stranger who had dropped on a mat in a helpless hopeless sort of way, all four feet spread out, sighing heavily. She settled her head on the pillow several times to show her little airs and graces, and struck up her usual whiney singsong before slumber. The stranger dog softly edged toward me. I put out my hand and he licked it. Instantly my wrist was between Vixen's teeth, and her warning *aaarh!* said as plainly as speech that if I took any further notice of the stranger she would bite.

I caught her behind her fat neck with my left hand, shook her severely, and said, "Vixen, if you do that again you'll be put into the veranda. Now remember!"

She understood perfectly, but the minute I released her she mouthed my right wrist once more and waited, with her ears back and all her body flattened, ready to bite. The big dog's tail thumped the floor in a humble and peacemaking way.

I grabbed Vixen a second time, lifted her out of bed like a rabbit (she hated that and yelled), and as I had promised, set her out in the veranda with the bats and the moonlight. At this she howled. Then she used coarse language—not to me, but to the bull terrier—till she coughed with exhaustion. Then she ran around the house trying every door. Then she went off to the stables and barked as though someone were stealing the horses, which was an old trick of hers. Last she returned, and her snuffing yelp said, "I'll be good! Let me in and I'll be good!"

She was admitted and flew to her pillow. When she was quieted I whispered to the other dog, "You can lie on the foot of the bed." The bull jumped up at once, and though I felt Vixen quiver with rage she knew better than to protest. So we slept till the morning, and they had early breakfast with me, bite for bite, till the horse came round and we went for a ride. I don't think the bull had ever followed a horse before. He was wild with excitement, and Vixen, as usual, squealed and scuttered and scooted and took charge of the procession.

There was one corner of a village nearby which we generally passed with caution because all the yellow pariah dogs of the place gathered about it. They were half wild starving beasts and utter cowards, yet where nine or ten of them got together they would mob and kill and eat an English dog. I kept a whip with a long lash for them. That morning they attacked Vixen who, perhaps of design, had moved from beyond my horse's shadow.

The bull was ploughing along in the dust, fifty yards behind, rolling in his run and smiling as bull terriers will. I heard Vixen squeal; half a dozen of the curs closed in on her; a white streak came up behind me; a cloud of dust rose near Vixen, and when it cleared I saw one tall pariah with his back broken, and the bull wrenching another to earth. Vixen retreated to the protection of my whip, and the bull padded back smiling more than ever, covered with the blood of his enemies. That decided me to call him "Garm of the Bloody Breast," who was a great person in his time, or "Garm" for short; so leaning forward I told him what his temporary name would be. He looked up while I repeated it, and then raced away. I shouted "Garm!" He stopped, raced back, and came up to ask my will.

Then I saw that my soldier friend was right, and that that dog knew and was worth more than a man. At the end of the ridge I gave an order which Vixen knew and hated.

"Go away and get washed!" I said.

Garm understood some part of it and Vixen interpreted the rest, and the two trotted off together soberly. When I went to the back veranda Vixen had been washed snowy-white, and was very proud of herself, but the dog boy would not touch Garm on any account unless I stood by. So I waited while he was being scrubbed, and Garm, with the soap creaming on the top of his

159

broad head, looked at me to make sure that this was what I expected him to endure. He knew perfectly that the dog boy was only obeying orders.

"Another time," I said to the dog boy, "you will wash the great dog with Vixen when I send them home."

"Does *he* know?" said the dog boy, who understood the ways of dogs.

"Garm," I said, "another time you will be washed with Vixen."

I knew that Garm understood. Indeed, next washing-day, when Vixen as usual fled under my bed, Garm stared at the doubtful dog boy in the veranda, stalked to the place where he had been washed last time, and stood rigid in the tub.

But the long days in my office tried him sorely. We three would drive off in the morning at half-past eight and come home at six or later. Vixen, knowing the routine of it, went to sleep under my table; but the confinement ate into Garm's soul. He generally sat on the veranda looking out on the Mall, and well I knew what he expected.

Sometimes a company of soldiers would move along on their way to the Fort and Garm rolled forth to inspect them, or an officer in uniform entered into the office, and it was pitiful to see poor Garm's welcome to the cloth—not the man. He would leap at him, and sniff and bark joyously, then run to the door and back again. One afternoon I heard him bay with a full throat—a thing I had never heard before—and he disappeared. When I drove into my garden at the end of the day a soldier in white uniform scrambled over the wall at the far end, and the Garm that met me was a joyous dog. This happened twice or thrice a week for a month.

I pretended not to notice, but Garm knew and Vixen knew. He would glide homeward from the office about four o'clock, as though he were only going to look at the scenery, and this he did so quietly that but for Vixen I should not have noticed him. The jealous little dog under the table would give a sniff and a snort, just loud enough to call my attention to the flight. Garm might go out forty times in the day and Vixen would never stir, but when he slunk off to see his true master in my garden she told me in her own tongue. That was the one sign she made to prove that Garm did not altogether belong to the family. They were the best of friends at all times, *but,* Vixen explained, I was never to forget Garm did not love me as she loved me.

I never expected it. The dog was not my dog—could never be my dog—and I knew he was as miserable as his master who tramped eight miles a day to see him. So it seemed to me that the sooner the two were reunited the better for all. One afternoon I sent Vixen home alone in the dogcart (Garm had gone before), and rode over to cantonments to find another friend of mine, who was an Irish soldier and a great friend of the dog's master.

I explained the whole case, and wound up with, "And now Stanley's in my garden crying over his dog. Why doesn't he take him back? They're both unhappy."

"Unhappy! There's no sense in the little man any more. But 'tis his fit."

"What *is* his fit? He travels fifty miles a week to see the brute, and he pretends not to notice me when he sees me on the road; I'm as unhappy as he is. Make him take the dog back."

"It's his penance he's set himself. I told him by way of a joke, afther you'd run over him so convenient that night whin he was drunk—I said if he was a Catholic he'd do penance. Off he went wid that fit in his little head *an'* a dose of fever, an' nothin' would suit but givin' you the dog as a hostage."

"Hostage for what? I don't want hostages from Stanley."

"For his good behavior. He's keepin' straight now, the way it's no pleasure to associate wid him."

"Has he taken the pledge?"

"If 'twas only that I need not care. Ye can take the pledge for three months on an' off. He sez he'll never see the dog again, an' *so,* mark you, he'll keep straight for evermore. Ye know his fits? Well, this is wan of them. How's the dog takin' it?"

"Like a man. He's the best dog in India. Can't you make Stanley take him back?"

"I can do no more than I have done. But ye know his fits.

161

He's just doin' his penance. What will he do when he goes to the Hills? The docthor's put him on the list."

It is the custom in India to send a certain number of invalids from each regiment up to stations in the Himalayas for the hot weather; and though the men ought to enjoy the cool and the comfort they miss the society of the barracks down below, and do their best to come back or to avoid going. I felt that this move would bring matters to a head, so I left Terrence hopefully though he called after me, "He won't take the dog, sorr. You can lay your month's pay on that. Ye know his fits."

I never pretended to understand Private Ortheris; and so I did the next best thing—I left him alone.

That summer the invalids of the regiment to which my friend belonged were ordered off to the Hills early, because the doctors thought marching in the cool of the day would do them good. Their route lay south to a place called Umballa, a hundred and twenty miles or more. Then they would turn east and march up into the Hills to Kasauli or Dugshai or Subathoo. I dined with the officers the night before they left—they were marching at five in the morning. It was midnight when I drove into my garden and surprised a white figure flying over the wall.

"That man," said my butler, "has been here since nine, making talk to that dog. He is quite mad. I did not tell him to go away because he has been here many times before, and because the dog boy told me that if I told him to go away that great dog would immediately slay me. He did not wish to speak to the Protector of the Poor, and he did not ask for anything to eat or drink."

"Kadir Buksh," said I, "that was well done, for the dog would surely have killed thee. But I do not think the white soldier will come any more."

Garm slept ill that night and whimpered in his dreams. Once he sprang up with a clear ringing bark, and I heard him wag his tail till it waked him and the bark died out in a howl. He had dreamed he was with his master again, and I nearly cried. It was all Stanley's silly fault.

The first halt which the detachment of invalids made was

162

some miles from their barracks, on the Amritsar road, and ten miles distant from my house. By a mere chance one of the officers drove back for another good dinner at the Club (cooking on the line of march is always bad), and there we met. He was a particular friend of mine, and I knew that he knew how to love a dog properly. His pet was a big retriever who was going up to the Hills for his health, and though it was still April the round brown brute puffed and panted in the Club veranda as though he would burst.

"It's amazing," said the officer, "what excuses these invalids of mine make to get back to barracks. There's a man in my company now asked me for leave to go back to cantonments to pay a debt he'd forgotten. I was so taken by the idea I let him go, and he jingled off in an *ekka* as pleased as Punch. Ten miles to pay a debt! Wonder what it was really?"

"If you'll drive me home I think I can show you," I said.

So he went over to my house in his dogcart with the retriever; and on the way I told him the story of Garm.

"I was wondering where that brute had gone to. He's the best dog in the regiment," said my friend. "I offered the little fellow twenty rupees for him a month ago. But he's a hostage, you say, for Stanley's good conduct. Stanley's one of the best men I have—when he chooses."

"That's the reason why," I said. "A second-rate man wouldn't have taken things to heart as he has done."

We drove in quietly at the far end of the garden, and crept around the house. There was a place close to the wall all grown about with tamarisk trees, where I knew Garm kept his bones. Even Vixen was not allowed to sit near it. In the full Indian moonlight I could see a white uniform bending over the dog.

"Good-bye, old man," we could not help hearing Stanley's voice. "For 'eving's sake don't get bit and go mad by any measley pi-dog. But you can look after yourself, old man. *You* don't get drunk an' run about 'ittin' your friends. You takes your bones an' eats your biscuit, an' kills your enemy like a gentleman. I'm goin' away—don't 'owl—I'm goin' off to Kasauli, where I won't see you no more."

I could see him holding Garm's nose as the dog drew it up to the stars.

"You'll stay here an' be'ave, an'—an' I'll go away an' try to be'ave, and I don't know 'ow to leave you. I don't think—"

"I think this is damn silly," said the officer, patting his foolish fubsy old retriever. He called to the private who leaped to his feet, marched forward, and saluted.

"You here?" said the officer, turning away his head.

"Yes, sir, but I'm just goin' back."

"I shall be leaving here at eleven in my cart. You come with me. I can't have sick men running about all over the place. Report yourself at eleven, *here."*

We did not say much when we went indoors, but the officer muttered and pulled his retriever's ears.

He was a disgraceful, overfed doormat of a dog; and when he waddled off to my cookhouse to be fed, I had a brilliant idea.

At eleven o'clock that officer's dog was nowhere to be found, and you never heard such a fuss as his owner made. He called and shouted and grew angry, and hunted through my garden for half an hour.

Then I said, "He's sure to turn up in the morning. Send a man in by rail, and I'll find the beast and return him."

"Beast?" said the officer. "I value that dog considerably more than I value any man I know. It's all very fine for you to talk—your dog's here."

So she was—under my feet—and, had she been missing, food and wages would have stopped in my house till her return. But some people grow fond of dogs not worth a cut of the whip. My friend had to drive away at last with Stanley in the back seat, and then the dog boy said to me, "What kind of animal is Bullen Sahib's dog? Look at him!"

I went to the boy's hut, and the fat old reprobate was lying on a mat carefully chained up. He must have heard his master calling for twenty minutes, but had not even attempted to join him.

"He has no face," said the dog boy scornfully. "He is a

punniar-koote.[1] He never tried to get that cloth off his jaws when his master called. Now Vixen-baba would have jumped through the window, and that great dog would have slain me with his muzzled mouth. It is true that there are many kinds of dogs."

Next evening who should turn up but Stanley. The officer had sent him back fourteen miles by rail with a note begging me to return the retriever if I had found him, and, if I had not, to offer huge rewards. The last train to camp left at half-past ten, and Stanley stayed till ten talking to Garm. I argued and entreated, and even threatened to shoot the bull terrier, but the little man was firm as a rock, though I gave him a good dinner and talked to him most severely. Garm knew as well as I that this was the last time he could hope to see his man, and followed Stanley like a shadow. The retriever said nothing, but licked his lips after his meal and waddled off without so much as saying "Thank you" to the disgusted dog boy.

So that last meeting was over, and I felt as wretched as Garm, who moaned in his sleep all night. When we went to the office he found a place under the table close to Vixen, and dropped flat till it was time to go home. There was no more running out into the verandas, no slinking away for stolen talks with Stanley. As the weather grew warmer the dogs were forbidden to run beside the cart, but sat at my side on the seat. Vixen with her head under the crook of my left elbow, and Garm hugging the left handrail.

Here Vixen was ever in great form. She had to attend to all the moving traffic, such as bullock carts that blocked the way and camels and led ponies, as well as to keep up her dignity when she passed low friends running in the dust. She never yapped for yapping's sake, but her shrill high bark was known all along the Mall, and other men's terriers ki-yied in reply, and bullock drivers looked over their shoulders and gave us the road with a grin.

But Garm cared for none of these things. His big eyes were on the horizon and his terrible mouth was shut. There was another

[1] a spaniel

dog in the office who belonged to my chief. We called him "Bob the Librarian," because he always imagined vain rats behind the bookshelves, and in hunting for them would drag out half the old newspaper files. Bob was a well-meaning idiot, but Garm did not encourage him. He would slide his head round the door panting, "Rats! Come along, Garm!" and Garm would shift one forepaw over the other, and curl himself around, leaving Bob to whine at a most uninterested back. The office was nearly as cheerful as a tomb in those days.

Once, and only once, did I see Garm at all contented with his surroundings. He had gone for an unauthorized walk with Vixen early one Sunday morning, and a very young and foolish artilleryman (his battery had just moved to that part of the world) tried to steal both. Vixen, of course, knew better than to take food from soldiers, and besides she had just finished her breakfast. So she trotted back with a large piece of the mutton that they issue to our troops, laid it down on my veranda, and looked up to see what I thought. I asked her where Garm was, and she ran in front of the house to show me the way.

About a mile up the road we came across our artilleryman sitting very stiffly on the edge of a culvert with a greasy handkerchief on his knees. Garm was in front of him, looking rather pleased. When the man moved leg or hand Garm bared his teeth in silence. A broken string hung from his collar, and the other half of it lay, all warm, in the artilleryman's still hand. He explained to me, keeping his eye straight in front of him, that he had met this dog (he called him awful names) walking alone, and was going to take him to the Fort to be killed for a masterless pariah.

I said that Garm did not seem to me much of a pariah, but that he had better take him to the Fort if he thought best. He said he did not care to do so. I told him to go to the Fort alone. He said he did not want to go at that hour, but would follow my advice as soon as I had called off the dog. I instructed Garm to take him to the Fort, and Garm marched him solemnly up to the gate, one mile and a half under a hot sun, and I told the quarter guard what had happened. But the young artilleryman was more angry than was at all necessary when they began to laugh. Several regiments, he was told, had tried to steal Garm in their time.

That month the hot weather shut down in earnest, and the dogs slept in the bathroom on the cool wet bricks where the bath is placed. Every morning as soon as the man filled my bath the two jumped in, and every morning the man filled the bath a second time. I said to him that he might as well fill a small tub especially for the dogs. "Nay," said he smiling, "it is not their custom. They would not understand. Besides, the big bath gives them more space."

The punkah coolies who pull the punkahs day and night came to know Garm intimately. He noticed that when the swaying fan stopped I would call out to the coolie and bid him pull with a long stroke. If the man still slept I would wake him up. He discovered, too, that it was a good thing to lie in the wave of air under the punkah. Maybe Stanley had taught him all about this in barracks. At any rate, when the punkah stopped Garm would first growl and cock his eye at the rope, and if that did not wake the man—it nearly always did—he would tiptoe forth and talk in the sleeper's ear. Vixen was a clever little dog but she could never connect the punkah and the coolie, so Garm gave me grateful hours of cool sleep. But he was utterly wretched—as miserable as a human being, and in his misery he clung so close to me that other men noticed it and were envious. If I moved from one room to another Garm followed; if my pen stopped scratching Garm's head was thrust into my hand; if I turned, half awake, on the pillow Garm was up at my side, for he knew that I was his only link with his master, and day and night, and night and day his eyes asked one question—"When is this going to end?"

Living with the dog as I did I never noticed that he was more than ordinarily upset by the hot weather, till one day at the Club a man said, "That dog of yours will die in a week or two. He's a shadow."

Then I dosed Garm with iron and quinine, which he hated, and I felt very anxious. He lost his appetite, and Vixen was allowed to eat his dinner under his eyes. Even that did not make him swallow, and we held a consultation on him, of the best human-doctor in the place, a lady doctor who had cured the sick wives of kings, and the Deputy Inspector-General of the veterinary service of all India. They pronounced upon his symptoms, and I told them his story, and Garm lay on a sofa licking my hand.

"He's dying of a broken heart," said the lady doctor suddenly.

" 'Pon my word," said the Deputy Inspector-General, "I believe Mrs. Macrae is perfectly right—as usual."

The best man doctor in the place wrote a prescription, and the veterinary Deputy Inspector-General went over it afterward to be sure that the drugs were in the proper dog proportions; and that was the first time in his life that our doctor ever allowed his prescriptions to be edited. It was a strong tonic, and it put the dear boy on his feet for a week or two; then he lost flesh again. I asked a man I knew to take him up to the Hills with him when he went, and the man came to the door with his kit packed on the top of the carriage. Garm took in the situation at one red glance. The hair rose along his back; he sat down in front of me and delivered the most awful growl I have ever heard in the jaws of a dog. I shouted to my friend to get away at once, and as soon as the carriage was out of the garden Garm laid his head on my knee and whined. So I knew his answer, and devoted myself to getting Stanley's address in the Hills.

My turn to go to the cool came late in August. We were allowed thirty days' holiday in a year, if no one fell sick, and we took it as we could be spared. My chief and Bob the Librarian had their holiday first, and when they were gone I made a calendar, as I always did, and hung it up at the head of my cot, tearing off one day at a time till they returned. Vixen had gone up to the Hills with me five times before, and she appreciated the cold and the damp and the beautiful wood fires there as much as I did.

"Garm," I said, "we are going back to Stanley at Kasauli. Kasauli—Stanley; Stanley—Kasauli." And I repeated it twenty times. It was not Kasauli really, but another place. Still I remembered what Stanley had said in my garden on the last night, and I dared not change the name. Then Garm began to tremble;

168

then he barked; and then he leaped up at me, frisking and wagging his tail.

"Not now," I said, holding up my hand. "When I say 'Go,' we'll go, Garm." I pulled out the little blanket coat and spiked collar that Vixen always wore up in the Hills to protect her against sudden chills and thieving leopards, and I let the two smell them and talk it over. What they said of course I do not know, but it made a new dog of Garm. His eyes were bright; and he barked joyfully when I spoke to him. He ate his food, and he killed his rats for the next three weeks, and when he began to whine I had only to say "Stanley—Kasauli, Kasauli—Stanley," to wake him up. I wish I had thought of it before.

My chief came back, all brown with living in the open air, and very angry at finding it so hot in the Plains. That same afternoon we three and Kadir Buksh began to pack for our month's holiday, Vixen rolling in and out of the bullock trunk twenty times a minute, and Garm grinning all over and thumping on the floor with his tail. Vixen knew the routine of travel as well as she knew my office work. She went to the station singing songs on the front seat of the carriage, while Garm sat with me. She hurried into the railway carriage, saw Kadir Buksh make up my bed for the night, got her drink of water, and curled up with her black-patch eye on the tumult of the platform. Garm followed her (the crowd gave him a lane all to himself), and sat down on the pillows with his eyes blazing and his tail a haze behind him.

We came to Umballa in the hot misty dawn, four or five men who had been working hard for eleven months, shouting for our dâks—the two-horse traveling carriages that were to take us up to Kalka at the foot of the Hills. It was all new to Garm. He did not understand carriages where you lay at full length on your bedding, but Vixen knew and hopped into her place at once, Garm following. The Kalka road, before the railway was built, was about forty-seven miles long, and the horses were changed every eight miles. Most of them jibbed and kicked and plunged, but they had to go, and they went rather better than usual for Garm's deep bay in their rear.

There was a river to be forded, and four bullocks pulled the carriage, and Vixen stuck her head out of the sliding door and

169

nearly fell into the water while she gave directions. Garm was silent and curious, and rather needed reassuring about Stanley and Kasauli. So we rolled, barking and yelping, into Kalka for lunch, and Garm ate enough for two.

After Kalka the road wound among the Hills, and we took a curricle [1] with half-broken ponies, which were changed every six miles. No one dreamed of a railroad to Simla in those days, for it was seven thousand feet up in the air. The road was more than fifty miles long, and the regulation pace was just as fast as the ponies could go. Here again Vixen led Garm from one carriage to the other, jumped into the back seat, and shouted. A cool breath from the snows met us about five miles out of Kalka, and she whined for her coat, wisely fearing a chill on the liver. I had had one made for Garm too, and as we climbed to the fresh breezes I put it on; Garm chewed it uncomprehendingly, but I think he was grateful.

"Hi-yi-yi-yi!" sang Vixen as we shot around the curves. "'Toot-toot-toot!" went the driver's bugle at the dangerous places, and "Yow! Yow! Yow! Yow!" bayed Gram. Kadir Buksh sat on the front seat and smiled. Even he was glad to get away from the heat of the Plains that stewed in the haze behind us. Now and then we would meet a man we knew going down to his work again, and he would say, "What's it like below?"

I would shout, "Hotter than cinders. What's it like above?"

He would shout back, "Just perfect!" and away we would go.

Suddenly Kadiar Buksh said, over his shoulder, "Here is Solon;" and Garm snored where he lay with his head on my knee. Solon is an unpleasant little cantonment, but it has the advantage of being cool and healthy. It is all bare and windy, and one generally stops at a rest house nearby for something to eat. I got out and took both dogs with me while Kadir Buksh made tea. A soldier told us we should find Stanley "out there," nodding his head toward a bare bleak hill.

When we climbed to the top we spied that very Stanley who had given me all this trouble, sitting on a rock with his face in his

---

[1] two-wheeled chaise, drawn by two horses abreast

hands and his overcoat hanging loose about him. I never saw anything so lonely and dejected in my life as this one little man, crumpled up and thinking, on the great gray hillside.

Here Garm left me.

He departed without a word, and as far as I could see, without moving his legs. He flew through the air bodily, and I heard the whack of him as he flung himself at Stanley, knocking the little man clean over. They rolled on the ground together, shouting and yelping and hugging. I could not see which was dog and which was man, till Stanley got up and whimpered.

He told me that he had been suffering from fever at intervals, and was very weak. He looked all he said, but even while I watched, both man and dog plumped out to their natural sizes, precisely as dried apples swell in water. Garm was on his shoulder and his breast and feet all at the same time, so that Stanley spoke all through a cloud of Garm—gulping, sobbing, slavering Garm. He did not say anything that I could understand, except that he had fancied he was going to die, but that now he was quite well, and that he was not going to give up Garm any more to anybody under the rank of Beelzebub.

Then he said he felt hungry, and thirsty, and happy.

We went down to tea at the rest house, where Stanley stuffed himself with sardines and raspberry jam and beer and cold mutton and pickles, when Garm wasn't climbing over him; and then Vixen and I went on.

Garm saw how it was at once. He said good-bye to me three times, giving me both paws one after another, and leaping onto my shoulder. He further escorted us, singing hosannas at the top of his voice, a mile down the road. Then he raced back to his own master.

Vixen never opened her mouth, but when the cold twilight came, and we could see the lights of Simla across the hills, she snuffled with her nose at the breast of my ulster. I unbuttoned it and tucked her inside. Then she gave a contented little sniff and fell fast asleep, her head on my breast, till we bundled out of Simla, two of the four happiest people in all the world that night.

Buried Treasure

BY PATRICIA LAUBER

C L A R E N C E was tracking. Nose to the sand, he was stalking a small sand crab. When the crab stopped, Clarence stopped and pointed. When the crab scuttled forward, Clarence followed. He was concentrating so hard that he didn't even notice when someone came over the dune and sat down beside Brian and me.

The new arrival was a boy we'd seen around. He was about our age, but he was much bigger than Brian. The boy said, "I'm Speed Armstrong. Who are you?"

172

When we'd told him, he looked at Clarence. "Is that your dog?"

"Yes," I said, "that's Clarence."

Speed hooted with laughter. "Clarence! What a name for a dog! Who ever heard of a dog called Clarence?"

"It's a very good name for a dog," Brian said angrily. "I bet you don't even have a dog."

"I've got something better," Speed said. "I'm building a rocket. As a matter of fact, you're sitting on my rocket site."

Brian and I looked around.

"I mean," Speed said, "when I finish building my rocket, I'm going to launch it from here."

"That's dangerous," Brian said. "You might blow yourself up."

"Of course it's dangerous," Speed boasted. "But I'm not afraid. I bet you're a sissy—and so's your dog. Any dog with a name like Clarence is bound to be."

Brian scrambled to his feet. "I'll show y—"

Speed paid no attention to Brian. "You should see Boy. He belongs to our next door neighbor, and he's a *real* dog. He's huge and he has great big bulging muscles that ripple when he walks."

"I imagine he's stupid," Brian said. "All muscle and no brain." As he spoke, he looked meaningfully at Speed's muscles.

"No, he isn't," Speed said. "He's very highly trained. All you have to do is say the word and he attacks."

"What word?" I asked.

Speed didn't answer.

"Yah!" Brian said. "You don't even know."

"Of course not," Speed answered. "Boy was right there while Mr. Gunn was telling me. If he'd said the word, Boy might have torn my arm off. Gosh, he's almost bitten the mailman, the milkman, and the boy from the grocery store. None of them will even deliver any more," Speed said admiringly. "Sometimes Mr. Gunn lets me take Boy out. I and he are the only two people who can handle Boy."

"Pooh!" I said. "Who wants a dog like that?"

173

"*I* do," Speed said. "When the Government buys my rocket plans from me, I'm going to buy a big dog just like Boy."

Brian and I looked at each other. Then Brian said, "I don't believe you have a rocket. I think you're making it up."

Speed laughed. "Well, I'm not going to prove it by showing you my rocket. All important rocket work is top secret. Nobody's seen my rocket and nobody even knows where I work on it, except Boy. Sometimes I take him along to stand guard." Speed looked back at Clarence. "What's he doing now?"

"He's tracking," I said.

"Clarence has quite a few kinds of very valuable dog in him," Brian said. "That's why he's such a good hunter and tracker. See how he points?"

"Points?" Speed said. "Dogs don't point with their hind paws. They point with their front paws."

"Most dogs do," Brian said, "because they only know how to point with their front paws. Clarence can point with any paw."

Just then the crab went down its burrow. Clarence began to dig furiously. Pretty soon all we could see of him was his hind quarters.

Brian said, "Clarence is a very good digger."

I said, "Clarence is good at everything."

Not to be outdone, Brian said, "In fact, Clarence is so good at hunting and tracking and digging that I'm going to use him to hunt buried treasure."

Speed howled with laughter and fell over backward. "Ah-ha-ha! That's the funniest thing I've ever heard—using a dog to hunt buried treasure."

"I don't see what's so funny about it," Brian said. "It's a good idea."

"That's all you know!" Speed snorted. "It's so silly that I'd bet my rocket Clarence couldn't find any buried treasure if he stayed here for a hundred years."

"All right!" Brian said. "We'll show you."

Just then Clarence gave up digging for the sand crab and trotted toward us.

For a moment, I almost wished Clarence was the kind of

dog who bit strangers. But he loves meeting people, so he jumped all over Speed and licked his face.

Speed held Clarence off and studied him. "He's pretty small," Speed said thoughtfully.

"But very intelligent," I said.

"His tail curls just right," Speed went on.

"Right for what?" Brian asked.

"Right for fitting into my rocket. You've got to have a small dog with a curly tail—the way the Russians did."

I gasped. Even Brian was speechless.

Speed got up. "Be seeing you," he said and strolled off.

Brian found his voice. "Not if we see you first," he said, but Speed was gone.

That evening we went to see Uncle Matt and told him the whole story. Uncle Matt didn't think we had much to worry about. "Speed's a regular teller of tall tales," Uncle Matt explained. "Just last year he told everybody he was raising a tiger. Turned out to be a plain, ordinary cat that was tiger striped. Like as not," Uncle Matt said, "Boy is a Pekingese and the rocket's a burned-out firecracker."

We felt much better after hearing that. So Brian brought up the matter of hunting buried treasure. He told Uncle Matt about the bet. "I was just boasting back when I said it," Brian confessed. "But it does seem like a pretty good idea."

Uncle Matt didn't know of any buried treasure around these parts. But he suggested we talk to Mr. Tolliver. "He's interested in the history of the Cape," Uncle Matt explained. "Maybe he's turned up something in all those old books and maps he has."

The next morning we went to see the Tollivers. Mr. Tolliver agreed with Uncle Matt that our chances of finding buried treasure were pretty slim. And he laughed at the idea of Speed sending Clarence up in a rocket. "Why," he said, "it would take the U. S. Army and half a dozen top scientists to do that."

Mrs. Tolliver, though, was indignant. "The very idea," she said. "Imagine even joking about sending Clarence up in a rocket!" Then she went away and brought out a big bone with huge chunks of meat on it. "I was going to make soup from this," she said, "but I can always get another one. May Clarence have it?"

It was the most beautiful bone Clarence had ever had. He took it into the shade and began to work on it. He was still chewing by the time Brian and I were ready to leave. The Tollivers said Clarence was welcome to stay and finish his bone. But Clarence decided he'd rather come with us and bring his bone.

It wasn't easy going, for the bone was big and Clarence's mouth is small. Clarence kept having to lay the bone down and take a fresh grip on it. Brian and I both offered to carry the bone. But Clarence thought so highly of it that he wouldn't trust it even to us.

We were heading home along the beach when someone hailed us. There was Speed coming down the dunes. Beside him, on the end of a chain, stalked a huge dog.

Brian and I stood and stared. Clarence, who was standing near us, laid down his bone on the sand. Then he went forward, tail wagging, to sniff at Boy.

Boy snarled.

Speed tightened his grip on the chain. "You better keep your dog away," he warned.

Brian scooped up Clarence.

"Isn't Boy something?" Speed asked. "Did you ever see such a dog?"

At that moment, Boy lunged. Speed managed to hang onto the chain, but it didn't matter. Boy had seized Clarence's bone.

Clarence squirmed and whimpered in Brian's arms. "You give that back!" Brian said. "That's Clarence's bone."

"Tough!" Speed said.

"That's stealing," I said. "Mrs. Tolliver gave that bone to Clarence."

"I can't give it back," Speed said. "You don't think Boy's going to give it up, do you?"

"I thought you could handle Boy," Brian said.

"I can!" Speed insisted. "But there's no need to. My

rocket's almost ready now. And there isn't room for Clarence *and* the bone." Speed strolled off with Boy and the bone.

We had to carry Clarence home to keep him from going after Boy. Clarence was very unhappy. We were unhappy, too. Speed hadn't been exaggerating. Boy was just as big and fierce as he had said. And this meant that he might be building an honest-to-goodness rocket.

When Aunt Jo heard what had happened, she gave Clarence a plate of chicken meat at lunch and promised him a new bone. Clarence soon cheered up.

Brian and I were still worried, though. And you can imagine what we felt like when Clarence disappeared. One minute he was poking around in some bushes. The next minute he was gone. We called and whistled, but he didn't come. We telephoned all the friends he might be visiting. But Clarence had vanished.

Brian was all for calling the police and having Speed arrested. I thought we'd better ask Uncle Matt first.

Uncle Matt listened to our story. Then he said, "Well, even if Speed wasn't exaggerating about Boy, that still doesn't prove he's planning to send Clarence up in a rocket."

"Then where is Clarence?" I asked. "He never goes wandering off for the whole afternoon this way."

"Please can't we call the police?" Brian begged.

Uncle Matt thought. "Tell you what," he said. "Suppose we start by calling Speed's family." He went to the phone. "Mrs. Armstrong?" we heard him say. "This is Matthew Gregory. Is Speed home? No, I wanted to ask him . . . What?" A look of concern came over Uncle Matt's face. "He did? No, Brian and Sis saw them this morning. Just a minute."

Uncle Matt turned to us. "Speed has disappeared," he said. "Boy came home alone before noon. But nobody's seen Speed since this morning. Where was he when you saw him?"

We described the place as best we could.

Uncle Matt repeated what we'd said. "All right, we'll meet him there." He hung up the phone. "Come on," he said to us. "Mrs. Armstrong called the police. We're going to meet Sergeant Wood on the beach where you saw Speed this morning."

177

The sergeant was waiting for us beside a jeep that he had driven along the wet sand. We told him the whole story.

The sergeant frowned thoughtfully and stared down the beach. "Did you think they were going to the secret rocket place this morning?"

"I thought so," I said, "but Speed didn't really say."

Uncle Matt had a suggestion. "What about getting this dog Boy to lead you to the place?"

"I tried that," the sergeant said, "but he just snarled at me and went back to sleep. He didn't seem to get the idea at all."

"Clarence could track Speed," Brian said. "If we could find Clarence, he'd find Speed. Can't we look for Clarence first?"

The sergeant grinned and ruffled Brian's hair. "We'll look for them both at the same time. Hop into the jeep and we'll take a drive along the beach."

As Uncle Matt, Brian and I watched for signs of Speed and Clarence, the sergeant told us that Speed's family didn't know anything about his rocket. What had started them worrying was Speed's absence at lunch. Speed might vanish for hours at a time, but he never missed a meal.

Sergeant Wood had hardly finished telling us all this, when Brian shouted, "Look, Sis! There's Clarence! I see him!"

Far down the beach a small dog was standing on the sand looking in our direction. The sergeant stepped on the gas. When he stopped, Brian and I piled out of the jeep. It was Clarence! He was perfectly fine except that he seemed a little tired. He also had something on his mind. As soon as he'd greeted all of us, he trotted off a few steps and then looked back at Brian and me to see if we were coming.

We followed him up the beach. The dunes here were very high. At their foot was a great pile of sand with some planks and beams sticking out of it. Clarence had spent the afternoon digging here. There were holes in the pile of sand, holes in the beach around it.

Uncle Matt and Sergeant Wood looked at all this. Then they looked at each other.

The sergeant said, "Wasn't there a hut here once?"

Uncle Matt nodded. "Belonged to some fisherman. Then in

that bad storm two or three winters ago, the dunes shifted. The hut was swallowed up in sand."

The sergeant said thoughtfully, "Do you suppose—"

"Might be," Uncle Matt said. "I don't think the whole hut collapsed."

Looking very concerned, the sergeant hurried toward the remains of the hut. "Ahoy!" he yelled.

A faint voice called, "Help!"

"Speed!" the sergeant yelled. "You in there?"

"Yes," the muffled voice replied.

Sergeant Wood ran back to the jeep for shovels. Then, working with great care, he and Uncle Matt began to dig.

Clarence was delighted. He began to dig, too.

In a matter of minutes, Sergeant Wood, Uncle Matt, and Clarence had made a big hole. Speed crawled out through it. Clarence went on digging as Sergeant Wood pulled Speed to his feet.

"You all right?" he demanded.

"I guess so." Speed was blinking and squinting in the light.

"Of all the fool things to do!" Uncle Matt said. "What did you do—blow the place up with your rocket?"

"No," Speed said in a small voice. "I couldn't. I mean, it wasn't a real rocket. It was just a model."

"Then what happened?" the sergeant demanded.

Speed explained that a few months ago he had discovered the hut buried in sand and tunneled into it. Part of the hut had collapsed but part was still standing. Speed had shored up the opening and used the hut as a secret place to keep his rocket. Everything had been fine until this morning.

"Boy found a bone," Speed said.

"He did not," Brian said. "He stole it from Clarence."

Speed blinked in Brian's direction. "Oh," he said, "are you here? I still can't see in the light."

"All right," the sergeant prompted. "Boy had a bone."

"Well," Speed went on, "I didn't see what happened, but I guess he decided to bury it. I heard him digging near me. The next thing I knew the tunnel was collapsing and Boy was gone."

"Weren't you scared?" Brian asked.

179

"A little," Speed admitted. "But I knew Boy would save me. First he went away. When he couldn't get help he came back. He's been trying to dig me out for two or three hours."

"Boy!" Sergeant Wood snorted. "It's Clarence who's been trying to dig you out. Boy buried you along with his bone and then went home and forgot about both of you. If it hadn't been for Clarence you might have been here for a week before we found you." He took Speed by the arm. "Come on. Your mother's sick with worry."

Uncle Matt drove off with them. Brian and I said we'd walk home with Clarence. This time Clarence let me carry the bone, which he'd found shortly after Uncle Matt and Sergeant Wood had rescued Speed.

The next day Mrs. Armstrong came to call on us, bringing Speed. She wanted to meet Clarence and Brian and me and to thank us for rescuing Speed. Then she made Speed apologize for having said he was going to send Clarence up in a rocket.

Red-faced, Speed said he was sorry. "I was only teasing," he explained, squatting and patting Clarence. "I like dogs. I wouldn't really do a thing like that." Clarence took a nip at Speed's nose. "Golly," Speed said, "Clarence likes me and I like him. We're friends. I wouldn't hurt him."

Mrs. Armstrong had brought Clarence a new collar. Attached to it was a little medal that read: CLARENCE—*for bravery*. She sent Speed to the car for a huge box, which he gave to Brian. It was a model rocket kit.

Brian didn't know what to say.

Mrs. Armstrong said, "Speed told me about your bet."

"But—" Brian began.

"Oh, I know," Mrs. Armstrong said. "You think of buried treasure as a chest of jewels. But Speed is my treasure."

Speed's face turned fiery red. "Aw, Ma," he said. "Cut it out."

For the first time I began to feel sorry for Speed. I mean, our mother may think Brian and I are treasures, but she'd never say so in public like that.

After the Armstrongs had left, Brian took me aside for a

talk. Finally we decided to put the problem to Aunt Jo and Uncle Matt.

"I don't think I should keep the rocket kit," Brian said.

"And Clarence isn't sure he should keep the medal," I said.

"Gracious," Aunt Jo said, "why not?"

"Because Clarence had tracked Boy and was just trying to find his bone," I explained.

"And neither the bone nor Speed is really treasure," Brian added.

Aunt Jo and Uncle Matt said nothing.

"Mother likes us to be honest," I said.

Aunt Jo smiled at us. "I think you could keep them," she said. "You must remember that treasure can mean different things to different people. Mrs. Armstrong would much rather have Speed than a chest of jewels. And Clarence would rather have his bone."

"Besides," Uncle Matt said, "you don't know that Clarence was just digging for his bone. He may have known that Speed was trapped. After all, he's a very intelligent dog."

That was certainly true. In fact, the more we thought about it, the more we began to believe that Clarence had been trying to rescue Speed. Anyway, that was the story printed in the town newspaper the following week. It had a big headline on the front page:

DOG SAVES LOCAL BOY

Then there was a long story about how Speed had been buried. It told how Clarence had tried to dig Speed out. Sergeant Wood told how Clarence had led the search party to the buried hut. Then Speed was quoted as saying what a fine, brave, intelligent dog Clarence was. At the very end, Speed said, "I'm going to get me a dog just like Clarence."

"Humph!" Brian said when he read that. "There aren't any dogs just like Clarence."

181

Dog of Good Omen

BY SHEILA BURNFORD

One Indian summer day, three animals—an aging English bull terrier, a young Labrador retriever, and a Siamese cat —set out across northwest Ontario for home 250 miles away. The strange trio had to cross a vast almost uninhabited wilderness and face many perils, including an attack by a bear cub on the old terrier.

T H E Y slept in the same place that night and most of the following day, and the weather mercifully continued warm and sunny. By the third day the old dog seemed almost recovered and the wounds were closed. He had spent most of the day ambling around and sleeping, so that by now he seemed almost frisky and quite eager to walk a little.

So, in the late afternoon, they left the place which had been their home for three days and trotted slowly along the track together again. By the time the moon rose they had traveled several miles, and they had come to the edge of a small lake which the track skirted.

A moose was standing in the water among the lily pads on the far shore, his great antlered head and humped neck silhouetted clearly against the pale moon. He took no notice of the strange animals across the water but thrust his head again and again under the water, raising it high in the air after each immersion, and arching his neck. Two or three water hens swam out from the reeds, a little crested grebe popped up like a jack-in-the-box in the water beside them, and the spreading ripples of their wake caught the light of the moon. As the three sat, ears pricked, they watched the moose squelch slowly out of the muddy water, shake himself, and turn, cantering up the bank out of sight.

The young dog turned his head suddenly, his nose twitching, for his keen scent had caught a distant whiff of wood smoke, and of something else—something unidentifiable. . . . Seconds later, the old dog caught the scent too, and started to his feet, snuffing and questioning with his nose. His thin whippy tail began to sweep to and fro and a bright gleam appeared in the slanted black-currant eyes. Somewhere, not too far away, were human beings—his world: he could not mistake their message—or refuse their invitation—they were undoubtedly cooking something. He trotted off determinedly in the direction of the tantalizing smell. The young dog followed somewhat reluctantly, and for once the cat passed them both, a little moon-mad perhaps, for he lay in wait to dart and strike, then streaked back into the shadows, only to reappear a second later in an elaborate stalk of their tails. Both dogs ignored him.

The scent on the evening breeze was a fragrant compound of roasting rice, wild duck stew and wood smoke. When the animals looked down from a hill, tantalized and hungry, they saw six or seven fires in the clearing below—their flames lighting up a semicircle of tents and conical birchbark shelters against a dark background of trees, flickering over the canoes drawn up on the edge of a wild rice marsh and dying redly in the black waters beyond, and throwing into ruddy relief the high, flat planes of brown Ojibway faces gathered around the centers of warmth and brightness.

The men were a colorful lot in jeans and bright plaid shirts, but the women were dressed in somber colors. Two young boys, the only children there, were going from fire to fire shaking grain in shallow pans and stirring it with paddles as it parched. One man in long soft moccasins stood in a shallow pit trampling husks, half his weight supported on a log frame. Some of the band lay back from the fires, smoking and watching idly, talking softly among themselves, while others still ate, ladling the fragrant contents of a black iron pot onto tin plates. Every now and then one of them would throw a bone back over a shoulder into the bush, and the watching animals gazed hungrily after. A woman stood at the edge of the clearing pouring grain from one bark platter to another, and the loose chaff drifted off on the slight wind like smoke.

The old dog saw nothing of this, but his ears and nose supplied all that he needed to know; he could contain himself no longer and picked his way carefully down the hillside, for his shoulder still pained him. Halfway down he sneezed violently in an eddy of chaff. One of the boys by the fire looked up at the sound, his hand closing on a stone, but the woman nearby spoke sharply, and he waited, watching intently.

The old dog limped out of the shadows and into the ring of firelight, confident, friendly and sure of his welcome, his tail wagging his whole stern ingratiatingly, ears and lips laid back in his nightmarish grimace. There was a stunned silence—broken by a wail of terror from the smaller boy, who flung himself at his mother—and then a quick excited chatter from the Indians. The old dog was rather offended and uncertain for a moment, but he made hopefully for the nearest boy, who retreated, nervously clutching his stone. But again the woman rebuked her son, and at the sharpness of her tone the old dog stopped, crestfallen. She laid down her basket then, and walked quickly across the ring of firelight, stooping down to look more closely. She spoke some soft words of reassurance, then patted his head gently and smiled at him. The old dog leaned against her and whipped his tail against her black stockings, happy to be in contact with a human being again. She crouched down beside him to run her fingers lightly over his ears and back, and when he licked her face appreciatively, she laughed. At this, the two little boys drew nearer to the dog and the rest of the band gathered around. Soon the old dog was where he most loved to be—the center of attention among some human beings. He made the most of it and played to an appreciative audience; when one of the men tossed him a chunk of meat he sat up painfully on his hindquarters and begged for more, waving one paw in the air. This sent the Indians into paroxysms of laughter, and he had to repeat his performance time and time again, until he was tired and lay down, panting but happy.

The Indian woman stroked him gently in reward, then ladled some of the meat from the pot onto the grass. The old dog limped toward it, but before he ate he looked up in the direction of the hillside where he had left his two companions.

A small stone rebounded from rock to rock, then rolled into the sudden silence that followed.

When a long-legged, blue-eyed cat appeared out of the darkness, paused, then filled the clearing with a strident plaintive voice before walking up to the dog and calmly taking a piece of meat from him, the Indians laughed until they were speechless and hiccupping. The two little boys rolled on the ground, kicking their heels in an abandonment of mirth, while the cat chewed his meat unmoved; but this was the kind of behavior the bull terrier understood, and he joined in the fun. But he rolled so enthusiastically that the wounds reopened; when he got to his feet again his white coat was stained with blood.

All this time the young dog crouched on the hillside, motionless and watchful, although every driving urgent nerve in his body fretted and strained at the delay. He watched the cat, well-fed and content, curl himself on the lap of one of the sleepy

185

children by the fire; he heard the faint note of derision in some of the Indians' voices as a little, bent, ancient crone addressed them in earnest anad impassioned tones before hobbling over to the dog to examine his shoulder as he lay peacefully before the fire. She threw some cattail roots into a boiling pot of water, soaked some moss in the liquid, and pressed it against the dark gashes. The old dog did not move; only his tail beat slowly. When she had finished, she scooped some more meat onto a piece of birchbark and set it on the grass before the dog; and the silent watcher above licked his lips and sat up, but still he did not move from his place.

But when the fires began to burn low and the Indians made preparations for the night, and still his companions showed no signs of moving, the young dog grew restless. He skirted the camp, moving like a shadow through the trees on the hill behind, until he came out upon the lake's shore a quarter of a mile upwind of the camp. Then he barked sharply and imperatively several times.

The effect was like an alarm bell on the other two. The cat sprang from the arms of the sleepy little Indian boy and ran toward the old dog, who was already on his feet, blinking and peering around rather confusedly. The cat gave a guttural yowl, then deliberately ran ahead, looking back as he paused beyond the range of firelight. The old dog shook himself resignedly and walked slowly after—reluctant to leave the warmth of the fire. The Indians watched impassively and silently and made no move to stop him. Only the woman who had first befriended him called out softly, in the tongue of her people, a farewell to the traveler.

The dog halted at the treeline beside the cat and looked back, but the commanding, summoning bark was heard again, and together the two passed out of sight and into the blackness of the night.

That night they became immortal, had they known or cared, for the ancient woman had recognized the old dog at once by his color and companion: he was the White Dog of the Ojibways, the virtuous White Dog of Omen, whose appearance heralds either disaster or good fortune. The Spirits had sent him, hungry and wounded, to test tribal hospitality; and for benevolent proof to the skeptical they had chosen a cat as his companion —for what *mortal* dog would suffer a cat to rob him of his meat? He had been made welcome, fed and succored: the omen would prove fortunate.

A clumsy dog can make things right

Marty and the Monster

BY VELA DePEUGH

This is the tale of a friendly pup,
Slightly smaller than a horse,
Who always tried to fix things up
But made them worse, of course!

"*MARTY!*" Lila's voice sounded like a surprised siren.

I thought about sticking my head under the pillow and trying to go back to sleep. But I knew it wouldn't work. Anyway, with only one eye open I could see it was a swell morning. No fog, like we have sometimes in California, and a mocking bird tottling away in the live oak.

So I rolled out and went to put my head in the window.

"Hi, Sis," I called. And then just stared. What looked like a small wet haystack was floating around the middle of our new swimming pool. Lila was in her yellow bathing suit, dancing around behind a chair and flapping a towel.

"Martha Jane Merritt!" she demanded in the voice she keeps for that name, "get this monster out of here!"

Lila will try to boss me, because she's nineteen and in college, while I'm only fourteen—well, almost. It's been worse than ever this past week, because our parents are on what Lila calls a second honeymoon. Actually it's just a trip back East, mostly on business. But Lila's the romantic type. She looks it, too. She's got Mom's curly black hair and goldy-brown eyes. My wild red mop and green eyes come from Dad's side of the family.

"It's not my monster," I told Lila when I ran out the terrace door. "First time I've seen it." Wow! In that little pool the dog looked like a whale with hair.

He was having a fine time, floating around and laughing up at us. Being wet, you could see which end was his head. Which is more than you can when he's dry.

Just then Bill Regan came plunging through the hedge.

"Lila! What's the—" He stopped with a grunt, like he'd been hit. One hand went up to his sandy hair as if he wanted to tug it, only it was cut too short.

"Monarch," he ordered the dog. "Come out of there."

Monarch gave a cheerful "Woof" and kept on paddling.

"Gee Lila, I'm sorry he scared you," Bill said. "He's gentle as a kitten. Friend of mine in the Air Force has been transferred and let me have him at a bargain." Bill stopped sounding apologetic and began sounding proud.

"Manchester's Mighty Monarch is one of the finest bred English sheep dogs in this country."

Lila hates to look undignified. She was never a tomboy like me. So I wasn't surprised the way she snapped at Bill.

"He didn't frighten me, I just screamed to exercise my vocal cords. If you bought that monster, you're even crazier than I've thought. Why is he in our swimming pool?"

"Because he wanted a swim." Bill grinned. He can usually kid Lila into seeing a joke. He's been in love with her forever.

Now he's got a keen job with Amber Electronics and he wants to get married. Lila does too, only not so much, I guess.

"Very funny." Lila's voice was right out of the deep freeze. "You can laugh about it all the time you're cleaning the pool. Oh-h-h!" She ended with a shriek.

Monarch had decided to get out and join the party. And right behind Lila he braced himself and gave a terrific shake.

She whirled around a couple of times, waving her arms and yelping. Then she took off for the house at a run.

"Hold it! Hold it!" Bill commanded, backing away from the free shower. I got my share, too. But I didn't mind, even if I was wearing my new blue bathing suit. I guess I shouldn't have laughed at Lila, but she did look funny.

"You'd better get something to dry him with," I told Bill, "before he rolls in the dirt. Where are you going to keep him? Gyp's old doghouse won't hold a fourth of him."

"I'll have to get one built. Maybe I'd better make it big enough for the two of us." He grinned at me. "You're on my side, aren't you, Red? Help me get Lila to appreciate Monarch. It's too bad she had to meet him like this. I put him in the tool shed but I guess he pushed the door open."

He'd pushed it open, all right. He'd taken it right off the hinges. He'd dug up half of Mrs. Regan's prize gladiolas, and made a new opening in the laurel hedge between our places.

Lila wasn't slow about reminding me of this at dinner that night. I'd spent most of the day fooling around with the dog, and he was sweet if sort of dumb. Like drinking out of the birdbath instead of his dish. And eating *everything*.

"But we need a watchdog," I argued. "With that mugger roaming around, who knows when he'll pop up here?"

Some creep had been jumping out from behind bushes and snatching women's purses. Sometimes he even choked the women. The police weren't having any luck catching him, so the paper had offered a reward of a thousand dollars.

"Watchdog!" Lila sniffed. "That's a wrecking crew. Talk about your white elephants. 'Friend' is not the word I'd use for the man who unloaded him on Bill."

Lila spent a lot of time working on committees and things. Especially the Day Nursery. Of course Bill was gone all day. His mother let me have Monarch whenever I wanted, which was whenever Lila was gone. I got real crazy about the dope, but I couldn't seem to teach him much. Not manners, anyway.

He'd chase a stick until my arm dropped off. And I could throw anything into the pool, point and say, "Get it," and he'd go right in and bring it out. He made up a game of hide-and-seek that was kind of startling the first time he played it. I'd step behind a bush and he'd gallop about sniffing and whining until he found me. Then he'd tear up barking like crazy and I'd better dodge quick or he'd knock me over.

We had a lot of fun with that until one day he saw the meter reader behind an oleander and thought he was playing the game. When he came at the man barking like mad the man tried to get away, but he twisted his ankle and Monarch knocked him over. He began jumping all over him, barking fit to kill. I guess the poor fellow thought he *would* be killed, the way he yelled. People came running from two blocks away.

Oh, it was a terrible hassle, believe me.

"That does it," Lila told Bill that night. "Either you get rid of that monster or *both* of you stay away from here."

So Bill promised he'd find a new home for Monarch in the next couple of weeks.

I couldn't get to sleep that night. Monarch was a crazy dog all right. He'd about wrecked the garden. I didn't dare eat anything within sniffing distance, he was such a pig. When Bill left him chained to the new doghouse, he'd just dragged it along after him—and what a hole that made in the hedge! Then Bill chained the doghouse to a tree and Monarch pulled his head through his collar. You had to practically choke him to keep it on. But it was just going to break my heart to lose him. I knew Bill felt the same way. He'd probably always hold it against Lila.

If only she could be half as crazy about Monarch as Mrs. Naylor was about the chihuahua she took every place with her. She was coming to talk to Lila about a contribution to the Nursery Fund the next day, and would expect a lot of fancy food.

191

She had the biggest appetite for sweets and the most money of anyone in LaLoma, but the only thing she loved was that nasty-tempered little dog, Don Juan.

Maybe the temper wasn't his fault. She kept him perfumed strong enough to give a rhinoceros a headache. I wondered if he wouldn't like a dip in the pool as much as Monarch did, and—POP—just like that I had it. My idea.

Mrs. Naylor came tippy-trotting out to the terrace the next afternoon, wearing enough jewelry to start a store, and carrying Don Juan. When I brought out the fancy little cakes and fresh strawberry ice cream, she put the dog down. I could see she was a lot more interested in the food than the Fund, so I thought maybe my plan would help Lila, too.

I began to lay a trail of cake crumbs over the edge of the pool and Donny Juanny, to quote his mistress, wasn't long in finding them. The thing I had to do next I didn't much like, though I didn't see how it could hurt. All dogs can just naturally swim—besides wasn't Monarch going to rescue him? That was the whole idea of the plot. I had loosened Monarch's collar to be sure it would work.

When Don Juan got right at the edge of the pool, I just moved one foot a little and shoved him off. He gave a yelp as he hit the water, and I made a ladylike scream. Then I began to yell "Monarch! Monarch!" real loud.

Monarch would rush over and I'd point to Don Juan in the water and say "Get it" and Monarch would jump in and carry him out. Mrs. Naylor would be so grateful she'd give even more than five hundred to the Nursery Fund, and Lila would be so happy about that she'd realize Monarch was a fine dog and let us keep him.

That's the way I had it planned.

Monarch came tearing over all right. Mrs. Naylor and Lila had jumped up and run to the corner of the pool, making frightened squawks. I started to yell at Monarch to "Get it" but I never really had a chance.

He went rocketing right past me and on around the pool toward the table. He must have sideswiped Mrs. Naylor who was teetering and screeching at the edge of the pool. She went in with a big screech and a terrible splash. Lila had been dancing around beside her. Now she gave a wild sort of scream and fell in, too. As if that wasn't enough, Bill came tearing across the garden and dived in after them.

Well, it was sure a mess. I just stood there petrified and watched them all plunging around in the water. I don't know who was rescuing whom, but Don Juan was the first one out—and he rescued himself. When I saw him crawl up the steps, I came to. I don't know what I meant to do, but I didn't get to do it. Monarch had cleaned up all the food and now he came galloping up and knocked me into the water and jumped in himself. Oh, *he* was having a fine time!

As for me, I just wanted to sit down on the bottom of the pool in the deep end and stay there.

"That's the end of any contribution from her," Lila said after Mrs. Naylor went home, wrapped in blankets and hysterics.

"We'll be lucky if she dosen't sue us. Why you had to let her dog fall in the pool! And then to call that monster!"

Bill gave me a few sharp words, too. It was lucky for me they didn't know it had all been my plot, gone wrong.

"It's time you learned responsibility," Lila went on. "From now on you'll spend two afternoons a week helping out at the Nursery. Beginning tomorrow."

"I'll miss Jeep's beach party," I protested. But my heart wasn't in it. I was too sunk to care.

Lila picked a fine time to break me in. They were having a bazaar the next afternoon and evening to raise money. I ran errands, carried trays, filled in at booths and washed dishes until I was really beat. I though they would never close.

Lila was the treasurer and she was real pleased with how much they made, nearly four hundred dollars. Of course, she wasn't too happy, remembering the day before. We had been as polite as strangers to each other all day.

I was one big ache when I crawled in the car to go home. We didn't say anything until we stopped in the drive.

"I'll put the car away later," Lila told me. "I want to get this money locked up in Dad's safe."

She had it in a little bag, and hopped out and started across to the terrace door. I slid over in the seat and started to get out. There was moonlight and I could see the garden real plain. So I didn't miss it when the hedge began to shake and Monarch burst through. He had heard the car and slipped his collar to come and meet us.

My throat got tight and hard and my eyes all bleary. So he was an idiot dog all right. So what! I loved him anyway. And now in a week or so he'd be gone forever. And not only would I miss him like crazy, I'd have to worry about whether or not the new owner would be good to him.

I blinked my eyes, and then I saw Monarch veer off suddenly and head for the hibiscus beside the terrace. Lila slowed down when she saw him. He raced past and dived at the bush with that roaring bark he has when he's excited. Then everything seemed to happen at once.

The bush seemed to burst apart. I could see it was a man, trying to run. Monarch knocked him flat, just the way he had with the meter reader. He kept him down, bouncing all over him with a run-together thunder of barks.

Like that other time, this man did a lot of yelling. The neighbors came pouring over, shouting questions. Bill was the first to get there. He pulled the man up while I calmed Monarch down, and by that time a police car rolled in.

And guess what? It was the mugger, and he'd been after Lila's Fund money. He'd have got it, too, but for Monarch. That dog's the town hero now. He even had his picture in THE PRESS, with the editor handing him the reward check. Bill said Monarch would donate it to the Day Nursery.

Lila and Bill are planning a June wedding. I wonder how Monarch will wreck it, but I'm not worried. Lila is almost as silly about him now as Mrs. Naylor is about her Don Juan.

No one but I seems to realize that Monarch, the sweet dope, wasn't really catching a prowler; he was just playing the game when he saw someone behind that hibiscus. But I'm not about to tell them the truth about Monarch; life is much simpler this way.

Partners getting old together

Reddy As Always

BY MARGUERITE HENRY

*Ever since Mr. Hoops' mother-in-law had come to live at
the house, Reddy and her pup, Snippet, had made their
home in the basement of Belleville's city hall. For Mr.
Hoops, the city treasurer, could not bear to put them in a
kennel.*

S*O M E T H I N G* was happening to Reddy. It
seemed every now and then as if her legs were not her own.
They refused to obey her will.

Mornings when she wanted to dance on her hind feet and
plant her forepaws on Mr. Hoops' shoulders, she could not
make it.

It was worse on a morning after a hard workout in the field,
especially if the weather had been frosty and the birds had fallen
in water. One morning she felt so stiff and sore that she could
not get up until the sun found her bed and toasted her bones.

195

Then, gradually, she limbered up and by noon she seemed as good as ever.

It was strange that Mr. Hoops suspected nothing. If Reddy failed to race and tear about the basement when he arrived, he laid it to sleepiness.

"Why, you lazy old girl!" he would say. "Pretty soft to lie abed all hours."

Then Reddy would make a great effort to rise.

"I declare!" Mr. Hoops would laugh. "You're as stilty-legged as a colt."

On dry sunny days, however, Reddy seemed livelier than ever before. She could put her paws clear up on Mr. Hoops' shoulders with no trouble at all. And she was so glad about it that she gave his ears and neck an extra good licking.

All through the hunting season Snippet gained in skill while Reddy seemed to let down, but Mr. Hoops admitted this to no one. He scarcely admitted it to himself. What if Reddy did not range out as wide as Snippet? What if she seemed to avoid fences and hedgerows? She still had a sure nose for birds and pointed them like an arrow.

One day several birds that Mr. Hoops hit fell into a creek swollen by fall rains. He watched amazed as Reddy just stood on the bank and let Snippet retrieve them. She made no move to help him.

Mr. Hoops had to call her name out sharply before she finally splashed her way into the water and did her share of the work. Even then Mr. Hoops did not suspect.

It was the last day of the hunting season before Mr. Hoops knew.

The weather was unpromising. In spite of a crust of snow on the ground, the air was dry with a wind so fierce that it scattered all bird scent. As Snippet dashed over the rough country, Reddy seemed almost to crouch along. Mr. Hoops wondered if rheumatism had at last caught up with her, but he closed the little shutters of his mind.

"She's just smart," he told himself. "Saving her strength for a real burst of speed when she needs it."

196

The day wore itself out. By twilight Mr. Hoops' game bag was still empty. "I know we should be getting home," he told Reddy and Snippet, "but I always like to take at least one bird to Mrs. Hoops. What do you say to working the alder thicket once more? The wind seems to be dying a little. Our luck is bound to change."

Snippet wagged his tail in agreement and Reddy seemed more eager than when they had started out. It was almost as if she knew that this was the last hour of the hunting season.

At a wave of the hat both dogs made a beeline for the alder thicket. Now Snippet was clearing a split rail fence. But Reddy! She was not going to clear it. Mr. Hoops watched horrified as she hit the top rail, was catapulted into the air, and then fell in a little heap in the leaves.

It was only a matter of seconds until he reached the spot where she lay, but to him it seemed hours. Snippet had already found her, and when Mr. Hoops reached them he was licking a tiny trickle of blood on her forehead.

He dropped to his knees beside Reddy and pillowed her head in his lap. "She tried to tell me in the only way she knew. Please, God," he prayed, "don't let her die."

He glanced about helplessly. The ground was hummocky, but between the hummocks were pockets of snow. With quick hands he filled his handkerchief with the snow and placed it on Reddy's head. She made no move then nor when he felt of her legs to see if they were broken. He listened to her breathing but could hardly hear it for his own.

"Reddy," he pleaded. "If you'll get well, we'll have the best of days together. I'll rub your legs with warm liniment night and morning. You'll never have to work the fields again. And when spring comes you can lie on a warm rug in the sun and watch me plant my garden. Why, you can sleep all day if you like!"

He took off his jacket and wrapped it closely about her. How quiet the world seemed! A squirrel came to look at them with an inquiring glance, but did not even scold.

Night was closing in when Mr. Hoops felt a stirring in his arms. He pressed his ear against Reddy's muzzle to hear any

197

faint cries of pain. There were none. Reddy was opening her eyes. She was trying to lick Mr. Hoops' face. She was trying to comfort *him!*

Joyously Mr. Hoops carried his precious burden to the car. Then he sped for the warmth of the city hall.

"Reddy's had an accident," he told Mrs. Hoops over the telephone. "I'll spend the night here. Yes, Hannah, there's a cot to sleep on. I'll be all right."

It was long past midnight before Mr. Hoops slept. He sponged the blood from Reddy's head and cut away some of her matted hair. He bathed the wound with flowers of sulphur. Then he wrapped her in his old hunting coat and placed her near the furnace. She fell into a fitful sleep while he and Snippet looked on.

Mr. Hoops could not help noticing how Snippet had changed. In just a few hours he had grown from a playful youngster into a responsible dog. It was as if he were the parent now and Reddy the overgrown pup to be watched over.

"Snippet," said Mr. Hoops softly, "it's time you had your supper. Nothing fancy tonight. Just dry crumbles moistened with beef tea."

While Snippet cleaned his bowl, Mr. Hoops heated some milk, beat an egg into it, and added a little beef tea. Then, very gently, he lifted Reddy's jowl and poured a teaspoonful of the warm liquid between her teeth. She swallowed it and then ever so faintly began to whimper. She could stand the scratch of briers and the thwack of a fence rail, but when the master bent over her in sympathy she cried.

Now Mr. Hoops moistened his finger in the liquid and let Reddy lick it as if she were a puppy. And soon she was lapping the milk not because she wanted it, but because it seemed to please him.

When she could drink no more, Mr. Hoops examined her carefully. Besides the gash on her head, the pads of her feet were cut by splinters and thorns.

She seemed very tired now, so Mr. Hoops covered her and let her sleep.

Meanwhile he made a table out of a barrel and spread open his dog emergency kit. With skilled fingers he cut and sewed four boots out of white leather. He made them long enough to fit well above Reddy's knees. Then he lined the insides of them with a layer of balsam salve and set them on top of the furnace to warm.

At midnight Reddy woke with a whining cry. She was ashamed of it immediately afterward, for she licked Mr. Hoops' hands as he took out the splinters and thorns from the feathering between her toes. At last he fitted her paws into the boots he had made and covered her again with his coat. In a very few minutes she began to snore.

With a deep sigh, Mr. Hoops tiptoed upstairs to finish the night on the mayor's cot.

Reddy's wounds healed like magic. Even her morning lameness improved now that she spent most of her time indoors where it was warm and dry. She could climb stairs as well as ever, and she could dance on her hind feet when she had a mind to. But in spite of all this, she was not happy.

All her life she had been a worker. As long as she could remember she had worked the fields for Mr. Hoops or helped him in the training of her puppies. And the harder she had worked, the happier she had been.

Now, all that was over. No one needed her, not even Snippet. She had nothing to do. And the days stumbled over each other endlessly.

Meanwhile, things began to go wrong at the city hall. It wasn't anything big or important that happened. Just little things that added up to something big.

The high school band began to practice on the second floor of the city hall, and every time the tuba hit a certain note Reddy and Snippet howled uncontrollably. It put the mayor and Bessie, his stenographer, and even the four commissioners, on edge.

Then Victoria had kittens in the coal room, and if either dog so much as passed her door, she leaped out like a tigress and clawed at them until the yelping was dreadful to hear.

199

On top of all this Reddy hunted in her dreams. Sometimes she found pheasant and partridge and quail. Then she would bark with joy. More often, however, she failed to jump over a fence, and moaned in a way that was half human.

But the final incident that brought in a score of complaints was when Snippet got his nose caught in a mousetrap. He let out such a bloodcurdling cry that a woman customer at Mr. Hoops' window fell to the floor in a faint.

"Adam," said the mayor as kindly as he could, "the time has come to find a kennel for your dogs." Then at an imploring look from Katy, the scrubwoman, he added, "Of course, you can wait for slightly warmer days."

Mr. Hoops was a man who never went to *meet* trouble. He waited for it to catch up with him and tap him on the shoulder. Sometimes he even waited until it whirled him about sharply.

"Time enough," he said to Reddy and Snippet one Saturday night soon after the mousetrap incident, "time enough to think about leaving here when warm weather comes. We got through yesterday, didn't we? All right, we'll get through tomorrow too. You'll see."

And he tried to whistle a gay tune as he stirred a pot of mulligan. But every now and then the whistling stopped and was a long time starting up again.

During one of these pauses, Officer O'Toole rattled the front door. Mr. Hoops let him in and invited him downstairs to sit awhile.

"Don't offer me any of that mulligatawny, Adam. I could clean the whole pot, and what would the dogs think if I did the like of that? It smells elegant!" he sniffed.

Mr. Hoops laughed. "Occasionally I sample it myself, but I always feel like a dog when I do."

Reddy and Snippet rubbed against the officer's legs.

"It was the mayor sent me," Officer O'Toole said, as he bent over to pat the dogs. "He stops me as he drives by and says 'O'Toole, would you be so kind as to drop in on Adam and tell him to be sure the safe is locked? I put some mighty important papers in it, O'Toole,' he says, 'and I can't remember for the life of me whether I locked it or not. 'Twould worry me all Sunday,' he says.

"Then I gives him the green light and away he goes," chuckled the policeman. "And now I've got to skedaddle too."

Mr. Hoops saw Officer O'Toole to the door. Then he tried the handle of the safe which he had locked when the five o'clock whistle blew. This was a firm habit with Mr. Hoops. He felt more responsibility for the city's money and papers than if they had been his own. Only the city treasurer and the mayor knew the combination of this safe.

With a little sigh of relief at the peace and quiet, he began to jot down all the things he wanted to do on Monday. At the very bottom of the list he wrote hurriedly, "Look up a good kennel man." He penciled this last quite faintly, almost as if he thought that the words and the need for them might vanish over the weekend.

When, that same evening, Mrs. Hoops saw Mr. Hoops come home without his hat, she knew that he was worried over something. Quite rightly, she suspected it concerned Reddy and Snippet.

And then Mrs. Hoops said something which gave Mr. Hoops a jolt. "Just because *Reddy's* hunting days are over," she remarked, "just because of that is no reason Snippet should be neglected. Don't you think you should be hardening him so he'll be in condition for the hunting season?"

Mr. Hoops looked at Mrs. Hoops in wonderment. Every now and again she would come out with a suggestion that showed she understood dogs too.

So it was that on the following day, which was Sunday, Mr. Hoops took Snippet out alone. Before they set off together he stooped down and had a word with Reddy. Then with his eyes carefully avoiding hers, he smoothed her head and said good-by.

Reddy made no move to follow. Yet she seemed to believe they could not really go off without her, for she stood up now, waiting to be invited.

As Snippet bounded up the stairs after Mr. Hoops, Reddy scarcely breathed. She heard the sound of their footfalls along the corridor. She heard the door to the street close with a terrible finality. She ran over to the window to hear her name, no matter how softly it might be called. But no voice came. Mr. Hoops' footsteps were growing fainter and fainter now, and the click of Snippet's toenails on the sidewalk could no longer be heard at all. She gave one loud bark as a reminder to them, but the only answer was her own echo. So she stood there for a long time nosing the air coming in through the window. She could smell spring, and a great longing filled her.

With Snippet gone, the basement suddenly seemed hushed and chill. The ticking of the clock on the wall upstairs only emphasized the quiet.

Reddy walked slowly to her rug, but she was restless and could not sleep. Trembling a little, she got up and made her way to the coal room. Even a scuffle with Victoria and her kittens was to be preferred to all this stillness. But a sniff around the coal room revealed that Victoria and her entire family had gone out too. Miserably, Reddy returned to her own quarters.

Minute after minute ticked by. Finally, with a sigh of weariness, she flopped down on her rug. She had almost fallen asleep when suddenly she twitched and was wide awake. The door upstairs was opening. Then it clicked shut, quietly and quickly. A stranger was walking overhead with hurried steps.

Reddy was alert at once. She crept cautiously up the stairs, her hackles rising. Unmindful of any danger to herself she went into Mr. Hoops' office. A man stood close to the safe, his back toward Reddy. Quietly she circled him, her nose reaching out to sift his scent from the familiar belongings of Mr. Hoops.

Instinctively she disliked him and let out a low warning growl. The man wheeled about, reaching for his gun. Then with frightening quickness he began beating at Reddy with the butt end of it. The hard steel hit her, now on the shoulders, now on the flanks. Yet the shock of the blows did not confuse her thinking. It whipped her into a fury of strength. She hurled herself at the prowler with such force that he was thrown against the wall.

And to a crash of glass and brass and bells that frightened Reddy more than the blows of the gun, the wall clock came bumping down on the thief's head. With a heavy thud, he fell to the floor.

The clock was in ruins. Coiled springs, wheels, pinions, and the big shiny pendulum were spilled over the thief's chest, and the hour hand was stuck through his hair. It gave him a rakish look.

Reddy stood there puzzled. She was covered with fine splinters of glass, but none had penetrated her coat. She shook herself, stepped carefully over the glass and wire, and made her way to the man. He lay very still.

She stood guard over him. Her shoulders ached from the blows, but she did not mind the pain at all. At last she had work to do. She must hold this stranger until her master returned. Steady. Steady. He would come.

How still everything seemed! Even the ticking noise had stopped. Outside, a Sunday quiet hung over the street. Only a few sparrows were making twittering remarks to each other. The prowler groaned, but made no move.

Finally the streets began to liven with men and women and children coming home from church. But Reddy never wavered. Even when the lock turned, she stood rigid, though she knew in a flash that it was Mr. Hoops and Snippet.

Anxious to see how Reddy fared, Mr. Hoops walked hurriedly down the corridor. He gave only a passing glance into his office, but that was enough to show him the opened safe and the thief with Reddy on guard.

At that very instant, the thief opened his eyes, but when he saw *two* red dogs where before he had seen only one, he closed them quickly again.

"Steady, partner! Steady!" breathed Mr. Hoops. He reached for the telephone and called Officer O'Toole and the mayor. Officer O'Toole came running, his dinner napkin still stuffed between his brass buttons. Close on his heels followed the mayor and two of the four commissioners.

There was such a hubbub in the crowded cage that Mr. Hoops and his dogs slipped downstairs unnoticed.

Reddy gave one glad cry when she and Snippet and Mr. Hoops were back together again. She began to leap and run in circles around Mr. Hoops, and there was an air of importance in the very way she wagged her tail. It reminded him of the way she used to act after a good day of hunting when things had gone just right.

Upstairs, Mayor Twitterton was saying to Policeman O'Toole, "I'm sorry I asked Adam to move his dogs out. Reddy has done the citizens of Belleville a great service today. I had no idea that the City Hall needed a watchdog. So long as I am mayor, she and her pup shall live right here in city hall."

And since he had already been mayor for a dozen years, and since his campaign for Congress was not going along too well, it looked as if he would go right on being mayor for another dozen years.

With the thief handcuffed and the two commissioners on watch, the mayor and Policeman O'Toole went downstairs to break the good news to Mr. Hoops.

But they got only as far as the landing. There they stopped suddenly, realizing that he must have overheard the mayor's announcement.

"Did you hear that? Everything's going to be all right," Mr. Hoops was telling Reddy. "Snippet can take over the field work, and you have a new job guarding city hall." Then a look of triumph crossed his face. "Why, you've got about the most important job in all Belleville!"

Too happy to say more, he swooped the great gangling dog into his arms and danced a funny little jig, in and out among Katy's mops and pails.

Gingersnap in name and deed

Snap

BY ERNEST THOMPSON SETON

I T W A S dusk on Hallowe'en when first I saw him. Early in the morning I had received a telegram from my college chum Jack: "Lest we forget. Am sending you a remarkable pup. Be polite to him; it's safer." It would have been just like Jack to have sent an infernal machine or a skunk rampant and called it a pup, so I awaited the hamper with curiosity. When it arrived I saw it was marked "dangerous," and there came from within a high-pitched snarl at every slight provocation. On peering through the wire netting I saw it was not a baby tiger but a small white bull terrier. He snapped at me and at anyone or anything that seemed too abrupt or too near for proper respect, and his snarling growl was unpleasantly frequent. Dogs have two growls: one deep-rumbled and chesty; that is polite warning— the retort courteous, the other mouthy and much higher in pitch. This is the last word before actual onslaught. The terrier's growls were all of the latter kind. I was a dog man and thought I knew all about dogs. So, dismissing the porter, I got out my all-round jackknife-toothpick-nailhammer-hatchet-toolbox-fire-shovel. It's a specialty of our firm, and lifted the netting. Oh yes, I knew all about dogs. The little fury had been growling out a whole-souled growl for every tap of the tool, and when I turned the box on its side he made a dash straight for my legs. Had not his foot gone through the wire netting and held him, I might have been hurt, for his heart was evidently in his work; but I stepped on the table out of reach and tried to reason with him. I have always believed in talking to animals. I maintain that they gather something of our intention at least, even if they do not understand our words; but the dog evidently put me down for a hypocrite and scorned my approaches. At first he took his post under the table and kept up a circular watch for a leg trying to get down.

I could have controlled him with my eye, but couldn't bring it to bear where I was, or rather where he was. Thus I was left a prisoner. I am a very cool person, I flatter myself; in fact, I represent a hardware firm, and in coolness we are not excelled. I got out a cigar and smoked tailor style on the table while my little tyrant below kept watch for legs. I got out the telegram and read it: "Remarkable pup. Be polite to him; it's safer." I think it was my coolness rather than my politeness that did it, for in half an hour the growling ceased. In an hour he no longer jumped at a newspaper cautiously pushed over the edge to test his humor; possibly the irritation of the cage was wearing off. By the time I had lit my third cigar he waddled out to the fire and lay down, not ignoring me, however. I had no reason to complain of that kind of contempt. He kept one eye on me, and I kept both eyes, not on him, but on his stumpy tail. If that tail should swing sidewise once, I should feel I was winning; but it did not swing. I got a book and put in time on that table till my legs were cramped

206

and the fire burned low. About 10 P.M. it was chilly, and at half-past ten the fire was out. My Hallowe'en present got up, yawned and stretched, then walked under my bed, where he found a fur rug. By stepping lightly from the table to the dresser and then onto the mantelshelf I also reached bed, and very quietly undressing, got in without provoking any criticism from my master. I had not yet fallen asleep when I heard a slight scrambling and felt "thump-thump" on the bed, then over my feet and legs; Snap evidently had found it too cool down below, and proposed to have the best my house afforded.

He curled up on my feet in such a way that I was very uncomfortable and tried to readjust matters, but the slightest wriggle of my toe was enough to make him snap at it so fiercely that nothing but thick woolen bedclothes saved me from being maimed for life.

I was an hour moving my feet—a hair's breadth at a time—till they were so that I could sleep in comfort; and I was awakened several times during the night by angry snarls from the dog—I suppose because I dared to move a toe without his approval, though once I believe he did it simply because I was snoring.

In the morning I was ready to get up before Snap was. You see, I called him Snap—Gingersnap in full. Some dogs are hard to name and some do not seem to need it—they name themselves.

I was ready to rise at seven. Snap was not ready till eight, so we rose at eight. He had little to say to the man who made the fire. He allowed me to dress without doing it on the table. As I left the room to get breakfast, I remarked:

"Snap, my friend, some men would whip you into a different way, but I think I know a better plan. The doctors nowadays favor the 'no-breakfast cure.' I shall try that."

It seemed cruel, but I left him without food all day. It cost me something to repaint the door where he scratched it, but at night he was quite ready to accept a little food at my hands.

In a week we were very good friends. He would sleep on my bed now and allow me to move my feet without snapping at them, intent to do me serious bodily harm. The no-breakfast cure had worked wonders; in three months we were—well, simply man and dog, and he amply justified the telegram he came with.

He seemed to be without fear. If a small dog came near, he would take not the slightest notice; if a medium-sized dog, he would stick his stub of a tail rigidly up in the air, then walk around him, scratching contemptuously with his hind feet and looking at the sky, the distance, the ground, anything but the dog, and noting his presence only by frequent high-pitched growls. If the stranger did not move on at once the battle began, and then the stranger usually moved on very rapidly. Snap sometimes got worsted, but no amount of sad experience could ever inspire him with a grain of caution. Once, while riding in a cab during the dog show, Snap caught sight of an elephantine St. Bernard taking an airing. Its size aroused such enthusiasm in the pup's little breast that he leaped from the cab window to do battle and broke his leg.

Evidently fear had been left out of his make-up and its place supplied with an extra amount of ginger, the reason for his full name. He differed from all other dogs I have ever known. For example, if a boy threw a stone at him he ran, not away, but toward the boy, and if the crime was repeated Snap took the law into his own hands; thus he was at least respected by all. Only myself and the porter at the office seemed to realize his good points, and we only were admitted to the high honor of personal friendship, an honor which I appreciated more as months went on. By midsummer not Carnegie, Vanderbilt and Astor together could have raised money enough to buy a quarter of a share in my little dog Snap.

Though not a regular traveler, I was ordered out on the road in the autumn, and then Snap and the landlady were left together, with unfortunate developments. Contempt on his part, fear on hers, and hate on both.

I was placing a lot of barbed wire in the northern tier of states. My letters were forwarded once a week, and I got several complaints from the landlady about Snap.

When I arrived at Mendoza, in North Dakota, I found a

fine market for wire. Of course my dealings were with the big storekeepers, but I went about among the ranchmen to get their practical views on the different styles, and thus I met the Penroof Brothers' cow outfit.

One could be long in cow country without hearing a great deal about the depredations of the ever wily and destructive gray wolf. The day had gone by when they could be poisoned whole-sale, and they were a serious drain on the rancher's profits. The Penroof brothers, like most live cattlemen, had given up all attempts at poisoning and trapping, and were trying various breeds of dogs as wolf hunters, hoping to get a little sport out of the necessary work of destroying the pests.

Foxhounds had failed—they were too soft for fighting. Great Danes were too clumsy, and greyhounds could not follow the game unless they could see it. Each breed had some fatal defect, but the cowmen hoped to succeed with a mixed pack, and the day when I was invited to join in a Mendoza wolf-hunt, I was amused by the variety of dogs that followed. There were several mongrels, but there were also a few highly bred dogs—in particular, some Russian wolfhounds that must have cost a lot of money.

Hilton Penroof, the oldest boy, "The Master of Hounds," was unusually proud of them and expected them to do great things.

"Greyhounds are too thin-skinned to fight a wolf, Danes are too slow, but you'll see the fur fly when the Russians take a hand."

Thus the greyhounds were there as runners, the Danes as heavy backers, and the Russians to do the important fighting. There were also two or three foxhounds, whose fine noses were relied on to follow the trail if the game got out of view.

It was a fine sight as we rode away among the Badland Buttes that October day. The air was bright and crisp, and though so late, there was neither snow nor frost. The horses were fresh, and once or twice showed me how a cow pony tries to get rid of his rider.

The dogs were keen for sport, and we did start one or two

gray spots in the plain that Hilton said were wolves or coyotes. The dogs trailed away at full cry, but at night, beyond the fact that one of the greyhounds had a wound on his shoulder, there was nothing to show that any of them had been on a wolf-hunt.

"It's my opinion yer fancy Russians is no good, Hilt," said Garvin, the younger brother. "I'll back that little black Dane against the lot, mongrel an' all as he is."

"I don't unnerstan' it," growled Hilton. "There ain't a coyote, let alone a gray wolf, kin run away from them grey- hounds; them foxhounds kin folly a trail three days old, an' the Danes could lick a grizzly."

"I reckon," said the father, "they kin run, an' they kin track, an' they kin lick a grizzly, *maybe*, but the fac' is they don't want to tackle a gray wolf. The hull darn pack is scairt—an' I wish we had our money out o' them."

Thus the men grumbled and discussed as I drove away and left them.

There seemed only one solution of the failure. The hounds were swift and strong, but a gray wolf seems to terrorize all dogs. They have not the nerve to face him, and so each time he gets away.

My thoughts flew back to the fearless little dog that had shared my bed for the last year. How I wished he was out here. Then these lubberly giants of hounds would find a leader whose nerve would not fail at the moment of trial.

At Baroka, my next stop, I got a batch of mail including two letters from the landlady; the first to say that "that beast of a dog was acting up scandalous in my room," and the other still more forcible, demanding his immediate removal.

"Why not have him expressed to Mendoza?" I thought. "It's only twenty hours; they'll be glad to have him. I can take him home with me when I go through."

My next meeting with Gingersnap was not as different from the first as one might have expected. He jumped on me, made much vigorous pretense to bite, and growled frequently, but it

210

was a deep-chested growl and his stump was wagging very hard.

The Penroofs had had a number of wolf-hunts since I was with them, and were much disgusted at having no better success than before. The dogs could find a wolf nearly every time they went out, but they could not kill him. and the men were not near enough at the finish to learn why.

Old Penroof was satisfied that "thar wasn't one of the hull miserable gang that had the grit of a jack-rabbit."

We were off at dawn the next day—the same procession of fine horses and superb riders, and the big blue dogs, the yellow dogs, the spotted dogs, as before: But there was a new feature, a little white dog that stayed close by me, and not only any dogs, but horses that came too near were apt to get a surprise from his teeth. I think he quarrelled with every man, horse and dog in the country, with the exception of a bull terrier belonging to the Mendoza hotel man. She was the only one smaller than himself, and they seemed very good friends.

I shall never forget the view of the hunt I had that day. We were on one of those large, flat-headed buttes that give a kingdom to the eye, when Hilton, who had been scanning the vast country with glasses, exclaimed: "I see him. There he goes, toward Skull Creek. Guess it's a coyote."

Now the first thing is to get the greyhounds to see the prey— not an easy matter, as they cannot use the glasses, and the ground was covered with sage brush higher than the dogs' heads.

But Hilton called, "Hu, hu, Dander," and leaned aside from his saddle, holding out his foot at the same time. With one agile bound Dander leaped to the saddle and there stood balancing on the horse while Hilton kept pointing. "There he is, Dander; sic him—see him down there." The dog gazed earnestly where his master pointed, then seeming to see, he sprang to the ground with a slight yelp and sped away. The other dogs followed after, in an ever-lengthening procession, and we rode as hard as we could behind them, but losing time, for the ground was cut with gullies, spotted with badger holes, and covered with rocks and sage that made full speed too hazardous.

We all fell behind, and I was last, of course, being least

accustomed to the saddle. We got several glimpses of the dogs flying over the level plain or dropping from sight in gullies to reappear at the other side. Dander, the greyhound, was the recognized leader, and as we mounted another ridge we got sight of the whole chase—a coyote at full speed, the dogs a quarter of a mile behind, but gaining. When next we saw them the coyote was dead, and the dogs sitting around panting, all but two of the foxhounds and Gingersnap.

"Too late for the fracas," remarked Hilton, glancing at these last foxhounds. Then he proudly petted Dander. "Didn't need yer purp after all, ye see."

"Takes a heap of nerve for ten big dogs to face one little coyote," remarked the father, sarcastically. "Wait till we run onto a gray."

Next day we were out again, for I made up my mind to see it to a finish.

From a high point we caught sight of a moving speck of gray. A moving white speck stands for antelope, a red speck for fox, and a gray speck for either gray wolf or coyote—which of these is determined by its tail. If the glass shows the tail down it is a coyote; if up, it is the hated gray wolf.

Dander was shown the game as before and led the motley mixed procession—as he had before—greyhounds, wolfhounds, foxhounds, Danes, bull terrier, horsemen. We got a momentary view of the pursuit; a gray wolf it surely was, loping away ahead of the dogs. Somehow I thought the first dogs were not running as fast now as they had after the coyote. But no one knew the finish of the hunt. The dogs came back to us one by one, and we saw no more of that wolf.

Sarcastic remarks and recrimination were now freely indulged in by the hunters.

"Pah! scairt, plumb scairt," was the father's disgusted comment on the pack. "They could catch up easy enough, but when he turned on them, they lighted out for home—pah!"

"Where's that thar onsurpassable, fearless, scaired-o'-nort tarrier?" asked Hilton, scornfully.

"I don't know," said I. "I am inclined to think he never saw the wolf; but if he ever does, I'll bet he sails in for death or glory."

That night several cows were killed close to the ranch, and we were spurred on to another hunt.

It opened much like the last. Late in the afternoon we sighted a gray fellow with tail up, not half a mile off. Hilton called Dander up on the saddle. I acted on the idea and called Snap to mine. His legs were so short that he had to leap several times before he made it, scrambling up at last with my foot as a half-way station. I pointed and "sic-ed" for a minute before he saw the game, and then he started out after the greyhounds, already gone, with energy that was full of promise.

The chase this time led us not to the rough brakes along the river but toward the high open country, for reasons that appeared later. We were close together as we rose to the upland and sighted the chase half a mile off, just as Dander came up with the wolf and snapped at his haunch. The gray wolf turned around to fight, and we had a fine view. The dogs came up by twos and threes, barking at him in a ring; last, the little white one rushed up. He wasted no time barking, but rushed straight at the wolf's throat and missed it, yet seemed to get him by the nose; then the ten big dogs closed in, and in two minutes the wolf was dead. We had ridden hard to be in at the finish, and though our view was distant, we saw at least that Snap had lived up to the telegram as well as to my promises for him.

Now it was my turn to crow, and I did not lose the chance. Snap had shown them how, and at last the Mendoza pack had killed a gray wolf without help from the men.

There were two things to mar the victory somewhat; first, it was a young wolf, a mere cub, hence his foolish choice of country; second, Snap was wounded—the wolf had given him a bad cut in the shoulder.

As we rode in proud procession home, I saw he limped a little. "Here," I cried, "come up, Snap." He tried once or twice to jump to the saddle, but could not. "Here, Hilton, lift him up to me."

"Thanks; I'll let you handle your own rattlesnakes," was the reply, for all knew now that it was not safe to meddle with his person. "Here, Snap, take hold," I said, and held my quirt to him. He seized it, and by that I lifted him to the front of my saddle and so carried him home. I cared for him as though he had been a baby. He had shown those cattlemen how to fill the weak place in their pack; the foxhounds may be good and the grey-hounds swift and the Russians and Danes fighters, but they are no use at all without the crowning moral force of grit, that none can supply so well as a bull terrier. On that day the cattlemen learned how to manage the wolf question, as you will find if ever you are at Mendoza; for every successful wolf pack there has with it a bull terrier, preferably of the Snap-Mendoza breed.

Next day was Hallowe'en, the anniversary of Snap's advent. The weather was clear, bright, not too cold, and there was no snow on the ground. The men usually celebrated the day with a hunt of some sort, and now, of course, wolves were the one object. To the disappointment of all, Snap was in bad shape with his wound. He slept, as usual, at my feet, and bloody stains now marked the place. He was not in condition to fight, but we were bound to have a wolf hunt, so he was beguiled to an outhouse and locked up, while we went off, I, at least, with a sense of impending disaster. I *knew* we should fail without my dog, but I did not realize how bad a failure it was to be.

Afar among the buttes of Skull Creek we had roamed when a white ball appeared bounding through the sagebrush, and in a minute more Snap came, growling and stump-waggling, up to my horse's side. I could not send him back; he would take no such orders, not even from me. His wound was looking bad, so I called him, held down the quirt, and jumped him to my saddle.

"There," I thought, "I'll keep you safe till we get home." Yes, I thought; but I reckoned not with Snap. The voice of Hilton, "Hu, hu," announced that he had sighted a wolf. Dander and Riley, his rival, both sprang to the point of observation, with the result that they collided and fell together, sprawling, in the sage. But Snap, gazing hard, had sighted the wolf not so very far off, and before I knew it he leaped from the saddle and bounded zigzag, high, low, in and under the sage, straight for the enemy, leading the whole pack for a few minutes. Not far, of course. The great greyhounds sighted the moving speck, and the usual procession strung out on the plain. It promised to be a fine hunt, for the wolf had less than half a mile start and all the dogs were fully interested.

"They've turned up Grizzly Gully," cried Garvin. "This way, and we can head them off."

So we turned and rode hard around the north side of Hulmer's Butte, while the chase seemed to go round the south.

We galloped to the top of Cedar Ridge and were about to ride down, when Hilton shouted, "By George, here he is! We're right onto him." He leaped from his horse, dropped the bridle, and ran forward. I did the same. A great gray wolf came lumbering across an open plain toward us. His head was low, his tail out level, and fifty yards behind him was Dander, sailing like a hawk over the ground, going twice as fast as the wolf. In a minute the hound was alongside and snapped, but bounded back as the wolf turned on him. They were just below us now and not fifty feet away. Garvin drew his revolver, but in a fateful moment Hilton interfered: "No; no; let's see it out." In a few seconds the next greyhound arrived, then the rest in order of swiftness. Each came up full of fight and fury, determined to go right in and tear the gray wolf to pieces; but each in turn swerved aside, and leaped and barked around at a safe distance. After a minute or so the Russians appeared—fine big dogs they were. Their distant intention no doubt was to dash right at the old wolf; but his fearless front, his sinewy frame and death-dealing jaws awed them long before they were near him, and they also joined the ring while the desperado in the middle faced this way and that, ready for any or all.

Now the Danes came up, huge-limbed creatures, any one of them as heavy as the wolf. I heard their heavy breathing tighten into a threatening sound as they plunged ahead, eager to tear the

215

foe to pieces; but when they saw him there, grim, fearless, mighty of jaw, tireless of limb, ready to die if need be but sure of this, he would not die alone—well, those great Danes—all three of them—were stricken as the rest had been with a sudden bashfulness: yes, they would go right in presently—not now, but as soon as they had got their breath; they were not afraid of a wolf, oh, no. I could read their courage in their voices. They knew perfectly well that the first dog to go in was going to get hurt, but never mind that—presently; they would bark a little more to get up enthusiasm.

And as the ten big dogs were leaping round the silent wolf at bay, there was a rustling in the sage at the far side of the place; then a snow-white rubber ball, it seemed, came bounding, but grew into a little bull terrier, and Snap, slowest of the pack, and last, came panting hard, so hard he seemed gasping. Over the level open he made, straight to the changing ring around the cattle-killer whom none dared face. Did he hesitate? Not for an instant; through the ring of the yelping pack, straight for the old despot of the range, right for his throat he sprang; and the gray wolf struck with his twenty scimitars. But the little one, if foiled at all, sprang again, and then what came I hardly knew. There was a whirling mass of dogs. I thought I saw the little white one clinched on the gray wolf's nose. The pack was all around; we could not help them now. But they did not need us; they had a leader of dauntless mettle, and when in a little while the final scene was done, there on the ground lay the gray wolf, a giant of his kind, and clinched on his nose was the little white dog.

We were standing around within fifteen feet, ready to help, but had no chance till we were not needed.

The wolf was dead, and I hallooed to Snap, but he did not move. I bent over him. "Snap—Snap, it's all over; you've killed him." But the dog was very still, and now I saw two deep wounds in his body. I tried to lift him. "Let go, old fellow; it's all over." He growled feebly, and at last let go of the wolf. The rough cattlemen were kneeling around him now; old Penroof's voice was trembling as he muttered, "I wouldn't had him hurt for twenty steers." I lifted him in my arms, called to him and stroked his head. He snarled a little, a farewell as it proved, for he licked my hand as he did so, then never snarled again.

That was a sad ride home for me. There was the skin of a monstrous wolf, but no other hint of triumph. We buried the fearless one on a butte back of the ranch house. Penroof, as he stood by, was heard to grumble: "By jingo, that was grit—cl'ar grit! Ye can't raise cattle without grit."

A lonely boy afraid of the dark, and a friend

A Pair of Lovers

BY ELSIE SINGMASTER

T H E first shadows from the western mountains fell upon the little farm at their foot. Often they seemed to chase James down the road. He had gone for the cows alone since he was six years old, but he had never grown accustomed to the queer shapes of the alder bushes in the evenings and to the dark masses which filled the fence corners. Even familiar Mooley and Daisy and Bess took on vast and unfamiliar proportions. James

218

did not often run, and having safely crossed the bridge over the stream which made his mother's land such fine pasture he grew bold. He could see from there the kitchen light, darkened sometimes as his mother passed before it, or he could hear the great tin pails rattling on her arm as she swung open the barnyard gate.

This evening James could not see the kitchen light or hear the pleasant clink of his mother's pails. Already the loud "Gee, Mooley! Haw, Bess!" with which he expressed his return to confidence in himself and in the reasonable structure of the world, was on his lips. But the shout died soundlessly away.

The light of his mother's lamp was lost in a brilliant glare. At first James was certain that the dreaded fire was at last consuming their dwelling and he began to run, crying frantically, "Oh, mother! mother!"

Then he stood still. The light was not in the house, but in the road; it was not the leaping red flame with which fire devours wooden walls and roof. It was a round, still white light, or rather two round, still white lights which illuminated the road to the bridge. James could count every nail in the railing, every knot in the floor. He could see also, as he looked down to gauge the astonishing power of the fiery eyes, his own bare feet, released today from their winter bondage of shoes. He could see the smooth, beautifully colored bodies of the Alderneys, moving placidly up the road in the face of the great light as though they were indifferent to the strange phenomenon.

James stopped so long in amazed contemplation that the cows were halfway to the barn. Then he ran at furious speed.

"It is one of *them!*" he cried, divided between fright and rapture.

At the gate of the house yard he stopped, breathless. The automobile lights were now behind him; he could see that the kitchen lamp was burning and that his mother stood in the doorway, her pails, one inside the other, in one hand, her lantern in the other. Facing her on the step was a stranger, a tall young man with an eager commanding voice.

"The dairyman told me about you. He said that you loved animals and were kind to them. Robin should be on a farm while we are away. I wouldn't have bought him if I had known

219

we were going so soon. He won't be any trouble, and I will pay you well."

Mrs. Schelling set the lantern on the sill beside her. She was a Pennsylvania German and spoke English with difficulty. She braced herself by putting her hand against the door.

"I could not say his name, to call him."

"Robin! Call him Bob, Bobby; anything you like!"

"I could not talk to him in English."

The young man laughed. "Then talk to him in German!"

Mrs. Schelling answered with a slow "Well." Two dollars a week would be a desirable addition to her income. Suddenly her face brightened. "The little one can talk to him!"

At this mention of himself, James withdrew to the shadows. But it was not at him that the stranger turned to look. The stranger gave a signal, a sharp stroke of middle finger against palm. In answer, a creature leaped in a single startling curve through the air. It hurled itself from the seat of the automobile and landed on the step between the stranger and James's mother. It was a collie dog, brown as a chestnut.

"Isn't he a beauty?" The young man did not wait for an answer. While James's mother gasped at the suddenness with which the dog had hurled himself at her, his master put him through a series of tricks. He said one word and the collie sat up on his hind legs, another and he leaped higher than his master's head.

"You will keep him?" said he, like one who is accustomed to obedience. "Robin, you are to stay here till I come."

Without another word, the young man stepped into his car. There was a whirring noise, a jolt of wheels, and the car moved. The ribbon of light rolled itself up until it vanished like the gloves of a magican. Loneliness and darkness descended once more upon the little farm; the spring evening seemed like a dark winter night.

"James!" called Mrs. Schelling.

James came out of his hiding place into the pale light by the door. His blue eyes almost popped from his head. He looked up at his mother and she looked down at him. Between them, the collie turned warm brown eyes from one to the other. Neither

220

mother nor son was given to speech, not because their minds traveled with especial slowness, but because their thoughts were alike.

"It is a dog!" said James's mother slowly in German, as though she could not believe in his presence.

"Will he stay all the time here?" asked James in the English which his mother required.

"Till winter. This was young Harmon from town."

"Will he bite?" asked James in dread.

"No, he is kind." Mrs. Schelling started with pails and lantern toward the barn. "You are to sit with him till I come back."

"He might run away from me!" objected James.

"Then call him! He will come if you call him. His name is Amshel in English. You can say it."

James sat on the doorsill and the dog lay on the step. James was in an ecstasy compounded of delight and terror. If he had ever desired a dog, he had not asked for one. He was a person who accepted the existent as the inevitable. Now he was afraid, not so much that the dog would bite him, as that the beautiful creature would scorn him. This was a rich dog, a proud dog. The Harmons lived in a great and wonderful house. James looked down embarrassed at his soiled bare feet, then solemnly back at the brown eyes.

For a long time he did not move. He could hear the sound of the milk streaming between his mother's strong fingers into the pails; he could hear an owl hoot in the distance and a whippoorwill call near at hand. At the latter dismal sound, accustomed as he was to it, he moved a little on the step, as though, under pressure of loneliness, he dared seek acquaintance with his proud companion.

"Robin!" said little James. "You—you doggy!"

Then the dog did a strange thing. James recounted it shyly to his mother when she came from the barn. Though speech was difficult, this pleasant experience must be imparted.

"Mother," said he. "I spoke to him by name and he licked me!"

James's mother looked down at the pair. The collie sat with his head on the little boy's knee, and James's arm was round his neck. The tears gathered in her eyes as she carried the heavy pails into the kitchen. Perhaps she thought of the human playmates whom James might have had if life had been dfferent.

For a week the collie was not allowed to leave the yard. When James started for the cows, the dog accompanied him to the gate and waited there till he came back. He did not seem to miss his master, to whom he had belonged only a short time. When James came in sight he barked like mad.

One evening James started later than usual. The shadow of the mountain lay already on the farm; to go toward it was like entering a darkening cave. Mrs. Schelling came twice to the door to bid him go.

"Take him with you!" She never ventured upon the dog's name. The collie had become "him" as all masters of Pennsylvania German households are "him."

The little boy leaped and shouted.

"Dare I?"

"Why, yes. He knows enough to come back."

Then was the gate of Paradise opened. The two went down the lane with the speed of greyhounds, but with the erratic course of June bugs. They advanced and they receded, retracing their steps from pure joy. They screamed and barked together. The little boy was transformed; he behaved as though he had become insane. His mother called to him to drive the cows carefully, and as though to make up for the soberness of the return, the two behaved all the more crazily. The collie sprang over fences; he sprang over the little boy's head. The little boy, a week ago so sober and quiet, danced like a Maenad or like a fakir of India. He drowned out the cry of the whippoorwill with his wild clamor, his shrieks and song. The stories which his mother had told him were strange, superstitious tales brought almost two centuries ago from Germany; he shouted out the names of their heroes in foolish reiteration, "Old Till Eulenspiegel, Old Sir Devil, Old Till Eulenspiegel!"

The cows walked home slowly, but behind them were strange doings. The little boy danced into the shadows, apostrophizing them scornfully.

"Oh, you nix nutz under the tree! Oh, you black man by the wall! Oh, you fat pig in the corner!" He shrieked with laughter as though his sentiments were the wittiest in the world. He beat at the shadows and kicked them. There was nothing in the universe which he feared.

All the summer Paradise continued. The little boy explored the mountain upon which he had hitherto never dared to set foot. He went far from home along the country roads. When a man spoke to him roughly, the collie leaped at the stranger with the same curving swiftness with which he had leaped from his master's automobile.

When school opened, the dog went with the little boy to the schoolhouse and lay in the corner of the room, being often used as an example by the teacher. The teacher regarded James with astonishment. From the most quiet of her pupils he had become the noisiest.

When September changed to October, the cows were once more fetched at twilight. The progress to the pasture was still as wild as a June bug's flight. The evenings were cool; the two would have moved swiftly even if life had not danced within them.

The little boy had for some time crossed the bridge by walking on the handrail, with the dog barking in admiration or fright below him. The night of the first frost his foot slipped and he plunged head first into the dark pool. He could swim, but the icy water bound him with fetters. He sank and rose and sank again in spite of all his frantic efforts to strike out with feet and hands. Then, beside him, he felt a support at which he could clutch, his fingers sank into a shaggy coat, and in an instant his feet touched the rising bank.

Foolishly, he went on for the cows, not dashing about and shaking himself as the collie did, but walking slowly, and trying to choke back his sobs. He could scarcely pull the pasture bars out of their sockets or follow the slow pace of the cows. They had crossed the bridge before he had left the shadows of the alders.

When he reached the bridge he gave a sharp cry. Again the light in his mother's kitchen was invisible; again there stretched

223

to his feet a broad, shining ribbon up which Daisy, and Mooley and Bess were making their placid way. He called the dog in terror but he did not come. Already four flying feet had carried the collie up the lane to the side of the young man on the step. Mrs. Schelling faced him, her lantern in one hand, a roll of money in the other.

"I do not like to take it," said she. "He was like a person to us." She could see the little boy creeping along the edge of the lighted road.

"I'm much obliged to you," said the young man. "There is something for your little boy, too." He gave a brisk command and the dog hurled himself into the car. There was a whir, a jolt of wheels, and the ribbon of light rolled itself up once more.

Mrs. Schelling waited for the little boy on the doorstep.

"Come in, little James." She laid her hand on his shoulder. "My child, you are wet!"

The little boy could make no answer, but stood with contorted face, trembling. His mother felt of him, questioning him wildly. "What has happened? You were in the water? What ails you?"

At last the little boy found his voice.

"I fell in the creek. He pulled me to the bank! Oh, mother, mother, mother!"

Mrs. Schelling stripped off his clothes and began to rub the shivering body. Then she wrapped him in a blanket and took him in her arms. Daisy and Mooley and Bess waited long to be milked.

In the frosty morning the little boy went for the cows. His icy plunge had not hurt him, but he moved slowly. In the evening he cried softly all the way to the pasture and all the way home, too smitten with grief to observe the threatening shadows.

But the next evening the shadows were in their places, darker, more terrible than ever. They seemed like sentient beings who would remember that he had mocked this one, had thrust that one with a sword of wood. They had grown larger; he could scarcely find a path between them and the fence. When he came

224

to the house his face was so white that his mother was frightened.

"I could get you a dog," said she.

"Oh, no!" cried James. "Oh, no, mother!"

By November, darkness had fallen completely when the little boy came home with the cows. There was still green pasturage in sheltered places, but it was far away. The little boy had to go around the enormous, rustling crown of a fallen tree; he had to encircle a pile of huge boulders. The autumn wind made crackling noises in the underbrush; the shadows thrust out arms to seize him. He dared not run and he was afraid to walk slowly. He tried to keep between the cows, but they wandered uncertainly from side to side, stupidly unaware of his human need.

One evening the cows were restless. James was late, having postponed his journey as long as he dared. The sky was black and the air was full of threatening sounds. When James thought he heard padding feet and panting breath he stood still and screamed. Then his cry changed to a shout.

"Is it thou!" laughed he. "Thou! Thou!"

His mother waited for him at the barn gate and did not see his shining eyes till he came into the kitchen.

"What ails you?" she asked.

"He was here," answered the little boy.

"He? Who?"

"*He,* mother! He brought me till over the bridge, then he went home."

"It cannot be!"

"He was here," insisted the little boy.

The next evening James came home again with shining eyes. His mother looked at him in terror.

"He was here again," said James quietly. "He was here with me till the bridge. He remembers about the bridge."

In the morning, Mrs. Schelling went out in the starlight to talk to the dairyman who fetched her milk cans.

"Do you think I could buy this dog?" she asked. "My little one is—is—" she could not say the dreadful thing she feared.

The dairyman shook his head.

225

"That dog cost two hundred dollars. If that young fellow wanted the moon he could have it. All his life he has everything."

Mrs. Schelling was now terrified because she had had in her house so valuable a creature. She wished that she had never seen the young man and his dog.

That afternoon the young man himself rode up the lane and beckoned Mrs. Schelling to the gate.

"My dog runs away every day. Does he come here?"

"The little one says he does." Mrs. Schelling drew a deep breath of relief.

"Where is the little boy?"

"At school."

"Tell him to drive the dog home." The young man spoke angrily. It was easy to see that he had always had everything. "Tell him to throw a stick at him. He's cunning as a fox about getting off."

Having issued his commands, the young man pulled a lever and the car slid down the hill.

Mrs. Schelling gave James the young man's order.

"You are to throw him with a stick and drive him off."

James laughed. "He would only fetch the stick!"

"I will drive him off. The man talked as if we would steal him!"

The next evening Mrs. Schelling crossed the bridge to meet the returning procession. The cows moved placidly along, behind them the little boy laughed and waved his arms, beside him leaped the collie. The litle boy did not see his mother until he was almost upon her.

"Mother!" he screamed. "Do not hurt him!"

The collie ran forward and took Mrs. Schelling by her apron and skirt. When he could release her for an instant, he barked for joy.

"You lump!" cried Mrs. Schelling in a furious tone. "You bad dog!" Mrs. Schelling's voice weakened a little. "You rascal! you scoundrel! Go home!" The last words were as weak as the chirp of a sparrow. Mrs. Schelling had seen suddenly over her shoulder the black pool beside the bridge. "Oh, *please* go home!" she cried.

At the end of another week the young man came again. This time he waited until James came from school.

"You must drive him home," he commanded sternly. "I can't keep him penned up night and day. He's growing to be a tramp dog. Do you feed him?"

"No," answered Mrs. Schelling

"I save him sometimes a little something from dinner," confessed James.

"You're ruining him. He'll have to be beaten if he doesn't stay at home. Remember! I'm determined to conquer him."

That evening the collie waited at the bars.

"Tomorrow I will chase him," said the little boy. The next day he said again "tomorrow," and the next. When six days had passed he still had done nothing. Then the collie came panting, walking heavily, with welts from a whip on his back.

"Oh, you must stay home!" wailed the little boy.

To his terror the collie would not leave him at the bridge. But if he did not go home he might be killed. James picked up the end of a fence rail and threw it with all his strength and the collie dropped as though he had been shot.

Somehow the little boy and his mother got the dog to the kitchen. His eyes were open and he breathed, otherwise he gave no sign of life. James sat beside him on the kitchen floor, speechless with woe. Suddenly he began to cry.

"The man is coming!"

Mrs. Schelling met the stranger at the door in the glare of light from the automobile lamps.

"The little boy threw him with a stick," said she.

The young man crossed the room and knelt down and passed his hand over the thick coat and the sleek legs. The cruel welts were still there; it was not the little boy who had hurt the dog.

"He's not badly hurt; he's only tired out."

Then the young man moved his hand quickly away from

227

a wet, warm, forgiving touch, and got to his feet. He looked about the simple room, bare of everything but the necessities of life, at the hardworking woman and at the little boy in his homemade clothes. He was himself not much more than a boy, and indulgence and prosperity had not yet so hardened him that his heart could not be touched. Now if he conquered anything it was a creature much harder to conquer than a dog.

"You may keep him," said he, in his clear sharp way.

James gave a startled cry. "For always?"

"Yes," said the young man, "for always."

Truest of the Breed

BY JACK O'BRIEN

*T*HE log house near which the dog kennel stood was long and wide, with one end open, through which could be seen on either side square pens separated by a central aisle. The only other building on the property was a small cabin snuggled deeply in the shadows at the farther end of the grove, perhaps a hundred yards distant from the largest one. Along the outer wall of the cabin climbed a rudely constructed stone chimney and from this blue-gray smoke drifted lazily out on the breeze. Four windows, one in each wall, square-cut and edged with heavy wooden shutters which swung outward, permitted sunshine to

229

filter within the hut. The one door to this building now stood open. Leaning easily against its frame were two men. Both were dressed as ranchers in soft wide-brimmed hats, boots, well-worn overalls and heavy shirts.

Abruptly leading the way to the kennel yard, the tall man dug into the pocket of his overalls and produced materials for a cigarette. As he dusted tobacco into the brown paper, he asked, "What do you think of them, Willis? Looks like we'll get one dog out of the bunch, eh?" He sealed the cigarette with his tongue and fumbled for a match.

Willis shoved his hat back on his head; a mop of pale yellow hair fell loosely over his forehead. "Yeah, but he ain't goin' to be any good," came the reply in a harsh, rasping voice. "You can't get a good sheep dog out of that lot. Take my tip and get rid of them all, Trent."

"No, Willis, I think you are wrong," Trent replied, as he blew forth a column of smoke. "Look at that pup! Small as he is, he's the picture of his mother and she was the best sheep dog in Australia, and I've never yet seen one here in the States to equal her. When Strand gave her to me, he told me what she'd be like. He said I'd never have to worry about her turning killer. Though the truth is, Willis, there's really no special brand of dog you can say will make a sheep dog. Shucks! I remember Bill Watson had a little bobtailed mutt over in Ranger Basin that could do anything with the band but shear 'em, and he was a mixture of everything under the sun. The whole thing depends on the dog's nature and how he is handled at first." He puffed for a minute, then walking away, turned his attention to other things. In the meantime, through the fence, Sultana and her babies watched the two men.

That the small dog mentioned was the single one of the litter who had bred true to the blood of Sultana, the mother, was certain. From the very first this fact was evidenced in different ways. He was the only male of the four and from the time his eyes opened, the difference between him and his sisters was startling in physical characteristics as well as in disposition.

Some unaccountable throwback in the processes of nature

230

had robbed the little females of that heritage of beauty and symmetry which distinguished their mother. This was manifested differently in each—in the dull, mottled coat of one, the short, blunt muzzle of another, the floppy ears and ropelike tail of the third. All these things gave the lie to purity of strain.

But this was not so with the male. The stamp of the true German shepherd was on him. From Sultana, through whose veins surged the purest blood of generations of that stock, he had inherited the well-shaped head, small, pointed ears, long sensitive nose, and gracefully molded legs. From his father, Fangs, a Mexican shepherd who had been killed by a wolf several weeks earlier, he had received a rare gentleness of disposition. This quality was not to be confused with timidity, but was rather an understanding of and a consideration for weakness, characteristics sometimes found in a brave man.

His development, too, was more rapid than that of his sisters. Tumbling about in the warming rays of the sun which flooded the valley, the little pups throve and grew, pulsating to the wondrous chemistry of light and heat, thrilling in every fiber, squealing in delight at the tingling sensations of just being alive. In the beginning the sun's brilliance dazzled them uncomfortably, and the male's eyes were the first to become focused and farseeing. Even during the preceding period of darkness he was able to identify his sisters as well as the mother who fed them and cuddled them protectingly to her warm side. He could tell one from the other by pressing his cool little nose along their necks or jaws. Thus did the senses of smell and touch receive their first training, and in much the same manner was hearing developed.

When the mother grew weary of the pups' constant tumbling and restless shifting about her, the little dog soon learned from the growl vibrating in her throat that she was losing her temper and that the danger of a quick reprimand was imminent. If the youngsters had already been fed and there was no reason for restlessness, Sultana's growl became more menacing, and when her repeated signals were not heeded, she would cuff the puppies smartly with her paws and send them sprawling in a heap until they were none too gently chastised into submission. After the little females had dozed off into fretful sleep, the mother would sound a low rumble of approval and contentment, and from this tone her son, still half awake, would know that once again all was well.

For perhaps a month the limitation of their world was the fence about the small yard encircling the kennel. Here a man appeared regularly and handed down a pan of milk or a plate of meat to Sultana. At first sight this strange figure terrified the puppies, and they would scurry in fright through the door of their house to seek refuge on the straw in the far corners, their faces resting on small outstretched paws as they whimpered for their mother to protect them. Surprisingly, the latter seemed not in the least alarmed by this being who brought her food, and she would stand for long minutes while the man talked to her, petting her smooth sides and stroking her head. At last the pups began to understand that the man signified kindliness rather than harm and they allowed him to pick them up and fondle them. As they grew accustomed to his presence, they would climb on their hind legs against the fence, and peering through the cracks of the boards, await his approach which was greeted by a terrific din of yelps and squeals.

Now and then Sultana would leap swiftly over the wall and disappear. This was terrible for her family. Their mother was gone and that ended everything, as far as they could reason. To them there was no world except the small enclosure of their yard tented by the blue sky overhead. When their mother vanished over the fence, she became a part of some other existence which they did not share. All they knew was that she was gone, and they sprawled on their haunches and howled sadly of their plight to all the world. Then suddenly she was back. For a brief startled second the little animals would be quiet, but this interlude of bewilderment passed quickly as they swarmed about their mother in rejoicing. Before long, however, these things took on a definite meaning in the consciousness of the dogs and they came to accept them without question.

With growth each puppy began to assume an individuality

in appearance, and the male's resemblance to his mother increased steadily. A solid black hue, which glistened in the sun, began at his haunches and ran forward to a point just behind his shoulders. There the color changed to a golden tan, extended downward on all four legs and, encircling his neck and chest, formed a handsome light-brown collar. The black which wrapped his back like a blanket occurred again in a well-defined triangle on his forehead and, at first glance, looked as if a mask had been placed on the brown head and muzzle. Tan was again predominant, although in a darker shade, on the tail which was thickly furred and carried high in a plume.

The rest of the litter were not as distinctive. Each had a dull, gray-black coat, metallic in tone, on legs, chest and belly, and deepening somewhat across the back and upper haunches. This coloring bore so little resemblance to either Sultana or the dead Fangs that one found it difficult to believe that these youngsters were of the same parentage as their brother. As they grew older, this relationship was even harder to understand, for he shared few of his sisters' characteristics. Even in their play they showed a viciousness almost never found in him. They attacked each other in terrible rages, sinking their small teeth into collars and ears, tumbling and mauling and squealing for hours at a time. Then tiring of this and eager for excitement, they would finally descend on their mother in a body until she cuffed them across the yard where they sprawled, yipping to themselves and eying her with an aggrieved air.

Their brother seldom entered into their play. He spent most of his time sniffing about the kennel, exploring the small yard, digging at the base of the fence in an unceasing search for something which he never seemed to find. When he rested, it was to lie between Sultana's paws and doze in the warm sunlight. Once in a while the other pups would break through this apparent aloofness and swarm over him. Perhaps because he was larger, perhaps because of innate gentleness or some desire for companionship, he permitted them many liberties. As they grew too fierce, he had a trick of clamping his teeth suddenly on an aggressor's foreleg which brought forth an immediate howl of pain. This punishment was so unpleasantly similar to that which they were used to receiving from their mother that they learned gradually to leave him to his own devices. As a result, he experienced a faint loneliness, but this was tempered by satisfaction in being undisturbed at moments when his nose, sniffing about the quarters, would seem to be on the verge of a great discovery. That nothing ever came of these quests bothered him little. He had too many other things to think about. Daily, in his limited confines, he was learning facts that were to stand him in good stead later on.

The first rainfall caught him in an exposed corner of the kennel yard and left him wet, cold and miserable. What had happened he had no idea, but when the second shower came he looked about, noticed that his mother entered the kennel at once, and followed her within. Inside the shelter his body remained comfortable, and after that the first sign of falling water led him to seek protection.

The second lesson concerned successful avoidance of pain. From the time that the puppies were able to eat solid food, their rations were brought to them in a deep metal dish, large enough for all to gather about and yet sufficiently shallow for them to reach its contents. One day when the meal was finished and the others had gone off to lie down, the little male returned to the plate and was rewarded by the sight of a juicy morsel resting on the bottom at the side farthest from him. He plumped his heavy paws on the metal lip and stretched his neck toward the scrap. At once the dish rose at a right angle and hit him sharply on the nose. Yelping, he fell back from this assault, raced over to his mother, and flopping down beside her, whimpered his complaint about the thing that had hurt him. Never again would he eat from a container of any sort or shape, and he attempted to satisfy hunger by the bits that others dropped about the yard, until this habit of self-imposed starvation was noticed and his portion tossed on the ground at feeding time. For the rest of his life he approached food with wariness.

Daily, although he knew nothing about any existence outside the fenced-in yard, he became more interested in extending

234

his environment. Without question he accepted the kennel and the earth on which it stood, the vastness of air and sky across which moved a circle of dazzling brightness which in some un-accountable way poured warmth on his plump, furry body, the regular appearance of food, the occasional loss of his mother's companionship when she leaped over the fence, the unpleasant dropping of water on him from above. These things were for the first weeks not a part but the whole of his life. Beyond them, however, was a restlessness somewhere within him that led him into the constant exploration of the enclosure.

One morning, sniffing as usual at the base of the fence boards, the little dog felt a sudden cool breeze touch his nostrils. Interested, he stretched a paw toward the narrow crack which was opening between the wooden panel and the ground, and with a vague, halting motion began to scratch. His claws sank into the soft earth and as he drew them back a small depression appeared, permitting not only wind but light to filter beneath the barrier. Excited by this, he began digging wildly with both paws. The tunnel swiftly grew larger and the loosened dirt flying back between his legs proved a delightful diversion.

With no warning of any kind, a blow struck him which sent him spinning across the yard. Bruised and dazed he struggled to his feet only to have his mother march up and cuff him painfully about the head. When he managed finally to slip away from her into a dark corner of the kennel, he crouched there trembling with fear and bewilderment.

Sultana at once returned to the excavation, pawed vigor-ously at the loosened earth, padded it down, and then stretched out on these repairs. This time her prone position did not mean sleep. Instead her eyes sought out her son's hiding place and concentrated on that spot. Each time he moved a muscle, his mother growled warningly—certain evidence of disapproval. Why digging earth under the fence should have brought such severe punishment, the little dog had no way of telling, but one thought became clear in his brain: he would not do so soon again. These incidents were but the first of similar ones, com-mon to the life of any animal.

At various times in the future he would find himself innocently enough engaging in activities which brought swift, sure punishment in their wake. His own intelligence would have no way of warning him to avoid these infringements on the rules and standards set by the human creatures who ran his world, nor would he ever be able to understand the pain and disgrace that followed such courses of action. One fact only he would learn from each experience: that it must never be repeated. And this ability to gain wisdom from a first lesson set him, even in his earliest puppyhood, head and shoulders above his playful and unheeding sisters.

Exhausted, he fell asleep, and his mother, after a time, left the repaired break in the fence and stretched beside her son. Years earlier in far-off Australia, when she was not much older than this small dog of her own, she, too, had delighted in digging beneath fences. In doing so she had broken a law of the ranch on which she lived and in penalty she had been lashed. That agony had never been forgotten, and today, in order to save the favorite in her litter from the same possible fate, she had used her only method of warning him in time. It was the worst punishment she had ever given him and he would not soon forget. Her duty done, she leaned over and began to lick him gently with her tongue.

A new life in Alaska

Trail of Danger

BY ESTHER BIRDSALL DARLING

When Blake Carson joined his mining father and new stepmother, Paula, in Alaska he brought along a mongrel waif dog he had found on the pier in Seattle. Luck became his close companion in the raw new land, and a good trail dog. As this story opens Blake's father has gone out to his mine, leaving Paula and Blake in Nome.

T O WA R D the end of March there were many cases of influenza in Nome and in the smaller interior villages. It was decided to close the schools for a week or two, as many of the pupils were ill and there was much talk of a general epidemic.

One night about ten o'clock, as Paula and Blake sat reading, the telephone bell rang and Blake answered. "Oh, Moose, she's here; just a minute." Moose Jones, an old friend, had gone out to the mine with his father. There had been a haste that was almost curt in his request to speak to Paula at once, with no usual words of greeting to the boy.

Paula listened tensely and then said in a voice that was not quite steady, "I think so, too, and we *could* start at once. No? Tomorrow, then, as early as possible. Yes, I think I have everything, but I'll speak to the doctor."

She hung up the receiver, and Blake saw that she was pale and greatly disturbed. "Your father has influenza and is at the Polar Star."

"Is he very sick?" Blake asked.

"Moose is afraid so, and he's not inclined to be nervous about such things. It seemed a very light case until this morning, when my brother and Moose became worried and took him by dog team to the roadhouse."

"Did they think that was better than keeping him at the mine?"

"It's easier to get a doctor there if he requires one and a nurse if I need help. I told Moose we could start immediately, but he said to talk to Dr. Sloane about medicines and bring them with us. It's so late he thought we'd better wait until morning. Night driving isn't easy with the trails in bad shape."

She rang up the doctor, and Blake jotted down his instructions as Paula repeated them. "He says he has some serious cases in the hospital here and he doesn't want to leave them unless it's absolutely necessary. I'm to let him know when we arrive there tomorrow night."

Paula found that she had in the house all the remedies the doctor had suggested. She packed them in a small box, wrapping it carefully in oiled silk and then in canvas. "We don't want anything to get damp, and we may have to go through overflows that would wet everything in the sled that is not protected."

By six o'clock in the morning their bags were packed and the dogs harnessed. It was cold and dark, and the sky was covered with black clouds. "We may be in for a blow before the day is over," Paula remarked as she put on a fur parka and covered it with one of drill. "Have you on your heaviest clothes, Blake?"

"Yes, and I'm so cluttered up with them that I can hardly move. If it should be warmer after a while I'll have to peel them off in layers, like an onion."

238

Before they started, Paula rang the Polar Star and asked for Moose Jones. When she came out to the kennel, Blake asked eagerly, "Any better news?"

She shook her head. "No. He had a restless night and they can't seem to break the fever. Moose is much relieved that we're coming. He told your father but was not certain that he understood. That sounded to me as if he might be delirious. Oh Blake, I'm terribly worried."

The streets were empty at that hour, and only an occasional light gleamed from the windows of some house where there were early risers. Blake had never seen Nome look so dreary. Perhaps it was partly because he himself was depressed and knew how anxious Paula was. They hardly spoke except when he asked her if she was comfortable or she suggested that she drive for a while.

As they passed through Fort Davis there was no one stirring; and the tiny shacks of fishermen and Eskimos dotted along the coast were as quiet as if they had been permanently deserted. It was only when they reached Cape Nome roadhouse, several miles beyond the fort, that there were signs of life.

"We'll go in and have coffee, Blake. Mushers stop here constantly; we may pick up valuable information from them."

They found a man at breakfast who was on his way from Council to Nome. Paula asked him if he had had any trouble.

"I'll say I had, ma'am, a lot. I ain't stuck on traveling in this country in spring; worst season of the whole year. You can't ever depend on anything. Weather changing every few minutes, ice getting rotten, snow slushy because of thaws, sun so strong you get snowblind from the glare; or maybe no sun at all, just a fog like the one I struck yesterday. It was so thick I felt like I was wrapped round tight in a dirty gray blanket. Believe me, if I didn't have business in town I wouldn't have left home till after the breakup when the water's running and you know just what's ahead of you. Ice that's uncertain ain't no joke in the North. You'd better not start on a trip now if you don't have to."

On most of the streams, however, and on the lagoons near

239

Solomon they found the ice still capable of bearing the weight of the loaded sled. Often they halted the team, and Paula and Blake went ahead to see if there were any visible indications that it was unsafe. "Many of the older dogs, the really experienced leaders," Paula said, "would know such a thing instinctively. But we can't expect Tom to be so wise; he's too new at the game. And as for Luck—well, he's a cheechako yet."

"How can *we* tell if it's not all right, Paula?"

"I'm afraid I'm not very good at it myself. But if there are cracks beginning to appear and water oozing through them from below, we'll try for a spot that looks more solid. At that people have traveled a long distance over ice that has shallow water all over it and have had no serious difficulty. But we want to keep our medicines and supplies as well as ourselves dry, so we'll be careful. We can't afford to take any unnecessary chances."

Because of the softness of the trail their progress was slow and tedious. The dogs frequently sank to their shoulders in mushy snow, and Paula and Blake pushed the sled from the back to ease their burden. It was later than they had planned when they stopped for lunch at Solomon. Here, too, they rang up the Polar Star. Sandy Watson, who worked at the roadhouse, answered. "Moose is up with Mr. Carson. I don't want to scare you, but we're afraid it's pneumonia. We're sure glad you're coming, and the sooner the better. Moose Jones is doing all he can, but Tom Barstow's not much good at nursing, and I've got to run the place and do the cooking."

Paula tried to persuade herself that Sandy was *always* an alarmist, even over unimportant things. But there was an anxiety in his voice that she could not dismiss from her mind.

At the Solomon roadhouse were several mushers who had come up the coast that morning. All reported hard sledding.

"We're only going as far as the Polar Star," Paula explained to one of the men, "and we want to make the fastest time possible. Someone told me once that you can save several miles by taking to the ice of Bering Sea below here, instead of following the shore line. Did you do that?"

"Not me," the man answered emphatically. "There is a

240

trail across the ice that's shorter, and I guess a lot of people use it in midwinter. But"—he shook his head discouragingly—"you know how treacherous ice is at this season; and the warmer weather we've been having the last couple of weeks eats into it quick. Besides, I wasn't in any hurry."

"But we are in a hurry—in a terrible hurry," Paula exclaimed.

"Well, you can give it the once-over when you get to the place where the trail branches and make up your mind then. But I can't say I'd choose it for myself."

Their pace was slower than ever after they left Solomon, for the dogs were plainly growing tired. Several times they had to rest, and the weary dogs threw themselves down in the damp snow while Paula and Blake sat in the sled. They were tired, too, for they had continued to push whenever possible; but they were nervously eager to get on, and the necessary delays were almost unbearable to them.

From the time they left Cape Nome the weather had been variable. Slight flurries of snow changed to sleet, the moist dampness being more penetrating than clear cold would have been at a much lower temperature. From the deep, funnel-like draws that ran back into the mountains on their left came fierce gusts of wind that made it difficult for the dogs to keep their feet. But worst of all was the icy fog that occasionally blotted out everything about them. They could not see Luck at all, and even Jimmy and Pete, in the wheel,[1] were like blurred shadows.

The fog had lifted when they reached the point where the trail over the ice separated from the main one along the coast. They stopped again at Paula's order to Luck. "Blake," she said, "we'd better talk this over. I've no idea just how much time we'd save by going over the ice, but every minute may count. If your father really has pneumonia I might be able to do something for him that those men would not know about. I've had quite a bit of experience as a nurse. But you heard what that man said at Solomon. He evidently thinks there's some risk. I'd be willing

---

[1] *in the wheel:* the positions next to the sled. The miners used wagon team expressions in referring to sled dog teams.

241

to take it for myself, but it's not fair of me to decide the matter for you."

"Gee, Paula, you don't think I'm scared to tackle anything you're ready to try, do you? I don't see what could be really dangerous about it. The worst thing that could happen, I guess, would be to strike heavier going than we've had already; and I don't believe there *is* any, any place. I'm game for it."

Paula still hesitated. "You don't know the North. A lot of things that you've never heard of can happen here. Not often, perhaps, but——"

"Well, let's not think of them. It's late, and we want to reach the Polar Star before dark, if we can. Come on, let's go!"

"Very well," she replied slowly, "but I *do* know the possible dangers, and if we find we've done the wrong thing I'll feel responsible."

"You needn't. I want to take the short cut as much as you do."

They turned directly to the right, running through many small pools that did not, however, come up to the body of the sled, so that the robe and bags in it, carefully covered, were still dry.

"The ice has rotted here worse than in any place we've seen yet," Paula remarked. "We may be making a mistake in keeping on it; but we've gone over a mile already, I'm sure, and *such* a mile, and I'd hate to go back over it. It may be better farther on."

The new trail had evidently not been used very much lately, for it was not at all as clearly defined as the one they had left; and because it was temporary there were no stakes and flags to outline it. For a short distance it led straight out from shore and then continued southward between tall ice hummocks that towered beside it, grotesque and ghostly in the coming dusk.

Blake felt sorry for the dogs, who panted and strained, but nothing could be done except to let them halt frequently. Luck, who had none of the burden of pulling, was far fresher than the others. He ran ahead as usual, and was often out of sight behind the pinnacles of rough ice through which they slowly wound their way. But always he came back and stayed with the team long enough to pace Tom encouragingly.

Suddenly Pete gave a yelp of pain. Blake called, "Stop!" and he and Paula bent over the dog, who was whimpering pitifully. There was a vivid stain on the snow beneath him. They examined his feet and took from the right forepaw a triangular piece of glass that had cut deeply into the pad.

"Oh, Blake," Paula cried in dismay, "how careless people are to throw a broken bottle on the trail. Just see what trouble it causes. Poor Pete can scarcely take a step, and he'll have to ride in the sled. Even if it makes it a lot heavier, the rest of the team can't drag him along in harness, and it would be cruel to try to keep him on his feet."

Paula took a roll of bandages from her bag. She probed the wound but finding no more glass, skillfully bound up the injury. They lifted Pete into the sled and made him as comfortable as possible.

"We'll have to shift the dogs into different places," Paula said. "Harry must go into the wheel with Jimmy and Tom beside Dick. Then if there's any leading to do, it's up to Luck."

Just then Luck, who had disappeared for an instant, came toward them barking in the greatest excitement. He tugged at Blake's parka and ran again in the direction from which he had just come, repeating this several times.

"Go and see what's the matter, Blake, while I change the dogs."

Blake followed Luck but returned with him shortly. "I don't understand it, Paula, but just beyond the next line of hummocks there's water."

"Water! You mean an overflow—larger than the pools we've crossed?"

"No, I mean——"

But Paula did not wait. She dashed ahead, and when Blake caught up with her she was standing, tense and motionless, looking at a wide strip of water on the edge of which the trail ended abruptly.

When she turned, her face was white and her voice was

243

unsteady. *"This* is one of the dangers of which I spoke, Blake. The ice of Bering Sea has begun to break, and the lead between this floe and the next must be two or three hundred feet wide. There's no possible way of our crossing it, and even if we did, it may be broken in a dozen places beyond."

"What can we do, Paula?"

"We must go back the same way we came and see if we can't reach the other trail before this field becomes entirely separated from the coast. When once the ice begins to rot through, a stiff offshore wind will move it rapidly. Only last year I went to bed with the sea in front of Nome covered with large floating floes, and in the morning they were entirely out of sight; so you see how necessary it is to hurry."

They began retracing their way, but it was slower work than ever. The dogs plodded along wearily, feeling the added burden in the sled. Paula and Blake pushed from the rear, rarely saying a word. Then at last, emerging from the high ridges of ice that had hid all but what was immediately before them, they stopped short, appalled. Here again was open water which stretched, a long thin line as far as they could see, between themselves and land. It was dotted sparsely with small bergs which had become detached from the main field.

Paula gazed in consternation at the shore, now growing slightly indistinct in the twilight. "I'm sure it's not half a mile away, perhaps much less—it's difficult to tell about distances over water," she said finally. "But so far as our being able to get across, it might as well be ten miles."

"Someone may see us from the trail and go and get a boat," Blake answered hopefully. "All of the roadhouses and Eskimo settlements along here have them."

"If only it were daylight that might be possible. We could stand the sled upright and put my red sweater on top of it as a signal—it would show plainly against the white of the ice and snow. But it'll be dark soon—if we could build a fire, it might attract attention, but there's nothing to burn but the sled, and that's hardwood and there's no paper or kindling."

"Not a thing, not even a bit of driftwood."

244

"This field must have been blown free of land just after we took to it, Blake. I remember there was a strong seaward wind then. We've lost a lot of time since because of the bad trail and poor Pete's accident, and the high ridges that were between us and shore kept us from seeing what was happening. Oh, if it hadn't been for me we would have been perfectly safe now and near the Polar Star."

"See here, Paula, please don't feel that way. I was as keen as you to come this way. I told you so then, and I meant it. Something'll turn up for us. Why, it *must!*"

The dogs had again thrown themselves down to rest a short distance from the rim of the floe. "We'll see if we can't figure out something," Paula said as they went to the sled. The boy pushed Pete to one side so that Paula could get in and, spreading the canvas near, he dropped on it.

"Well, it's not very cold, and with all our clothes and the fur robe we can't freeze. That's one good thing."

"I'm not afraid of that. There are other dangers more likely. Listen!"

There was a complete silence, and then Blake could hear, at intervals, a sharp, crackling sound followed by a soft, dull splash.

"That's what I mean. You can't tell when or where these cracks will come, or how wide they'll be. See"—she pointed to a little berg a few yards away—"that broke off from the very place where we were standing a few minutes ago. Wherever we go it may be to a spot that will give way at any instant. And if we should be blown still farther out———" Her eyes filled with tears. "Oh, Blake, it's too terrible!"

"But, Paula, the wind seems to have died down. I don't believe we're moving at all. And the little berg you showed me— it's floating, but not drifting away. As soon as it's light they'll be out looking for us, and they'll see the signal we'll put up."

"Yes, you're right," Paula agreed, recovering herself. "I'm sorry"—she smiled wanly—"that I lost my nerve for a moment. I was thinking of your father and of my foolish haste that brought you into this awful mess. Of course when we don't show up at the Polar Star by the time we're expected, allowing for the heavy going, I'm sure they'll give a general alarm by telephone and a search will be started. There's every chance for us if—if only the wind doesn't come up again and carry us far out, and if the ice beneath us holds firm."

It grew slightly more chilly as the darkness came, but their furs kept them comfortable, and the dogs, unhitched, stayed close together for warmth. There was no fog, and the stars were brilliant in the clear sky.

"Soon there'll be a moon, too," Paula remarked as she walked toward the bank of the floe. "There it is now, coming over the horizon."

"Don't you think you could get some sleep?" Blake asked as he followed her. "You're dead tired, and Pete and the rug'll keep you snug."

"No"—she shook her head—"but I wish you could. There isn't a thing we can do till daylight." She peered across the water toward shore. As the moon rose higher, the coastline with its background of mountains was plainly visible. "It seems so short a distance, Blake, and yet——" Paula gave a startled cry as the snow-covered ice on which she was standing crumbled without warning. Blake, just behind her, grasped her parka and pulled her back from the brink. Her head and shoulders scraped the jagged edge, and when he had dragged her a few yards to safety he saw that there was a deep gash on her forehead from which blood was flowing freely.

"Paula, are you badly hurt?" She did not reply, and Blake saw that her eyes were closed. He carried her to the sled and laid her in it, pillowing her head on Pete's back. Chafing her hands, he tried again and again to rouse her, but there was no response. He wet his handkerchief with snow and bathed the wound till the blood almost ceased and then clotted. Covering her with the robe, he sat beside her. His arm ached from the sudden wrench he had given it when he held her from slipping entirely into the water, but that was nothing in the overwhelming anxiety that confronted him. Adrift on a field of ice; the dangers of which Paula had spoken, that might mean certain death in

Bering Sea. And nothing to do but wait—for what? For any of these things to happen?

He leaned over Paula. She was breathing irregularly and now and then gave a low moan. At least she was alive. If only there was something he could do for her! She'd been a darned good sport always, and kind to him and to Luck from the very first. And his father—a great guy, but he'd only found it out lately, since he came to Alaska. If he ever got out of this jam he'd tell them both all they meant to him. . . .

Blake gazed across the stretch of water. It was absolutely calm, and in the brighter light the land looked nearer than ever. If the field moved no farther, surely they would be sighted the next morning. But the unexpected blows that came down from the mountains and lashed the sea into fury—what of them? They had passed through several earlier, and the man at Cape Nome had said (he remembered the very words) that at this season "the weather changed every few minutes." Of course it didn't quite do that, but in a few hours—an hour, maybe . . .

Luck was pressing close to the boy, and the contact with the dog's sturdy body was comforting. Blake stroked the rough coat, and Luck's tail wagged happily in response. *He* didn't know what they were up against. He—— Then an idea flashed through Blake's mind. Would it be possible to carry it out—would Luck understand?

He quickly returned to the sled. Paula was still very white, and while she did not speak, her breathing was more even. Blake found the box of medicines they had packed the night before. Only twenty-four hours ago! Why it seemed ages and ages. Removing the oiled silk he laid it aside, and with the aid of his flashlight he wrote hurriedly on a page torn from his pocket notebook. Folding this into a compact wad, he wrapped the silk around it many times and tied it tightly with a strong string he had also taken from the box. He drew Luck to him and with trembling fingers fastened it securely to the top of his collar.

With dragging footsteps he went again to the edge of the floe, from which a shining path of light led to the shore. Blake dropped to his knees beside Luck and put his arms around the dog's neck. "It's not so *very* far; not so far as it was from the *Victoria* to Nome. And this time it may—— Oh, Luck, I can't send you like this. I *can't*. You've been the very best friend I've ever had. You saved me the night of the storm, and now I'm——"

Luck placed his paws on the boy's shoulders and licked his cheek.

"Maybe you'll never get there. The water's cold and you're tired." Blake's voice quivered. But there was Paula, himself, the dogs. In Luck lay their one chance, perhaps, for life.

Blake rose slowly to his feet. "Luck," he said solemnly, "you *must* go." The dog, knowing the word so well, pricked up his ears and moved a yard or so toward the team. Apparently it was the only direction he could take, for in the other lay the sea. Blake did not move, and Luck came back to him. What did his master mean? "Go" was plain enough, but where?

"Find 'em—find Moose—find 'em!" Then, with the strength of desperation, he pushed the dog over the brink of the ice, sobbing wildly, "Go, Luck! Go!"

With one uncertain backward look the dog struck out boldly, his dark head rippling the smoothness of the water and his cockade of white and gold glistening in the moonlight.

At the Polar Star Tom Barstow and Sandy Watson had finished their supper, and were waiting impatiently for the arrival of Paula and Blake Carson.

"You'd better keep things hot, Sandy, and I'll go and sit with Mr. Carson while Jones gets something to eat."

Moose Jones came down presently and said, "He's sleepin' quiet an' I reckon that means he's better. He ain't tossed round ner fretted all afternoon."

Sandy brought him food, and when he had finished he glanced at the clock and then out into the darkness. "I'm afeered, Watson, that Mrs. Carson an' the kid's had a bad time of it today, but they'll be here soon now. While Tom's on the job I'll lay down an' take a little snooze. I didn't git much rest last night, and I'll want t' relieve Mrs. Carson when she comes. She'll be all tuckered out, likely."

Sandy read a Seattle newspaper that was two months old and fairly snorted with disgust as he noticed the date. It had come only a few days before. He went to the kitchen from time to time to keep the fire in the range replenished. It was growing late, and he was beginning to worry because the mushers had not arrived. He wondered if he'd better wake Moose to see what he thought about telephoning to Solomon. Maybe they'd decided to make a two day trip of it instead of one. But in case of a change of plans surely they'd have rung up. No, of course it was just some delay along the way, natural enough at this season.

There was furious barking outside, answered by a chorus from the kennel. Sandy went to open the door. "Well, look who's here, Jones. Luck—so the others can't be far behind. I sure am glad, for I was getting fussed about them."

Luck was shivering. He shook himself vigorously, and they saw that he was dripping. Moose Jones came to him and felt of his back. "Why, there ain't a dry hair on him. They must've got into some deep overflows somewheres, an' Mrs. Carson an' Blake'll be chilled t' the bone. How's the fire, Sandy?"

"Pretty nigh red hot. And there's plenty of coffee and steaming food ready."

Luck stood nervously alert, in spite of his evident fatigue. "That's all right," Moose said soothingly, "we know they're comin'. What is it, old scout, want me t' go an' meet 'em?"

Luck dropped to the floor but wagged his tail continuously and looked appealingly into Moose Jones' face, giving sharp, short barks every moment or so.

"He's got somethin' on his mind, Sandy, but I can't figger out what 'tis. His bein' here means the trail was passable, so if he could git through, the others could, too. Now what do you s'pose he's tryin' t' tell us?"

Clara Bow, Sandy's cat, jumped from her basket and came toward Luck amiably, but he did not look at her. Attracted by a yellow object, almost round, on his collar and much like the ball she rolled when she played with him, she touched it; but it was wet and cold, and she drew her paw away quickly. But not before Moose, who was still regarding the dog curiously, discovered it. He bent down and tried to untie the string that held it in place, but it was knotted securely. "Here's something queer, Sandy. Give me a knife."

Sandy handed him a sharp bread knife from the table and, cutting the cord, Moose hastily unwrapped layer after layer of oiled silk, revealing a bit of paper. "Good God, Watson, listen to this:

On ice that has broken from land. Not far out yet but afraid of wind or fog. Writing on chance someone will find message. Come quick with boat. Get word to Polar Star. Moose Jones will know what to do. Just now about opposite place where trail over ice separated from one on shore. Mrs. Carson hurt. Lose no time.

BLAKE CARSON

Tom Barstow came downstairs. "What's all this racket about? Mr. Carson's asleep, but he won't be long if——"

Then Tom saw Luck, and Moose handed him Blake's note. "Well, I'll be——"

"You got a boat here, haven't you?" Moose interrupted.

"Yes," Tom nodded, "it's in the barn and in fine shape. I was overhauling it only a day or so ago."

"Any others near? There's Mrs. Carson, Blake, the dogs an' the sled t' be brung back."

"There's a couple of fishermen not more'n a mile from here right along the trail," Sandy answered, "and they have two big dories."

"Good!" Moose exclaimed. "We'll take one o' theirs an' the men'll go, too. I wish George West hadn't went back t' the mine with our dogs; but you got enough fer two teams ain't you, Tom?"

"Such as they are," Sandy muttered.

"And you, Watson, had better go up to Carson. If he should wake an' ask fer me, say I'm dead tired an' havin' a nap down here. If he asks fer Mrs. Carson an' Blake—— But I don't reckon he will. I don't think he rightly understood they was expected. If

250

he does, though, jest tell him they was delayed at Solomon. We'll be as quiet gittin' ready as we kin."

Moose and Tom went to the barn and loaded the boat on one of the sleds. Luck followed them about slowly and stiffly. He had ceased barking and seemed less disturbed after the message had been taken from his collar; but he did not let Moose Jones out of his sight.

The moon had gone down before they left the roadhouse, but it was still bright starlight and they had no difficulty keeping to the trail, though they found it heavy and hard pulling for the dogs.

When they reached the cabin of the fishermen, the men were still in bed; but they dressed at once and cooked a hearty breakfast. "We might as well eat something," Barstow said. "We need it, and we'll have to wait till daylight anyway. No use in cruising around Bering Sea in the dark."

They placed the smaller of the dories on the extra sled and by dawn had started up the coast.

At last one of the fishermen called, "Here's the spot, Jones, where the ice trail began. I know every inch of this shoreline, and I'm sure this is right."

Luck showed signs of great excitement and leaped from his place in the sled with Moose, running up and down and looking across the water impatiently. "I guess this is just about where he landed last night," Tom Barstow observed. "See him sniffing —finding his own tracks, I'll bet. Nobody's come over it since he did."

They led the teams to the shelter of some leafless willows nearby and left them with the sleds. It took but a short time to launch the boats, as there was no surf, only a gentle lapping of ripples against the snow-covered beach.

The fishermen used their own dory and Moose and Tom Barstow the other. As they pushed off, Luck, in spite of his stiffness, scrambled in with them. "Let him come," Moose said. "It was him that give the alarm an' he sure should share in the rescue operations."

251

The boats were heavy, and with but two oarsmen in each they went slowly. It was quite light, and before long they could see a dark patch against the highest hummock on the edge of the field. "The signal!" Tom exclaimed. "Something red." Then a figure waving to them became clear. "It's the kid, Moose, but Mrs. Carson ain't with him. His message said she was hurt, but I do hope it ain't serious."

The next time they looked, another figure was there. "She's all right, Tom, she's wavin', too."

Luck faced the floe from the bow of the boat and commenced to bark wildly as soon as he sighted Blake. The men renewed their efforts, and shortly they were greeting the Carsons with relief and joy.

While Paula was asking about her husband (she was told that he was much better), and insisting that her wound was nothing, Blake held Luck in his arms. Tears of happiness fell on the dog's head as the boy whispered, "You're the best Luck in all the world!"

New test for Jimmy and Pat

Crisis in the Storm

BY COL. S. P. MEEK

Jimmy Trainor, blinded in a Japanese ambush that killed his valiant patrol dog, Pat the First, found new faith and a new life through his Seeing Eye dog, Pat the Second. He became a successful salesman, married and had his own home. Then, during a hurricane that disrupted both lights and the phone, his wife, who was about to have a child, tripped and fell.

J I M M Y Trainor went to the telephone and dialed slowly and carefully. His hands were trembling so that he knew his movements were clumsy, uncertain. He could hear no sound from the telephone and he replaced the receiver with a groan.

"I'd forgotten the phone was out," he muttered. "What the devil am I to do? I've got to get hold of Dr. Talbot, but I don't dare leave her alone. Oh, why didn't Mother come down this week instead of next?"

He gripped his head with both hands and battled desperately with the problem.

"Mrs. Walsh!" he cried in relief. "She's had two children and she'll have some idea what to do. Eileen, honey, are you feeling better now?"

"Yes, just now I'm feeling okay."

"Fine. Now honey, I've got to leave you alone for a couple of minutes while I get Mary Walsh."

"Jimmy! You can't go out in this storm. Listen to that wind!"

The wind had risen steadily to a howling crescendo and the whole house was shaking and quivering. Eileen shuddered.

"You can't go out," she repeated.

"Nonsense, I've got to go out. Now just relax. I'll be back in two or three minutes. Come, Pat."

With hands that he forced to steadiness by sheer will power he adjusted the dog's harness, put on his slicker and opened the front door. The wind tore it from his grip and slammed it against the building, and it required all of his strength to close it again.

"Forward, Pat," he said.

Pat hesitated. He had been taught that he was responsible for his master's safety and that it was his duty to disobey Jimmy's commands when those commands would lead them into danger. This, he was afraid, was one of those times. It certainly did not look safe to the dog to go out in the face of that storm with the wind howling and the rain driving before it in solid sheets. He ignored the command and sat down.

"Phui!" Jimmy explained sharply. "Forward!"

He shook the harness but Pat did not stir. Jimmy realized that there might be a real obstacle before them and his feet swept the ground as far as he could reach. He could feel the top step and, by reaching, the second, but there was nothing else. Suddenly he understood the dog's reasoning. He sat down beside the shepherd and put his arms around him.

"Listen, Pat," he said earnestly. "We must go on. It may not be safe, but safe or not, we've got to get to Walsh's. I'll have to go alone if you won't come with me. We've got to get help for Eileen."

He hugged the dog close to him, Pat rapidly licking his face.

"We've got to go, old fellow," he repeated. He stood up and took the handle of the harness in his hand.

"Forward," he said sharply. When Pat sat stubbornly still, Jimmy deliberately released his hold on the harness and started alone down the steps to the walk. Instantly Pat was in front of him, crowding him back.

"Phui!" Jimmy cried sternly, shouting to make his voice heard over the howl of the wind. "Phui!" Once more he gripped the harness. "Forward, Pat!"

The dog hesitated a moment, then started forward. Never before in their two-year association had his master spoken so sharply or insisted that the dog obey a command he had once refused. After all, there was no obstacle ahead and no danger immediately threatening, so Pat relegated his judgment of the weather to the background of his canine mind and took up his appointed task of guiding his master where he wished to go.

"Good boy. Good old Pat," Jimmy cried as he stooped and stroked the dog. "We'll do it, storm or no storm. Left," he commanded as they reached the sidewalk.

The wind suddenly died down to a velocity of thirty miles, and it was only a matter of minutes before Jimmy was hammering at the Walsh's door.

"Hello, Jimmy, come in. Why, what's the matter?"

"It's Eileen. She had a fall, and I'm afraid something's going to happen."

"Oh, my Lord!" Mary gasped. "I'll come right over. Wait a minute, let me think. I'd better get some things together."

"I think we've got everything we need, except some help."

"I'll get all the candles we have anyway. I suppose, of course, your lights are out."

"Yes, they are."

Joe Walsh appeared in the doorway.

"What's up?" he asked.

"Eileen Trainor. She is in trouble. I'm going right over."

255

"Of course. I'll go too. Maybe I can help some."

"We can't leave Caroline and Frances alone, Joe. You go to Owens' and get Bill or Hazel to come and stay with the girls, then come over."

Three minutes later Mary Walsh was bending over Eileen, her gentle fingers removing some of the garments whose fastenings had proved too intricate for Jimmy in his excitement.

"I think you're right, Jimmy," she said. "We'll have to have the doctor right away."

"I'm going after Dr. Talbot now."

"In this storm? Jimmy, you're silly. Just hear that wind, it's coming up harder than ever. And it's dark as pitch, too. Wait until Joe gets here and he can go."

"No, I'm going, Mary. I can find my way much easier than Joe. The darkness would confuse him, but it's the same as midday to me."

"Of course it is, I hadn't thought of that angle. It's as dark as midnight out and I know you get all over town. Maybe you're right, but it seems terrible to let you go alone. Let Joe go with you."

"I think he'd just handicap me. Besides, I'm not going alone, Mary, I'm taking my eyes with me, eyes that can see in the dark better than yours or Joe's, ears that can hear better, and a nose that tells things neither eyes nor ears can know. Don't worry about us, Mary. Pat will get me through. Come, Pat, let's go!"

Jimmy settled his hat firmly on his head and mentally reviewed the route he must follow to reach the physician's house.

"Left to the corner, then forward three blocks to Currile. Left for six blocks to Pine and cross street. Right two blocks, then back three houses," he said to himself. "That's not complicated. It would be easy but for this wind."

The wind, which had lulled temporarily, came again with renewed force. The house shook and trembled under the constant blasts. Already most of the blinds had been torn off and carried away into the darkness, and as he listened there was a ripping sound as another broke loose and sailed away on the wings of the storm.

Repeating the directions to himself again as a final check, Jimmy opened the front door. The wind dragged it from his hand and slammed it back against the building. It took all of his strength to fight it back into place. He gripped the handle of Pat's harness and set his back squarely to the house.

"Forward, Pat."

The shepherd did not hesitate. No matter how bad the storm might be Pat realized that his master meant to face it, and it was not for Pat to question the decision. In the face of any obstacle or immediate danger the dog would act, but if Jimmy insisted on plunging into the storm Pat would go with him, to lead him where he wished to go and to guard him from danger along the route. Leaning hard into the wind, he started forward down the path to the sidewalk at his usual trot, a gait which made Jimmy walk briskly to keep from dragging back on the harness.

"Left, Pat," Jimmy commanded as they reached the walk. The wind caught the words and forced them back into his throat, but Pat's sharp ears caught the command and he turned left, directly into the wind.

Jimmy caught his breath with a gasp. This was even worse than he had bargained for. For a moment he leaned into the wind, unable to make any forward progress. His grip tightened on Pat's harness and he knew that he was nanging back. He stooped so that his body would offer less resistance and, a step at a time, fought his way forward. There was a steady pull on his left hand and he knew that Pat was lunging ahead, dragging his master after him.

The wind snatched away his hat and Jimmy felt the hammering of the rain on his head like a shower of small pebbles. His right hand instinctively went to his face to protect it from the battering and to keep rain-drops from being driven up his nostrils. Farther and farther forward he leaned into the on-coming blasts, fighting his way yard by yard. The wind was

257

catching the skirts of his raincoat and they acted like sails, threatening at times to completely halt his progress, even to drive him backward.

"No percentage in this," he grunted. "Anyway, I can't get any wetter than I am, Sit, Pat."

He unfastened the buttons of his coat. The wind grabbed at it gleefully, tore it from his shoulders and whirled it away into the night.

"Forward, Pat."

That was better. Freed from the drag of the coat he found he could go steadily ahead, if not at his usual brisk gait, at least in a steady manner that would not confuse Pat and make the dog think his master was signaling a halt.

"One," he counted as Pat stopped at the first curb. "All right so far. Three more and then left. Forward, Pat."

The dog did not move. Evidently there was a block of some sort which prevented further progress. Jimmy thrust forward an inquiring foot, but he could detect nothing except the curb he had already located. He thrust his foot still farther and enlightenment came. The heavy rain was too much for the drains to carry away and next to the curb was a six-inch-deep stream of rapidly running water. In a moment he was on his knees, feeling ahead. Yes, that was it. The street was flooded. He rose and grasped the harness handle.

"It's okay, Pat," he said. "Forward."

He stepped down confidently. The dog no longer hesitated. He had shown his master an obstacle and his master had investigated it. Evidently it was not a real block. He led Jimmy across the street, stopping at the far curb.

"Forward, Pat," Jimmy said as he stepped up and they resumed their progress.

The next street was flooded also, but they splashed their way across it. In what Jimmy judged was the middle of the next block, Pat stopped. Jimmy felt ahead anxiously, then felt a sense of relief. It was only a downed tree.

"Forward, Pat."

A fallen tree was nothing to worry about; they might en-

258

counter a dozen such obstacles before they reached their goal. Pat led his master out into the street and around the obstacle, then back to the sidewalk and forward in the original direction.

"Two," Jimmy counted as they reached the next cross street. "Forward, Pat."

The wind came in the strongest gust he had yet faced and lean into it as he would Jimmy could not force himself a foot forward. Then, with dramatic suddenness, the wind ceased. Jimmy strove to catch himself but it was too late. He fell sprawling into the water. As he fell, he instinctively released his grip on the harness and he lay there in the wet and darkness, helpless.

For a moment panic gripped him.

"Pat!" he cried. "Pat!"

A strong, hairy body pressed against him and Pat's tongue rapidly assured his master he was not deserted.

"Oh, Pat!" Jimmy cried as he hugged the shepherd. "You good dog. You most awful good dog!"

He regained his feet, the harness gripped in his hand, but, to his horror, he was completely confused in his directions. He could not tell whether he was facing in the same direction he was before he fell or whether he had been turned to the right, the left, or even clear around. The wind had stopped and he no longer had it as a guide. If he told Pat, "Forward," the dog would go in the direction he indicated, which might be altogether wrong. If there were only someone to ask. Jimmy had not thought that the time would come that night when he would pray for wind, but a fervent prayer rose to his lips, then he stopped. Even if wind came, he had experienced hurricanes in the tropics and he knew that sudden calms often presaged a change in the wind's direction, sometimes even a complete reversal. He pressed his hand to his head and thought furiously. Perhaps Pat would maintain his original direction if he were told to go forward. At any rate, it seemed the only hope. With a prayer in his heart, Jimmy spoke.

"Forward, Pat."

The dog went obediently forward and stopped at a curb.

Jimmy's foot told him it was at a right angle to the course they had pursued and the distance seemed about right. They were still on Castner Street, but whether they were going in the right direction or had completely turned around, he could not tell. He started to step up and then struck his hand against his forehead.

"Dumbbell!" he cried. "I deserve to get lost."

Quickly he stooped and held his hand in the water. It had been running to his right, down toward the river which bisected the town. To his relief it was still running to his right. Pat had taken him in the correct direction.

"Good boy," he said as he stroked the dog's wet side. "Forward."

In the middle of the block the wind came again. First a light puff, then a stronger one, then with a roar the full force of the hurricane struck. Again Jimmy found himself leaning into the wind, fighting his way forward literally foot by foot.

"Three," he counted at the next curb. "One more and I turn left."

He could tell by the devious, twisting route Pat was taking that the sidewalk must be littered with debris and he marveled that neither of them had been struck by flying objects. Repeatedly the dog crowded his master to the right or left around some obstacle which lay in their path, and twice he took him off the sidewalk in a wide detour, but each time they came back to the walk.

Above the roar of the wind Jimmy heard an ominous creaking, then a sharp crack. Pat sprung in front of him, crowding him back. Jimmy turned and the dog pulled on him as through to drag him along. The wind was on his back now and he seemed to fly through the air. Behind him came another sharp crack and then a crash. Something struck Jimmy between the shoulder blades and he heard a sharp yelp from Pat. A few feet further the dog slackened his gait, then stopped. Jimmy turned again into the wind. He suspected what had happened and when Pat took him only a few feet into the wind before he stopped, Jimmy's inquiring hands told him he was right. A big elm had given up the struggle against the wind and had crashed down across the sidewalk. But for the shepherd's quick action Jimmy knew he would have been caught under the tree and probably badly hurt. His heart swelled with gratitude as Pat led him out into the street around the obstacle and back in safety to the walk. Pat paused again and Jimmy's foot told him he was at a curb.

"Four," he counted. "Left, Pat."

The wind was no longer directly in their faces and progress was easier, although Jimmy knew that there were more road blocks than before, for twice in the first block Pat took him on wide detours around some obstacle he knew his master could not surmount. The road had a slight upgrade and Jimmy knew he was going in the correct direction, for Dr. Talbot's home was on the upper side of the town.

In the middle of the second block, Pat stopped. Jimmy thrust his foot forward to learn the nature of the obstacle, but Pat jumped before him, crowding him back.

"What is it now, I wonder?" Jimmy exclaimed. "Forward, Pat."

The dog hesitated. This was something new in his experience and he was momentarily undecided. He took his master a few paces to the left, then stopped again. Now he turned completely around and took Jimmy back, crossing the street they had been following. Nor did he stop there. Jimmy could feel grass under his feet and he knew that he was on a lawn. Still Pat went steadily ahead, fighting his way into the wind. Presently he turned right, then left again. Jimmy followed him confidently. What the obstruction was that forced Pat to this devious route he had no way of knowing, but one thing he did know and know thoroughly. Pat had a good reason for his actions and it was not for him, Jimmy, to question the shepherd's guidance.

The route twisted and turned. Jimmy was sure they had gone far beyond the line of houses and were prowling through back yards, areaways, alleys and he knew not what else. But for the wind Jimmy knew he would be hopelessly lost, for he could not keep the constant twists and turns straight in his mind.

261

At last Pat turned his back to the wind, and in a few minutes he crowded his master to the right. Jimmy was certain they were back on their original route.

"Three," he counted as Pat paused for a curb. "We're getting there."

The terrific blast which had torn down the big elm and almost pinned Jimmy and Pat under it had marked the height of the hurricane's fury. The wind was still blowing with such force that it was difficult for Jimmy to push his way into it when an obstacle made Pat turn for a short distance directly into its teeth, but it did not have the wild note of fury it once had held. Pat zigzagged back and forth, frequently leading his master up onto a lawn or out into the street to avoid some fallen object.

"Six," Jimmy counted at last. "Right, Pat."

Once more they were heading straight into the wind, but the worst was over. The storm had abated so that, by using his best efforts, Jimmy was able to proceed at something approaching his normal gait. Two more blocks of twisting and turning and then Pat stopped at a curb.

"Left, Pat," Jimmy said. "Left, Pat," he repeated when the dog had completed the first turn. "Now, it's the third house."

He went what he estimated was the correct distance, then told Pat, "Right." The shepherd led him forward five steps, then turned right into what Jimmy knew was the path leading to a house. A moment later he was pounding on the door.

"I want Dr. Talbot, please," he said when he heard the door open a crack.

"You're on the wrong street," a man's voice answered. "He lives on Pine. This is Oak."

"Wait a minute, please!" Jimmy cried as the door started to close. "Where is Pine?"

"Next street over."

Again the door started to close.

"Please," Jimmy cried, placing his hand against the door. "Which direction is it from here?"

"That way. Where I'm pointing. Are you blind?"

"Yes, I am."

"What?" The door suddenly swung open. "Good Lord, it's Jimmy Trainor. I've seen you in town lots of times. What are you doing out a night like this? Come in out of the rain."

"I can't, thanks, I've got to get Dr. Talbot right away. My wife is ill."

"Wait till I get my hat. I'll take you there."

"That's not necessary. I've come this far with Pat."

"Pat?"

"My dog, my eyes."

"You came out in this storm with just a dog? And you blind? Lord," the man's voice held a note of amazement. "Let me get my hat."

"No, just tell me how to get there. I can find it."

"You go down to the corner—"

"Wait." Jimmy turned and put his back to the house. "When I reach the sidewalk, which way do I go, right or left?"

"Left is the shortest. At the corner turn right for one block, then turn right again. Doc Talbot's house is on the same side of the street as this one, the third house from the corner. You'd better wait and let me go with you."

"No, I can find it. Thanks a lot."

Jimmy followed the route with no difficulty, but he was sorely puzzled. He had kept careful count of the blocks and he could not believe he had made a mistake, yet he had gone one block too far. Sudden understanding flooded his brain. When Pat had led him twisting and turning through back yards they must have crossed a street, possibly along an alley where there were no curbs, without his realizing it and when they came back to their original direction on the sidewalk, they were one block farther along than he had thought. A minute later he was pounding on Dr. Talbot's door.

"What happened?" Dr. Talbot asked when Jimmy had explained the emergency. "I wasn't expecting anything to happen for at least a week, probably two."

"Our lights were out and she tripped and fell."

"Heavens, then it's a rush. What did the streets look like? Can I get my car through? Oh, excuse me, of course you couldn't see."

"I can tell you there isn't a chance, Doctor. The streets are blocked by fallen trees a dozen places between here and there. We'll have to go on foot."

"What a night! And you came here alone? Why didn't you send someone?"

"I'd trust Pat quicker than anyone else."

"I hope we don't get lost," Dr. Talbot exclaimed anxiously as they left his home. "It's dark as the inside of a tomb and I've got just one flashlight."

"Follow right behind me, Doctor. Put your hand on my shoulder if you like. We can trust Pat to guide us."

He felt Dr. Talbot's hand grip him. At the sidewalk he said, "Right, Pat" confidently and stepped briskly out. The wind was on his back now and he had trouble in holding his gait down to normal, or rather he would have had but for the doctor. Dr. Talbot kept his flashlight playing on the footing before him and moved hesitatingly, stumblingly, along the route, which, to Jimmy under Pat's guidance, presented no difficulty.

They turned left down Currile Street. At the third block Dr. Talbot stopped, pulling back on Jimmy.

"Look out!" he cried. "The power line's down and there are live wires all over the street. We can't go through here, a touch from one of them would electrocute us."

Jimmy's stomach muscles tightened, then came quick relief, relief and an overwhelming gratitude to Pat. That was why the dog had taken him on that devious twisting route, the route that had made him lose track of the number of blocks he had gone. Elation surged in his heart. Here was an obstacle that would stop a man with sight, might even make him turn back, but nothing could stop a man with eyes like he had, four-legged eyes named Pat.

"Just follow close behind me, Doctor," he cried. "Pat will take us safely around them. He brought me past here once tonight, you know."

Dr. Talbot swore with frightened reverence as he followed Pat along the devious twisting route over which the dog had previously taken his master. He knew that he was seeing a miracle, and he felt a sense of awe as he thought of the daily miracles the dog performed, unknowing that he was a hero, just that he was doing the job for which he had been trained, content with the praise and affection of his master.

"This should be Castner," Jimmy said as Pat paused.

"It is."

"Good. I was afraid I might have lost count again on that detour. Right, Pat."

Five minutes later Jimmy opened the door of his home.

Hours later, Eileen's weak voice summoned him to her side.

"Yes, honey?"

"I want to ask something of you."

"Anything in the world, honey."

"Let me choose her name. I don't like Eileen Junior."

"Why, of course, honey. What do you want to name her?"

"I want to name her after the one we both owe so much to. Would you mind very much if I name her—Patsy?"

Dr. Talbot's hearty laugh boomed from the doorway.

"You stick to that, Mrs. Trainor," he said. "It's a dandy name. There's only one trouble with it. That young lady is going to have an awful lot to live up to when she grows up."

Turtle Hound

BY ZACHARY BALL

I T   W A S   the hottest part of summer and the sun
on my back was digging in its claws like a scared tomcat as I
trudged down the dusty road, heading north. I didn't know
where I was going. I reckon in the back of my head I was thinking of Memphis, better'n two hundred miles away I'd been told.
I'd never lived anywhere but on one-mule farms, and I didn't
hardly know what Memphis was except that it was a whopping
big town and lay off to the north.

It was the middle of the afternoon of my second day of
walking. Yesterday I had finished off what little grub I'd started

out with, and today I had stopped at a little sawed-plank house to ask the woman if I could do some work for a bait of grub. Looking me over she'd swung her head pitying-like and clucked her tongue. Then she told me to come on in and eat. That was about three hours ago, and I was hungry as a hog again already. I was tired too. Real tired.

I left the road, sat down on top of a low cutbank, laid back in the grass and wished I had my home and my ma and pa back again. While I was stretched out there thinking like that I heard a kind of whiffing, snuffing, snorting sound. It was somewheres behind me, but I couldn't tell just where. As I listened it stopped for a minute, then started again. This time it was a kind of scratching sound. Then that stopped and the snuffing and snorting started again.

I got up feeling kind of goose-pimply, being alone there with that funny sound so close by. I stood real still looking amongst the brush and small tree growth, listening. Pretty soon I saw some dirt pitch up into the air. More little spurts of it followed, then I saw something move. I watched it for a minute and was sure I knew what it was. It looked like a dog digging in a hole with only the top of his hips showing.

I walked over there and sure enough that's what it was. Even down in that hole like he was, all except his hind parts, I could tell he was a right big dog. I stood watching him for a little, and pretty soon he started backing out of the hole. He didn't come out empty-mouthed, either. He brought out a tortoise, one of those dry land box turtles.

Well, that dog had almost that whole turtle in his mouth, that's how big it was. His mouth, I mean. When he saw me he acted like he'd known me all his life. He came over and dropped his turtle at my feet, then backed off grinning, his big blanket of a tongue dripping. He waited for me to tell him how proud I was of him.

I swear, I never before saw such a dog as he was. I could tell by his strong white teeth that he was just a young dog, but he didn't look young; he looked like he was maybe ten years old. That was because of the kind of dog he was. He looked like he had started out to be a hound then decided he'd look better as a porcupine. His face looked like somebody had stuck pine needles all in it. Big old stiff hairs were growing out of it that looked exactly like pine needles. And his eyes were not like any dog's eyes I'd ever seen. They were glassy looking—like two glass marbles—and kind of whitish-gray. I stood there looking at him and for a minute I misdoubted he was really a dog at all.

He kept looking first at me, then at the tortoise, still waiting for me to say something about it. Finally I picked it up and said, "You did all right, feller. I wish I could eat the thing." That made him as happy as a pullet that's just laid her first egg, and he went flopping around and around in the grass and bouncing up as high as my head to show me how glad he was that I liked it.

I dropped the turtle back in the hole and said, "Yeah, you done a good job, all right, but I've got to be on my way," and I went back down onto the road. Right behind me came a sound like somebody dropping blocks of wood as that dog's big paws hit the ground. I looked around and his glassy eyes were shining and he was still grinning, with his tongue lapping up his slobbers. I think I knew right then I wasn't going to have to go any farther on my trip alone.

I stopped and looked for a collar, but he wasn't wearing one. His feet and legs had some cuts on them like maybe he'd climbed out of a pen to run away.

"You better go back," I said to him, and pointed down the road the way I had come. All the time I was hoping down inside that he wouldn't leave me—I was that lonesome for some kind of a friend. "Go on! Go on home!" I told him.

He bounced up and down, long ears slapping his jaws, happy as could be, just like I'd said he could go along with me. Then he hit out down the road ahead of me. He loped along for a few yards, then came back to me, pounding along in the dust with those big clumsy feet. He stopped there in front of me and the sassy way he looked up made me laugh. My laugh really tickled him, and he started jumping up and trying to slap my face with that foot-long tongue of his.

"All right, Bristle Face," I said to him. "Maybe you ain't got any place to go either. Maybe you've had to run away from somebody that got drunk and clubbed you, too. We'll go on to Memphis together."

So we went on along that winding, dusty country road. Roads were nothing to brag about in Mississippi back in 1900, but this one suited us fine. We went on and on together, and it seemed to me I couldn't remember being as happy as I was then. I had me a friend. Once I looked down at that hairy-faced old coot and he winked at me. I reckon his eye blinked on account of having some dirt in it from the tortoise hole, but it looked just like he winked because he was glad he'd found me, too. I took hold of one of his long hound-like ears and we walked on down the road.

As we plodded along, Bristle Face would stop every little while and lift his big black muzzle and twitch it like he was pleased with the smells coming from the weeds and brush along the sides of the road.

Once a half-dozen quail started across the road ahead of us. He spread his front paws out and brought his head down low and studied them like he was thinking maybe he ought to do something about them but didn't know what. Another time he stopped to watch a butterfly, then looked up at me and those glassy eyes asked me what I thought about it. When I told him that no proudful dog would ever low-rate himself by pranking with butterflies he paid it no more mind.

We slept that night in a shock of hay out in a field, and at daylight hit the road again. Seemed like it didn't take the sun no time at all to climb high enough to be hot, and I got so hungry my stomach felt like there was a big auger boring in it.

Along about eight o'clock I stopped at a house and asked the woman there if I could trade her some work for grub. She said her yard man kept the place up but like the other woman gave me a meal anyway, and Bristle Face too. I was full when we left, but Bristle Face wasn't. She hadn't fed him nowheres near what I figured would fill him up.

We walked all that day without any more food, and slept under a pine tree that night. The next day Bristle Face trailed another box turtle to a hole and I couldn't get the hairy old savage to leave it. So I had to sit down and wait till he dug it out. Finally he dropped it at my feet and winked at me, tickled as a pig that's found its lost mammy.

A little after noon I bought me some cheese and crackers at a sawmill store a little ways off the road. Now I had only fifty cents left, which I wrapped up good in my handkerchief and stuffed deep into my overalls pocket. Down the road a ways we flopped down in the shade of a pine tree and I shared the cheese and crackers with Bristle Face.

About the middle of the afternoon we came to another store. It was just a little old building with a sign over the porch that I could hardly make out: SWANK'S STORE. The building had no paint on it at all, just the weathered boards, and this little porch across the front of it. I stood there a minute looking the place over, trying to make up my mind if I should spend another dime for some more grub or not. Finally I started toward the building. Just as I came to the porch steps a man came out the door. He was about thirty-five, I figured, tall and lank, but with a good pair of shoulders on him. His skin was dark and he had a hooked nose that had a comical slant to one side. His wide face was friendly and he had dark eyebrows that kind of flared up like a bird's wings.

He leaned against a porch post, took a sack of tobacco and cigarette papers out of his shirt pocket and started rolling a cigarette. While he was doing that he was looking down at me and Bristle Face.

"Howdy, boy," he said, real drawly. "Looks like you ought to pull them porcupine quills out of that old dog's face. I got some pliers if you want to use 'em."

"He ain't got any quills in his face," I told him. "Those are just hairs. Just big stiff hairs, growin' out."

He stooped a little to look at Bristle Face and said, "Well, danged if they ain't! I swanie! I've seen a heap of dogs in my time, but never such a prickly old wretch as that." He shook his head like he couldn't believe what he was seeing, then he lit his cigarette and said, "What's he good for?"

"I don't know," I told him.

"Can he trail anythin'?"

270

"I couldn't say. He finds box turtles and digs them out, that's all I know."

"Box turtles! Well, he looks like trackin' a turtle would be about the best he could do. Where'd you git him?"

"South from here," I told him. "He was diggin' out a turtle and I stopped to watch him. Then he just followed me."

The man had been mostly paying attention to Bristle Face but now he level-looked at me for a minute. Just talking to him that little bit and looking up at him, I knew I liked Lute Swank, which is what he told me a little later his name was. When he spoke again, I noticed for the first time what a rumbly voice he had. It was a heavy voice, but still it had a woman kind of gentleness to it.

"Boy," he said to me, "if ever I seen anybody with the miss-meal colic, you've got it. I'd bet a purty you ain't been eatin' regular lately. How long you been trampin' the road?"

"Three, four days."

"Goin' where?"

"I don't rightly know. Memphis, maybe."

He shook his head and said, "Come on in here." He turned and went into the store.

I went up onto the porch, Bristle Face right behind me. Beside the door I noticed a school slate and a piece of chalk tied to a string. I wondered what they were for. We went on in, and saw Lute Swank piling a bunch of crackers on a tin pie plate. He added a big hunk of cheese, a half-dozen slices of bologna and some pickles.

"Now git busy," he said to me, sliding the plate across the counter.

While I was eating I looked around the store. It was just one little old room, and I didn't see how anybody could make a living selling what was there. A few shelves of canned stuff, some side meat and hams hanging from rafter pegs, some boxes of crackers and cookies and such as that, brooms and kerosene cans, harness straps hanging on a back wall with some horse collars, a barrel of sugar and one of salt and one of potatoes— that was about all there was.

271

When I'd eaten everything Lute gave me he said, "Around back is a box with some meat scraps and stuff in it that you can give that stickery old hound of yours. What's his name?"

"I call him Bristle Face," I told him.

"Why now, I never heard a more fittin' name," he said, and smiled his gentle smile.

I took Bristle Face outside and around to the back and fed him. Then I went back in and told Lute that I didn't have much money, but that I'd give him whatever I owed him for the food. He was shaking his big bushy head before I finished saying it.

"You can run a errand for me, though," he said. "You see, if folks come along 'fore I'm out of bed or when I'm not around, they write what they want on that slate by the door out there— iffen they know how to write. Them that can't write draw pictures —which I can't always make out. So you can run down to Miz Wogan's, just around the next bend of the road, and take her some hominy."

By the time I got back to the store with Mrs. Wogan's fifteen cents, it was coming on sundown. As I handed the money to Lute he said, "Where you fixin' to sleep tonight?"

"Ain't been studyin' on it," I told him.

"I have," he said. "I got me a room back there." He pushed a thumb at the door behind the counter. "Sleep and eat in there. Got a extra cot."

"I'd be mighty pleasured to stay the night, sure-enough," I answered.

"Reckon I'll fix some hot vittles," he said. "Come on."

As me and Bristle Face followed him into the sleeping and eating section of the building, I told him I'd had my fill of grub awhile ago.

He was busy taking the lids off a little cookstove and putting wood into the firebox. "You can eat some more," he said. "Boy your age has got one thing that's man-size about him—his stomach."

After supper I went out to milk Lute's cow for him. There was a small stable and barnlot out back of the store, with a mule and a riding horse in the lot. Off to one side was a granary. On

272

past the stable was a small pasture, where the cow was standing. I let her into the stable and fed her and milked her. Then I fed the mule and the horse.

All the time I was doing the chores Bristle Face was following me around. The other animals paid him no mind so when I went back to the house I asked Lute if I could fix a bed for Bristle Face in the stable.

"What's your name, boy?" he asked, like he hadn't heard me.

"Jase Landers," I told him.

"I'd say you're risin' thirteen, maybe?"

"I'm past fourteen."

"Well, Jase," he said, "about your old Bristle Face, he can sleep right on the floor there by your cot."

"That pleasures me aplenty." I told him. "And likely it will Bristle Face, too."

Nobody had come to the store from the time I first stopped until Lute shut the front door and locked it for the night. As we were getting ready for bed I said, "In five or six hours nobody's come to your store to buy anything."

He grinned and said in that deep-gentle voice of his, "Boy, I've seen five, six days go past and nobody come in."

"Don't look to me like that would be very profitin'," I said.

"Why now, it ain't much of a livin', that's for sure," he said, "but I don't need much to keep me. What little business I do is cash; I don't have no accounts to fret about. Could be I'll have more income next year, though. I'm fixin' to run for high sheriff, come fall. Done paid my fee and all."

I told him I hoped he'd get elected. And thinking ahead to the fall, I wondered where I'd be by then.

As if he was reading my thoughts, he said, "When I start 'lectioneerin', it's goin' to keep me away from the store a good bit. You want to stay here and look after it for me?"

For a minute his question kind of knocked the breath out of me. There wasn't anything I wanted as much as a home—a place to live and somebody around that wasn't going to beat me if I did something that didn't just suit him.

273

Finally I said, "I sure-enough would!"

"I figured you wasn't goin' no place in particular. Where'd you come from?"

Then I told him how my ma and pa had died two years before and how I went to live with pa's brother, a farmer that lived alone, and how he would come home drunk and whale me with a trace strap.

Lute listened to all I had to say, then blew out the lamp. "I'd be pleasured to have you stay here with me," he said as he climbed into bed. "I can pay you a little, not much. But you'll have a place to eat and sleep."

"Why—why, I wouldn't want any pay," I told him. I wanted to thank him proper, because I was feeling mighty beholden to him, but gladness was making a lump in my throat until I couldn't say any more at all.

I lay listening to the night sounds outside the window and thinking how lucky I was to have stopped at Lute Swank's little store. For now I had a home—at least for the time being. I was mighty thankful to Lute for taking me in. He was a good man, anybody could see that, and the knowing was in me that I liked him better than I'd liked anybody since I'd lost my pa and ma.

I began feeling drowsy. I heard Bristle Face get up and turn around a couple of times, then drop his hairy old carcass back down on the bare floor and let out a big sigh. I closed my eyes. I reckon I sighed too, for the world was being mighty good to me that night.

Friendship or the country's need

Dog for Defense

BY RUTH ADAMS KNIGHT

Unable to enlist in World War II because of a twisted shoulder, Larry Hanson threw his energies into directing the training program for dogs for defense. Now he had to train his own dog Count, the magnificent collie Larry had raised from a sickly pup, for a special military detail.

WHEN Larry cleared his desk and started for the training ring Count always went with him, sometimes carrying the record book in his mouth, sometimes with the training leash trailing behind him. At the gate he would pause, nudge whatever he was carrying into Larry's hand, and stand ready for his orders.

In the old days he had gone to classes like all the other collies. But lately he'd frequently been allowed to stay and help

Larry, and though he was too obedient and well behaved to presume, his eyes always begged for the privilege.

Today, when Larry finally got to his feet, Count followed him out as a matter of course. But at the gate Larry gave him none of the familiar commands. Instead he snapped a training leash onto his collar and went with him out beyond the corral, where a new trainer was inspecting a strange-looking uniform that resembled a football suit.

"Better put on plenty of padding, Jack," Larry called. "I'm going to try Count on attack work."

Teaching attack work always presented a problem at Bay Lane, and very little of it had been done before the war. With dogs such as these, successful instruction in attacking a man meant forcing them to go against their strongest instincts. The animals here, well fed and well cared for and looking upon every man as their friend unless he menaced someone they loved, were not belligerent by nature, though extremely high spirited. Courtesy and good manners had been bred into them for generations, and prodding them to attack without cause was difficult. It frequently took a long time for them to understand what was wanted of them.

The trick was to make them realize what was to be done—when to strike, when to release, and when to hang on and fight to the death. They must learn to do these things also with no sense of true animosity, but only as a job to be accomplished. And it was work in which sometimes the most intelligent dog failed, because in spite of all a trainer could do, it was never possible to get the animal to make the first move and close his teeth on anything which would form a basis for encouraging him to further attack.

The knowledge of this was clear in Larry's mind as he stood waiting for Jack to get ready. That it might be true of Count was his one hope. In all basic requirements Count already qualified as a perfect war dog. He had been trained as a watchdog, and it would be simple to ready him for sentry duty. With that nose of his he could follow any trail without difficulty once he was taught the system; he could locate persons or articles; he could learn very quickly to carry communications. But Dave had said the dog must be trained for attack. Count liked people, and teaching him to attack a human being on signal and without apparent provocation might be a different matter. If Count couldn't qualify for that, Dave couldn't use him for this special service, whatever it was. Then he needn't go immediately, and he and Larry would at least have a little more time together.

Jack, the new trainer, had been hired especially for this job when Larry had begun to teach attack work in earnest. Jack had not been allowed to make friends with any of the dogs. It would have been practically impossible to persuade untutored collies to go after a man they knew and liked. Though they were taught to work with no rancor and to regard the attack only as a routine piece of work, it was difficult enough to encourage them to leap and hold a stranger. Once they got the idea, however, Jack's job wasn't one many people envied.

But now, as he pulled on his grotesque-looking suit, he grinned at Larry cheerfully.

"Going to make an attack dog out of Count?" he asked with surprise in his voice. "I thought his long suit was retrieving."

"That hasn't anything to do with this," said Larry. "He can be a fighter too, can't he?"

Jack looked at Count with respect.

"I'd hate to have him come at me when I didn't have my football clothes on," he said. "I'll bet he could lick his weight in wildcats if he ever got started. Only he's so gentle it seems a shame—"

"He'll stay gentle," said Larry. "This will only be a job—if he'll do it."

"You think he might refuse?"

"I—don't know. That's what we're going to find out. He's smart enough to get the idea after a while, but whether he'll carry on with it . . . Well, let's see."

If Count was good at this he'd have to send him—he'd have to. And he wanted him to be good. He didn't want Count to fail as he had failed, and be only on the side lines. If Count knew, he'd want to fight, just as Larry wanted to. Only, separation would be tough.

He tried to imagine the ranch without the great gold and sable body streaking across it to greet him—a place with hundreds of dogs and yet to him completely empty. Well, meet that when he came to it. Get on with this now.

Count had obviously been puzzled but interested as he and his master entered the yard. Dogs come to be creatures of habit, and this was not the usual plan. Ears at alert, he was trotting about, wagging his tail and investigating every corner of the place thoroughly. The new lad, struggling into the outfit which made him resemble a mattress more than a man, startled him and he eyed him warily. When he was finally in readiness and Larry gave Jack the nod to begin, Count backed away from him in sheer amazement.

Jack wore not only the thickly padded suit, but a helmet and long heavy gloves which covered hands and wrists. In his hand he held a stout piece of sacking. The steps to be taught were three. First the dog must grip the sacking, then the padded arm, then learn to attack with full force. As Count retreated Jack advanced, waving the sacking back and forth in front of Count's face, barely missing his nose. Startled, Count backed and growled, and backed and growled again, louder. But there was disdain rather than challenge in his attitude. Who this strange person was, behaving in such a peculiar way, he did not know. But since Larry gave no order, he was evidently to be tolerated, though his manners were, to say the least, questionable. If Larry permitted him there, Count would permit him too, though his clothing was queer and his actions annoying. There was great dignity in Count's restraint as he turned and moved away, avoiding the sacking which was still being insolently snapped again and again in his face.

But the strange man followed him, and Larry, though making no move, was hissing between his teeth with an encouraging sound. And then the sack caught Count across his sensitive nose and hurt a little. This time his growl was unmistakable.

This idiot better be warned. But the stranger paid no attention. He only struck out with the sacking again and again, flapping it before Count's eyes until he was dizzy.

Count's hackles rose. This was new and unpleasant and not understandable. A growl, warning of his displeasure, had always been sufficient before to frighten off any threat. He circled, looking at Larry. Larry nodded to him. Obviously his master wanted him to do something about this, take some action. But he didn't know what.

He tried barking, at first only once or twice, sharply, then long and continuously. But the annoying monstrosity never even hesitated. Noise evidently served no purpose and was not what was required of him. Completely confused, Count circled again and snarled. The sacking flapped again and again.

Finally, in utter desperation, Count leaped at it.

Immediately Larry's voice reached his ears, jubilant, approving.

"That's the stuff. Good boy—go after it, Count. Go get it!"

Unbelievable as it seemed, his master evidently *wanted* him to go after this flapping burlap. It was contrary to all his former training, but if that was the way it was . . .

He heard Larry's voice, low and commanding now: "Count, strike!"

There was a low growl, a streak through the air, and sixty pounds of concentrated fury struck and began reducing the sacking to a mangled pulp. The man fell back, and Larry's voice rang out again: "Bravo, Count! Good boy. You get it. I knew you would. Try it again, Jack."

An hour later a weary but comprehending dog was making attack after attack. The padded sleeve of the intruder had been substituted for the sack and he was gripping it between his jaws and holding on for dear life as long as he was resisted, releasing it instantly when the man stopped fighting. It was a queer game, and Count didn't understand it too well, but if Larry wanted him to play, he'd play. The trick apparently was to catch this person's clothing in his teeth but not to close his jaws completely, just keep him prisoner until Larry ordered him freed or until he was quiet. If the man struggled, it seemed it was Count's duty to subdue him; if he tried to run away, Count must bring him back.

It was noon when Jack, practically on the verge of collapse, staggered out of the pen, and Larry fell on his knees, his arms around Count's neck.

"Good boy," he said chokingly. "Good fellow. You'll go in my place, Count. You show 'em."

Battle Tactics

BY FARLEY MOWAT

*A*FTER several years in Saskatoon, my family
moved into a new neighborhood. River Road was on the banks
of the Saskatchewan River, but on the lower and more plebian
side. The community on River Road was considerably relaxed
in character and there was a good deal of tolerance for indi-
vidual idiosyncrasies.

Only three doors down the street from us lived a retired
schoolteacher who had spent years in Alaska and who had
brought with him into retirement a team of Alaskan huskies.
These were magnificent dogs that commanded respect not only

281

from the local canine population but from the human one as well. Three of them once caught a burglar on their master's premises, and they reduced him to butcher's meat with a dispatch that we youngsters much admired.

Across the alley from us lived a barber who maintained a sort of Transient's Rest for stray mongrels. There was an unkind rumor to the effect that he encouraged these strays only in order to practice his trade upon them. The rumor gained stature from the indisputable fact that some of his oddly assorted collection of dogs sported unusual haircuts. I came to know the barber intimately during the years that followed, and he confided his secret to me. Once, many years earlier, he had seen a French poodle shaven and shorn, and he had been convinced that he could devise even more spectacular hair styles for dogs, and perhaps make a fortune and a reputation for himself. His experiments were not without artistic merit, even though some of them resulted in visits from the Humane Society inspectors.

I had no trouble fitting myself into this new community, but the adjustment was not so simple for Mutt. The canine population of River Road was enormous. Mutt had to come to terms with these dogs, and he found the going hard. His long, silken hair and his fine "feathers" tended to give him a soft and sentimental look that was misleading and that seemed to goad the roughneck local dogs into active hostility. They usually went about in packs, and the largest pack was led by a well-built bull terrier who lived next door to us. Mutt, who was never a joiner, preferred to go his way alone, and this made him particularly suspect by the other dogs. They began to lay for him.

He was not by nature the fighting kind. In all his life I never knew him to engage in battle unless there was no alternative. His was an eminently civilized attitude, but one that other dogs could seldom understand. They taunted him because of it.

His pacific attitude used to embarrass my mother when the two of them happened to encounter a belligerent strange dog while they were out walking. Mutt would waste no time in idle braggadocio. At first glimpse of the stranger he would insinuate himself under Mother's skirt and no amount of physical force, nor scathing comment, could budge him from this sanctuary. Often the strange dog would not realize that it *was* a sanctuary and this was sometimes rather hard on Mother.

Despite his repugnance toward fighting, Mutt was no coward, nor was he unable to defend himself. He had his own ideas about how to fight, ideas which were unique but formidable. Just how efficacious they actually were was demonstrated to us all within a week of our arrival at our new address.

Knowing nothing of the neighborhood, Mutt dared to go where even bulldogs feared to tread, and one morning he foolishly pursued a cat into the ex-schoolteacher's yard. He was immediately surrounded by four ravening huskies. They were a merciless lot, and they closed in for the kill.

Mutt saw at once that this time he would have to fight. With one quick motion he flung himself over on his back and began to pedal furiously with all four feet. It looked rather as if he were riding a bicycle built for two, but upside down. He also began to sound his siren. This was a noise he made—just how I do not know—deep in the back of his throat. It was a kind of frenzied wail. The siren rose in pitch and volume as his legs increased their r.p.m.'s, until he began to sound like a gas turbine at full throttle.

The effect of this unorthodox behavior on the four huskies was to bring them to an abrupt halt. Their ears went forward and their tails uncurled as a look of pained bewilderment wrinkled their brows. And then slowly, and one by one, they began to back away, their eyes uneasily averted from the distressing spectacle before them. When they were ten feet from Mutt they turned as one dog and fled without dignity for their own back yard.

The mere sight of Mutt's bicycle tactics (as we referred to them) was usually sufficient to avert bloodshed, but on occasion a foolhardy dog would refuse to be intimidated. The results in these cases could be rather frightful, for Mutt's queer posture of defense was not all empty bombast.

Once when we were out hunting gophers Mutt was attacked by a farm collie who, I think, was slightly mad. He looked mad, for he had one white eye and one blue one, and the combination gave him a maniac expression. And he acted mad, for he flung himself on the inverted Mutt without the slightest hesitation.

Mutt grunted when the collie came down on top of him, and for an instant the tempo of his legs was slowed. Then he exerted himself and, as it were, put on a sprint. The collie became air-borne, bouncing up and down as a rubber ball bounces on the end of a water jet. Each time he came down he was raked fore and aft by four sets of rapidly moving claws, and when he finally fell clear he was bleeding from a dozen ugly scratches, and he had had a bellyful. He fled. Mutt did not pursue him; he was magnanimous in victory.

Had he been willing to engage deliberately in a few such duels with the neighborhood dogs, Mutt would undoubtedly have won their quick acceptance. But such was his belief in the principles of nonviolence—as these applied to other dogs, at least—that he continued to avoid combat.

The local packs, and particularly the one led by the bull terrier next door, spared no pains to bring him to battle, and for some time he was forced to stay very close to home unless he was accompanied by Mother or by myself. It was nearly a month before he found a solution to this problem.

The solution he eventually adopted was typical of him.

Almost all the back yards in Saskatoon were fenced with vertical planking nailed to horizontal two-by-fours. The upper two-by-four in each case was usually five or six feet above the ground, and about five inches below the projecting tops of the upright planks. For generations these elevated gangways had provided a safe thoroughfare for cats. One fine day Mutt decided that they could serve him too.

I was brushing my teeth after breakfast when I heard Mutt give a yelp of pain and I went at once to the window and looked out. I was in time to see him laboriously clamber up on our back fence from a garbage pail that stood by the yard gate. As I watched he wobbled a few steps along the upper two-by-four, lost his balance, and fell off. Undaunted he returned at once to the garbage pail and tried again.

I went outside and tried to reason with him, but he ignored me. When I left he was still at it, climbing up, staggering along for a few feet, then falling off again.

I mentioned this new interest of his during dinner that night, but none of us gave it much thought. We were used to Mutt's peculiarities, and we had no suspicion that there was method behind this apparent foolishness. Yet method there was, as I discovered a few evenings later.

A squad of Bengal lancers, consisting of two of my friends and myself armed with spears made from bamboo fishing rods, had spent the afternoon riding up and down the back alleys on our bicycles hunting tigers (alley cats). As suppertime approached we were slowly pedaling our way homeward along the alley behind River Road when one of my chums, who was a little in the lead, gave a startled yelp and swerved his bike so that I crashed into him, and we fell together on the sun-baked dirt. I picked myself up and saw my friend pointing at the fence ahead of us. His eyes were big with disbelief.

The cause of the accident, and of my chum's incredulity, was nonchalantly picking his way along the top of the fence not fifty yards away. Behind that fence lay the home of the huskies, and although we could not see them, we—and most of Saskatoon —could hear them. Their frenzied howls were punctuated by dull thudding sounds as they leaped at their tormentor and fell back helplessly to earth again.

Mutt never hesitated. He ambled along his aerial route with the leisurely insouciance of an old gentleman out for an evening stroll. The huskies must have been wild with frustration, and I was grateful that the fence lay between them and us.

We three boys had not recovered from our initial surprise when a new canine contingent arrived upon the scene. It included six or seven of the local dogs (headed by the bull terrier) attracted to the scene by the yammering of the huskies. They spotted Mutt, and the terrier immediately led a mass assault. He launched himself against the fence with such foolhardy violence that only a bull terrier could have survived the impact.

We were somewhat intimidated by the frenzy of all those dogs, and we lowered our spears to the "ready" position, undecided whether to attempt Mutt's rescue or not. In any event, we were not needed.

Mutt remained unperturbed, although this may have been only an illusion resulting from the fact that he was concentrating so hard on his balancing act that he could spare no attention for his assailants. He moved along at a slow but steady pace, and having safely navigated the huskies' fence, he jumped up to the slightly higher fence next door and stepped along it until he came to a garage. With a graceful leap he gained the garage roof, where he lay down for a few moments, ostensibly to rest, but actually—I am certain—to enjoy his triumph.

Below him there was pandemonium. I have never seen a dog as angry as that bull terrier was. Although the garage wall facing on the alley was a good eight feet high, the terrier kept hurling himself impotently against it until he must have been one large quivering bruise.

Mutt watched the performance for two or three minutes; then he stood up and with one insolent backward glance jumped down to the dividing fence between two houses, and ambled along it to the street front beyond.

The tumult in the alley subsided and the pack began to disperse. Most of the dogs must have realized that they would have to run halfway around the block to regain Mutt's trail, and by then he might be far away. Dispiritedly they began to drift off, until finally only the bull terrier remained. He was still hurling himself at the garage wall in a paroxysm of fury when I took myself home to tell of the wonders I had seen.

From that day forth the dogs of the neighborhood gave up their attempts against Mutt and came to a tacit acceptance of him—all, that is, save the bull terrier. Perhaps his handball game against the fence had addled his brain, or it may be that he was just too stubborn to give up. At any rate he continued to lurk in ambush for Mutt, and Mutt continued to avoid him easily enough, until the early winter when the terrier—by now completely unbalanced—one day attempted to cross the street in pursuit of his enemy and without bothering to look for traffic. He was run over by an old Model T.

Mutt's remarkable skill as a fence walker could have led to the leadership of the neighborhood dogs, had that been what he desired, for his unique talent gave him a considerable edge in the popular game of catch-cat; but Mutt remained a lone walker, content to be left to his own devices.

He did not give up fence walking even when the original need had passed. He took a deep pride in his accomplishment, and he kept in practice. I used to show him off to my friends, and I was not above making small bets with strange boys about the abilities of my acrobatic dog. When I won, as I always did, I would reward Mutt with candy-coated gum. This was one of his favorite confections and he would chew away at a wad of it until the last vestige of mint flavor had vanished, whereupon he would swallow the tasteless remnant. Mother thought that this was bad for him, but as far as I know, it never had any adverse effect upon his digestive system, which could absorb most things with impunity.

Justice in
the Painted Hills

BY ALEXANDER HULL

*L*IN TAYLOR had murdered his partner.
He had known he was going to do that for three days, ever
since in the rotten, friable detritus of the mountain meadow they
had found the fabulously rich deposit of gold. The source of the
stream upon which this placer gold lay was so near at hand, the
high valley so restricted in area, that the finding of the lode from
which the deposits had disintegrated and been washed into the
little basin seemed a practical certainty, and the task, it might
be, merely of days, certainly of no more than a few weeks.

288

Both men had been experienced prospectors, partners for more than three years—years, however, that had never paid out in more than day wages. Late in the preceding fall, pronounced traces of color in lower Paint Creek had sent them climbing through the next spring, farther and farther toward the headwaters among the mountain summits which, rising steep and snow-garbed out of the high plateau, gave the stream its name. Convinced at length that they were near the mother lode, that it must, in fact, lie up this particular branch, they had built a cabin at the foot of the meadow within sight of the marvelous peaks of the Painted Hills, which gleamed in red and green and blue and yellow, mingled with the white and violet and rose of the snow fields, like some incomparable color scheme of a superhuman futurist painter.

Three days ago their theory had found confirmation. In the very roots of the meadow grass and flowers they had discovered pay dirt, literally thousands of dollars' worth of loose gold in a plot scarcely half as large as a city lot! Moreover, just upstream there was certainly the vein which, discovered, would make them rich as the dreams of avarice.

From that dizzy moment Lin Taylor had known that he alone must profit by that wealth. If by some malevolent stroke of fate he failed to find the vein from which this gold had come, why there was altogether too little in the meadow washing to be shared with another man. And even if he did locate the mother lode— No! John Harvey must die!

That they had broken bread together for years, shared the same cabin, the same fire and tobacco, that Harvey believed him to be his friend—that Harvey actually was *his* friend—none of these things mattered for an instant compared to the insatiable and ferocious lust that had lighted its fires in his veins at the sight of those big yellow flakes in his gold pan. Mingled with those furious flames there was the ice of an implacable determination to kill; there was no heat in that. It was a cold, deliberately planned, irrevocable intention.

This morning as they rounded a spur high up on Firetop Mountain, a massive dome which took its name from the scarlet

289

rock of its peak, his chance had come. At a critical moment he had suddenly halted in the trail and thrust out a foot. Harvey, stumbling upon the edge of a yawning abyss, tottered for seconds which seemed like infinity to Lin Taylor, and then pitched downward in utter silence, but with a look on his face of horror and incredulous amazement.

Lin Taylor stood alone on the trail, breathing heavily from sheer nervousness and excitement. His knees were trembling. He leaned back against the scarp of rock that towered upward from the trail. Here, in a moment, his strength and determination came back to him rapidly, and with them a feeling of intense exaltation.

He was a rich man at last! Forty-three years he had been the world's underdog, but now—

He straightened up confidently, stood away from the wall behind him. Kneeling in the trail, he leaned far over the edge and peered down into the chasm. Far below, lying like a heap of old clothing, he discerned upon the jagged rocks of the canyon floor all that remained of John Harvey.

Yes, he told himself as he got to his feet, the job was done—and well done! And there was never a chance that the way it had been done ever would come to light. No living being knew, or would ever know.

Close upon that thought he noticed how very still it was. It was always still in the high mountains, though, and for weeks one might hear no human sound. It was suddenly impressed upon him that he would hear none from this moment, save those which he made himself. . . . But there was one sound now afloat upon the clear high atmosphere, a distant, faint baying, miles away to the south; Shep, John Harvey's dog, was on the trail of a rabbit or a coyote.

Just then a pressure of wind came off the ice fields of Blue Peak in the opposite direction and passed, sounding and cold, over Lin Taylor, the canyon, and the dead man, and was gone. It had blown for a minute, perhaps, with a low keening moan, blotting out the other sound, that of the hunting dog. And when it was gone there was no sound at all, neither wind, nor bird, nor dog—utter silence, complete and somehow menacing.

Lin Taylor stirred from his immobility and, turning, made his way back in the direction from which he had come. Not long after, he reached the floor of the canyon, and threading his way among massive boulders and sharp outcroppings of the stratified bedrock, he came at length to the huddled heap that had been John Harvey, his partner.

If there had been an eye to see him, the eye of an intelligence that hoped or expected to see him flinch, it would have been disappointed. Lin Taylor was not a man to feel remorse. There are such men who, committing a murder in a passion, are driven, harried and hounded by their own thoughts and imaginations, into betraying themselves at last to punishment. Lin Taylor was not that sort of man. Introspection as a word was unfamiliar to him; the process itself was scarcely less so. He would never betray himself. He would never see ghosts. It takes the eye of belief to see ghosts, and Lin Taylor believed only in the things that can be handled—food and drink, women, gold. The things of the spirit (and ghosts are essentially things of the spirit) did not exist for him.

And now, at the side of his victim, he felt neither remorse nor fear. Bending over the bloodstained and broken thing, he ascertained that there was nothing of value in its clothing and drew from its belt a prospector's pick. Then, catching the body handily by the boot, he dragged it a few feet away to a shallow depression in the floor and set about heaping over it a cairn of rocks. Stones of every size were plentiful and half an hour saw his work done.

An hour later Lin Taylor entered his cabin. Hurriedly getting together the dead man's effects, he loaded them upon one of the two pack mules grazing beside the cabin and, packing the saddle bags of the other animal with some food, he was in less than half an hour on his way out of the Painted Hills. With him he took nothing more to show for the season's work than one small bag of dust and nuggets, about the same number of ounces in weight that he and Harvey had averaged for the last three seasons.

The third day he reached Nordness, a settlement of three

291

hundred inhabitants, the link between civilization and the mountain fastnesses, where for three seasons he and John Harvey had wintered, and whence in the first thawings of spring they had set out again on their quest for gold.

There was no questioning of his story of John Harvey's death, and he had known there would not be any. A careless step on the edge of a perilous cliff, a little loose rock underfoot—how often that had happened. Harvey's nearest relative, a cousin in New York, would never question the manner in which he became the receiver of some seven hundred unexpected and welcome dollars, half the proceeds of the dust which Lin Taylor had brought in. There was little interest anywhere in John Harvey, the poor and unimportant prospector. He had always been a silent man, sitting by the hotel stove through the winter days with his dog at his feet as silent as himself, smoking his pipe—not surly, but uncommunicative in the extreme.

Lin Taylor himself, because of a bluff and hearty manner that gave him at least the appearance of cordiality, was the better liked of the two. And rather than suspicion he encountered sympathy. Dan Blake, who owned the general store in Nordness, mentioned the loss thus the first time Lin entered the store.

"Mighty hard luck, losing Harvey. Quiet sort of man, but I always had a notion he'd be a mighty good, dependable sort of fellow, if a man knew him. Makes it right hard for you, I guess."

Lin Taylor nodded.

"Fell off a cliff, I heard say? How'd it come to happen? Did you see it?"

Lin answered without hesitation: "No, I didn't see it. Must've happened that day, though. He started out to climb Firetop pretty early in the morning, and I figured he'd be back by noon or a little after. It's a good trail, you know."

"Never been up there," said Blake.

"Well, it is. I don't know what it was—presentiment, I guess. But along about three in the afternoon I began to get uneasy. So I started out. Well, I found him. Foot of a cliff about three-four hundred feet high—all broken to pieces. Slipped, I suppose."

"Mighty hard luck," said Blake again. "You'll miss him a lot. Been working together quite a spell, haven't you?"

"Going on four years," said Taylor shortly, with the manner of one who had rather not go on with the topic under discussion.

Blake perceived his reluctance, said to himself that Taylor was pretty hard hit by the accident, and forebore to question him further in that way, but asked briskly: "Well, what can I do for you?"

"Want to get a few supplies."

"Going out again?"

Taylor nodded.

"Pretty late in the season to be starting out, ain't it?"

"Yes, but I've got a good cabin that me and Harvey built."

"Going back up *there?*" queried Blake, in surprise.

It was obvious that he thought it odd. He was recalling all that he had heard said about the Painted Hills country, that prospectors hereabouts were universally agreed that it was poor prospecting ground. True, a few colors had been found in the lower reaches of Paint Creek, as they had been in every stream in this part of the country, but no one had found more than that, despite the fact that the stream had been overrun with prospectors thirty years before and had been tried from time to time, as a forlorn hope, by a good many men since. Lin Taylor and his partner had got barely day wages out of it this season. And those mountains should now be doubly distasteful to Taylor because of the death of Harvey. It did look odd. Blake, pondering, wondered if Taylor was going to turn "queer." He saw no signs of it in the man's appearance; but, anyway, prospectors were pretty nearly all queer. Losing his partner that way was no doubt going to make Lin Taylor like the rest of them.

"Yeh, I guess I will."

"Get snowed in, won't you?"

"Won't likely be much snow for another month. Anyway, I've got a notion to winter it up there."

"Man! They say the snow gets thirty feet deep in that country!"

"I'm used to snow country. Take a few traps, maybe, and

293

get some fur. Plenty of firewood up there. And if I don't like it, why, I can come out on snowshoes or skis."

Blake shook his head, now thoroughly convinced that Taylor had gone queer. "You don't really think there's gold in that country, do you?"

"Think?" said Lin. "No! I know there is. How do you suppose the lower creek gets its colors? It's bound to be there, somewhere. The only trouble is finding it. It's there though. It's got to be. It's got to wash down from somewhere, hasn't it?"

"Oh, sure," said Blake indulgently. "Sure, I admit there's gold up there. It's all around in these hills, for that matter; but it's badly spotted. Nobody has located a good vein yet. Little pockets now and then; but that ain't what I mean. The big strike—"

"It's there," said Taylor stubbornly. "It's got to be. All you say doesn't prove anything except that nobody's made it yet."

"That's right," admitted Blake. "In theory, anyway. But it's a big country, too."

"I know that," said Taylor. "But if it's in the water, it's got to come from somewhere the water drains, hasn't it? Thunder! We worked pretty well up to the headwaters, Harvey and me. Harvey, he had a hunch we were going to find it this summer. I didn't take much stock in it right at first, but—I tell you, Blake, it looks mighty promising. It's awful good-looking country. There ought to be gold in it."

"I wish I had a dollar for every square mile of good-looking country I've seen," said Blake.

Taylor laughed grudgingly. "Me too, for that matter. But I've got a hunch I'm going to strike it—'fore I come down again. Maybe Harvey passed the hunch on to me—I don't know —but I've got that hunch."

Blake nodded. He well knew it. They all had that hunch. They kept going back into those lean mountains until they were grizzled and old, and their joints were swollen with rheumatism, and their bones rasped as they walked, and their eyes were bleared and half blind. And Blake, perhaps a little pharisaically, thanked God that he was a sensible man without the gold fever.

"Well," he said, "I hope your hunch is good, Taylor. I'd sure like to see you make the ten-strike."

"Thanks," said Taylor. "Now then. Let's see. Tobacco, first of all. There'll sure be plenty of time for smoking if I don't come out till the spring."

For an hour he made purchases, and when he had finished he asked Blake if he had extra pack horses, and finally completed arrangements by which Blake's son was to take the stores in as far as the north branch, where they could be cached in a lean-to, from which Taylor could pack them to his cabin. He turned to go, but at the door paused, halted by Blake's inquiry:

"Say, Taylor! Whatever became of Harvey's dog?"

"Why—nothing. He's still up there."

"He is?"

"Yes. He's a great hunter, that dog. Goes out by himself, maybe gone all day, maybe two days. Hear him baying off on the mountain somewhere. He was gone that way when I came down."

"Didn't know about Harvey being dead, then?"

Taylor shook his head.

"Wonder how he'll take it?"

"Darned if I know."

"He'll be all broke up over it, shouldn't wonder."

"H'm." The monosyllable might have meant anything.

"That was the darnedest, smartest dog I ever saw," pursued Blake. "He was the same one that tended that bunch of sheep over the Cascades, wasn't he?"

Blake was referring to the time, some years before, when Shep, working with a grazing outfit, had become separated in a heavy fog from the main bunch of animals, and had disappeared with fifty of the sheep that were being brought down from the high country into the lowlands for the winter. That was early in October, and neither dog nor sheep were seen for almost five months and a half, and it was supposed they had perished in the cold, or had become the prey of coyotes, wolves or cougars. But one morning in April the band of sheep appeared at the ranch house, seventy miles from the spot where they had been lost, every sheep plump and well-conditioned, not one missing. Shep had wintered them alone, no man knew how nor where.

Taylor admitted it was the same dog.

295

"And that's some dog." said Blake admiringly. "Did you know Harvey—of course you did, though—refused a thousand dollars for him?"

"Yeh, I knew it. Sure."

"Not much to look at, either," Blake went on. " 'Bout half collie and half something else."

"Airedale, I guess," said Taylor.

"Just goes to show," said Blake, the true Philistine. "You can talk about your thoroughbred dogs all you want. And after all what are they good for? Why, to take a blue ribbon at a swell dog show. Then you take a dog like Shep— Say, I'd like to see some of these pure breds put that stunt over.

"A dog like Shep, though, he's been up against things; he understands. He's got the experience of life. He savvies. That was the most knowing dog I ever did see.

"Wouldn't make up to me, though. Oh, he wasn't ugly, of course. Only, he just wasn't very friendly. Let me pet him, all right, but he wouldn't wag his tail while I was doing it. One-man dog, I guess. That's the airedale in him, I suppose."

"He was always friendly enough with me," said Taylor.

This was a lie, but it seemed best to him to say it. That a dog should not be friendly with those with whom he is in daily contact is unusual, so unusual, indeed, that it awakens our distrust of the person for whom the dog shows distrust. There had never been any liking between Taylor and Harvey's dog. Taylor was that anomalous being, the man who didn't like dogs. Shep reciprocated the dislike, certainly. The antagonism had never been open, for at the slightest show of restiveness on the dog's part there had always come the quick sharp command of Harvey, whose slightest word was the dog's law. But Taylor did not intend Blake should know that; the instinct of self-protection warned him against it.

"He's always been friendly enough with me," he repeated.

"Of course. He knew you mighty well, he'd lived with you," nodded the storekeeper. "Well, I can't help wondering— You really aim to stay the winter out?"

296

"Going to make that ten-strike. Before the snow flies, if I can; if not, I'll surely stay."

"Luck to you!" said Blake. "No man I'd rather see make it!"

That was the perfunctory cordiality of the shopkeeper, however, and he probably would have said the same to any other prospector whom he hadn't personal reasons for disliking.

The last wash of gold was pouring over the marvelous domes and spires of the Painted Hills three days later when Lin Taylor entered his cabin. He had no eye for the ineffable beauty of that moment, however. He was dead tired; moreover, he meant to be up early in the morning and on his search for the vein of gold. That, he had determined, should be his first concern. The flakes in the roots of the meadow grass were already found, and could wait. He unpacked his supplies and picketed the mules. After a hurried supper he turned into his bunk and lay there, smoking his pipe, with the door open, for the night was strangely mild. When his pipe went out, he went to sleep.

Something woke him.

He lay still, listening. He could hear the lazy "champ-champ" of the mules at the grass near the cabin. It couldn't have been a prowling wild animal, or they would have been disturbed. He decided finally that it had been nothing. He did not sleep immediately, though, and after a little he rose and went to the door to look at the big misty stars. It must be, he decided, after eleven. And then again he heard the sound that, however faint, had awakened him.

Far away, yet distinct, a long mournful howl . . . repeated . . . and repeated again. . . . Shep, his murdered partner's dog!

He listened for a few moments while he smoked another pipe. The mournful cadence was lifted again, and then again. He was not moved by it. It was now so far away; now that he had identified it, it would not again disturb his sleep, and, since it was so far away, let the dog howl!

With grim lines about his mouth, Lin Taylor climbed again into his bunk. But the door was no longer open to the night. He had closed it. And now, with one ear buried in his pillow, he could not be sure whether he heard the desolate keening of the animal, or imagined it. If it was imagination . . . well, he was not strong on that! He drifted into a dreamless sleep.

He was up with the dawn, and could scarcely wait to consume his breakfast, so intense was his excitement. This morning he meant to follow the trail that he and Harvey had taken the morning he had murdered Harvey. The night preceding, the two men had lain awake until nearly daylight, prospecting in advance the ensuing day's search.

"High up—probably just below the bend at the edge of Gray Spur," Harvey had said at last. "And there'll be a lot of loose stuff down at the edge of the water, and up somewhere a scar, a new one, for there are flakes almost on top of last year's dead grass. We can take the Firetop trail and catch the branch just below the Spur."

They had taken the trail, and for Harvey it had led to eternity. Today Lin Taylor meant to take it alone, and for him it would lead to fortune!

When he opened the cabin door he saw that Shep had come back. The dog rose from the beaten area before the door, a big-shouldered, magnificently built animal, and stood silent, looking into his face. Taylor spoke, but the dog made no reply; there was no friendliness in his attitude, no stirring of his body, no wagging of his tail. Taylor had a queer feeling for an instant as if he were facing some searching inquiry. . . .

With an effort he shook off the absurd notion, and set out on his day's search. Shep followed at a discreet distance, followed up the trail on Firetop, and down into the canyon, making no advance toward friendliness, but keeping always in sight.

Lin Taylor, after the first hour, paid the animal scant heed. He had other work on hand.

But he did not discover the vein that day, and though in the morning he had told himself that he would, at sunset he told himself that he hadn't really expected to find it the first day. That would have been too absurdly easy. Tomorrow . . . ay, tomorrow!

He came down to his cabin, his mind preoccupied with the problem. He had been looking too far down the gash in the mountainside, he decided. Five hundred, a thousand, yards higher up—

Entering the cabin, he had left the door open, and disturbed by a sound behind him as he was kindling the fire, he turned and saw that Shep had followed him in and was nosing at Harvey's bunk.

"Get out of here!" said Taylor sharply, making a movement toward the dog as he spoke.

Shep half turned and stiffened, bristling.

Taylor paused with an instinctive feeling that it would be better to let the animal alone, and went back to his stove, saying nothing more.

Shep, after deliberately "smelling out" the cabin, turned and stepped slowly over the threshold and lay down outside.

Taylor closed the door, making a mental note that he wouldn't leave it open again, and then prepared his supper. He did not see the dog again that evening, but once when he wakened late in the night, he heard it howl in the distance.

In the morning he set out early again and climbed steadily up the Firetop trail to resume his search farther up the canyon. When he reached the treacherous place where Harvey had lost his life, moved by some obscure impulse, he leaned over and looked down from the precise spot where his victim had gone over. He saw the cairn . . . yes, and there was something on it! Shep! The dog had found at last its master's grave, and it lay stretched upon the boulders, perhaps sleeping.

But no, not sleeping. For as the man looked down, the dog suddenly rose and looked up. Lin Taylor moved quickly back out of sight, compelled by a feeling that he scarcely understood. Fear? Absurd! What had he to fear from a dog? And yet, if he had a gun with him . . . but he hadn't. He moved on.

When he returned from his second day's vain search for the lode he found the dog lying beside the cabin, and as he entered the door, glancing down, he noticed, lying between its paws, Harvey's prospecting pick. He recognized it at once by the thong of buckskin that Harvey had bound around the lower part of the handle, and he remembered that in burying Harvey he

299

had taken the pick from the dead man's belt and dropped it beside the cairn and then had gone off, forgetting it. The dog, of course, had found it, scented its master, and brought it up. It was a good pick, too. . . . He stepped toward the animal and bent over.

Suddenly Shep rose and stood over the pick he had been nuzzling, stiff-legged, bristling, his teeth bared.

Taylor straightened up angrily. "Get out of here," he shouted furiously. And at the same moment he let drive a kick.

The dog moved so that the blow was only a glancing one, then crouched and sprang.

It was Taylor's good fortune, unprepared as he was for the suddenness of the onslaught, to catch the dog's leap with a straight blow of both arms that flung the animal to the earth, snapping vainly as it rolled over and over. Before it could rise he had stooped and picked up a heavy piece of three-foot firewood. On the next lead the dog grazed his arm but received a stunning blow from the club, and then, dazed, a second still more deadly.

In a blaze of passion now, Taylor yet hesitated at actually beating the dog to death. . . .

He went to the cabin for his gun. The magazine was empty. He filled it; but the delay had cost him his victim.

The dog was gone. An incredible, almost miraculous recovery from the two blows on the skull. Far down the meadow, disappearing in a clump of trees, he saw it. He flung the gun to his shoulder and fired—once, twice. But in vain. Then in the flush of his anger he fired twice more at the spot where he had last seen it.

When his rage had somewhat cooled he thought of what might have happened if he had not found the piece of wood so ready to his hand, and a cold, sickly sensation permeated him. If he had not found the means for protection he would certainly have been cut to pieces by those slashing fangs. But this, he told himself, was a known danger and easily met. He had only to go armed hereafter, and at the first encounter—why, Shep would be a good dog because he would be a dead one!

So in the morning as he set out he buckled his pistol holster to his belt and put in the belt a dozen extra cartridges. And for three days, as he searched the upper end of the stream from the snowfields of Firetop down to the first bend, and searched vainly, he watched for Shep as well. But he did not see him—unless a brown shadow, half imagined, slinking through the rocks of the canyon at a great distance was the dog. It might as easily have been a coyote, or a cougar, or nothing at all. He thought with a sense of violent relief that perhaps his blows had been more deadly than he supposed, that the dog had lost itself in the forest to die.

But his relief ended that very night when, far and mournful as he had first heard it, Shep took up his dirge once more upon his master's grave.

Well, if he kept that far away, Taylor said to himself, it was all right. And closing the door he got into his bunk and muffled his ears in the blankets, and drifted into a sound slumber that lasted until just before dawn. Then, in the dim cold grayness close by the cabin, there came a different note, a hoarse, menacing burst of sound that could not be ignored or shut out by the door or the bedclothing. With a start and an oath he got out of his bunk and caught up his automatic. From the windows he could see nothing. The dawn was yet thick and formless. He unbarred the door and emerged.

A full-throated cry to the right of the cabin announced that Shep had seen him; but he could not discern the dog, strain his eyes how he would. He fired at random in the direction in which he had heard the bark—a second time—then a third. But it was without result, he was well aware. There was no sound from the animal now, and yet he had a feeling that it had not left the vicinity. Three times he circled the cabin, revolver in hand, each time a little farther afield, but he did not see Shep. Finally, he returned to the cabin, angrily muttering to himself that he was a fool. There was no need for hunting the dog; sooner or later they would meet without hunting. Until that time it was folly indeed to waste his time and energy in such pre-dawn, mad activities as he had just engaged in.

301

Moreover, he needed all his energy for the search for the mother lode. If he could find it before the snows began to fly— No. Let the dog go. Every hour must be given to the search for the big vein that lay waiting for him on the red slope of Firetop.

Yet on the trail that morning he turned not less than a dozen times, the very hairs of his head tingling with the feeling that the dog was behind him and very near. But he could actually see nothing of it; and once, a little after noon, he again heard the distant baying in the south that told him that Shep was hunting. Yet again, as he took the trail down to his cabin, he found his hand ready at his holster, his eyes alert ahead, and his body turning frequently so that he could look back.

A dull rage was burning in him that night as he went to bed, only to be wakened toward morning again by the threatening challenge of Shep near by. This morning, however, he did not get up, but lay there awake and angry, catching, each time he drifted to the verge of sleep, the strident reiteration of the dog's bark. And again that day, another day of failure on the mountain, he had the same uneasy feeling that he was being constantly shadowed. . . . He remembered, with curses upon his monumental folly, that he had had an opportunity to slay the dog, that he might have beaten it to death when he had stunned it with the length of wood, and that he had through some crazy compunction, hesitated.

And again the following morning, before the light came, the dog found and haunted the vicinity of the cabin, growing bolder, coming closer, until Lin Taylor at one time could have sworn he heard its breath puffing at the threshold, the sniff of its hot nostrils. He fired a shot through the door and sprang up quickly and threw it wide open.

Nothing.

The dog was not at the door, had not even been at the door. There was not a single trace of his pads in the clean-swept, fine, damp dust before the cabin.

So it went through another week, and it became increasingly difficult, and at last intolerable. Only once had he got a fair shot at the dog, having surprised it at the rock cairn, and then he had not scored a hit. The dog had leaped as he fired and had been lost almost instantly among the boulders of the canyon.

He knew now that the dog was shadowing him, for he saw it often, just out of range. He realized, too, that his prospecting was becoming less and less a search for the vein of gold, and more and more a tense watch for the dog. It could not go on so. He had a terrible feeling that if he failed to watch for the animal it would in some inexplicable way ambush him, and he could not keep his mind from that horrible contingency.

There was only one thing to do, he decided finally, and that was to hunt for the dog and kill it. Until that was done he would never be safe, never be at ease. And until that was done—here a thread of superstition wove through his mental processes—until that was done, he would never find the vein of gold that was to make him rich and powerful. He knew it. John Harvey, he muttered to himself, Harvey first, then Harvey's dog, and then—and only then—peace. Peace and riches. But there would be neither as long as the dog was living. That was written. It was Fate.

He was waiting, the next dawn, fully clothed, his pistol in his hand, his belt filled with extra cartridges, for the sound of the avenger, and at the dog's first bark he stepped from the door and took up the challenge that God had flung him

All through the morning he trailed the animal, glimpsing him now and then, firing often, though the range was so great as to be prohibitive of surety. He followed him up the first gentle slopes of Blue Peak, through the sparse forest clover, to the timber line, and beyond. He saw him far ahead on a snow field, his head hanging low, his pace slow and laborious. He kept up the chase across the high ridge that intervened between Blue Peak and Firetop Mountain, and he plodded wearily after in the waning of the afternoon light as the dog found again the trail that led down Firetop to the valley. And now he saw that the animal was going faster and faster, that to hope to overtake him was madness, and that he would never come within shooting range of the dog again that day.

Tomorrow he would begin again. His mistake today had been that he was too impetuous, too determined to get the thing done. A stern chase was always a long chase. Tomorrow he would hide somewhere in the valley and watch for the dog . . . which now had completely vanished among the crags of the lower spur.

He was horribly tired. He had been on edge all day. He paused for a moment to rest before beginning a steep descent along the edge of the deep canyon where all week he had been looking for the baffling vein of gold. And as he paused, reflecting how tired he was, he noticed his revolver was still in his hand, clutched tightly, almost painfully, and he realized that he had been holding it so, almost continuously ready, since early dawn. What a fool he had been, to let his nerves play fast and loose with him—over a dog! Just a dog! And when he tried to let go of the revolver he could only do so with an effort, for his fingers seemed paralyzed, frozen to the grip. He stuck the automatic in his holster and began, a moment later, to descend the trail. Tomorrow, after a night's sleep . . . tomorrow—

He rounded a sharp turn of the trail and suddenly faced Shep, his enemy, whom he had given up for that day.

The dog stood rigid and menacing, athwart his way. In a terrified flash Lin Taylor saw that the dog would be upon him before he could draw his revolver from its holster with his clumsy stiffened fingers. He uttered a sharp cry, wheeled about, and fled back up the trail. His foot turned on a loose bit of rock. He spun around, swayed for an instant on the edge of the cliff, and then, as John Harvey had done before him, he pitched over, his body hurtling through space, to land far below upon the deadly jagged rocks of the canyon, broken, bloody and lifeless.

And it was here that the searchers in the spring found his rotted remains, here with the broken bones of his hands actually clutching the crumpled outcropping of the richest vein of gold that the Painted Hills had ever offered, or perhaps ever would offer, to men.

A surprising solution to terror

Hector

BY H. C. BUNNER

*I*T *W A S* such a quiet old home, so comfortably covered with wistaria from basement to chimney-tops, and it stood on the corner of two such quiet, old-fashioned streets on the East Side of New York that you would never have imagined that it held six of the most agitated and perturbed women in the great city. But the three Miss Pellicoes, their maid, their waitress and their cook could not have been more troubled in their feminine minds had they been six exceptionally attractive Sabines with the Roman soldiery in full cry.

For twenty years—ever since the death of old Mr. Pellicoe

305

—these six women had lived in mortal fear of the marauding man, and the Man had come at last. That very evening, at a quarter past eight o'clock, a creature who called himself a book agent had rung the front doorbell. Honora, the waitress, had opened the door a couple of inches, inquired the stranger's business, learned it, told him to depart, tried to close the door, and discovered that the man had inserted his toe in the opening. She had closed the door violently, and the man had emitted a single oath of deep and sincere profanity. He had then kicked the door and departed, with a marked limp. . . .

The eldest Miss Pellicoe, who was the head of the household, had decided forthwith what was to be done.

"Sisters," she said to her two juniors, "we must keep a dog."

"A dog!" cried Miss Angela, the youngest. "Oh, how nice!"

"I do not think it is nice at all," said Miss Pellicoe, somewhat sternly, "nor would you, Angela, if you had any conception of what it really meant. I do not propose to keep a lap dog, or a King Charles spaniel, but a *dog*—a mastiff, or a bloodhound, or some animal of that nature, such as would spring at the throat of an invader and bear him to the ground!"

"Oh, dear!" gasped Miss Angela. "I should be afraid of him!"

"You do not understand as yet, Angela," Miss Pellicoe explained, knitting her brows. "My intention is to procure the animal as a—in fact—a puppy, and thus enable him to grow up and to regard us with affection, and be willing to hold himself at all times in readiness to afford us the protection we desire. It is clearly impossible to have a man in the house. I have decided upon a mastiff."

When Miss Pellicoe decided upon a thing, Miss Angela Pellicoe and her other sister promptly acquiesced. On this occasion they did not, even in their inmost hearts, question the wisdom of the decision of the head of the house. A man, they knew, was not to be thought of. For twenty years the Pellicoe house had been a bower of virginity. The only men who ever entered it

306

were the old family doctor, the older family lawyer, and annually, on New Year's Day, in accordance with an obsolete custom, Major Kitsedge, their father's old partner, once junior of the firm of Pellicoe & Kitsedge. Not even the butcher or the baker or the candlestickmaker forced an entrance to that innocent dovecote. They handed in their wares through a wicket gate in the back yard and were sent about their business by the chaste Honora.

The next morning, having awakened to find themselves and the silver still safe, Miss Pellicoe and Miss Angela set out for a dog store which they had seen advertised in the papers. It was in an unpleasantly low and ill-bred part of the town, and when the two ladies reached it they paused outside to note, with lengthened faces, the combined clamor and smell that emanated from its open door.

"This," said Miss Pellicoe, after a brief deliberation, "is not a place for *us*. If we are to procure a dog, he must be procured in some other way. It need not entail a loss of self-respect.

"I have it!" she added with a sudden inspiration. "I will write to Hector."

Hector was the sole male representative of the Pellicoe family. He was a second cousin of the Misses Pellicoe. He lived out West—his address varying from year to year. Once in a long while Miss Pellicoe wrote to him, just to keep herself in communication with the Man of the family. It made her feel more secure, in view of possible emergencies. She had not seen Hector since he was nineteen. He was perhaps the last person of any positive virility who had had the freedom of the Pellicoe household. He had used that freedom mainly in making attempts to kiss Honora, who was then in her buxom prime, and in decorating the family portraits with cork moustaches and whiskers. Miss Pellicoe clung to the Man of the family as an abstraction; but she was always glad that he lived in the West. Addressing him in his capacity of Man of the family, she wrote to him and asked him to supply her with a young mastiff, and to send her bill therefor. She explained the situation to him, and made him understand that the dog must be of a character to be regarded as a male relative.

Hector responded at once. He would send a mastiff pup within a week. The pup's pedigree was unfortunately lost, but the breed was high. Fifty dollars would cover the cost and expenses of transportation. The pup was six months old.

For ten days the Pellicoe household was in a fever of expectation. Miss Pellicoe called in a carpenter and, chaperoned by the entire household, held an interview with him and directed him how to construct a dog house in the back yard—a dog house with one door about six inches square, to admit the occupant in his innocent puphood, and with another door about four feet in height to emit him when, in the pride of his mature masculinity he should rush forth upon the burglar and the book agent. The carpenter remarked that he "never seen no such dorg as that," but Miss Pellicoe thought him at once ignorant and ungrammatical, and paid no heed to him.

In conclave assembled, the Misses Pellicoe decided to name the dog Hector. Besides the consideration of the claims of gratitude and family affection, they remembered that Hector was a classical hero.

The ten days came to an end when, just at dusk of a dull January day two stalwart expressmen, with much open grumbling and smothered cursing, deposited a huge packing case in the vestibule of the Pellicoe house and departed, slamming the doors behind them. From this box proceeded such yelps and howls that the entire household rushed affrighted to peer through the slats that gridironed the top. Within was a mighty black beast, as high as a table, that flopped itself wildly about, clawed at the sides of the box, and swung in every direction a tail as large as a policeman's billy.

It was Hector. There was no mistake about it, for Mr. Hector Pellicoe's card was nailed to a slat. It was Hector, the six-months-old pup for whose diminutive proportions the small door in the doghouse had been devised, and for whom a saucer of lukewarm milk was even then waiting by the kitchen range.

"Oh, Sister!" cried Miss Angela, "we *never* can get him out! You'll have to send for a *Man!*"

"I certainly shall not send for a *Man* at this hour of the evening," said Miss Pellicoe, white but firm; "and I shall not leave the poor creature imprisoned during the night." Here Hector yawped madly.

"I shall take him out," exclaimed Miss Pellicoe, *"myself!"*

They hung upon her neck and entreated her not to risk her life, but Miss Pellicoe had made up her mind. The three maids shoved the box into the butler's pantry, shrieking with terror every time Hector leaped at the slats, and at last, with the two younger Pellicoes holding one door a foot open, and the three maids holding the other door an inch open, Miss Pellicoe seized the household hatchet, and began her awful task. One slat! Miss Pellicoe was white but firm. Two slats! Miss Pellicoe was whiter and firmer. Three slats!—and a vast black body leaped high in the air. With five simultaneous shrieks, the two doors were slammed to, and Miss Pellicoe and Hector were left together in the butler's pantry.

The courage of the younger Pellicoes asserted itself after a moment, and they flung open the pantry door. Miss Pellicoe, looking as though she needed aromatic vinegar, leaned against the wall. Hector had his forepaws on her shoulders, and was licking her face in exuberant affection.

"Sisters," gasped Miss Pelicoe, "will you kindly remove him? I should like to faint."

But Hector had already released her to dash at Miss Angela, who frightened him by going into such hysterics that Miss Pellicoe was obliged to deny herself the luxury of a faint. Then he found the maids, and after driving them before him like chaff for five minutes, succeeded in convincing Honora of the affectionate purpose of his demonstrations, and accepted her invitation to the kitchen, where he emptied the saucer of milk in three laps.

"I think, Honora," suggested Miss Pellicoe, who had resumed command, "that you might perhaps, give him a slice or two of last night's leg of mutton. Perhaps he needs something more sustaining."

Honora produced the mutton leg. It was clearly what Hector

wanted. He took it from her without ceremony, bore it under the sink and ate all of it except about six inches of the bone, which he took to bed with him.

The next day, feeling the need of masculine advice, Miss Pellicoe resolved to address herself to the policeman on the beat, and she astonished him with the following question:

"Sir," she said, in true Johnsonian style, "what height should a mastiff dog attain at the age of six months?"

The policeman stared at her in utter astonishment.

"They do be all sizes, Mum," he replied, "like a piece of cheese."

"My relative in the West," explained Miss Pellicoe, "has sent me a dog, and I am given to understand that his age is six months. As he is phenomenally large I have thought it best to seek for information. Has my relative been imposed upon?"

"It's har-r-d to tell, Mum," replied the policeman, dubiously. Then his countenance brightened. "Does his feet fit him?" he inquired.

"What—what do you mean?" asked Miss Pellicoe, shrinking back a little.

"Is his feet like blackin'-boxes on th' ind of his legs?"

"They are certainly very large."

"Thin 'tis a pup! You see, Mum, with a pup 'tis this way. The feet starts first, an' the pup grows up to 'em, like. Av they match him, he's grown. Av he has arctics on, he's a pup."

Hector's growth in the next six months dissipated all doubts as to his puphood. He became a four-legged Colossus, martial toward cats, aggressive toward the tradesmen at the wicket gate, impartially affectionate toward all the household, and voracious beyond all imagining. But he might have eaten the gentle ladies out of house and home, and they would never have dreamed of protesting. The house had found a Head—even a Head above Miss Pellicoe.

Loved by an army but loyal to one

Verdun Belle

BY ALEXANDER WOOLLCOTT

I *FIRST* heard the saga of Verdun Belle's adventure as it was being told one June afternoon under a drowsy apple tree in the troubled valley of the Marne.

The story began in a chill grimy Lorraine village where, in hovels and haymows, a disconsolate detachment of United States Marines lay waiting the order to go up into that maze of trenches of which the crumbling traces still weave a haunted web around the citadel bearing the immortal name of Verdun.

Into this village at dusk one day in the early spring of 1918 there came out of space a shabby, lonesome dog—a squat setter of indiscreet, complex and unguessable ancestry.

One watching her as she trotted intently along the aromatic

311

village street would have sworn that she had an important engagement with the mayor and was, regretfully, a little late.

At the end of the street she came to where a young buck private lounged glumly on a doorstep. Halting in her tracks, she sat down to contemplate him. Then, satisfied seemingly by what she sensed and saw, she came over and flopped down beside him in a most companionable manner, settling herself comfortably as if she had come at last to her long journey's end. His pleased hand reached over and played with one silken chocolate-colored ear.

Somehow that gesture sealed a compact between those two. There was thereafter no doubt in either's mind that they belonged to each other for better or for worse, in sickness and in health, through weal and woe, world without end.

She ate when and what he ate. She slept beside him in the day, her muzzle resting on his leg so that he could not get up in the night and go forgetfully back to America without her noticing it.

To the uninitiated onlookers her enthusiasm may not have been immediately explicable. In the eyes of his top sergeant and his company clerk he may well have seemed an undistinguished warrior, freckle-faced and immensely indifferent to the business of making the world safe for democracy.

Verdun Belle thought him the most charming person in all the world. There was a loose popular notion that she had joined up with the company as mascot and belonged to them all. She affably let them think so, but she had her own ideas on the subject.

When they moved up into the line she went along and was so obviously trench-broken that they guessed she had already served a hitch with some French regiment in that once desperate region.

They even built up the not implausible theory that she had come to them lonely from the grave of some little soldier in faded horizon blue.

Certainly she knew trench ways, knew in the narrowest of passages how to keep out from underfoot and was so well aware of the dangers of the parapet that a plate of chicken bones up there would not have interested her. She even knew what gas was, and after a reminding whiff of it became more than reconciled to the regulation gas mask, which they patiently wrecked for all subsequent human use because an unimaginative War Department had not foreseen the peculiar anatomical specifications of Verdun Belle.

In May, when the outfit was engaged in the exhausting activities which the High Command was pleased to describe as "resting," Belle thought it a convenient time to present an interested but amply forewarned regiment with seven wriggling casuals, some black and white and mottled as a mackerel sky, some splotched with the same brown as her own.

These newcomers complicated the domestic economy of the leathernecks' haymow, but they did not become an acute problem until that memorable night late in the month when breathless word bade these troops be up and away.

The Second Division of the A.E.F. was always being thus picked up by the scruff of the neck and flung across France. This time the enemy had snapped up Soissons and Rheims and were pushing with dreadful ease and speed toward the remembering Marne.

Foch had called upon the Americans to help stem the tide. Ahead of the marines, as they scrambled across the monotonous plain of the Champagne, there lay amid the ripening wheat fields a mean and hilly patch of timber called Belleau Wood. Verdun Belle went along.

The leatherneck had solved the problem of the puppies by drowning four and placing the other three in a basket he had begged from a village woman.

His notion that he could carry the basket would have come as a shock to whatever functionary back in Washington designed the marine pack, which, with its neat assortment of food supplies, extra clothing, emergency restoratives and gruesome implements for destruction, had been so painstakingly calculated to exhaust the capacity of the human back. But in his need the young marine somehow contrived to add an item not in the regulations— namely, one basket containing three unweaned and faintly resentful puppies.

313

By night and by day the troop movement was made, now in little wheezing trains, now in swarming lorries, now afoot.

Sometimes Belle's crony rode. Sometimes (under pressure of popular clamor against the room he was taking up) he would yield up his place to the basket and jog along with his hand on the tailboard, with Belle trotting behind him.

All the soldiers in Christendom seemed to be moving across France to some nameless crossroads over the hill. Obviously this was no mere shift from one sector to another. They were going to war.

Everyone had assured the stubborn youngster that he would not be able to manage, and now misgivings settled on him like crows.

He guessed that Verdun Belle must be wondering too. He turned to assure her that everything would be all right. She was not there. Ahead of him, behind him, there was no sign of her. No one within call had seen her quit the line. He kept telling himself she would show up. But the day went and the night came without her.

He jettisoned the basket and pouched the pups in his forest-green shirt in the manner of kangaroos. In the morning one of the three was dead. And the problem of transporting the other two was now tangled by the circumstance that he had to feed them.

An immensely interested old woman in the village where they halted at sunup, vastly amused by this spectacle of a soldier trying to carry two nursing puppies to war, volunteered some milk for the cup of his mess kit, and with much jeering advice from all sides, and, by dint of the eye dropper from his pack, he tried sheepishly to be a mother to the two waifs. The attempt was not shiningly successful.

He itched to pitch them over the fence. But if Verdun Belle had not been run over by some thundering camion, if she lived she would find him, and then what would he say when her eyes asked what he had done with the pups?

So, as the order was shouted to fall in, he hitched his pack to his back and stuffed his charges back into his shirt.

314

Now, in the morning light, the highway was choked. Down from the lines in agonized, grotesque rout came the stream of French life from the threatened countryside, jumbled fragments of fleeing French regiments. But America was coming up the road.

It was a week in which the world held its breath.

The battle was close at hand now. Field hospitals, jostling in the river of traffic, sought space to pitch their tents. The top sergeant of one such outfit was riding on the driver's seat of an ambulance. Marines in endless number were moving up fast.

It was one of these who, in a moment's halt, fell out of line, leaped to the step of the blockaded ambulance, and looked eagerly into the medico top sergeant's eyes.

"Say, buddy," whispered the youngster, "take care of these for me. I lost their mother in the jam."

The Top found his hands closing on two drowsy pups.

All that day the field hospital personnel was harried by the task of providing nourishment for the two casuals who had been thus unexpectedly attached to them for rations. Once established in a farmhouse (from which they were promptly shelled out), the Top went over the possible provender and found that the pups were not yet equal to a diet of bread, corn syrup and corned willy. A stray cow, loosed from her moorings in the great flight, was browsing tentatively in the next field, and two orderlies who had carelessly reminisced of life on their farms back home were detailed to induce her cooperation.

But the bombardment had brought out a certain moody goatishness in this cow, and she would not let them come near her. After a hot and maddening chase that lasted two hours, the two milkmen reported a complete failure to their disgusted chief.

The problem was still unsolved at sundown, and the pups lay faint in their bed of absorbent cotton out in the garden, when, bringing up the rear of a detachment of marines that straggled past, there trotted a brown-and-white setter.

"It would be swell if she had milk in her," the top sergeant said reflectively, wondering how he could salvage the mascot of an outfit on the march.

But his larcenous thoughts were waste. At the gate she halted dead in her tracks, flung her head high to sniff the air, wheeled sharp to the left and became just a streak of brown and white against the ground. The entire staff came out and formed a jostling circle to watch the family reunion.

After that it was tacitly assumed that these casuals belonged. When the hospital was ordered to shift further back beyond the reach of the whining shells, Verdun Belle and the pups were intrusted to an ambulance driver and went along in style. They all moved—bag, baggage and livestock—into the deserted little Château of the Guardian Angel, of which the front windows were curtained against the eyes and dust of the road, but of which the rear windows looked out across drooping fruit trees upon a sleepy, murmurous, multicolored valley, fair as the Garden of the Lord.

The operating tables, with acetylene torches to light them, were set up in what had been a tool shed. Cots were strewn in the orchard alongside. Thereafter for a month there was never rest in that hospital.

The surgeons and orderlies spelled each other at times, snatching morsels of sleep and returning a few hours later to relieve the others. But Verdun Belle took no time off. Between cat naps in the corner, due attentions to her restive brood and an occasional snack for herself, she managed somehow to be on hand for every ambulance, cursorily examining each casualty as he was lifted to the ground.

Then, in the four o'clock dark of one morning, the orderly bending over a stretcher that had just been rested on the ground was hit by something that half bowled him over.

The projectile was Verdun Belle. Every quivering inch of her proclaimed to all concerned that here was a case she was personally in charge of. From nose to tail tip she was taut with excitement, and a kind of eager whimpering bubbled up out of her as if she ached to sit back on her haunches and roar to the star-spangled sky but was really too busy at the moment to indulge herself in any release so satisfying to her soul. For here was this mess of a leatherneck of hers to be washed up first. So

316

like him to get all dirty the moment her back was turned! The first thing he knew as he came to was the feel of a rough pink tongue cleaning his ears.

I saw them all next day. An ambling passer-by, I came upon two cots shoved together under an apple tree. Belle and her ravenous pups occupied one of these. On the other the young marine—a gas case, I think, but maybe his stupor was shell shock and perhaps he had merely had a crack on the head—was deep in a dreamless sleep. Before drifting off he had taken the comforting precaution to reach out one hand and close it tight on a silken ear.

Later that day he told me all about his dog. I doubt if I ever knew his name, but some quirk of memory makes me think his home was in West Philadelphia and that he had joined up with the marines when he came out of school.

I went my way before dark and never saw them again, nor ever heard tell what became of the boy and his dog. I never knew when, if ever, he was shipped back into the fight, nor where, if ever, those two met again. It is, you see, a story without an end, though there must be those here and there in this country who witnessed and could set down for us the chapter that has never been written.

I hope there was something prophetic in the closing paragraph of the anonymous account of Verdun Belle which appeared the next week in the A.E.F. newspaper, *The Stars and Stripes*. That paragraph was a benison which ran in this wise:

Before long they would have to ship him on to the evacuation hospital, on from there to the base hospital, on and on and on. It was not very clear to anyone how another separation could be prevented. It was a perplexing question, but they knew in their hearts they could safely leave the answer to someone else. They could leave it to Verdun Belle.

BIOGRAPHICAL NOTES: *About the Authors*

About the Authors

ZACHARY BALL writes of the people in "Turtle Hound" from his own experience. He was born in a log cabin and lived in the Blackjack Hills of Missouri until he was six, when his family moved to Kansas. After several years of schooling he worked at various odd jobs, until he was given the juvenile lead in a traveling "rag opera" company's tent shows. He toured all over the South, getting to know the people and the country at first hand. During World War II—Mr. Ball had lost the sight of one eye and so could not enlist—the actor turned writer. He has since published numerous books for young people.

It took emigration to America to turn LUDWIG BEMELMANS' sense of fun into artistic and literary channels; that it did was fortunate both for him and his readers. He was born in the Austrian Tyrol, the son of an artist. As a schoolboy his exploits so exasperated his parents that they sent him to work for his uncle, who in turn contrived to send him to America. His first job, in the dining room of a fashionable New York hotel, is delightfully chronicled in *Hotel Splendide,* and his army service in World War I (he became a United States citizen in 1918), is irreverently described in *My War With the United States.*

Every experience was material for his writing and drawing facility, and soon he was turning out sketches, cover illustrations and articles like "Dog Story" for The *New Yorker* magazine and others. His whimsical writing lent itself easily to both adult and children's books like *Madeleine,* which he illustrated in color. A recognized gourmet and gourmand, Bemelmans was manager and host for a time of a small Viennese restaurant in New York, where his drawings still decorate the walls.

H. C. BUNNER, author of "Hector," loathed his given names (Henry Cuyler) but loved New York, the city in which he grew up and, like O. Henry, never tired of writing about. Young Bunner prepared for college, but finding it beyond his parents' means he went to work. After trying various jobs he joined the staff of *Puck,* America's earliest weekly devoted to wit and sophisticated humor, and became its chief editor at 23. For many years he wrote the major portion of every issue—poems, parodies and short short stories, the first of their kind. Until his health failed, at 40, Bunner's witty conversation, phenomenal memory and strong likes and dislikes made him the center of a brilliant social group that flourished in New York in the 1880's.

SHEILA BURNFORD burst into the bestseller list with her very first book, *The Incredible Journey,* from which "A Dog of Good Omen" was taken. This is perhaps characteristic of a woman whose life has brimmed with activity. Scottish-born, she is the mother of three children and a regular contributor to such magazines as *Punch, Canadian Poetry* and the *Glasgow Herald;* she has her pilot's license, and can outshoot most men. During World War II she served in a Royal Naval Hospital, and after a short leave to marry her pediatrician-husband, returned to service as an ambulance driver.

Although the incredible journey in Mrs. Burnford's book is imaginary, the animals are not. Luath, the Labrador retriever, is her own gun dog, and the cat and bull terrier are real animals. They have been faithfully portrayed in a noted motion picture version of *The Incredible Journey.*

The setting for "A Hunter's Horn" comes naturally to BILLY CLARK. Like his young hero Jeb, the author, one .of a family of eight children, grew up near the Ohio and Big Sandy rivers at the foot of the Kentucky hills. Young Clark had to struggle for his education. He walked a 14-mile trap line every morning before school. He sold pelts, planted and hoed corn in the river bottoms, hunted fish, turtles, bullfrogs—and combining these sources of income, managed to stay in school. As he grew up Mr. Clark wrote about the hills he knew so well and how they influence the people who live in them. He continued his writing while working his way through college and in 1957 published his first book, *Trail of the Hunter's Horn*. Since then Mr. Clark has published several novels for young people.

ESTHER BIRDSALL DARLING wrote "Trail of Danger" from her own years of living in Nome, Alaska. For three years following her graduation from Mills College in California Mrs. Darling traveled widely—in Europe, the Near East, and in Hawaii and Mexico. Then she married an Alaskan merchant and settled in Nome, where she came to know and admire the great work dogs of the north. She founded the Nome Kennel Club and wrote several books about the sled dogs, of which *Luck of the Trail* is best known today. Mrs. Darling now lives in California, one of the few people who know and remember what Alaska was like in the years just following the great Klondike gold rush of the 1890's.

VELA DePEUGH, author of "Marty and the Monster," and Tiger, her first dog, were born on the same day. Tiger was her close companion when she was growing up in Iowa, and once held a strayed and angry bull at bay until Miss DePeugh, then aged five, could flee to safety in her grandmother's house. The author's home, when she was a child, was always filled with pets —cats, birds, a rabbit, a pig, and of course various dogs of pure and mixed breeds. Later the family moved to southern California where Miss DePeugh now lives. She has written several mysteries, a result, perhaps, of living for a hair-raising period during her school days in a haunted house.

323

Although WALTER A. DYER's "Gulliver the Great" is an exciting story of the high seas, Mr. Dyer in his lifetime never strayed further from western Massachusetts than Long Island. He was an inspired journalist and imaginative writer from his grade school days, when he founded, edited and for two years ran a paying newspaper singlehandedly. After graduation from Amherst College he became managing editor of *Country Life in America,* an illustrated magazine devoted to country homes.

Several years later, he and his wife settled in their own country home near Amherst, and Mr. Dyer devoted much of his time to writing—historical fiction and dog stories. The Dyers had several dogs, but their favorite was given them by their neighbor, Robert Frost. A huge black dog, gentle, intelligent and kingly, he may have suggested the idea of the story, "Gulliver the Great," for which, until his death in 1943, Mr. Dyer received countless fan letters each year.

MARGUERITE HENRY, author of "Reddy As Always," is the loving owner of numerous dogs and horses, as well as the nation's most popular writer of stories about them. A native of the midwest, and one of a large happy family in Milwaukee, Wisconsin, Mrs. Henry early developed a love of literature and writing. Her father, who also wrote, would often read Shakespeare aloud to the family, and her sister Gertrude was and still is her most trusted critic.

After graduation from Milwaukee State Teachers College, Mrs. Henry married and began to write stories and articles for magazines, then turned to books for young readers. Her *Misty of Chincoteague* won the Lewis Carroll Shelf Award, was made into a film, and has become one of the best-loved, most widely read books of our time. For her material Mrs. Henry lived for a while on Chincoteague off the Virginia coast, getting to know at first hand the island, its people and its famous herd of wild horses. Mrs. Henry finally yielded to countless pleas for a sequel to her famous story, when Misty foaled during a storm and tidal wave. Its title: *Stormy, Misty's Foal.*

ALEXANDER HULL led an unusual life for a writer of adventure stories. A versatile and successful musician, he was concert singer, music teacher, composer, cellist and pianist before turning author. Shortly after graduation from the University of Pennsylvania Hull went to the Pacific coast, where he was to spend the rest of his life and in whose magnificent settings his most exciting stories were laid. He was head of the music department of a college in Oregon for many years; then in 1939 he moved to Seattle where he wrote scripts for commercial radio. Meanwhile, a novel which Hull had written during a period between careers, *Shep of the Painted Hills,* was made into a motion picture. Hull remained in Seattle, dividing his time between writing and conducting a radio program of classical music and commentary. Before his death in 1953 he had published more than 50 adventure stories, of which "Justice in the Painted Hills" is best known today.

Thanks to RUDYARD KIPLING, English life in India under British rule is as familiar to Americans today as American history. "Garm—A Hostage" is one of his best tales of that period. Kipling was born in Bombay and learned Hindustani from his *ayahs* before going to school in England, where he edited his school paper. Upon returning to India, his news assignments as youthful reporter for the *Lahore Civil and Military Gazette* gave him the opportunity to travel throughout India and gather first-hand material for his own writing. Later he met and married a girl from Vermont, where he lived for awhile and where he wrote his famous Jungle Books, "Garm—A Hostage," and other stories.

Kipling finally settled in Sussex, England, frequently interrupting his writing to cover news assignments—notably, the Boer War and World War I. Although critics tended to treat him lightly, Kipling's immense popularity extended far beyond England, and he became the first English writer to receive the Nobel Prize. Until his death in 1936 he continued to write the poems, stories and novels that have made him one of the world's favorite authors.

JIM KJELGAARD grew up on a farm in the Black Forest region of Pennsylvania. Between school sessions he and his brothers ran trap lines, shot deer and fished for trout, and once spent an entire season in the woods with a friend, hunting and trapping.

After high school Kjelgaard was, at one time or another, a laborer, teamster, factory worker, plumber's apprentice, and surveyor's assistant. His writing career began when he sold his first story to a magazine that paid for it with a two-year subscription. Undiscouraged, he kept writing. By the early 1940's, "Pat'tidge Dog" and other stories were appearing in national magazines, and *Forest Patrol,* the first of more than 40 books he has written for young people, had been published. As often as possible, Kjelgaard is off on a hunting and fishing expedition to the wilderness areas of the United States and Canada.

ERIC KNIGHT was born in 1897 in Yorkshire, England, where he held various factory jobs before coming to America at 15. After serving in World War II Knight was a reporter, drama critic and Hollywood film writer until he settled in Pennsylvania as a free-lance writer. It was then that he created Sam Small, the doughty farmer and soldier, famous for his flying feats. These stories, like Knight's now classic "Lassie Come Home," were set in his native Yorkshire.

When the United States entered World War II Knight was commissioned as a major in an army film unit. During the war he continued to write, but his career was ended when he was killed in the crash of a military transport plane.

RUTH ADAMS KNIGHT has combined her twin talents for journalism and fiction in many of her books, including *Valiant Comrade* from which "Dog for Defense" was taken. A native of Ohio, she wrote prize-winning stories at an early age, and while a journalism student at Toledo University began writing

326

special features for the Toledo *Times*. Before long she was covering news beats and editing the drama, motion picture and book sections for that paper.

In New York she wrote scripts for popular radio shows like *Cavalcade of America* and *Dr. Christian*, and has since written many articles and books based on her travels and research.

PATRICIA LAUBER started writing about her dog Clarence because, she says, "he expected it of me." All the adventures in the book *Clarence Turns Sea Dog*, from which "Buried Treasure" is taken, "either have happened to Clarence or might very well happen to him tomorrow," she says. Miss Lauber's enthusiasm and understanding for animals, people and science run through her more than twenty books that deal with such diverse subjects as the planets, dolphins, the sea, penguins, the changing face of North America, and the Scottish highlanders.

JACK LONDON crammed into his short life all the adventure and excitement he put into his stories. He went to sea on a sealing schooner; he hoboed his way across the country; he was an oyster pirate in San Francisco bay, and he sailed to the South Seas in his own yacht. He was born in 1876 in San Francisco, where his childhood was spent in poverty. As a boy he took all kinds of odd jobs to keep alive, and at sixteen was a longshoreman on the waterfront. To enter college he crammed four years of high school reading into one, then left in his freshman year and joined the gold rush to Alaska. He found no gold there, although his books about Alaska—like *The Call of the Wild*, from which "For the Love of a Man" is taken—are his best, and made his fortune. London built his own yacht in which he sailed across the Pacific, and a number of his stories are set in the South Seas. When he died, at 40, he had written more than twenty volumes of novels and short stories and hundreds of magazine and newspaper articles.

DON MARQUIS always wanted to be a serious writer and to have a column with a byline. Fortunately for the millions who read his columns in the New York *Tribune* and *Sun,* he failed in the first but brilliantly succeeded in the second. His genial folk stories and commentary were always entertaining, and their high literary quality never overshadowed their lively humor. Joel Chandler Harris, with whom he had worked on *Uncle Remus's Magazine* in Atlanta before coming to New York, had encouraged his flair for fantasy and for creating wonderful animal characters. Some of Marquis' best stories dealt with Archy the cockroach who inhabited the *Sun* office and typed up the ashcan adventures of Mehitabel the *toujours gai* alley cat. Although he suffered tragic personal losses in the death of his son, daughter and wife, Marquis' keen wit and colorful personality influenced journalistic circles in New York for many years. Marquis' serious writing is largely ignored today, but his *Lives and Times of Archy and Mehitabel* and his stories such as "Blood Will Tell" are as fresh and entertaining as when he wrote them.

It is not surprising that Col. S. P. MEEK has preferred to write about working dogs, since his own life has been crowded with activity. A star athlete in college, he won his Phi Beta Kappa key before specializing in chemical and metallurgical work and joining the army in 1917. He began to write fiction during a long army career that took him to posts throughout the United States, Hawaii and the Canal Zone. While stationed at Picatinny Arsenal in New Jersey he became fascinated by the Seeing Eye dogs he saw at work on the streets of nearby Morristown, and wrote *Pat: The Story of a Seeing Eye Dog,* from which "Crisis in the Storm" is taken. In 1943 he was crippled by an ammunition explosion, and since his retirement has devoted himself to books about sheep dogs, patrol dogs, coast guard dogs, circus dogs and hunting dogs. Hunting, raising setters and judging dog shows are his favorite hobbies.

FARLEY MOWAT, who wrote the foreword as well as "Battle Tactics" in this book, was born in Canada in 1921. His idyllic boyhood in Saskatchewan, spent with his unusual parents and Mutt, an unusual dog, is warmly recounted in *The Dog Who Wouldn't Be*. His was an outdoor life, of growing up on the great plains of Canada, hunting in the fall and sailing in summer on the unpredictable Saskatchewan River. During World War II he served as platoon commander and officer in Sicily and Northern Europe, and began his career as a free lance author following two years spent in the Arctic with the remaining members of a lost Eskimo tribe. Winner of several awards for his work in the field of race relations and for juvenile literature, he is one of Canada's outstanding authors.

As a boy in Scotland, JOHN MUIR wanted more than anything to explore the wilderness of North America. In the 1840's his father moved to a farm in Wisconsin, and after Muir left the University there he began exploring the country on foot. He traveled thousands of miles through the Great Lakes area, Canada and the West, and on one journey walked all the way from Indiana to Mexico.

One of our country's greatest naturalists, Muir first made the public aware of the need for a conservation program, and saw a system of national parks established under his friend President Theodore Roosevelt. He loved animals and disliked the notion of a world made for men alone, with animals to serve them. "Stickeen" is his tribute to the half-wild little dog who accompanied him in his explorations.

JACK O'BRIEN was one of those soldiers of fortune to whom adversity, hardship, danger and romance are everyday encounters.

As the chief surveyor for the Byrd Antarctic expedition,

he was in charge of the dogs taken along on the trip. He drove huskies on prospecting trips into northern Canada and worked with the big sled dogs for such a long time that he came to know them as few men do.

"The Truest of the Breed" is taken from his book *Valiant, Dog of the Timberline*. Set in northern Montana, it recreates the era of the old West when sheepmen and cattlemen fought for possession of the land.

ALFRED OLLIVANT was brought up in the best British tradition. He attended Rugby and the Royal Military Academy at Woolwich, and was commissioned in the Royal Artillery. Then an accident turned him abruptly from a military career to writing; a fall from a horse injured his spine and forced him to resign. It was while lying flat on his back that he wrote his first and best-known book, *Owd Bob,* published with spectacular success in America as *Bob, Son of Battle.* "Red Wull," Owd Bob's enemy, is a story from this book.

Ollivant was extremely sensitive to criticism. On one occasion he requested his publisher to print four copies of a new book—one each for himself, the publisher, a friend who liked the manuscript, and the public. Fortunately his publisher did not agree, and Ollivant, before his death, had published 14 books for children and adults.

ERNEST THOMPSON SETON was one of the few men, wholly dedicated to nature and animals from an early age, who was also able to communicate his love easily to others. As a child in Ontario he spent countless hours studying the birds and animals in the forests, and later, when tuberculosis interrupted his college studies, he went camping and hunting to regain his health.

In 1898 Seton collected eight of his realistic animal stories and published them under the title *Wild Animals I Have Known.* Another collection was called *Animal Heroes;* one of the heroes

330

was "Snap," the selection included in this book. Seton's stories were an immediate success, and he continued to publish as fast as he could write and illustrate. But he remained above all a naturalist, and spent long periods exploring and hunting. Seton felt a sense of mission about Americans growing up with a love for their outdoors, and was instrumental in establishing the Boy Scouts of America. In 1930 he moved to New Mexico, where he lived until his death in 1946.

ELSIE SINGMASTER spent much of her life in and around the Pennsylvania Dutch country. Her father was of Pennsylvania German stock; her mother was a Quaker. Both of these traditions later became background for her writing, and Gettysburg, her home for many years, provided ample inspiration for stories set in Civil War times.

Although she started writing when she was eleven, it was not until she was taking a theme course in college that Miss Singmaster hit upon her subject. A new topic was required every day in the course, and after a few weeks of racking her brains for far-flung subjects and settings, she began to see that the people she had known all her life were most interesting to her. From that time until her death in 1958 most of her stories reflected the Pennsylvania Dutch background of "A Pair of Lovers."

JOHN STEINBECK was born in Salinas, California, in 1902. After leaving college he held an assortment of jobs: he was a fruit picker, bricklayer, ranch hand, and unpublished but ambitious writer. He earned nothing but rejection slips until finally, in 1929, *Cup of Gold* was published and Steinbeck turned his full attention to writing.

In 1940 Steinbeck published *The Grapes of Wrath,* a story of migratory workers which became the most famous novel to emerge from the depression. Over the next fifteen years he published many successful books, notably *East of Eden* and *Tortilla Flat*. Recently he traveled over the entire country to rediscover the land, accompanied by Charley, the intelligent poodle of "Mind-Reading Dog." Mr. Steinbeck won the Pulitzer Prize in 1940 and, in 1962, the Nobel Prize for Literature.

RUTH TANNER, at the age when most little girls are playing with dolls, was most likely to be found chasing rustlers or branding cattle, accompanied by Tip, the faithful shepherd collie of "Wild Dog." She grew up on a Colorado cattle ranch—along with Tip, three brothers, assorted calves and ponies, a bear cub, wild prairie chickens, and a pet goat. Tip, she says, "helped Dad and Mother ride herd on us." He acted as their protector, too, saving Ruth's life one summer by grabbing a rattlesnake just as it struck at her ankle.

Miss Tanner now lives in Kansas, where she spends much of her time writing tales of adventure in the West—in her case, likely to be first-hand.

ALBERT PAYSON TERHUNE acquired his love of writing from his mother; his father taught him to handle and understand dogs. Shortly after Terhune was first published, he devoted himself to writing almost exclusively about dogs—usually collies, which he raised and sold all over the world. To him the reason was simple: "We like to talk and write about the things which interest us most. That is why I always craved to write about animals, chiefly dogs."

After the success of *Lad: A Dog* in 1919, other tales of canine loyalty and resourcefulness, among them *The Heart of a Dog,* from which the story "One Minute Longer" is taken, gained for Terhune a following among dog-lovers everywhere. By the time of his death in 1942 on the farm where he had raised his pedigreed collies, Terhune's reputation was firmly established as the best-loved of all dog-story authors.

JAMES THURBER grew up near the turn of the century in Columbus, Ohio, in a family whose experiences were the source of some of his funniest essays—among them the "Snapshot of a Dog." A childhood accident cost him the sight of one eye and caused the poor vision which eventually led to blindness. But it is characteristic of Thurber that, in an essay on the impossibility of seeing anything under a microscope, he was capable of treating his poor eyesight humorously.

The beginning of Thurber's long association with *The New Yorker* is now a legend: he came in the door to ask for a job, and left as managing editor. Thurber soon resigned from this position, but he continued writing for the magazine, and almost all his fables, tales, drawings and essays appeared there first. The unique quality of these pieces earned Thurber an unchallenged position as the leading humorist of his age.

As a boy LOUIS UNTERMEYER wrote poetry and dreamed of becoming America's leading orchestral conductor or the world's greatest pianist. Instead, after leaving high school as the result of trouble with mathematics ("x to me," he has said, "was not an unknown but an unknowable quality") he found himself a salesman in his father's jewelry store. He continued writing poetry, however, and finally left the jewelry business in 1923 to study in Europe for three years. He is now one of America's foremost poets and its most noted anthologist.

While in Europe Untermeyer visited the small museum at Pompeii, where a plaster cast of a dog captured his imagination. "The Dog of Pompeii," Untermeyer's contribution to this anthology, was the result.

ALEXANDER WOOLLCOTT was a prominent and controversial figure of the American literary scene for many years of this century. Drama critic, author, and radio broadcaster, he became famous for his barbed wit, often directed at public personalities. He could also "take it." Although he was the model for the self-centered Sheridan Whiteside in *The Man Who Came to Dinner,* Woollcott accepted the characterization as a tribute and played the role himself in a touring theatrical company.

Woollcott used his national radio program, "The Town Crier" to comment on anything or anyone he chose, and to promote favorite causes. One of them was The Seeing Eye, partly, perhaps, because he himself suffered from poor eyesight. He became The Seeing Eye's best friend, lecturing for the organization and promoting its work. His story, "Verdun Belle," although not involved with The Seeing Eye, reflects this kindlier side and is one of many outstanding stories he wrote in a fiercely articulate lifetime.